PearlHeart Book 2

The Constellation Caves

Keilani McConnell

To everyone who went

on the first journey!

Also by Keilani McConnell

Novels

PearlHeart Series
Journeys of PearlHeart

Graphic Novels

Silent Comics Series
Gem Music and Other Silent Comics
Turtle Journey and Other Silent Comics

Art Books
Snakes in Hats: 2024 Artwork

Delphy

Meridelle Village
Vera Town
Archen Town
Tema Island
Solene City
Ferillis Town
Kel City
Marchand's Bay
Alianne Village
Meran Town
L'öeile Village
Priage
Akkan City
Melrin Village

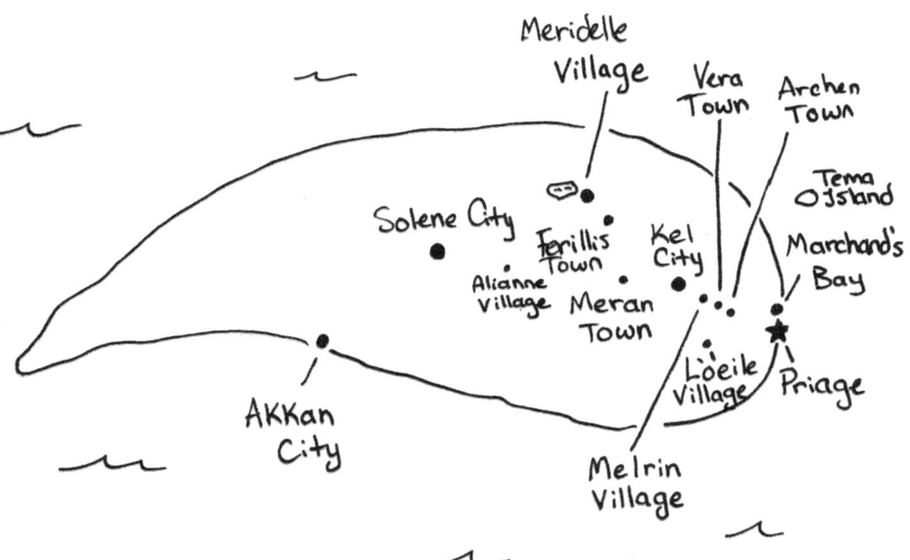

1

On Delphy, Captain Rath and Marchand, the god of the country, walk up the hill leading to Marchand's Bay.

Behind them, *PearlHeart* bobs peacefully at Priage Port and a maintenance team is already at work on repairs from the crew's most recent journey.

Marchand says to Rath, "I think it's a good thing you're all taking a break – even if it's not as long as usual – and I'm glad to hear you've chosen to spend it on Delphy. Can I ask where you'll be staying?"

"Yes. Franz and Velt were very kind to offer their homes to me, the Pagu, and One-Eye for the Summer."

Marchand raises an eyebrow. "One-Eye, too?" He rubs his chin. "Although, I would guess none of the ports are hiring right now with the sailing season already underway."

Rath nods. "His current housing at Leighran Port on Delphy is only available during our off-season in the Winter."

They reach the bay and Marchand pauses for a moment.

He asks, "Has One-Eye given any thought to a permanent home here? He could apply for citizenship."

Rath looks surprised. "That would be wonderful." He flushes. "That is – I speak from my point of view, not One-Eye's. I do not know what he would think."

Marchand pats his shoulder. "Ask him. I'd be more than willing to sign the paperwork and I know Georgio would be as well." He suddenly sighs. "I wish you could stay with Garreth, but I know that even the visit you make each year during the Winter was difficult enough to convince Merp to allow you to do. Your grandfather likely would have too much paperwork right now – with Summer being the Wedding Season – to enjoy your visit anyway. And now I'm leaving him with all of Delphy to watch after." He exhales, brightening. "Well, it's good that you have a place to stay. I knew I wouldn't have to worry, but I'm happy to hear you're staying with friends. And … as I recall, Velt's sister – Vann – will be getting married next month. Will you all be attending?"

"We are. Carlos and Phillip will be as well when they return from their trip."

They hear a splash from the bay, then a gasp. "Oh dear, have I arrived too soon?"

Marchand says, "No, you're just in time."

Berceuse, the God of Oct, is in the water in his octopus form. He glows and turns into his human form, appearing on the shore with them. "I do not want to interrupt, however … "

His brother nods. "If we're going to make it to Haliae, we should get going."

"Yes. Vocalise, Belle, and the others have already left."

Marchand hugs Rath. "You take care. I can't say when we'll be back from helping Elvin with Haliae – or offering our help to Pantha – but I'm sure it'll be before the holiday."

"I look forward to it," Rath says. "And thank you very much for helping them. May I ask if there is anything I can do?"

Both gods' eyebrows raise, then they smile.

Marchand shakes his head. "No – relax. Take a break. You and your crew deserve it after the past two years."

Berceuse says, "I fully agree. Even my dear ones are doing so, correct?" Rath nods and the god claps his hands together.

"That is wonderful! I am sure they will enjoy it. I believe it has been some time since they have seen Delphy."

Marchand says to Rath, "Let Garreth know if you or anyone else needs anything. He'll be the acting representative on Delphy until I return."

"I understand. Please have a safe journey."

Berceuse envelops him in a hug. "Ohh, I will miss you, my dear Captain." He pulls back and winks. "Remember – relax!"

"Yes, Berceuse."

The two gods wave to Rath, then dive into the water. They glow blue-green and purple, then Rath watches a dolphin and an octopus travel away from Delphy, swimming northeast.

2

One-Eye waits with Flower-Pagu, Bucket-Pagu, Well-Pagu, and his Spirit Lion near the docks of Priage Port.

As his Lion looks around inquisitively, One-Eye reaches down and pats his mane. "I don't think you're going to find any gossip right now." His Lion says something and One-Eye frowns. "Wedding Season?"

At that moment, Flower-Pagu says, "Oh! There's Rath!"

He trots down the hill and joins them. "Thank you for waiting."

One-Eye says, "Sure. Why is it the Wedding Season?"

"It is because the Summer months are a very popular time for them to be held. Marchand believes part of it is due to the flowers that begin to bloom with the warmer weather and that his constellation – *Marchand's Message* – is the most visible in the sky, right above Delphy. It is believed to be good luck for newlyweds. Recently, they say it is also because the Constellation Caves are accessible for those without

Marchand's Traits." He flushes happily. "Father tells me that he proposed to Mother there. She cannot breathe underwater like he can and the entrance is submerged due to the tides all year except for Summer."

The Spirit Lion listens intently. One-Eye says, "I haven't heard of the Constellation Caves before. Have you been there?"

"Yes. With my parents when I was very young. However, I have not been since I lost my traits." He thinks. "Actually, these two months will be the longest that I have been on my homeland in a long time. I am very excited for it."

Suddenly, they hear a familiar voice shout, "Rath, One-Eye, Pagu!" and turn to see Franz – one of the helmsmen aboard *PearlHeart* – running up to them. "Velt and I just found a ship. Are you all ready to go?"

They agree and follow Franz through the crowded streets. The group passes smaller waterways where people swim, stone arches glittering with Delphaen crystals, and bright flowers that One-Eye's Spirit Lion looks at with interest. The path descends and at the bottom, they see a waterway stretched beneath the shade of Delphaen Palms. There, Velt – a sailor on the lines on *PearlHeart* – is standing on a dock next to a small Delphaen ship.

They meet her and all get settled – Velt at the lines and Franz at the tiller, while Rath, One-Eye, and the Pagu sit on the seats near the stern.

As the ship starts to move, Rath says, "It is a three-day journey. Should we take turns sailing?"

One-Eye says, "I sailed ships like this last year at Leighran Port. I can help, too."

"Naw – Franz and I have it handled," Velt says. "You, One-Eye, and the Pagu did a lot in the past two years. Think of this as us doing it for you so you can take a break."

The waterway widens until there are two lanes, both going in the same direction. While they travel, One-Eye's Spirit Lion peers over the side at the Delphaen ships sailing underwater, One-Eye looks at the hills on either side of the waterway, and the Pagu sit in Rath's lap, enjoying the breeze. Rath watches the other ships near them, however after an hour, he seems restless.

One-Eye notices and after Rath shifts one more time, he says, "Relax."

He starts. "I … I suppose I am tense."

"About what? We can rest now."

"That is true. And I am very thankful for it. I am just used to helping on journeys."

One-Eye sighs, sitting back. "That makes sense. I don't like not doing anything for a long period of time either – I'd rather be working – but … these past two years were difficult." He ruffles his Lion's mane. "If there's anything I can appreciate about Pantha culture, it's that you rest when you're tired." His Lion nods emphatically.

Rath exhales. "That is true. I apologize for not being grateful for this time. Marchand and Berceuse encouraged me to do the same – relax, that is. Thank you. I will do my best."

"No. Just … do nothing."

Rath frowns, confused.

One-Eye nods at the Pagu. "Be like them."

The Pagu are talking quietly with each other as they look up at the sky or the trees or the water as it sparkles in the sun.

Rath laughs happily. "I see! I will do so." He relaxes more and falls silent as he turns his attention to the water all around them, blue-green and glittering in the alternating sun and shade.

They travel for another hour. Above, the sun shines brighter as it approaches noon. The Pagu leave Rath's lap to have a snack on the rail. One-Eye's Spirit Lion yawns and settles by his feet for a nap. He opens one eye, however, to ask One-Eye a question. He listens, then says to Rath, "There aren't many Spirit Dolphins around right now, are there?"

"I cannot say," he says. "I have not been able to see them since I lost my traits, which Carlos says is likely the cause."

One-Eye's eye widens. It flicks down. "Sorry."

"It is … " Rath hesitates. "I miss seeing them, however, I was not as close to one as you seem to be with your Spirit Lion. I hope I am not making an improper assumption."

"You're not."

Rath nods, then says, "It would be better to ask Franz or Velt. They can see them."

"I will later." One-Eye thinks.

When they stop for lunch, Velt and Franz turn the ship into a smaller waterway, then to a set of docks where other ships have pulled off into as well. One which had sailed underwater surfaces and those aboard talk as they tie off the lines and dry off in the warm sun.

The docks look older here and the wood creaks as Rath and One-Eye step off onto them. While the Pagu look around at the bright foliage and Flower-Pagu points out the plants they remember, Franz ties off the ship and Velt stretches her arms. Her Delphaen tattoos start glowing and she kneels by the water, dipping her hand in.

After she reads the message, she says, "Vann is wondering when Carlos and Phillip are arriving."

"They said they would be here the day of the wedding," Rath says.

As she sends the reply to her sister, Franz asks, "They went to Tema Island, right?"

"Yes, to the underground gardens there. They were both very interested in seeing them. Carlos thought he would restock on herbs after our last journey, as well. It seems that he ran very low on lavender in particular by the end."

One-Eye crosses his arms. "Probably all that tea. The gods drank a lot, too."

"That is what Carlos said."

"They should have paid for it."

Rath frowns. "They were guests. And worked for a long time to disperse Ara's Storm around Pica Pica, Daerce, Pantha, and Haliae."

One-Eye holds his expression for a moment longer, then says, "At least Ara compensated us."

Rath coughs. "He did, yes. I am still startled by the amount. However, it will help with *PearlHeart's* repairs and maintenance for many coming years."

One-Eye nods.

After Velt finishes with her message, they walk on a small dirt path up a nearby hill to Archen Town, with low buildings, sloped tiled roofs, and small community gardens tucked into corners with stone borders.

Franz says, "Velt and I know this really good place to eat nearby. I think you'll all like it. It's called *Melta's* – privately owned and run by the family there."

"I am looking forward to trying it," Rath says.

As they enter the town, One-Eye's Spirit Lion searches for other Spirit Animals, but after a few minutes, he pouts up at One-Eye, who says, "If you don't see them, there's likely not many." The Lion huffs, saying something else. "That's Cunica. They're *Rabbits*."

Beside them, Bucket-Pagu flies beneath an archway shaped like a wave. "Archen Town doesn't seem to have changed much. I always liked how everything's close together so it doesn't feel so big."

"I agree," Rath says. "Father, Marchand, and I visited to do some repairs one year. I always thought it felt very … comfortable. I do not recall *Melta's* being here, however, at that time."

Franz says, "It's relatively new – in the last decade definitely."

Velt says, "Vann and I heard about it from her betrothed, Merlin. Melta is his aunt."

They pass under a shaded pavilion where a weaver is working on small colorful mats, then more archways carved with designs and dotted with small Delphaen crystals. A stone mason with Maro's Traits carefully touches up one with a crumbling edge, merging it with a handful of raw stone.

One-Eye asks Rath, "What were the repairs you did here?"

"They were for a Signal Fountain. I believe … Yes. There is one right over here." He walks over to it and the others join him. A small waterfall flows down a rock wall, its water supplied by a large glass globe suspended above it. "Actually, I believe this is the same one we helped. You see, Marchand's Traits can be used to send a Delphaen message up the water to the globe, which causes it to glow. It can be used to help families find one another in crowded places and alert the Butej Guard of any problems. It is the duty of the town to keep them serviced. However, even though the globe was full, the water was not running down properly. We discovered that, over time, it had eroded the stones and was leaking through the cracks instead. This is one of the oldest fountains on Delphy, so it needed to be resurfaced. Now, routine checks are made to ensure it does not happen to others."

Franz says, "I didn't know about that. Though, Velt and I did see someone work on the fountain near our houses a while ago. It's old, too, so that's maybe what they were doing."

"It is likely."

Flower-Pagu says, "I think it was a wonderful idea of Marchand to make these!"

"I agree."

They walk past one more Signal Fountain – One-Eye's Spirit Lion looks at it with more interest – and a few more shops with different glass-blown items – One-Eye sees a small bauble filled with water dangling in the window of one –

before they arrive at a building half the size of the others with the title *Melta's* over its awning. Beneath it is an open window looking into a small but organized kitchen.

A woman with red hair tied back with an embroidered bandana is inside talking with a young man at a stove. Her hand is dipped into a pot, now glowing orange-pink as she uses Penelope's Traits to purify the water inside. However, when she sees the group, she walks up to the counter, saying, "Franz! Velt! Wondered when you would be here. Luta got your message that you would be on Delphy this Summer."

"Yup!" Velt says. "Our last journey ended in the Spring, so we're on break for two months before leaving again."

"I see. I'm sure your family's happy about it so you can be here for Vann's wedding." She nods to the others. "Who are these? I'm Melta, the owner."

They introduce themselves. When she meets the Pagu, her face brightens with delight. "Oh my! And three of you, too! That can mean good luck! It's a pleasure to meet all of you." But then her eyes go back to Rath and she gasps. "Why, you're Councilman Georgio's son, aren't you? You, he, and Marchand fixed that Signal Fountain down the way not too long ago."

"I believe it was over ten years ago," Rath says.

Melta laughs. "Well! Shows how much I pay attention. Though, you do look older. I remember you only having a few Delphaen tattoos. On your wrists, right?"

"Ah, they were. I do not have them anymore."

"Don't have … " She shakes her head, exhaling. "I have missed a lot." She smiles. "You likely don't remember me – it was before I finally started up this restaurant. And – well, let me get you something. Free of charge for the work you did all those years ago – I insist."

"Thank you," Rath says, flushing a little.

"Of course. Franz, Velt, do you want dinner to take with you all as well?"

"Yes, please!" Velt says.

Melta leaves and soon comes back with a large tray of food. "This is what Franz, Velt, and Perri always order, so I thought you'd all like it, too." She calls behind her, "Luta! Come say hi to Franz, Velt, and meet the others!" The younger man by the stove looks over. His messy orange hair is held back by a headband similar to his mother's bandana.

"But the food – " he starts to say.

"I'll take care of this. Go on."

"Thanks, Mom." Luta comes over to the counter. A Spirit Dolphin is with him that Franz, Velt, the Pagu, and One-Eye's Spirit Lion can see.

After Rath, One-Eye, and the Pagu introduce themselves, he says, "It's great to meet you all. Velt, Franz, and Perri have told us a lot about *PearlHeart*. Did Perri not come with you?"

"No," Velt says, "she decided to go to Pantrog with Isaac last minute."

"Oh!" Luta's eyebrows raise, then he grins. "She's told me about Isaac."

One-Eye's Spirit Lion says something to him and he says, "Sure. If it's all right with her."

At the same time, Luta looks at his Spirit Dolphin. "Of course you can. I'll be fine." He suddenly flushes. "I-I won't forget the recipes!" The Dolphin smiles as she swims away and the Lion trots off with her to discuss.

While they do, Luta returns to the kitchen to help his mother and the rest of the group sit nearby to eat their meal.

"I forgot they can talk to each other," Franz says, referring to the Spirit Animals.

Velt nods. "Phillip says One-Eye's Spirit Lion and his Spirit Rabbit are talking all the time on *PearlHeart*."

"Gossiping," One-Eye says.

Rath chokes a little beside him.

"It's the truth."

"You have told me. I do not know how to feel about it."

One-Eye shrugs. "It's how I heard about you. Also how I knew that it was you when we met." At Rath's surprised look, he explains, "He'd heard a captain was looking for a first mate – he got us in the right town to apply for the position. Told me that you had a good reputation and that it'd be a much better situation than what we had before."

"I see. I am very thankful for him doing so." Rath takes a thoughtful bite. "However, when you explain it in such a way, it sounds more like information, not gossip."

One-Eye sighs. "Trust me. It is."

Rath frowns, but accepts it.

Over by *Melta's,* a line begins to grow. Franz says, "It's gotten really popular. Velt, Perri, and I try to tell people about it when we can."

"We appreciate it!" Luta says, balancing a tray he is carrying over to another group. When he comes back around, he says, "Mom's telling me to go on break soon – Dad just got home from the market – so I'll be able to talk more. I've only heard from your messages a little bit of why your journey was so long this year – I want to hear more about it."

Once they finish eating and are waiting for Luta to come back, they look at one of the nearby gardens, mostly with flowers native to Delphy, but also a few from Campi.

"I believe these are Perin," Rath says as he gently touches the small light blue flowers.

One-Eye smiles at his expression.

His Spirit Lion returns, looking smug. As he licks his paw, One-Eye says, "Find a friend?" and the Lion opens one eye in response.

At the same time, Luta walks over to them, carrying a large wrapped package. He says to his Spirit Dolphin, "They went *where?*" The Dolphin's eyes gleam. He sits with them and tells One-Eye, "She really enjoyed talking with your Spirit Lion."

"He liked it, too. Thanks. There aren't a lot of Spirit Animals we've encountered on Delphy yet. He misses talking to them." He grins at his Lion. "Finding out more *information*."

The Lion flicks his tail at the back of One-Eye's calves and he laughs.

Then, Luta listens as they all share with him their most recent journey to Draconi.

By the end, he blows out a breath."It sounds incredible. And kind of terrifying."

Franz nods. "I fully agree."

Velt says, "We had Marchand with us – and a lot of the other gods – to keep us safe. Rath, One-Eye, and the Pagu, too."

"That's true," Luta says. He looks at Rath, hesitates, then says, "I remember you coming to Archen Town before with Marchand and Councilman Georgio." He rubs his arm. His Delphaen tattoos only reach to his forearm. "It was really neat seeing someone without strong traits do a lot of good for the town. And now it sounds like you're still doing amazing things. I'm glad I got to meet all of you. I've only ever been around Delphy and Campi to visit some of my mom's family – I haven't even been to Pantrog, where Merlin's family is – so I always like hearing about the different places people go. Maybe I'll trave more some day, but it's a little hard with the restaurant here."

"Luta! Could you help?" Melta suddenly calls. The line of people is now stretched across the small seating area.

"Coming, Mom!" He lifts up the package, saying to the others, "Here's the dinner you ordered – I hope you all like it." He runs off, saying, "Come by again some time – we'll make sure you get something free. See you at the wedding!"

As they leave, Melta and her husband Tierth wave to them, then turn their attention back to the people waiting.

3

As they travel away from Archen Town, Rath sits with the Pagu in his lap again.

Franz looks over. "They look really comfortable there."

"They have told me they enjoy it," Rath says.

Flower-Pagu says, "We do!"

Bucket-Pagu says, "We feel safe here."

Well-Pagu says, "Group."

Rath says, "Yes, we are all in a group. And, I am glad that you feel safe. I do as well."

Over the next hour, the Spirit Lion takes a nap, One-Eye looks around at the different ships and branching waterways, and Rath talks with the Pagu.

Bucket-Pagu says, "I definitely want to see the Constellation Caves again. That is at the top of my list."

"Mine as well," Rath says. His eyes flick over to One-Eye, then he flushes. He continues, "There is an entrance to them near Franz and Velt's homes."

Velt hears and says, "We could take a trip there – I'm pretty sure Vann and Merlin were going after their wedding, but we could go before. It's like a day's hike or so."

Bucket-Pagu says, "That's not far at all!"

Flower-Pagu says, "It would be really fun to see them together!"

"Hike," Well-Pagu says.

Rath says, "That is a great idea."

One of the Spirit Lion's ears flick and One-Eye says, "'An entrance.' Are there multiple ones?"

"Yes. There are twelve. They are along the northeastern coast. The caves are beneath all of eastern Delphy."

One-Eye listens to his Lion again, then says, "They show the real constellations?"

"Yes, on a smaller scale, however. Marchand told me it was important to him to acknowledge all of his siblings' stories."

One-Eye and his Lion nod.

They go under a large patch of shade, but come out into the sun not long afterward. All around them, the water sparkles. They stop briefly in Vera Town to eat the dinner Luta packed for them, sitting by a large fresh water lake, then set out again. Three hours later, close to evening, Velt says, "We'll stop at the next docks. There's a way station nearby."

When they arrive, Franz ties off the lines and Velt locks up the ship for the night. Nearby, a man is lighting lanterns and their warm glow flickers on the calm waterways.

After they gather their bags, they follow the path to Melrin Village, with tall buildings covered in ivy and flowers. A small fair is going on in the main square and the Pagu look up at the ribbons tied in between the houses in delight.

They go to a three-story building with a waterway running through it. Above the front doors, there is a painted dolphin leaping over a ship, designating it as a way station.

The rooms are free to travelers, so after receiving their

key, they all start heading up the stairs. Rath pauses, however, when he sees something on a table by the front desk.

It is a small basket full of colorful squares of fabric. A sign above it says, *Haliae and Pantha Relief Effort Blankets – Take One and Sew!*

When he joins the others in their room, One-Eye sees it and asks, "What's that?" After Rath explains, he frowns. "I'm still not used to them accepting help," he says, but his Lion looks interested.

The Pagu fly over to Rath and Flower-Pagu says, looking at the fabric squares, "They're all such pretty patterns!"

Bucket-Pagu says, "I hope they keep people very warm!"

"Soft," Well-Pagu says.

"They are," Rath says. He sits on his bed and pulls out two squares, then prepares a needle and thread as he continues, "Marchand tells me that although Ara's Storm has ended in the North the weather there is still very cold and is expected to be through the Fall and Winter when these blankets should arrive."

He works on it for the rest of the evening while the Pagu read next to him, One-Eye and his Spirit Lion take a run in the area around the village, and Franz and Velt go downstairs to the waterway on the first floor to send Delphaen messages to their families, updating them on where they are.

By the time they have all returned, Rath has finished the first two rows. He folds it carefully and sets it in the basket by his bed before he and the others go to sleep.

In the morning, they decide to have breakfast outside before continuing to travel.

Franz says, "There's a really nice place nearby."

They get food from one of the vendors that is still there from the fair the previous day, then Franz and Velt lead them to a grassy hill overlooking an area with fountains and pools for children to play in or send Delphaen messages through.

Many trees nearby provide shade for their parents.

As the group sits beneath one, eating and talking with one another, One-Eye's Spirit Lion goes off to look for Spirit Animals and soon finds two Spirit Dolphins and one Spirit Rabbit to talk with.

After they finish eating, Franz and Velt go down the hill to say hello to some people they recognize and the Pagu fly around the trees. One-Eye sits next to Rath while he sews the blanket for Haliae and Pantha.

"You're nearly done," One-Eye says, surprised.

"Yes," Rath says. "I thought of asking the way station clerk for another basket." He finishes before they leave and One-Eye helps him fold it.

Franz, Velt, and the Pagu join them, then they all go back to the way station where Rath turns it in and asks for another basket which the clerk happily gives him.

Then, they gather their things and board the Delphaen ship again.

Flower-Pagu sits on the edge of the basket while they sail. "What about this one?" they ask, holding up a square.

"Yes, please," Rath says. "Would you set it on top?"

"Of course!"

The Pagu take turns pulling out the remaining squares for Rath to use and by the time they are stopping for lunch, he has finished. However, when he gives it to the clerk at the next way station, there are no more baskets to take, so he spends much of the afternoon of travel speaking with the others and looking out at the clear water.

Near evening, the sound of water grows louder and One-Eye's Spirit Lion pricks his ears forward. He turns to One-Eye for a moment, who says, shaking his head, "Stay here with us." He asks Rath, "What's up ahead?"

"The Wishing Fountain. It is very beautiful."

Velt says, "Have you seen it before, One-Eye?"

"No. My Lion and I were further south before."

Franz asks the Pagu, "What about you three?"

Flower-Pagu says, "I remember it!"

Bucket-Pagu says, "I wonder if it's changed since the last time we saw it."

Well-Pagu nods.

The waterway narrows until only one ship can travel at a time. Above, the large leaves of Delphaen Palms drip water over them. After One-Eye's Lion asks a question about them that One-Eye relays, Rath explains that Marchand designed them to hold onto moisture long after rain falls and they both listen.

Thirty minutes later, they arrive at a wide ring with multiple lanes that ships can sail around, then exit from the various branches. In the center is a large fountain with water shooting up and flowing down its sides into lower tiers before joining the water in the ring. As people sail close to it, they pause and dip their hands in the water to send Delphaen messages. There, they are sent into the sky as droplets, the water glowing blue-green for a few seconds with Marchand's Traits before it fades.

One-Eye's Spirit Lion has his paws on the edge of the ship, his nose raised up as he watches. He turns back to One-Eye to ask him something.

One-Eye listens, then says to Rath, "Where do the Delphaen messages go?"

"To Marchand. They are wishes that he listens to."

One-Eye frowns, but nods. He sits back. "It's amazing."

"I believe so as well." Rath tucks his hands in his lap, enjoying the sight of the fountain while the Pagu raise their hands to the glowing droplets.

As they make their way around the ring, they see an older woman standing on the surrounding walkway. She is looking up at the fountain and rubbing her hands. She sighs.

Velt reduces their speed. "Are you waiting for a ship?"

The woman looks over, then smiles kindly and shakes her head. "No, no … just thinking. Well – " She bites her lip. "Perhaps one of you would have an idea. Are you in a hurry?"

"No, we've got time."

With Franz's help, they pull into the outside lane and Velt quickly ties off the ship so they can climb out and join her.

She extends her hand to each of them. Her tattoos run up all the way to her shoulder, exposed in her sleeveless dress. "I'm Nera. And you?" After they give their names, she explains, "You see, my daughter will be delivering her first baby with my son-in-law. He offered to take me on his ship for my wish, but … I'm not steady enough for that now. I was going to use one of the raised bowls, but as you can see," she says, pointing to a blocked off area with two people wearing uniforms who are looking at something on the ground, "they've closed them off. It seems a large crack was found near them. They're repairing it right now, but no one can go there until they're finished. I need to return to my family soon, but I truly want to send my wish first. Would any of you have an idea?"

"I may," Rath says. "Have you sent Delphaen messages through water droplets before?"

She blinks. "I've heard of it – my mother could do them through rain." She gasps and looks at the fountain, then Rath again. "Do you think – could that work?"

"I believe so. Given your tattoos, your traits from Marchand are very strong."

"I'll try it then." She frowns. "I never asked my mother how she did it – now I wish I did."

"That is all right. I can teach you. I cannot do it myself, but my grandfather has taught me."

She nods quickly. "If you do not mind, I would love to learn."

As Rath does, she listens carefully. Franz and Velt listen,

too, looking amazed.

Once he finishes, she says, "I think I understand it. Let's see … " She steps forward to where there are more droplets. Her tattoos glow and she tries to send a message to one, but it misses.

Rath says, "Try thinking more of where you would like the message to go at the end. My grandfather also told me the more emotion you put behind it, the easier it will travel in between the drops."

She tries again. This time, the message connects two droplets for a brief moment.

"I did it!" She shakes out her hands. "A little tiring, though. The fountain is a long way … "

Franz says, "Rath, is it possible to send a carrier message with it?"

"Definitely."

Stepping next to Nera, he says, "Then if you don't mind, I can help."

"I'd more than appreciate it," she says.

Velt hops over. "I can, too! Franz, teach me how to do carrier messages in the next two seconds!"

"Uh – " But he explains and she practices a few times before giving him a thumbs-up.

Then they all work together, Nera sending the message while Franz and Velt strengthen it with their own traits from Marchand.

Nearby, One-Eye's Spirit Lion's ears flick as he follows the messages. He says something to One-Eye, who asks Rath, "What are carrier messages? My Lion and I want to know."

"They are used to help the original message travel further than one's own traits may allow. The Delphaen Relay uses them to help send messages all over the world. Franz was part of the relay here on Delphy before he joined *PearlHeart*."

Suddenly, they hear Nera, Franz, and Velt gasp and look

just in time to see a bright blue-green message go through the falling droplets, connecting them like dots, all the way to the fountain. It joins the water there, then shoots up into the air, raining glowing blue-green drops over everyone.

Velt cheers. "Me next!"

Franz exhales. "I don't know if I can do that again."

Nera laughs. "I certainly can't." But she closes her eyes, smiling happily for a moment. She says to all of them, "Thank you so much. My daughter and her husband won't believe it. I'm only glad that it was sent before she gave birth. Now, I'd best return to them. Thank you again!" She waves to them as they board their ship and rejoin the other lane.

When they are near the fountain, both Franz and Velt dip their hands in to send their own wishes.

Velt says, "You know, I recently learned a lot more fun way of doing this … "

Franz shakes his head. "I've only got enough energy for a normal message right now." But as they leave, he laughs a little. "I kept asking you before if you wanted to learn how to send carrier messages – you always said no!"

"I didn't see a reason to! I need a reason!" As they sail to one of the exits, she says, "Rath, you said Lord Garreth taught you?"

"Yes, it was startling. He showed me during a rainstorm. His messages were very bright."

"I can only imagine," Franz says. "His traits are really strong."

One-Eye says to him, "Rath told me you were part of the Delphaen Relay."

"Yeah! Most people request to travel to different countries, but I decided to stay here to be close to my family."

"And me! And my family, too!" Velt says.

"That's true." He tells One-Eye, "Our homes are literally right next to each other, so we grew up together. Actually, it was Velt who convinced me to go to Pantrog to learn how to sail Pan ships."

"It sounded fun!" she says.

"We also met Rath there when he was hiring for his crew."

Rath nods. "I had earned enough from working on ships to have *PearlHeart* built. Besides Carlos, Phillip, and Fenrir, Franz and Velt were the first sailors I hired – and the first to see *PearlHeart*."

"It was incredible," Franz breathes.

Velt says, "And then he hired you on Pantrog, too, One-Eye!"

Franz says to Rath, "Didn't you also meet Isaac there?"

"Yes. Actually, it was when I was still working on *HighTree*, Captain Larox's ship, as his sailmaster." He flushes. "Isaac mistook me for the captain."

"I remember him telling me! He said he saw how you worked with the lines and asked if you were hiring."

"I was not – *PearlHeart* was still being built and I would remain on *HighTree* for one more year as first mate. However, we did have lunch together that day and when I told him about *PearlHeart*, he was very excited. We stayed in touch since then, however, it was only three years ago that he told me he wished to apply as sailmaster. Alya, too, had decided to move on to another ship. She was our previous sailmaster."

They sail quickly through the afternoon until they encounter a long line of ships ahead and need to slow down to a pace they keep for several hours. One-Eye stretches his legs, getting impatient.

Velt says, "At this rate, we won't be able to stop anywhere to get something to eat."

"Is there a town nearby?" One-Eye says. "I could get something and run back. I want to move around."

Franz says, "Kel City is."

Rath rubs his legs. "I would like to move as well. May I go

with you, One-Eye? I remember the way to the city from here."

He agrees and they both carefully step off of the ship onto the path next to the waterway.

Velt says, "We'll catch up with you later."

Franz says, "Though we might be in the same place when you get back."

"Hopefully not," One-Eye says.

Rath asks, "Is there anything in particular we could get for everyone?"

Velt shakes her head. "Naw, we're open."

The Pagu – who are staying on the ship – confer quietly, then Well-Pagu says, "Delphy … Fruit?"

Rath says, "Definitely! I would like some as well. It is a good month for them so I am sure that they will have them."

He and One-Eye walk down the path, crowded with people walking to and from the Wishing Fountain. The roofs of tall buildings begin to appear over the trees and the waterway they have been following divides into many smaller ones that run into the city, creating fountains and waterfalls over stone arches.

As they enter Kel City and Rath guides them through the narrow streets of shops, One-Eye sees one with a display of small glass-like shapes filled with water. He says, "I saw those in Archen Town. Meant to ask you what they were."

Rath looks. "They are called Water Pendants. They allow you to store a Delphaen message in them and only release it when it has been thrown into the water."

"It shatters?"

"Yes. It is made out of Rulo – a mineral that is very strong until it comes into contact with water. The inside of the pendants are coated with wax to protect them when they are filled with water."

They soon find a place with small stuffed bread rolls filled with shredded vegetables, then stop at another stall for a few

Delphy Fruits.

As they are returning to Franz and Velt, Rath suddenly stumbles forward and One-Eye catches him. "Are you all right?"

"Yes. Thank you." However, he looks down and frowns.

There is a long crack in the stone stretching across the walkway. Rath kneels and touches it.

The Spirit Lion says something and One-Eye says, "My Spirit Lion says this crack wasn't here when we walked through earlier."

"Really? That is concerning. We should let Leader Leytel know. He will be in the city hall."

They quickly go back into the city and to a tall building with many windows reflecting the bright sunlight.

Once inside, they find a group of workers clustered around a tall man who says, "I've told you – we can't contact Marchand until he returns from Haliae and Pantha. Yes, I've sent a Phoenae message to Councilman Georgio, however, it will be several months before his response." He looks past them and gives a start. "Why – Rath." He moves through the crowd of disgruntled workers. "It is good to see you. Who is this with you?"

After One-Eye gives his name, the man smiles. "Welcome. I am Leytel, the leader of Kel City. Rath and I know each other from when he was training to be councilman. Was there something either of you needed?"

Rath says, "There is a large crack on the walkway leading out of the city."

One-Eye says, "My Spirit Lion says it only appeared recently."

"*Another?*" Leytel turns around. "Lana – would you?"

Lana, one of the workers, sighs and picks up a sign from a freshly painted stack. "On it."

As she leaves, Leytel says to Rath and One-Eye, "That's our

current problem – these cracks. We have no idea why they have been appearing and have yet to find a pattern for them either." He raps his fingers over the Delphaen tattoos on his arm. "Marchand would likely know what to do and Georgio might as well, but neither of them are here. Rath, I hate to ask you – you're likely on your way somewhere – but would you have any advice?"

He thinks. "Have you compared them with the underground waterways?"

"I'm trying to. Each time I begin, another report comes in. We've had a few searched with Marchand's Traits, thinking perhaps the rain had caused them – we've had a lot recently – but they're dry. It's not just here either – other places nearby are having a similar problem. There was even one near the Wishing Fountain. It's caused a lot of trouble for people wanting to send messages, but just earlier this morning – " He stops suddenly. "Did you teach someone how to send messages through the droplets? I couldn't believe it when I heard about it. It's not a very common skill."

"I did. Grandfather had taught me that anyone with strong traits could – as long as their feelings behind their messages were as well."

"I'm sure they were, given they were able to do it. Thank you for teaching them – we may have to consider that as an alternative until the crack is repaired. I've already put in a request to the Delphaen Relay to help people with their carrier messages. Now, if I could just have a moment to study those maps – " But his tattoos glow and he exhales. "That's from the leader of Archen Town." Then his eyes light up. "Would you have time to look at the maps for me? There should be enough cracks marked to find a possible cause."

"I can, however, I cannot stay in Kel City for very long. We are traveling with friends to Meridelle Village."

"Not a problem." Leytel quickly asks one of his staff to

retrieve the maps which he hands to Rath. "These are copies, so don't worry about returning them soon. Just look at them when you have time."

After Leytel leaves to check his message, Rath and One-Eye walk back to the main waterway leading out of the city.

They find Franz, Velt, and the Pagu and board the ship again. After they exit the area, they enter a large bay where ships can idle and eat their lunch while Rath explains the situation.

"That *is* worrying," Velt says.

Franz says, "I might send my family a message – see if they've seen anything in Meridelle Village."

They finish eating and rejoin the waterway. While they travel, Rath studies the maps.

When he takes a break, One-Eye asks, "Have you found anything?"

"No. None are near any major underground waterways. However, neither of these maps include the Constellation Caves – I would like to compare them as well. My grandfather would have one. I will send him a letter to ask to borrow it. I need to update him on the situation as well, if he does not know."

He puts away the maps for the rest of the afternoon and One-Eye starts to ask him about different areas in Delphy while his Lion listens intently. The Pagu are closer to Velt, asking her about Meridelle Village.

At the way station that night, Rath looks at the maps one more time before One-Eye – who had been playing cards with the others at the table – says, "We're starting a new round – do you want to join?"

"Yes, please."

However, as he walks over, the Spirit Lion says something and One-Eye says to Rath, "My Spirit Lion wants to know if he can look at the maps."

"Of course. Where would he like me to place them?"

"Just spread them on the floor."

Rath kneels and does so. "There." The Lion grins at him, but Rath does not see it. He then stands and says to One-Eye, "Thank you for letting me know," before joining the others at the table.

The Lion studies the maps, his tail swishing as he concentrates.

4

Rath sends a letter to his grandfather the next morning and then they are sailing again, traveling swiftly on the waterway. They are only one day away from Franz and Velt's homes in Meridelle Village. There are more hills here and the trees on top of them sway in the breeze. Behind them, darker clouds are building.

It rains later and they stop briefly to put on their rain gear. The Pagu sit on Rath's shoulder beneath his hood, watching the drops.

Beside them, One-Eye stares ahead, wet despite his own rain hat and parka, and his Spirit Lion crouches under his legs.

Later, all of them dry off in front of the fire in the common room of the next way station. The Pagu hold out their hands to it happily.

Franz says, "It won't be long until we're in Meridelle Village."

Velt flaps out her parka. "I wonder if it's raining there, too."

She turns to Rath. "Were you able to find out anything from the maps Leytel gave you?"

"No. I have decided to wait until I hear back from my grandfather to see if he would be willing to send his Constellation Caves map. I would like to compare the map of the cracks to it."

Franz says, "I'm sure you'll figure it out."

As they eat breakfast, the rain patters outside the large window.

The Lion looks at it, then walks dejectedly over to the fire and flops down in front of it. While Franz and Velt go to return the dishes, Rath pulls out the maps again and looks at them.

One-Eye says, "I thought you were waiting for your grandfather's letter."

Rath raises his head quickly. "I had a thought … " He scans the maps, then pauses. "I should put these away." One-Eye nods and Rath slowly rolls them up again.

After Franz and Velt return, they set out. The rain has stopped and the sun has returned. They travel quickly through the morning, but when they reach a crossroads, they find the ships in front of them at a standstill. The waterway to the south is open, but crowded, and the waterway to the north has been dammed off. Workers are walking alongside it, looking at something.

Another worker is standing on the small grassy hill dividing the two waterways. When he sees their ship, his shoulders slump. "Stay right there!" he tells them. "Catch the General Delphaen Message for more information." Then he goes back to trying to direct the other ships ahead.

Velt slows them and Franz releases the tiller to stick his arm in the water. A blue-green message rushes toward him and his tattoos glow as he reads it.

Velt asks, "Is it flooding? We did get a lot of rain earlier this morning."

"No – the opposite. The waterway is almost completely drained ahead. Apparently there's a crack in it and the water has been leaking out. It's fixed now, but the water level is too low for safe travel. It sounds like it happened in the middle of the night and was only discovered early this morning. They closed it off before anyone was near, so no one got hurt. We'll have to go through the southwest waterway instead and go around."

Velt says, "That'll take us another two days to get home!"

Franz shrugs and gets ready at the tiller.

Rath pulls out the maps. "May I ask where the crack is?"

"The message said it was just a quarter mile beyond this point."

"Thank you." He measures the area, then makes a careful mark with his pen. "It is also not above an underground waterway." He suddenly asks Franz, "Was there anyone in the Constellation Caves at the time? The water would go straight to them in this area."

"I'm not sure."

Another group has heard him, however, and a man says, "I asked the same thing earlier – they said they searched but found no one. Some damage to the cave, but they think it's fixable."

"I am glad to hear that. Thank you … "

The man smiles and reaches his hand over. Rath takes it. "Soren. Seems like we'll be here for a while. I doubt any of us will get much further at this rate. What is your name?"

"Indeed. And it is Rath."

As the lanes continue to back up and workers stand on the nearby hills trying to direct them, many ships idle and people begin talking to one another or playing cards. A shout of "Marchand's Twist!" rises up, followed by laughter.

From their ship, One-Eye frowns and his Spirit Lion paces restlessly.

One-Eye says, "Is there another waterway we can take beside these two?"

Franz says, "Back at the last divide – or even further at the Wishing Fountain – but they'll both take us much longer to get to Meridelle Village."

Rath says, "It is getting near lunch. Should we sail back to the way station nearest here?"

"Maybe." Franz turns to Velt, who is talking with someone in the ship in front of them. "Should we go back to the way station?"

"We could." She grins, nodding to the woman across the water. "Though, I guess it sounds like the Butej Guard is coming with camping gear and food. It's not like everyone here is going to fit in a way station. Or two."

"That is true," Rath says. "That is very kind of the Guard to do."

Franz says to Velt, "When are they going to get here? Do you know?"

In response, she turns to the woman, who says, "Should be any minute now." Suddenly, a few small shadows go over them and they all look up at the sky. "Ah, there they are."

Above, small Butej skyships fly, kept aloft by the guards who are using Fierce's Traits to fill the sails with wind. The workers below sigh in relief and one of them calls out, "We'd advise you come to shore now and help the Guard set up camp. No more ships will go on from this point." Some of the travelers look disappointed by this, but most nod and do so, tying them off to the edge of the waterway or to their neighbor's ship to keep them from drifting off.

They all climb ashore and gather where the Butej Guard is currently unpacking food to distribute to everyone there.

After everyone gets lunch, they spread out around the grassy slope, eating while their ships bob in the water.

Soren's group joins Rath's. While Velt talks with the woman

she spoke with before and Franz talks with a man from the same ship, Soren discusses with Rath, One-Eye, and the Pagu. He says, "I'm surprised to see Pagu here. I've heard of them, of course, but have never seen any."

Flower-Pagu says, "It's been a while since we've been on Delphy."

"Really? I'm glad you're here. I hope this situation hasn't disrupted your plans too much."

"A little bit," Bucket-Pagu says. "But, I'm sure we'll figure it out."

"Crack," Well-Pagu says.

"It was certainly surprising," Soren says. "My grandmother did repair work for a while – I wonder what she'd say … "

One-Eye asks, "Do you do the same work?"

"No, I work down at Tyan Port." He nods to the man and woman talking with Franz and Velt. "But, I've taken time off for my brother Dereth's wedding. Mirani is his betrothed. Where are you all heading?"

Rath says, "We are going to a wedding as well, in Meridelle Village. It is for Velt's sister, Vann and her betrothed, Merlin."

"Velt had told Mirani you all work on a Pan ship together?"

"Yes. I am the captain of *PearlHeart* and everyone is part of the crew."

Soren looks startled. "*PearlHeart*? The ship that sailed with the Gods?"

"Yes."

He laughs. "And you're the captain! Never thought I'd get to meet any of you. Thank you for your work. Who knows if Ara's Storm really would have hit Delphy if you hadn't helped."

He asks more about their journey to the North, shaking his head in amazement as he listens.

Afterward, he goes to tell Dereth and Mirani about it and Velt and Franz sit with Rath, One-Eye, and the Pagu.

Velt says, "I just heard they're opening up the other

waterway again to people who want to go on, but the one with the crack won't be accessible until later tomorrow."

Franz says, "What does everyone want to do? I say we just wait for the one we were going to take – especially if they think it'll be safe to travel on tomorrow."

One-Eye eyes the ships still bobbing in the waterway. "We likely won't be traveling fast either way, but I'd go for waiting until tomorrow over another two days."

The others agree.

Several of the ships leave, taking the open waterway. To the east, the waterway has been blocked off with rope and General Delphaen Messages shimmer in the water to prevent any more ships from arriving. To the north, the waterway is being filled again by slowly lowering the barrier damming it.

Rath is watching when Soren joins him.

"Have you heard about the other cracks that have been appearing?" he asks. "It seems like nearly every town, city, and village has at least one now."

"I have," Rath says. "Leader Leytel of Kel City asked if I would try to find a reason for them occurring. I have not."

Soren hums, looking at the waterway. "Well, I don't know if this will help you, but my grandmother always said the waterways were the most reinforced parts of Delphy – they have to be. The only way for a crack to appear like that would be if it was caused by something underground."

"In the Constellation Caves?"

"Seems like it."

Rath looks thoughtful.

Not long afterward, Soren and his group board their ship. He asks Rath and the others, "Will you be going on, too?"

Velt says, "Nope. We're staying until the other waterway opens up."

"Oh, I see! It was nice meeting you all."

"You too! Congratulations on the wedding!"

"Thank you!" Dereth, Soren's brother, calls back and Mirani says, "To your sister as well!"

The Butej Guard brings around tents for those who are staying through the night. The group puts theirs up – one for Franz and Velt and another for Rath, One-Eye, and the Pagu – then go retrieve their dinner.

While they eat, Rath tells the others what Soren had told him.

"Underground?" Franz says. "Maybe the Constellation Caves should be checked."

"I agree," Rath says. "This crack was above them, however, I will not know about the others until I hear back from Grandfather and if he is willing to allow me to borrow his map of them."

They talk about other things until the sun goes down. Then they climb into their tents and go to sleep.

5

The following morning, Garreth sits in his home in Priage. He is at his desk going through marriage announcements between those of different races and approving almost every one.

A Butej guard knocks on the door.

"Come in already. I knew you were out there."

Wincing, a guard named Lez enters. He is carrying a crate. "This just arrived from Phoenae."

Garreth snorts. "Well! It's golden, where else would it come from?"

Lez frowns. He sets it down, then straightens, arms behind his back beneath his Butej Guard cloak. "I also wished to tell you that a Paradi letter arrived for you. From your grandson, Rath."

At that, Garreth's eyebrows go up and his expression eases. Then he gruffly pushes himself out of his chair, moves past Lez without another word, and exits. The guard follows him, shutting the door behind him.

By the time Lez reaches the foyer, Garreth is already outside and down the steps to where a woman and her bird partner are waiting.

The woman holds out the letter. "From your grandson, Rath, Lord Garreth."

"Thank you," he says quickly. He begins to open it, then hesitates. "He's all right, isn't he?"

"I would not know."

Garreth sighs. "Guess not." He starts to turn, then pauses. "Thanks Hera, Morenid."

She smiles. "You are welcome, Lord Garreth." Her bird partner gives a "Caw!"

Garreth smiles a little. He walks back into the house, opening the letter as he does so and ignoring the Butej guards at watch. He is halfway up the staircase when he shouts, "What!" and the nearby guards jump.

Lez – who was carrying in another crate of paperwork – asks, "Is there something wrong, Lord Garreth?"

He grunts. "None of your business. What are you doing still in here?"

"Bringing more crates. I have set them in your office."

Garreth shakes his head in response. He starts to walk past the guard, then stops and says, "Actually – you might know. What was your name again?"

"Lez."

"Right – you heard anything about cracks appearing around Delphy?"

"I have not," he says and Garreth frowns.

Another guard clears her throat. "Lord Garreth, if I may."

"Speak already."

"Yes, Lord Garreth. I have heard from family of mine that cracks have been appearing around Delphy from an unknown source for the past week."

Garreth waves the paper. "Yeah – I get that. Rath's already

told me. Do you know why?"

"No."

Garreth huffs. "I'll be in my office. Lez – go out and tell Hera to stay where she and Morenid are. I'm going to reply to this immediately. My grandson needs one of my maps."

"Yes, Lord Garreth."

He quickly writes his response and finds the map of the Constellation Caves Rath asked for. Then he seals the letter and carries both it and the map outside.

Hera takes them and Morenid flies off with them in their talons to the nearest Paradi Message Tower to be carried further west.

Instead of returning to his office, Garreth goes to the terrace in the back. He tromps down the steps and to the beach. He is about to put his hand in the ocean to deliver a message to Marchand when he stops and shakes his head. His Spirit Dolphin looks at him curiously.

Garreth stands up and crosses his arms. "No, the old dolphin would worry himself all the way home. Rath will figure it out." He looks out at the ocean, where his god is somewhere, still swimming to Haliae and Pantha. "You hear that, Marchand? You're needed *there*. Not … " He looks back at his home. " … here." He pauses for a long moment, frowning.

Then he walks up the stairs again, headed toward his office to continue working on his paperwork from Phoenae.

That same morning, the waterway with the crack has been reopened and Rath's group is on their ship, ready to leave.

As they sail, One-Eye sighs. His Spirit Lion, refreshed after some time off, is facing the warm breeze, his mane blowing behind him.

They have breakfast at the next way station and Rath sends his letter to Leader Leytel at the nearby Paradi Message Tower. Afterward, he plays cards with everyone in the common room.

Franz lays down his hand, "Teclan Shuffle!" he says.

"Excellent job," Rath tells him.

Velt says to the Pagu, "Thanks for teaching us this game! It's really fun."

Bucket-Pagu says, "Of course! We're happy to have more people to play with!"

A pair of Paradi messengers enter and go over to their table. "Rath Lewis?" he asks.

"Yes. That is me."

The messenger holds out a thick bundle. "From your grandfather, Lord Garreth."

"I see. Thank you very much."

After the messengers leave, One-Eye asks, "Is that the Constellation Caves map?"

"Yes." Rath reads over his letter from his grandfather, then unfurls the map carefully.

Velt asks, "Was he aware of what was going on?"

"No. However, he has been very busy with looking over wedding announcements. He has asked that we all be careful while investigating this." He flushes. "He also asked if this was not my break and why I was working, although he is thankful for it."

The others smile.

After Rath sends a reply letter to his grandfather, thanking him, he joins the others at their ship.

They stop in Ferillis Town for lunch and eat in the plaza, sitting on one of the many low stone walls.

Before they go back to the ship, they browse the different shops in the town.

One-Eye and his Lion are looking at some woven scarves when a man suddenly exits a nearby building with his Spirit Lion.

"No, it's fine," he says to the proprietor. "I'll keep looking." He crosses his arms, thinking, then his Spirit Lion nudges him and he sees One-Eye and his Lion.

He walks over to them. "You looking for work, too? I've been all over Delphy and no one's hiring."

One-Eye shakes his head. "No. I already have a job on a Pan ship – I'm on break now."

"Here?" the man says, raising an eyebrow. "If you have the money, why not go back to Pantha?"

One-Eye opens his mouth. His Spirit Lion looks at him. "Don't want to. The break isn't long and I wanted to see Delphy."

The man brightens. "It's nice, isn't it? Warm. I came from Cunica recently, but it's a lot hotter here."

They step aside, leaning against a stone wall while their Spirit Lions converse with one another. After a moment, they begin to tussle and both One-Eye and the man smile.

"She's going to win," the man says.

One-Eye does not say anything to that. Instead, he says, "Why Cunica?"

"My wife's there." He beams. "She's the most amazing person I've ever met. We met on Pantrog. A few years later, we went to Cunica, got Rella's blessing, and were married." His eyes soften. "She wants to go back to Pantha with me and help with those farms King Faerohr is starting. That's why I'm here – we can't go to Pantha without both of us working for money to get passage."

Next to them, One-Eye's Lion wins. The Lions go into another bout right afterward.

One-Eye asks the man, "Did you have a job in Cunica?"

"Of course. On a farm for a bit."

"Why didn't you stay there?"

"Thought about it, but … Primrose said it might be good for me to see more of the South before we went to Pantha. Don't know when we might come back down here with all the work that's to be done there. Always wanted to see Delphy."

He smiles. "And – my Spirit Lion really wanted to go here. She didn't know much about it."

The man's Spirit Lion has won this time. She hops off, trots over to the man and begins licking her paw as he pets her head. "Good work there." She gives him a look, then continues grooming.

One-Eye's Spirit Lion drags his paws over and sits down with a *whump,* shoulders hunched. "It's even now," One-Eye tells him.

His Spirit Lion suddenly straightens and looks over at the other Lion as if awaiting the next bout. One-Eye laughs and ruffles his mane. He then sees the man extend his hand to him. "Relanor."

He smiles and takes it. "One-Eye."

Relanor blinks. "Interesting name."

"You should try the docks – they usually hire more in the Winter, but there could be an opening now."

Relanor snorts. "And work around all those ships with *sails?* No way. Can you imagine depending on something *else* to carry you through the ocean but your own arms and your oars? Weaklings." He pauses, looking at One-Eye. He says, "You're a sailor."

"Yeah."

"Not one of those Delphaen ships?"

"No. A Pan ship with a Delphaen captain."

Relanor looks surprised. "Huh. Didn't know that was possible."

"There's a lot of different people on *PearlHeart.* People from Delphy, Paradi, Pantrog, Cunica" – Relanor brightens – "Pertes, Ullia, and three Pagu, too."

Relanor nods seriously. "The Pagu are good. Lionel loves them."

One-Eye frowns. "Right."

Relanor jostles him with an elbow. "You think you'll ever

go back to Pantha?"

"Not if it isn't for work."

"Why not? King Faerohr's there. I'm definitely going to fight him when I get there. Primrose said she'd watch."

One-Eye opens his mouth for a second, then shuts it. "It's not home to me." He looks around at Delphy, petting his Spirit Lion thoughtfully. "I'm happy on *PearlHeart* – with the people, too. It isn't like I would be on Pantha for long with our route. We're typically only on land for the Winter."

"Fair enough. You know of any farming here on Delphy? I'm good at that – Primrose taught me everything."

"I don't. Rath would – he's the captain of *PearlHeart*. I'll ask him."

"Thanks." Relanor steps away from the wall. "I'm going to check a few more shops. Hoping to find one with food. I know what good produce looks like. Come find me after you talk to your friend. Our Spirit Lions should know where each other is."

One-Eye's Spirit Lion looks intent with anticipation. "He will."

Relanor grins. Then, with a much lighter demeanor, he waves and walks off with his Spirit Lion, One-Eye and his Lion doing the same.

They find Rath sitting to the side of the plaza near a flowerbed, studying the maps from Leytel and his grandfather.

They wait while Rath thinks, then looks up. "One-Eye. I apologize. Was there something you needed?"

"Yeah. Didn't want to disturb you. Did you find anything?"

"I believe so. I just compared the new cracks with the underground waterways. They are not the cause. I was going to take a break before comparing the Constellation Caves map when you came."

One-Eye offers his hand and Rath takes it as he stands up. "Good. There's someone I want you to meet."

As they walk, One-Eye tells Rath about Relanor and his Spirit Lion. "Are there any farms on Delphy?" he asks Rath.

"A few – most are for the specialty produce that is grown here. They are further north, however."

"I don't think he or his Spirit Lion will have a problem with traveling."

One-Eye's Spirit Lion, his ears pivoting, leads them through the streets.

As they approach a shop, they see Relanor walking outside while a woman holds the door open behind him. "Sorry. We just don't have any room for more workers at the moment."

"That's all right. Keep in mind?"

"Someone with Rella's approval? Absolutely."

Relanor grins, but it fades as the owner walks back in. He turns, sees One-Eye and his Spirit Lion, and immediately grins. "You're back!" He walks over to meet them. "This your friend?"

One-Eye nods and Rath extends his hand. "I am Captain Rath of Delphy."

"Relanor. One-Eye said you'd know about some farms here."

"Yes." They step out of the way of others entering the shop and Rath pulls out one of his maps. "There are several on the northern coast."

Relanor nods over his shoulder. "Not too far." He smiles, saying to both of them, "Thanks for the help." He pets his Spirit Lion. "Better get started – Primrose can work sunup to sundown, so I've gotta do the same. Nice meeting you both." One-Eye's Spirit Lion speaks and Relanor laughs. "Bet you'll get your next bout another time."

As they are walking back to the plaza, One-Eye says, "I can't believe he's going back to Pantha."

Rath says, "May I ask if you will go there?"

"Not unless *PearlHeart* does."

They find Franz, Velt, and the Pagu, then all return to their ship where Rath compares the map with the cracks with the one of the Constellation Caves as they travel.

After he puts away the maps, One-Eye asks Rath, "Any more thoughts?" His Spirit Lion looks up at them.

"Many." Rath frowns. "A great deal of the cracks line up with walls in the Constellation Caves which could mean that there is structural damage, however, it is not something I am knowledgeable about. I thought I would send a letter to Leader Leytel to notify him of this."

6

They enter an area where the waterway narrows and private docks begin appearing on the shore. Smaller waterways run in between the hills at the top of which are homes.

One-Eye asks the Pagu, "Have you been to Meridelle Village before?"

They nod and Bucket-Pagu says, "It was a really long time ago, though."

Flower-Pagu says, "I think it was right after it was started, too! You see, the village was named after Marchand's First, Meridan, who founded it."

Turning to Rath, One-Eye says, "Then why did your family live in Priage?"

"I am told that when Merp agreed to the creation of the Alliance, that he asked all of the councilpeople – all were their god's Firsts at that time – to reside in the first site their god claimed their land. On Delphy, it was Priage. Although, Grandfather thought it was very arbitrary to ask for this."

"I can see why," he says and Well-Pagu sighs, saying, "Agree."

As they come to two hills very close to one another, they slow down and Velt says, "Here we are!"

While Franz and Velt secure the ship, Rath, One-Eye, and the Pagu wait on the wooden planks.

One-Eye asks Rath, "Have you met their families before?"

"Yes. They are all very kind."

Franz joins them and they start to walk up the hill on the right. "Mine were a little awkward at first, though. They kept trying to call Rath 'Lord' until my mom set the rest of them straight. I think you'll like her, One-Eye. She's bonded to a Spirit Dolphin."

One-Eye nods. His Spirit Lion looks interested.

Velt says, "I think you'll like my sister, Vann, too." She grins. "Actually, you kind of reminded me of her when we first met."

"They'll definitely all love the Pagu," Franz says.

Flower-Pagu twirls. "We can't wait to meet them!"

They are halfway up when they hear a voice say, "Franz? Is that you and Velt?"

"Yeah! We're all here, Aunt Fiona!"

When they reach the top, they see an older woman with a high bun standing in front of a home. As they join her, she looks around at the group. "Velt, of course, and Lord – rather, Rath, too." Her eyes widen. "And Pagu! And … One-Eye. You told me he was arriving as well." She pats her hair down, then straightens, hands clasped in front of her. "Welcome, all of you. Come inside, we have dinner prepared."

"Thank you," Rath says.

As they follow Fiona, Flower-Pagu looks at the home on top of the other hill. They ask Velt, "Is your family coming, too?"

She shakes her head. "Naw – they're all working right now."

One-Eye says, "What do they do?"

"My family runs a ship maintenance shop. My dads do the building and teach the classes. Vann does the repairs."

"What about you?"

"A bit of everything. I'm pretty talented, you know?"

The corner of One-Eye's lip quirks up for a moment.

Velt continues, "Vann's betrothed, Merlin, is probably there, too. He's from Pantrog and has been helping our dads with building ships."

Ahead, a voice calls out, "Fi – I told you I'd meet them. My Spirit Dolphin is the one who said they were here."

Franz's mother, Joseline, rolls forward in a wooden wheelchair. She looks remarkably similar to Fiona, but her gray hair is done in a looser bun at the base of her neck. A Spirit Dolphin swims beside her.

Fiona rushes forward and tries to take the handles but Joseline swats her hand away. "None of that." She nods to the group, her eyes crinkling near the edges. "Good to see you all. How was the journey?"

Franz hugs his mother. "Great! We got a bit delayed with the whole waterway thing, but we made it here all right."

"I'm glad to hear it!"

Fiona sniffs. "Yes, the waterway. It was truly worrying to hear about."

"It all worked out," her sister tells her.

"Very true." Fiona sighs and says to Rath, "And it is relieving to hear that Leader Leytel has asked for your advice on this matter."

Joseline, however, raises an eyebrow. "I thought you were on break."

Rath flushes. "Ah – "

Joseline laughs and rolls over to him. She grasps his forearm. "Don't worry – I understand." She rubs her leg. "Trust me. I do." Then she turns to One-Eye and the Pagu. "Now –

I don't think we've been introduced yet. I'm Joseline, former Captain of *WindCurrent,* a Delphaen ship." She nods to each of them. "I believe you are One-Eye, Well-Pagu, Bucket-Pagu, and Flower-Pagu. Is that right?"

Bucket-Pagu says, "Yes! It's wonderful to meet you."

"You as well. One-Eye, my Spirit Dolphin tells me you have a Spirit Lion with you."

"Yeah." Beside him, his Lion looks inquisitively at the Dolphin.

He does a loop and Joseline smiles. She waves her hand. "Now, come on – it's been a long journey for them – longer than most years."

"Oh! With Ara's Storm!" Fiona follows Joseline back into the house. "It sounds absolutely terrifying."

Before the others enter, Franz faces the group. "I'm going to warn you all now – most of this will probably be them hearing about our journey with Ara's Storm. I told them some at the time, but there were definitely some parts I left out … "

Velt pats his shoulder. "We're here for you!"

Franz's family home is small, with two levels. The upper level is a loft, where four beds can be seen. Two of Franz's younger cousins race down the stairs, giggling as they chase one another.

Fiona says, "Max! Mimi! Be careful!"

"Sorry, Mom!" they say in unison, then continue to run outside.

Mimi pokes her head back in. "Can we look at the ship they took?"

Max says, "We won't touch it."

"No, no," Fiona says. "We're having dinner now. And we're hearing Franz's story about their journey through Ara's Storm."

Max sighs. "But we've already heard it!"

"Where?"

Mimi says, "Everyone talks about it in the village. They say Captain Rath stood up to Ara and said 'No. More. Storm!'"

Rath flushes deeply. "Th-That is not what I said. Ara agreed to end it on his own."

Max tilts his head to the side. "Really?"

But Mimi gasps and begins punching her brother's arm quickly. "That's right! *He's* Captain Rath!"

"I am. Max, Mimi, I do not believe we have seen each other for several years. From what I remember, you were … this big the last I saw you."

Mimi shouts in delight. "I was right! Carry me!"

"Y-Yes."

Mimi leaps into his arms. Max tugs on his pant leg. "Me too!"

Rath ducks down. "Of course." Soon, both of them are holding onto his neck.

Fiona, hands on her hips, sighs. "You indulge them, Rath, and now they won't let go of you."

Rath pauses. "I … I see." He does not seem to know what to do.

Mimi says, "Did you really meet Amara?" and Max says, "So what was Draconi like?" but Fiona begins ushering all of them to one large table in the center of the room, saying, "You'll hear about it while we eat. Now, come on, it's time to sit down."

"Yes, Mom!" Max and Mimi say. They leap out of Rath's arms so suddenly, he stumbles. Then the two hop into their chairs, hands in front of them, ready for the story.

An older man – Franz's grandfather, Mattias – walks by, handing them both a plate with food on it.

Max says, "Thanks, Grandpa!" and Mimi digs in.

Joseline brings by a bowl of fruit for all, then Fiona gives out glasses. Franz's younger brother, Mallo, fills everyone's cup with juice, looking very serious as he does. However, after the

Pagu thank him, he brightens and flushes happily as he fills the rest.

After everyone has been served, Joseline says, "Franz, would you like to start?" She nods to the whole group. "And do feel free to jump in. I want my son to eat, too."

He starts with their departure from Priage and their stops at Lotinx, Tecla, Lady Azalea's Island, and Cunica before finding out that they would be taking the delivery for Haliae to Pica Pica instead.

Joseline frowns. "We had heard about Haliae's evacuation."

"It sounded terrible," Fiona says.

Franz turns to Rath. "You probably know this part better. It was you the gods wanted to talk to."

Fiona gasps. "I had heard as much! It's true, then … *do* go on, Rath!"

"Mom," Max says, "that's what he's trying to do."

She shushes him.

Rath says, "That is true. Elvin carried me to the Clock Tower on Pica Pica where the other gods were."

Joseline raises an eyebrow. "*All* of the gods? The stories differ here, I'm afraid."

"No. Only Berceuse, Marchand, Vocalise, Belle, Elvin, Maro, and Oracle were present."

Franz's family looks surprised.

Fiona exhales. "Well! I suppose it is only to be expected that you would speak with all of them. You would have been working with them had things been different, as Councilman Georgio's son."

But next to her, Joseline's eyes twinkle. "I don't think that's why. What happened next, Captain?"

Rath continues, telling them about the storm arriving on Pica Pica and Amara's appearance.

"So, she ordered you to go." Joseline frowns. "That wasn't very kind."

Fiona looks at her sister. "Joseline!"

She shrugs. "It's the truth."

Rath asks One-Eye to continue with the journey to Draconi and when all went dark. "I saw it with Lionel's Traits," he says. "Belle jumped overboard and turned into his shark form. He pushed *PearlHeart* the rest of the way."

Joseline and Fiona both look shocked. Joseline says to her son, "You did not tell us it was so close," and Fiona just says, "Franz!"

Franz says, "I didn't think it was a good idea at the time! And – honestly, I wasn't sure exactly what happened. It was dark and none of us – but One-Eye and Evermore, really – could see."

One-Eye says, "I offered to tell you."

"I really didn't want to hear at the time. All I wanted to hear was that we were safe."

Joseline sighs. "Fair enough."

Velt tells them about the Three Dragon Guardians and Rath being carried to Draconi on top of South.

Max says, "Finally! Draconi!"

Velt asks Rath, "Do you want to tell this part?"

"I can."

Rath shares how he met Ara, Krir, and Niven and the meals they had together. He speaks of Ara's garden of Frost Flowers and the table goes very quiet when he does.

Then he tells them about leaving Draconi, Ara's choice to go to Pica Pica instead, their meeting with Merp, and the gods going on to Haliae to clear away the storm.

Joseline nods. "*That* the stories get right. It was the gods that helped clear the storm – why it disappeared in that area so quickly."

They all add into the last part of their journey, traveling back to Lady Azalea's Island, finding the seed, and Ara's departure back to Draconi as well as how the other gods decided to help Haliae and Pantha, where they were traveling to now.

"I am told Rella went with Ara to Draconi," Rath says. "She has agreed to help him build new gardens suitable for each season. I think it is a wonderful thought."

Joseline smiles. "It truly is." She looks at her niece and nephew. "Well? What did you think?"

Max shrugs. "It wasn't as much action as I thought there would be."

Mimi punches him. "Don't you remember the previous year? Captain Rath *fell off his ship*."

Rath says, "I would rather not think about that."

Joseline asks, "Is your shoulder all right now? I would expect with someone like Carlos, you had a full recovery."

"I did. He, River-Pagu, and One-Eye helped heal it."

Joseline's eyebrows raise. "Really. A healer, too?" She looks at One-Eye. "Sounds like a wonderful first mate."

After dinner, they all help clean up. Rath and One-Eye wash dishes while Franz keeps the cake for dessert away from his younger brother and cousins. Velt helps Fiona put the clean dishes back in the cupboards while Joseline wipes off the table. When they are done, Mattias cuts the cake and hands out slices, then they all eat comfortably in the living room, talking more about what Franz's family has been doing.

Mimi says, "I've decided that I'm gonna be a sailor, too! Just you wait!"

Fiona drops her fork. "Mimi, that is a very dangerous profession. Just – " She glances at Franz, then Joseline, who gives her a hard look. "Just be careful."

"Of course I will, Mom!"

Looking at One-Eye, Max says, "I think I might travel around a lot. Learn how to fight and stuff."

Fiona says, "Max!"

He scoots over to One-Eye on his knees. "Will you fight

with me?"

"No."

Max points. "But – you've got that knife in your boot. Can't you at least show me how you use it?"

As One-Eye starts coughing, Fiona gasps. "A knife? Why in the world – "

Joseline raises her hand. "I want to know as well. That's a fair bit larger than one you'd have on a ship for repairs." One-Eye flushes a little. "Self-defense. Haven't used it since I was in Pantha."

Joseline nods.

Max says, "Is it really dangerous there?"

One-Eye does not respond.

"Would you tell me about it?"

"There's not a lot to say. It's dangerous, the people all expect a fight, and the Winters are difficult to survive." He pauses. "But – it's changing. I don't know if it's still like that."

"Don't you go back?"

"No."

"Isn't it your home? I'd always go back to Delphy in my adventures."

One-Eye's eye flicks over to Rath. "*PearlHeart* is the only place I've ever considered a home."

Rath's eyes widen, then soften.

Max says, "Then tell me more about *PearlHeart!*"

One-Eye eats his last bite. "You already heard about it."

"But – "

Joseline laughs. "I think it's about time for bed for the young ones. Franz, Velt, would you help?"

"Yes, Mom!" Franz says.

Velt hops up. "Gotcha!"

Fiona says, "I'll help Dad get settled."

Joseline says, "Thank you, Fi." Then she turns to Rath. "Would you mind talking for a bit outside? I'd like to hear about a few things that weren't recounted."

"Of course."

Joseline says to One-Eye, "Velt told me you, Rath, and the Pagu would be staying at her home, but you're welcome here whenever you like, all right?"

"Thanks."

Soon, the children are tucked into bed and Franz, Fiona, and Mattias are retiring as well. Joseline and Rath watch from the porch as Velt, One-Eye, and the Pagu go to Velt's home to get settled for the night.

Joseline's Spirit Dolphin – who was talking with One-Eye's Spirit Lion – swims back to her. Joseline listens, then says to Rath, "He's a good man. Your first mate."

"I believe so as well. I am very thankful to have met him."

Joseline smiles. She settles back. "Now, I know that Mimi, Max, and – yes – my sister, Fiona, were all interested in the more exciting bits, but what I want to know are some things that I think you and I are more interested in. How were the currents? And the weather? How was it to sail through Ara's Storm? I believe you would know all of those well."

Rath spends the next hour telling Joseline about *PearlHeart's* journey, the state of the waters, the effect Ara's Storm had on the currents, and how they all worked together with the gods to sail through the storm.

"I do not believe it would have been possible without everyone working together," he finishes.

"I agree fully." She pauses, taking in all Rath said, then asks, "What about Draconi? What was it like to sail near there – oh." She looks up. The moon has risen high. She looks apologetic. "I've kept you up far too late. And after such a long journey, too." She laughs. "I would be upset if someone had done that to me."

"It is all right."

Joseline shakes her head. "No, it's not. You're also doing

that business with the cracks and such for Leader Leytel. You've got a lot that you're doing. But, now it's time to get some sleep. Rest well, Rath. Thank you for telling me about the ocean – it feels like I'm in the water again just like before."

Rath quietly nods.

They squeeze one another's hands once, then Rath walks to Velt's house to rest. Joseline stays outside for a long moment, then looks up at the moon and the stars before wheeling inside.

She finds Fiona waiting for her. They exchange a long look, then Fiona smiles just a little. She helps her sister out of her wheelchair. "All right, let's get you to bed."

"Thank you, Fi."

7

The next day, Rath wakes up on a pallet next to One-Eye's. Velt's is empty and the Pagu's has been neatly folded up beside hers. Just as One-Eye is stirring, Rath sits up. He blinks when he sees someone in the front doorway.

Mimi trots in and holds out a plate of fruit pastries to Rath. Max comes in right after her, holding one out to One-Eye.

Mimi says, "We brought you breakfast."

"Thank you very much." Rath pauses. "I cannot eat this in bed."

"Why not?"

One-Eye – who had already started eating – puts his fork down slowly.

They end up at the table. Mimi and Max stay, telling them how their morning has been.

" … and then we ran down the hill to look at the ship," Mimi says.

"But we didn't touch it!" Max says.

Rath nods. "You said you would not."

At that moment, Velt and the Pagu come in. She is frowning, but brightens when she sees them. "Oh, hey! You're awake!" She ruffles the children's hair – one with each hand. "Thanks for bringing them breakfast!"

"Sure, Velt!" they say. Then they begin tugging at one another's hair, talking about whose is messed up more.

Velt sits down and the Pagu light on the table. "I was wondering when you two were going to get up. You must have been tired – I don't think I've ever seen either of you sleep for so long!"

Rath and One-Eye exchange a look.

"What time is it?" Rath asks.

"Ten in the morning."

Rath's eyebrows raise. One-Eye frowns. "Makes sense for the light outside." He asks his Lion, "Did you sleep longer, too?" and the Lion yawns as he nods.

Rath says, "I apologize for oversleeping."

Velt shakes her head. "No, no – it's all right." She laughs. "It was surprising, though. Even Mimi and Max were up before you."

Max, with the left side of his hair inexplicably in a tail with one of Mimi's hair ties, says, "I want breakfast at ten."

Mimi says, "Then when would you have lunch?"

"The same time, duh."

They scuffle a little, then run out of the room. Velt smiles at them, then turns back to the others, more serious. "A General Delphaen Message just went out. Yesterday, another crack appeared in a waterway not far from here, but it happened in the middle of the day – a lot of ships collided with each other and most of the ones sailing underwater had their hulls split when they hit the bottom. It flooded parts of the Constellation Caves, so the leader of Meridelle Village has disallowed everyone from entering them."

"Is everyone all right?" Rath asks.

"I think so. Mostly, my family's just heard about some bumps or scrapes – nothing serious. They kept the shop open through the night to help out. Right now, my parents are sleeping there while Vann and Merlin manage the shop today, but they only got a little sleep last night."

Flower-Pagu says, "Is there anything we could do to help? I don't know anything about repairing ships, though."

"That'd be great! I'm sure my sister could come up with something for you to do."

Rath looks at One-Eye – he nods – then says, "We can help, too."

"Great! I kinda already told her you might be willing and she's got an idea for what you can do."

After Rath and One-Eye finish eating, they find Franz and he brings his younger brother Mallo to go with them.

"I want to see Merlin," he says softly.

They walk together through the small paths of Meridelle Village, passing hills with calm waterways running in between them.

Thirty minutes later, they arrive at an inland sea which connects to many waterways. There is a small shop near a set of docks at its shore. While many people are in front of the building, others are listening to workers explain why they cannot use the cracked waterway.

As they join the crowd, Franz says to Velt,

"Wow … I didn't know it would be this bad."

"I didn't either. Though it was one of the larger waterways."

They reach the shop and have to push in through a line of people. When they come in sight of the desk, Vann – Velt's sister – a young woman with deep bags under her eyes, is saying to a traveler, "Yeah – it's almost done. Please go to the back. We'll find you when it's ready. Next." When she sees Velt and the others, her eyes light up and she quickly waves them over.

The man who was at the front gives them a surprised look, but when Vann says, "That's my sister. And her friends. They're here to help," the man's expression brightens considerably.

Velt asks her sister, "So – what can we do?"

"You and Franz handle the counter and take reports – make two lines." She says to the Pagu, "Actually … could you three do that, too? We could have more lines going and it'd go a lot faster. All you have to do is get a report of what's wrong with their ship and where it's docked. Here – I'll get you some paper." She digs under the desk.

Flower-Pagu says, "Thank you!" and Bucket-Pagu says, "We're here to help!", but Well-Pagu says, "Investigate?"

Vann blinks. "Huh?"

Well-Pagu looks to Rath, who says, "I believe they are asking if they can investigate the damage the ships have sustained."

"Oh." Vann nods quickly. "Yeah. That'd be great. You're more familiar with ships, right?" they ask Well-Pagu.

"Yes!"

"Great. Then we can go together. I'll be the one repairing them until Merlin wakes up. He's napping now. We've been taking it in shifts while our dads rest." She turns to Rath and One-Eye. "I trust your feel, Captain – mind testing out the ships with One-Eye once they are repaired?"

"Of course," he says and One-Eye nods.

Vann grins, relieved. "All right. Thanks – all of you. I am really looking forward to this day being over." She lets all of them behind the counter, then kneels next to Mallo and ruffles his hair. "You come to see Merlin?" The boy nods. "Sorry. He's gotta rest for a bit. But – why don't you come back with us and you can watch me work on some ships?"

"Okay."

They go through the back door, passing Velt and Vann's

dads and Merlin, all passed out in hammocks, then go outside. A few ships are on the shore and Vann gestures to them. "I managed to finish these before things got really busy inside. Test them out, then – if they're good – I'll mark them off and have you sail them back to their owners."

Rath and One-Eye agree, then go to the first ship.

While they do, Vann says, "This way, Well-Pagu, Mallo. Here's the one I was working on earlier."

They follow her to the ship and Well-Pagu looks it over carefully while Mallo sits on a box to watch them.

Nearby, Rath sails with One-Eye at the tiller. The sun is warm and the wind hits both of them.

They go further out into the water, testing out various turns and maneuvers. Rath asks One-Eye, "What do you think?"

"Tiller is stiff."

"I thought so as well from the turns. The rigging is sound. The mast and sail are in good repair." He pauses, then shifts his weight. "The hull … "

One-Eye shifts his own weight. "Lurches starboard."

"Exactly."

They return to Vann and give their report. She laughs and pats them on their shoulders. "Knew I could leave it to you. Well-Pagu and I will take a look at it after we finish this one. Go ahead and take out the next one." As they sail away, Mallo – who had been staring at them since they picked up speed on the first ship – says, "They're really good."

Vann grins. "Aren't they? Those two spend most of their lives on the ocean."

Mallo nods. "They remind me of your dads when they go out."

"Really?" She looks at the two again, thoughtful, then shrugs and – smiling – starts working.

Throughout the morning, Mallo watches Rath and One-

Eye, forgetting about the repairs, while Vann and Well-Pagu finish the ship they were on, then start on the first one that was tested. Well-Pagu studies the hull seriously, then points. Vann nods and begins sanding it down.

Back in the shop, Franz, Velt, Flower-Pagu, and Bucket-Pagu take reports from the people in the lines and outside, the docks fill up with more ships needing repairs.

Near noon, Merlin wakes up. He joins Mallo out on the beach. "Whatcha watching?"

"Ship."

Merlin raises an eyebrow, then follows his look. He brightens. "Ah." He turns to Vann. "Rath and One-Eye?"

"Yeah. He, Franz, Velt, Well-Pagu, Bucket-Pagu, and Flower-Pagu came to help."

Merlin nods to Well-Pagu. "Thank you very much."

"Welcome!"

To Mallo, Merlin says, "Did you come here for another block puzzle? I think I've got one around here."

Mallo blinks. "A … " He looks surprised. "Yes. I did."

Merlin smiles and Vann laughs, saying, "I think he's been too interested watching those two sail. I didn't think anything but your puzzles could keep his attention for so long."

Merlin says, "They do sail beautifully."

"Very thorough reports, too. I wouldn't have expected anything less from Rath, but I was happy to see One-Eye's the same, if more succinct than the Captain. He's got a good feel for sailing."

"He's from Pantha, too. That's pretty surprising." He kisses Vann on the cheek. "Thought you could all use lunch. I can manage things for an hour or so."

"Thanks." She turns to Mallo. "You ready for something to eat?"

"Yes, please."

Merlin leaves to relieve the others while Vann, Mallo,

and Well-Pagu wait for Rath and One-Eye to return and give their report. When they do, Vann tells them, "Thanks for your work. Merlin's up now, so we'll all be taking a break. It's nearly noon."

Together, with Franz, Velt, Flower-Pagu, and Bucket-Pagu, they sit on one of the hills nearby and eat lunch provided by a local sailor who brought it out of thanks.

Bucket-Pagu says, "I did not know that so many things could be wrong with a ship."

Rath says, "I find it very sad."

Vann sighs. "They're all from the cracked waterway. It's a larger one, too, and happened right in the middle of the day." She shakes her head. "Unfortunately, we weren't able to save some of the ships. The repairs we would do would amount to building a whole new one." She continues, "Velt said you were investigating the cause of them. You have any ideas?"

"No, only that they are being caused by something underground and that all of the ones I am aware of are on supporting walls of the Constellation Caves. May I ask if you know where the new crack is?"

"Yeah." She goes back into her family's shop and returns with a map of the waterways on Delphy. "It was here." She points to a mark to the north of the inland sea. "We've been trying to keep track of them to let other travelers know, too."

He thanks her, but frowns when he sees the crack is also on a supporting wall of the Constellation Caves.

After lunch, Vann takes a nap while the others work. Mallo watches Rath and One-Eye test the ships as Merlin and Well-Pagu fix more to be taken out. Franz, Velt, Bucket-Pagu, and Flower-Pagu are at the counter, talking to travelers or taking them out to the docks to their newly fixed ships. One traveler shakes Franz's hand enthusiastically, thanking him.

It is nearing dinnertime when Velt and Vann's parents walk inside. Niz, with graying hair and many Delphaen tattoos, takes Velt's shoulder. "We can take it from here, sweetheart." Velt gasps. "Dad!" She throws her arms around his neck. His husband Alfin, with short gray hair and dark blue eyes, gives Velt a warm hug, too.

"Good to see you," he says.

Niz claps his hands, facing the crowd. "Everyone! We'll be taking over – please stay in the lines you're at and we'll get to you in order."

Velt says, "We don't mind helping."

He ruffles her short hair. "No, no – go relax. We're planning on closing the shop for dinner – but we need to get these reports first. You and your friends go on ahead."

They all give their notes to Niz and Alfin, then leave through the back of the shop, where Vann is still sleeping. On the beach, Merlin is tightening a bolt while Well-Pagu checks the hull.

Rath and One-Eye come back and Velt waves to them. "Our dads say they're giving us the rest of the day off."

"I see. That is very kind of them," Rath says. He says to Merlin, "It seems to be sailing perfectly." One-Eye nods in agreement beside him.

"Great. Go ahead and sail it back to the front. I'll get it marked off."

As they board the ship again, Merlin pats Mallo's head. "Time for you to go, too."

"May I have a block puzzle?"

"Heeey? Watching ships *and* a puzzle?" He digs into his pocket. "Yeah, sure. Here." He tosses it.

Mallo catches it. "Thanks, Merlin!" Then he trots over to Franz and holds the block puzzle in one hand and his brother's in the other.

Merlin stretches out his back. "Thanks for your work, Well-Pagu."

"Happy!"

He grins. Then he tells Velt, "Go on with the others. I'll wait here until Vann wakes up, then we'll head out."

After they leave, Merlin flops down in the sand with his tools, resting.

The group meets Rath and One-Eye in front of the shop, then they all return to Franz and Velt's homes.

Merlin and Vann come later that afternoon and as it nears dinner time, Niz and Alfin arrive.

Niz says, "The shop is closed until we open at four tomorrow morning like usual!"

Merlin laughs. "How late!"

Alfin gives him a look, but smiles.

Everyone works together to prepare the food for dinner. Rath, Franz, the Pagu, and Mallo gather berries and nuts from the surrounding bushes and trees. Velt, Vann, and Merlin help Niz and Joseline prepare the side dishes while Alfin roasts the vegetables outdoors, Fiona gives him suggestions, and the rest of Franz's family bring out the dishes.

When it is all done, they eat outside, talking around the fire that Niz and Alfin built up in the clearing between the homes.

Rath tells the others, "I would like to go to the Constellation Caves and ask the workers there about the damage the caves have sustained. I believe my grandfather needs to be informed as well."

"I'll go with you," One-Eye says.

"Us too!" Velt says.

Franz and the Pagu nod beside them.

Fiona and Niz look concerned, however Alfin says, "It's a good idea."

Joseline adds, "You can also show them the connection with the cracks and the cave walls with your maps. Seeing all of them and not just the ones here in Meridelle Village might give them an idea of what's been causing them."

Shaking her head, Fiona says, "I still think it sounds dangerous."

"They'll be all right," Niz says. Then to their group, "Just be careful. All of you."

Velt says, "We will! Leader Peiera already disallowed anyone from entering, so we'll just find some workers outside we can talk to."

Niz asks Vann and Merlin, "Will you two be going as well?"

Vann shakes her head. "Not with the ship repairs we've still got. And a wedding, I guess." To the group, she says, "Actually, would you be able to help again for the next two days? It made a huge difference today."

Alfin says, "It'll give the workers time to finish any repairs with the caves and make them safer to travel to."

They all agree.

Niz sighs, patting Velt and Franz's shoulders. "Well, I guess I'll get at least two days with my dear daughter and her best friend."

Velt says, "Dad! We'll be back in a few days!"

Alfin says, "They'll be fine."

Niz says, "I know."

"You're worrying."

"You know."

Alfin smiles. Then he says, "Does Garreth know anything about this, Rath?"

"I have informed him of what I knew as of last week. I do not know if he has heard that Leader Peiera has disallowed travel to the caves in Meridelle Village, however, it is likely."

"I agree. He have any thoughts?"

"No. He only said to be careful while we are investigating this."

The next morning, they wake up at three, get ready, and go to the shop. At six, a pair of Paradi messengers arrive with a letter from Garreth for Rath, who is just returning from testing a ship with One-Eye.

Vann and Merlin – who are repairing the next ship together with Well-Pagu – notice and Vann tells Rath, "Go see what it is. We're not done with this one yet."

He thanks her, then steps aside to read his letter before returning to work.

At noon, the shop closes for an hour. There are fewer ships to repair now. The group sits in the back room at the table to eat lunch, then Rath composes his reply letter to his grandfather, which he then takes to the Paradi Message Tower by the docks.

They work for the rest of the day and walk back to Franz and Velt's homes that evening to have dinner prepared by Franz's family.

Afterward, Joseline is outside on her porch, looking up at the moon. Her Spirit Dolphin is chattering with One-Eye's Spirit Lion. She turns to One-Eye, who is sitting nearby. "Your Lion is quite talkative. My Dolphin enjoys it."

"I'm glad."

Joseline wheels closer to him. "Has he been with you your entire life?"

One-Eye nods. "Since I can remember."

Her look softens. "It was the same with me." She looks at her Dolphin, knowing the Lion is there too, even though she cannot see him. "Fiona thinks my Dolphin only came to me because of my accident – that they only go to people who will suffer some sort of tragedy. But, I don't believe that – I've had a very happy life, I believe."

One-Eye smiles briefly. "I don't either." He asks, "What happened to you?"

She presses her lips together. "Ten years ago, right when Franz was starting to learn how to sail, my ship went down in the Delphaen Trade Route. Pirates attacked us, wanting the cargo we were carrying. Neither of our ships survived.

The hull of mine was cracked in two. I lost the use of my legs helping my crew escape." Her eyes shine. "No one was killed. It truly was a miracle." She takes a shuddering breath. "But, Fiona didn't think so. She's been worried about all of us since – especially Franz. I was concerned after my accident that he'd give up on sailing or be afraid of it for the rest of his life. But, I talked to him and Marchand did, too … and Franz came to terms with it as well. Velt's been a support to him, just as Rath has." She sobers. "Your captain hasn't had an easy time of it either. Has he ever told you about it?"

"No." One-Eye's Spirit Lion pads over, satisfied, and he begins petting him. "He'd probably tell me if I asked, but I'd only be interested if he wanted to tell me himself."

She hums. "You take him as he is as he does for you."

He reddens, but does not say anything.

Joseline strokes her Dolphin for a moment, then says, "Years ago – when Franz introduced me to him – Rath told me something interesting about Spirit Animals. He said his grandparents could see one another's – Garreth's Dolphin and Azalea's Turtle. I had heard of such a thing happening, but never a real case."

One-Eye glances at his Lion, but he is quiet. "Did he say how?"

"He wasn't sure. According to his grandmother, it's very rare and if it does happen, it more than often involves someone who is from Sudines or with heritage from there." She shrugs. "Again – she didn't tell him why so he couldn't say how that would be a factor."

He nods, thinking.

After a few minutes, Joseline says, "I don't think Fiona's right about why Spirit Animals bond to the people they do – that it's because of tragedy or because they *will* experience tragedy. I believe they simply know this is where they need to be – and *who* they need to be with." She smiles. "They have an excellent sense for those sorts of things."

One-Eye returns it. "I think so, too." His Lion grins at him, saying something, and One-Eye shoves him, laughing softly.

Joseline and her Dolphin watch them, then look up at the moon together, remembering the ocean waves surrounding them.

8

The next day, they work at the repair shop again, but by the afternoon, Niz, Alfin, Vann, and Merlin send Rath and the others off.

"Go!" Niz says. "If you want an early start tomorrow to the caves, you'll want your rest today."

Velt says, "Thanks, Dad!"

When they reach Franz and Velt's homes, they all start packing for the trip. While the Pagu neatly fold their extra clothes and belongings into day packs, Franz tucks his own into his bag as Fiona hovers over him. "You're only bringing two shirts? Bring three," she says.

"Aunt Fiona … "

Joseline pats her sister's arm. "Fi, I think my son knows what to bring for a trip."

"But – that's for the ocean! This is different. And to somewhere dangerous."

Franz says, "We won't go into the caves, just talk with

whoever we can find outside of them."

They spend the rest of the day playing with Mallo, Mimi, and Max, then have dinner with everyone outside.

Velt sits in between her parents by the fire. They both have their arms around her. Niz says, "There she goes! Off again, my wayward daughter!"

Velt says, "Dad!"

Alfin squeezes her shoulder. "He says it because he's worried."

"We'll be fine."

He kisses her hair. "I know. He knows, too."

Niz says, "Do let us know if you run into any trouble. I'm just a Delphaen message away and you've seen how fast Alfin can run."

Velt laughs. "I know!"

Across from them, Joseline hugs Franz tightly. "You have become so brave."

"Thanks, Mom. It helps to have everyone else around."

"I'm sure. What was it that Well-Pagu said earlier? Something about 'together'?"

Franz grins. "Yup!"

She pats his arm, then watches as he rejoins the others, beaming with pride.

Early the next day, the group sets out. Both families see them off. Mimi and Max look very tired and yawn as they wave, but Mallo is surprisingly awake.

As they walk through the morning, fewer homes are seen until all that is left are large old trees and tall grass.

Flower-Pagu spins in the air. "Oh! I love this part of Delphy! It's been so long since I've seen it!"

Rath smiles. "I do as well. And it has been the same for me."

Franz says, "It's really nice. Velt and I always use this way to reach the Constellation Caves in the Winter." He frowns.

"Seems so weird they're closed now."

Beside them, One-Eye looks around and his Spirit Lion has his nose in the air, sniffing all the different scents. He sees two Spirit Dolphins who are not bonded to anyone move in arcs up in the sky and his ears perk up.

At noon, they take a break in an open field. The Pagu eat on a small checkered blanket and the others sit on the nearby rocks. The Spirit Lion studies one, then asks One-Eye who turns to Rath. "What kind of rock is this?"

Rath finishes his bite and says, "Miphrin." He looks down at the one he is sitting on and brushes his hand over a small part that has a mirror-like surface which has been exposed over time by the wind. "It is the same type of mineral that is in the ceiling of the Constellation Caves."

Well-Pagu softly says, "Stars."

One-Eye looks confused and Rath explains, "The Miphrin deposits are what create the constellations – as Well-Pagu said, they create the stars." He smiles and Well-Pagu beams as they nibble on their bread roll. "There are small streams in the caves and when Delphaen messages are sent through them, the light is reflected by the Miphrin. It is very beautiful to see."

They pack up and start traveling again. After a few hours, they come to a low valley.

Rath is walking down when One-Eye suddenly holds him back. "Wait."

As the breeze blows the tall grass, he sees a crack in the ground, far larger than any others. The Spirit Lion – who had alerted One-Eye – is crouched next to it.

Rath kneels as Velt, Franz, and the Pagu join them.

Franz says, "Another?"

"Is it also on one of the cave's supporting walls?" Velt asks.

Rath pulls out his maps, comparing their location with the crack. "Yes, it is. We need to report this in case it is not known by the workers yet."

Franz says, "There's a stream nearby, I can send a message to my family and they can inform Leader Peiera."

While he is gone, Rath, Velt, and One-Eye begin gathering sticks that the Pagu help find and put them around the crack to warn others of it. Velt ties napkins to them so that they are more noticeable in the tall grass.

Rath says to One-Eye, "Thank you for telling me to wait."

"My Spirit Lion told me. He wants to know why they've been appearing, too, and wants to help."

When Franz returns, they continue on, growing closer to the coastline.

Just as the ocean comes into view, they suddenly hear a shout and a man runs up the hill toward them.

He puffs a little, out of breath, then says, "You're not here to see the Constellation Caves, are you?"

Rath says, "Yes, however – "

The man straightens and shakes his head. "Absolutely not. This part isn't safe. The entrance just ahead collapsed."

They all look startled and Rath asks, "Are the workers inside all right?"

"We're not sure. I've been trying to get a message to them, but – well, I'll show you. Follow me – it's safer on the beach."

As he guides them around other cracks marked with sticks, he explains, "I'm Marn. I'm part of the communications team. We were all sent down to the caves when the crack appeared in the waterway in Meridelle Village, but other teams have already been sent down to areas where other waterways have been affected. It seems Rath Lewis – Councilman Georgio's son – was asked for his input by Leader Leytel of Kel City and found that most of the cracks are on supporting walls of the Constellation Caves. Now, that could mean a few things, but we're only going off of the cracks here in Meridelle Village. We've requested maps to be sent of other parts of Delphy, but they've been delayed with the waterways being damaged."

Rath says, "I have maps of them. And I am Rath."

Marn stops, blinks, then chuckles. "Well! It's great to meet you. I appreciate your help with this."

"Of course."

They reach the entrance and see large rocks have fallen over it, blocking it entirely. A pool has formed at their base with the water from the ocean that can no longer enter the cave.

"I'm just glad no one was near when it happened," Marn says. "Everyone was further inside. I've tried to contact them, but the messages are having a hard time getting through the rocks. I even tried wetting a rope and sending it down one of the cracks up on the cliff – that was when I saw you all. But, it kept drying out before I could find the stream in the cave.

Rath nods, thinking. "Have you tried the underwater tunnels?"

"I've heard of them, of course, but I thought they were too small to – ah!" He grins. "Good idea." He walks over to the ocean and dips his hand in. "It should go to one of the main pools in the cave – I'm sure the team will pass by it. I'll make it extra strong, just in case." He sends his message and it goes down, disappearing quickly.

When he rejoins them, he asks, "You wouldn't happen to know when those tunnels were created, do you?"

"No. Marchand does not know either. We explored them twelve years ago. Only a few were large enough to swim through, however, and he was unsure of their stability."

"That's what we were told, too." He wipes off his hands. "Well, all I can do now is wait for their response. Can I see those maps you mentioned?"

Rath gives them to him and he looks over each, comparing them carefully.

He shakes his head as he hands them back. "These cracks really are all over Delphy. I see what you mean about their placement, too – that in particular is highly unusual." He explains to all of them, "With the Constellation Caves, we would more expect the Miphrin deposits to be comprised – not the supporting walls. Miphrin is pretty, but also very fragile. It's long been a concern for how it would affect the stability of the caves, however, besides a few isolated incidents over the past centuries, there hasn't been anything serious until now. Those in the repair teams would know more. There might be another reason those areas sustained cracks that I'm unaware of." He chews his lip. "Actually, Dinra's group shouldn't be too far from here – just the next entrance. I need to stay here for when my team replies, so would you be willing to take your maps to her to look at? If you stay on the beach, you should be safe – none of us have heard of any cracks occurring here."

They agree to and he thanks them before they continue on east, following the coastline. Beside them, the waves hit the shore.

Franz says, "The water level is really high for Summer. Though, my family says there's been a lot more rain since Ara's Storm."

Velt says, "When Franz and I visited the caves two Winters ago, it was also up – it almost covered part of the cliff."

They walk for the rest of the day, then begin to set up their camp late that evening.

After Franz sends a message to his family to update them on what they learned from Marn, they all sit down for dinner around a fire they made in the sand.

Flower-Pagu looks out at the water, glittering under the moonlight. "The ocean is so pretty at night! All of the stars in the sky and on the water!"

Rath smiles. "I think so as well. Marchand tells me that how the ocean and sky looked at night was part of his inspiration for the Constellation Caves." His eyes fall. "I hope that the people inside are all right."

Franz's tattoos glow and he sets down his food to go receive the reply message from his family.

When he comes back, he looks nervous. "My family thinks we should come tomorrow morning. And not just Aunt Fiona – my mom, too."

The others lower their bowls and exchange a look.

Velt says, "We all told Marn we would bring the maps to Dinra's group. We have to at least do that."

"I agree," Rath says.

One-Eye looks at his Spirit Lion for a long moment, then turns to the Pagu. "What do you think?"

They pause. Then Flower-Pagu says, "We think it will be hard."

Bucket-Pagu says, "But, we also agree that we need to find Dinra's group."

Well-Pagu says, "Worried."

Rath understands. "About everyone in the caves?" Well-Pagu nods. "I am as well."

Franz and Velt look at one another, then Franz stands up again. "I'll send another message. I didn't really tell them about the people inside – thought it wouldn't help, but maybe it'd show them why we need to do this." He goes back to the ocean.

Velt says, "We'll just stay on the beach, like Marn said."

One-Eye asks Rath, "How far is the next entrance?"

"Only three hours."

Franz returns and sits back down. "Well – I've told them everything. I bet I'll hear something in the morning, then we can decide."

They finish their meal, talk a while longer around the fire, play a few rounds of Marchand's Twist – the Pagu suggested it – then tuck in for the night.

9

As they are packing up their camping supplies the next day, Franz's tattoos glow.

"It's my family," he says, trotting over to the ocean. Afterward, he says, "Well, my mom's agreed now. Aunt Fiona still doesn't, but … " He shrugs. Then he turns to One-Eye. "My mom says her Spirit Dolphin thinks we should keep going. She wanted to ask – if it was all right – what your Spirit Lion thought. She says to trust in what they say."

Beside One-Eye, the Lion straightens. They glance at one another, then One-Eye says, "He thinks we should keep going, too." He crosses his arms. "But, he also can't stand not knowing why the cracks are appearing." The Lion flicks his tail.

Rath says, "Is that all right with everyone?"

One-Eye and his Spirit Lion nod immediately, followed by Franz and the Pagu. Velt says, "Definitely!"

As they set out, Franz says, "My mom also asked we stay on the beach like we did yesterday. It's safer and we have easy access to the ocean to send any messages."

Throughout the morning, they see more small ships on the ocean and Velt says, "I wonder if they're all out there because of the waterways being unpredictable."

Franz says, "Not a bad idea for right now."

One-Eye and his Lion look at the landscape that is unfamiliar to them while Rath thinks. The Pagu fly alongside him and take breaks every so often on his shoulder, fanning themselves from the hot sun. An hour later, Franz is doing the same and they all decide to walk in the surf to cool off.

One-Eye's Spirit Lion goes to talk with a few of the Spirit Dolphins that were nearby and when he returns, he seems very pleased.

However, when they are nearly to the next entrance, the Spirit Dolphins return and speak quickly with the Lion, Franz, Velt and the Pagu.

One-Eye sees his Lion's expression and asks, "What is it?"

The Lion explains and One-Eye tells Rath, "My Lion told the Spirit Dolphins earlier to let him know about anything regarding the caves. They just came to tell him the entrance ahead has collapsed."

"That is very concerning. Do they … May I … "

Flower-Pagu softly says, "Ask whatever you need, Rath."

"Do they know if the people inside are safe? Or, where they are?"

One-Eye looks to his Lion, who turns to the Dolphins. They shake their heads, then swim off. One-Eye says, "They're going to go check on them."

"Thank you for telling me."

They pick up their pace for the next hour.

As they get close to the cave entrance, they see a group of workers up on the cliffside, talking seriously with one another.

One of them sees Rath and the others and shouts, "Hey! Didn't you hear Leader Peiera's warning? We don't want anyone near the caves right now."

However, one of the other workers says, "Were you sent by Marn? With maps?"

"Yes!" Rath says.

The group helps them up a steep path on the cliffside. As they set down their bags, they see that they are all standing near a large crack in the ground and a woman with dark hair is next to it, repairing it with Maro's Traits. She looks very tired.

The second one who spoke tells them, "I am Dinra. I can look at the maps in just a moment." She kneels, handing the worker more stone to meld to the other, filling in the gap. "While the other teams have been inside, we have been tasked with fixing as many cracks from outside." She sighs. "However, we will need far more help to clear the entrances – we know of two that have been blocked as of right now. Two Spirit Dolphins just informed us of the second – we are all hoping the team Marn is from is all right. It sounds like he was able to reach them, however – "

The ground beneath them shudders.

The worker filling in the crack immediately removes her hands. Dinra quickly pulls her to her feet and they both step back, the rest doing the same.

With another shudder, a second crack appears further inland. It splinters twice, edging toward them before connecting with the one they were trying to fix.

As soon as it does, the ground breaks loose.

They all move away. The Pagu fly toward the edge of the cliff with Franz and Velt. One-Eye grabs Rath's hand to pull him to safety.

Abruptly, the land gives way beneath Rath's feet. As One-Eye tries to pull him back up, the ground underneath him collapses too and he falls with Rath into the cave. One-Eye's Spirit Lion leaps after them.

10

Below the surface, One-Eye holds onto Rath. They tumble into the rubble and he lands hard on his back. They roll for a few feet, then stop. Rocks continue to fall from above.

Rath pulls himself up onto his knees and shakes One-Eye's shoulder. "One-Eye. We need to – " The man's eye is closed. "One-Eye?" Another large sound causes Rath to look up and he sees another part of the ceiling give way. He picks up One-Eye and runs, the Lion on his heels, toward the nearest tunnel.

Almost as soon as he reaches it, the rest of the ceiling in the previous chamber falls, filling the cave for several deafening moments. When it stops, Rath can only see tiny sparks of sunshine through the collapsed rocks.

One-Eye stirs in his arms, then opens his eye. It glows blue with Lionel's Traits, allowing him to see in the dark. His Lion is licking his hand. "Back," he says.

"I'm sorry?"

One-Eye coughs the dust out of his throat. "My back. Lie

me down on my stomach." After Rath does, he sighs. "Where are we?"

"In the Constellation Caves. I do not know any more than that. What do you see?"

"Cave. Tunnel. Whatever it is." He groans. "What happened?"

"We fell. When we landed, you were unconscious."

"I'll be fine. What about you?"

"Only a few cuts. I am all right."

One-Eye smiles a little. "Good." As his Spirit Lion lies across his legs, he says, "My Lion says I need to be here for a while. Sevran's Traits are healing my back, but it's going to take a while. Will probably go faster if I sleep. Can you find out exactly where we are while I do?"

"Yes. Please rest."

"Thanks. It'll just be a few hours." He closes his eye and falls asleep.

Rath stays with him for a minute longer, then stands up. It is too dark to see in the tunnel, however he can hear water, so he walks toward it. Next to the wall, there is a stream that runs through all of the Constellation Caves. He kneels next to it and picks up two dry rocks beside it. He flicks them together. A small spark erupts from them, brightening the water for a moment. He does it again, but this time, he looks up.

Faint stars flash above.

For the next thirty minutes, he moves beside the stream, scraping the rocks together to create enough light to cause the Miphrin to light up, building a constellation.

When he comes to the last star, he stops. "*Marchand's Message.*"

He walks back, counting his steps. He listens for One-Eye's breathing, then sits near him again. He closes his eyes, picturing the map of the Constellation Caves and keeping it in his mind for when One-Eye awakes.

The Spirit Lion, who is still lying over One-Eye's legs, looks at Rath curiously. Then he focuses on One-Eye again as the man rests, his traits healing his injuries.

Back outside, Dinra gapes at the disappearing dust cloud. "They – "

Bucket-Pagu says, "They're okay."

Flower-Pagu says, "One-Eye's Spirit Lion is with them. He won't let anything happen."

Dinra bites her lip. She looks at the whole group, then bows. "I am sorry. I am responsible for this. I promise to do all that I can to ensure their safe exit."

Well-Pagu shakes their head. "Communicate."

Dinra looks confused, but Velt says, "I think I understand. It might be better if you focus on communicating with the other groups that are near entrances – get them out before something else happens. Right, Well-Pagu?"

They nod.

Velt continues, "While you're doing that, we'll find Rath and One-Eye. Rath has been studying those maps all month – I'm sure he remembers the one of the Constellation Caves well enough to get him and One-Eye to the nearest exit."

Franz says, "He might, but we don't. We don't even know where they are down there."

"No – but we can make a guess." Velt walks over to the bags near the edge of the cliff. She hesitates, then asks Well-Pagu, "Do you think he'll mind if I look at his grandfather's map?"

Well-Pagu gives her a thumbs-up. "Okay!"

"Thanks." Velt very carefully takes it out. Franz leans over her shoulder.

Dinra says, "Were those the maps he mentioned? That Marn wanted me to see?"

"Oh right!" Velt shows her while Franz gets out the others.

"Here."

"Thank you." She looks at each, her frown deepening. With a bewildered look, she hands them back. "No cracks have touched the Miphrin? Given the number of deposits … it's remarkable. Not only that, but them appearing over the supporting walls and what happened to the entrances should be highly unlikely – they should be the strongest parts of the caves." She sighs. "I'm afraid I do not know why they would appear in those areas – someone from Ullia might. Erole's Traits allow them to sense any structure – including any hidden weak points. I apologize I could not offer more." She straightens. "As Well-Pagu said, we will now focus on communicating with others so that they exit safely. We will start with contacting Marn to see if he has reached his team." She nods to them. "Be careful. I am sorry again."

They all go down to the beach, bringing their packs with them and Dinra's group gathers by the ocean where she sends a Delphaen message.

While she does, Franz, Velt, and the Pagu study the Constellation Caves map.

Velt says, "It looks like Rath and One-Eye ended up in one of the larger chambers. Here."

Franz says, "It looks like there's three different tunnels off of it. Which one do we follow?"

"I'm not sure … " She bites her lip, then says, "This definitely counts as an emergency, right? I could use Belle's Traits."

Franz nods encouragingly and she closes her eyes, concentrating.

She frowns as if startled, then points east. "That way."

Franz looks at the map. "So … this tunnel. Is something wrong?"

"I could only sense One-Eye. Rath has to be down there too, right?"

"I'm sure he is. Well-Pagu, Bucket-Pagu, and Flower-Pagu said they both were okay." He shoulders his pack and One-Eye's. "I mean, Evermore has never been able to sense Rath with Erole's Traits either, right?"

"That's true." She takes up Rath's pack as well as her own and the Pagu shoulder theirs as well, then they travel along the coast together.

In the caves, Rath waits for One-Eye to wake up. All he can see is the yellow glow of Sevran's Traits. The Spirit Lion lies across One-Eye's legs protectively.

Suddenly, the Lion's ears twitch and he faces the blocked entrance. After a moment, Rath hears voices and turns as well. He stands up, feeling his way toward them. When he reaches the rubble, he says softly, "Hello?"

The voices go silent immediately.

Then, very quietly, he hears, "How many?" and a reply of, "Only one. From Pantha."

"What is he doing down here?"

"The cave-in. Wasn't supposed to be so large … "

The voices fade and their footsteps retreat away.

"Excuse me," Rath says, but they are gone. He returns to One-Eye's side, thinking.

The Lion looks in the direction of the voices for a few more moments, then settles down on One-Eye.

They wait for another hour and a half.

Footsteps approach them.

In the dark tunnel, Rath sees two pairs of pale yellow eyes glowing in his direction, bouncing as they approach. They remind him of Evermore's.

He stands and walks over to two people wearing hoods.

They study him and one says, "You are not from Pantha."

"No. I am from Delphy."

The pale yellow eyes squint and in the darkness, both

frown, exchanging looks. "But … "

Rath starts to say, "May I ask who you are?" when he feels a small electrical charge and his eyes flutter closed.

The two catch him, then one carries him down the tunnel with the other following, saying, "I can't sense him at all!"

"Neither can I." The one carrying Rath pauses. "We should take him to Lura."

The other nods.

Nearby, One-Eye's Lion sees and hears all of this. He stands, but does not leave One-Eye's side. He paces in a circle then lies back down, looking tense.

Thirty minutes later, One-Eye wakes up. As his Lion steps off of him, he looks around carefully, still feeling tense from the dull ache in his back. He stiffens. "Where's Rath?" The Lion tells him quickly.

One-Eye tries to stand up – his Lion helps him. "Why didn't – " He rubs his face, then exhales. "I get why you didn't wake me up. We'll find him." He peers into the tunnel ahead. "Do you know where they went? Or where we are?" He sighs. "Rath was supposed to figure that out."

As they start to walk, his Lion gives a nod.

"He did?" One-Eye starts to smile, then frowns. "*Marchand's Message.* How did he figure that out without his traits? I thought they were supposed to make the stars glow." The Lion explains and he says, "Rocks? That's really smart."

They reach a divide in their path. One-Eye asks, "What way do you think?"

The Lion looks down both helplessly.

"I thought you saw the map." When the Lion pouts, One-Eye strokes his mane. "I know you're not a navigator. But, if the tunnel we were just in was *Marchand's Message,* then maybe we can figure out the rest like Rath did – with the rocks." He then asks, "Where would those people take him? To their god's constellation? Isn't that Erole?" The Lion nods and One-Eye thinks some more, then shakes his head. "I'm not as good with the constellations as Rath, but I think I can tell which path we should go down."

Being supported by his Lion, One-Eye finds two rocks. He scrapes them together, creating a spark. When he sees the Miphrin flash above, he grins. Walking more steadily, he moves along the left tunnel, watching the stars light up. His smile fades as they reach another fork in the path. Looking back the way they came, he asks his Lion, "Do you know what that constellation was?"

After a moment, the Lion shakes his head.

One-Eye drops the rocks. "Neither do I. Let's try this a different way. Rath says that the constellations down here are just like the ones up above in the sky." The Lion nods. "I think … I remember seeing Erole's more to the east – does that sound right to you?"

The Lion thinks intently, then nods again.

"Thanks. I'm glad you're here," he says, scratching behind the Lion's ear. They start walking. "I always am." After a few minutes, he continues, "If *Marchand's Message* is behind us, we must be heading east now. We won't worry about which path – just try to stay in this direction and … " He does not finish.

The Lion understands.

He pads beside One-Eye, watching him grow stronger with each step.

Rath wakes up in a cave full of pale yellow eyes staring at him. He gives a start when he feels a hand on his arm.

A man knelt next to him helps him to his feet. "You are all right? You are unharmed? We are always very careful with a shock like that." Rath sees him frown in the dim yellow light caused by the many eyes. "We do not like to, but we did not wish to risk waking the man from Pantha."

"The man … " Rath gasps. "M-May I ask … where is One-Eye? He is hurt."

"Hurt? I thought such things never happened to those from Lionel's country. They are" – the man brings up an arm and flexes it – "strong."

"One-Eye is. However, that does not mean he cannot be injured."

"We left him in the cave." The man glances around. "I suppose we could find him. He is likely the only one with Lionel's Traits there."

"If you are willing, I would greatly appreciate it."

The man hesitates.

Ahead, the group begins to part to either side as a woman with large yellow eyes comes forward. She has blond hair in a long tail over one shoulder, as is customary for those from Ullia. She leans close to Rath and his green eyes widen. Then she takes his chin and turns his head left and right. She moves back, saying to the others, "You are right. I sense nothing." To Rath, she asks, "Why is this? It is as though you are not there."

"As though … " He understands. "Evermore has told me the same. He believes he cannot sense me with Erole's Traits due to my lack of traits."

"Your … " However, his second sentence registers and she says suddenly, "You know Evermore? How is my son? It has been so long since I have seen him … " She lays a hand on her chest and bows. "I am Lura. Mother of Evermore. One of Erole's own." She thinks. "You are … You would be Rath, correct? The kind captain Evermore was assigned to."

"I am. I cannot say if I am – "

She laughs. "You are kind! We all know this. It is dangerous to speak of those we care about on Ullia – Erole may grow interested in them and we do not want that. Evermore has spoken nothing about you but your name – to keep the rest a secret would mean he truly and deeply respects you." Her eyes dance. "But, we are all very close – we have lived very similar lives – and even if I have not seen my son, others have, and they tell me that as of seven years ago, Evermore has had a new light in his eyes. A much happier and peaceful light." She beams at Rath. Her expression abruptly falls. "We have taken you unjustifiably. It was due to a … curiosity. Something Evermore has noticed, as you have said. I am afraid that if Erole were to learn of it, he would be very interested in you. We all thought – "

Someone new enters the chamber. "Lura, they *will not* leave. How are we to do our task now?"

"I do not know. However, we cannot risk angering Erole." She turns back to Rath. "I am afraid that our god was very displeased when Evermore did not return the year … " She pauses, then nods quickly. "Let us not call your ship by its name. All are trusted here, but … " She sighs. "What I was saying was that Erole was angered when Evermore did not return to Ullia for his yearly report. We all understood – you were in Draconi, aiding the Elder God, Ara. However, when Evermore did not return … I am told that my son has not been allowed out of his presence until he gives his report in full. I worry for him." She takes a deep breath. "But, he is strong – we all are. We will … be all right."

They hear footsteps and voices above them.

One says, " … the entrance we used has been blocked and another chamber has completely caved in – just heard from Marn, Dinra, and her group."

Another says, "Are they safe?"

"Yeah. They're staying outside to warn others and find a safe exit for everyone."

They continue on, their voices fading.

Rath says to Lura, "Are we in the lower levels of the Constellation Caves?"

"You know of them?"

"Yes. Marchand and I investigated them years ago. The underwater tunnels lead to them."

Lura bites her lip. "Erole knows of those. He is who suggested we use them to enter the Constellation Caves so that we did not have to officially announce our presence on Delphy while completing our task."

Another person with a hood comes forward. "They seem to have all gathered in the chamber above. We could continue our studies."

Lura says, "Good. We will do so."

As she starts to leave, Rath says, "May I ask where the exit is? My friend is injured and I need to return to him."

She looks pained. "I am sorry, Rath. I need to ask you to stay here for now. If we fail in our task, then – " She shakes her head quickly. "Miv, Pel, make sure he does not leave."

"Yes, Lura," they say in unison – Miv being the man Rath spoke to at first and Pel who had been nearby.

Rath says, "Wait – " but Lura and over half of the group have left. Without the light from their eyes, the lower cave becomes very dark. He says to the others, "I need to find One-Eye and the group still inside. With the cracks that have been appearing, I do not believe it is safe for anyone to be here."

Miv shakes his head. "We cannot leave until our task is finished."

Pel says, "And we can assure you this area of the caves is secure." Her hand brushes the cave wall and Rath sees a yellow pulse go through every surface, briefly illuminating them.

Rath says, "I trust you. I am concerned for other areas." He then asks, "Would you be able to use your traits to find weak areas in the caves? It may help the workers here determine the cause of the cracks."

The two avert their eyes.

Finally, Pel says, "Rath … we know of these weak areas. We used them to create the cracks."

Miv says quickly, "We needed to. The people would not leave. Couples and groups and families … " He seems to struggle over the last word. "We only wished to make them think the area was unsafe so they would exit. We did not want to harm the caves. They are a beautiful creation." The others near them nod. "That is why we chose only hard rock and stayed away from the Miphrin deposits – the … stars as the people here call them." He sighs. "However, it seems all of us had the same thought and our cracks caused the overall integrity of the caves to weaken as a result."

Pel says, "We did not intend the entrances to cave in … or the chamber in which you and – One-Eye? – fell into. But, the other people – those who have started investigating the caves – they make it very difficult for us to make accurate readings with our traits. Erole wants a perfect map of these caves."

Miv sighs. "After the most recent cave-in – a far larger result than even we expected – Lura has told us to only use it as the very last option. Harming the caves would not help us achieve our task. Yet we must have the people leave in order for us to complete it. Lura knows that as well. She worries for Evermore and what Erole may do to him and all of us if we ultimately fail this task he has given us. He is already too angry."

"What may he do?"

They collectively flinch.

Pel says, "He will not hurt us – he cannot. That is a rule of the Gods that even Erole cannot disobey. But he will do more – take us away from families, give us tasks in areas where they are impossible to reach or even send a letter to, *forbid* us to send letters if we can."

Rath's eyes look wet in the dim light. He lowers them. "I am very sorry to hear that. Is there anything I can do?"

Pel recoils as if struck. "Anything … We hold you here, yet you wish to help?"

"I do not believe what Erole is doing is right."

Pel stares at him for a moment longer, then says, "You come from a kind god – Marchand. Erole is not the same."

Miv says, "If we ultimately fail this task as it seems we will, we hope that meeting you will appease him – that is why we cannot let you leave. As Lura said, he would find you and our inability to sense you very interesting and will hopefully disregard our failure."

"We all hope that such a thing will not be necessary." Pel wrings her hands. "If the other people would leave these caves so that we could finish our studies, then … perhaps we can all go back to where we are supposed to be."

Not far from them, in the Constellation Caves, One-Eye walks with his Spirit Lion. He is moving faster now. They reach another branching path and, trusting they are still going east, continue down the straight path. They follow it for a while longer.

At the end, the tunnel splits out to the left and right. There is no forward path.

One-Eye looks down at his Lion. "What do you think?" The Lion sniffs the air. He looks right, then left. His ears perk up.

"You see a Spirit Dolphin?"

The Lion nods, his nose pointed down the left path.

"That should be north. We weren't far from the coastline initially, so it should at least take us to an exit. Let's go."

Unseen by One-Eye, the Spirit Dolphin continues forward, guiding them.

The dark tunnel becomes brighter and they arrive in a large chamber filled with baskets of glowing Delphaen crystals. Many people are sitting around, discussing quietly while they eat.

A man that was placing more crystals in a basket sees

One-Eye and gives a start. "What are you doing down here?"

One-Eye bites back an irritable response and says instead, "Fell. There was a crack where I and some friends were traveling – "

"We've been trying to tell people to stay away!"

One-Eye grits his teeth. "Rath. I was traveling with Rath."

The man blinks. Then he nods. "Lord Georgio's son. Everyone says he's been investigating what's causing the cracks. Marn said he was bringing maps to Dinra."

"Right."

The man flushes. He holds out his hand awkwardly. "Sorry. It's been stressful. I'm Harton, lead geologist."

"One-Eye," he says, not taking his hand.

Harton pulls his back and clears his throat. "I'll get you our team lead." He calls behind him, "Brinz!"

Brinz, a man who was just about to take another bite of his meal, frowns, and stands up. As he goes over to join them, his Spirit Dolphin – the same one who guided One-Eye and his Lion – speak to him, explaining the situation. "One-Eye. Traveling with Rath." To One-Eye, he says, "My Spirit Dolphin says you and Rath fell. Are you both all right?"

"He was when I last saw him. I injured my back and had to rest. He was gone when I woke up. My Spirit Lion said two people from Ullia knocked him out and took him."

"Ullia?" Harton says.

Brinz says, "That is concerning. We'll see what we can do to find them. They may be the answer to this."

Harton starts. "You don't think that *they* caused the cracks?"

"It's possible. Erole's people are very knowledgeable about caves, tunnels, and other structures. They would know where the weak points are."

"And if they knew that, it wouldn't take much force to cause a crack."

"Exactly."

One-Eye frowns at both of them as they discuss. His Spirit Lion flicks his tail impatiently.

Brinz turns to him. "You mentioned your back. We have a doctor here if you want to have it looked at."

"I'm fine."

"Well, you've certainly helped us. Thank you. If this was all caused by people with Erole's Traits, which seems highly probable now, I think I know what we need to look for to confirm it."

Harton says, "But we were directed to find the nearest exit by Dinra."

"If those people are purposely causing the cracks, I want to meet them. Us leaving could very well be what they want. Now – it doesn't explain *why* they're here, they're typically – "

One-Eye thrusts out his hand. "All I need is a map and compass." The two men stare at him. He says, "Please."

Harton and Brinz exchange a look. Brinz nods to Harton and the man trots off. "He'll retrieve them. May I ask why?"

"To find Rath. I thought you said you were concerned about him."

"I am. But, people from Ullia tend to be non-violent – that's what I had been about to say. They won't hurt him if that's what you're worried about."

"They didn't have any issue with knocking him out."

Harton returns. "Map and compass," he says.

One-Eye takes them. "Thanks."

Brinz continues, "Even if those people are dangerous, I don't want to miss this chance to find them. Given it's the first I've heard of them, it's clear they want to keep secret whatever they're doing."

"I get it," One-Eye says. He takes a look at the map, his Lion tells him their current location – he had asked Brinz's Spirit Dolphin – then he confirms their direction with the compass and starts out.

Brinz says, "I'm sorry, One-Eye. Our priority here has to be to determine the cause of these cracks and what you've told us is a lead."

One-Eye does not reply. He walks down the dark tunnel and his eye starts to glow blue, Lionel's Traits allowing him to see. His Spirit Lion walks alongside him with purpose.

Brinz, his Spirit Dolphin, and Harton watch him. Brinz speaks silently with his Dolphin, then sighs. "I know – but if we can find evidence of those people tampering with the caves, we might finally figure all of this out." He says to Harton, "Let's gather everyone up. I want to set a watch. Hopefully, we'll either encounter those people or at least deter them from doing anything more. We'll start at this point, then stretch out – there won't be an area that doesn't have at least one of us. We'll communicate with each other with Delphaen messages. Once we're sure the tunnels have been cleared and we're in no danger of another collapse, we'll start evacuating everyone. Hopefully, by that time, One-Eye has found Rath."

Harton nods and together they explain the plan to their team.

One-Eye walks through the caves. Instead of using the constellations, he uses the map and compass. Together with his Spirit Lion, they reach another branching tunnel and start down it.

Below, Rath hears footsteps. He looks at Miv, then Pel, then all of the people who are blocking him from leaving, but they do not move.

All around the caves, Delphaen messages are being sent out. They travel at varying speed and brightness, illuminating the constellations in the ceiling – *Hep's Home* and *Elvin's People*.

As the messages are received, the plan is relayed to

everyone and soon the cave workers start walking through the tunnels, holding glowing Delphaen crystals.

Lura's eyes widen when she sees one.

She and her group return to the lower caves quickly, lighting the area with the pale yellow glow from their eyes.

Rath asks, "Are you all right, Lura?"

She runs a hand through her hair. "No … no … they're everywhere now. They're not leaving."

"The workers in the caves?"

"Yes. They must know about us."

Someone beside her speaks up. "They do. I don't know how they found out, but they are angry, Lura."

She looks afraid for a moment, then shakes her head. "Erole will be more so. We need … we need to … " She glances at Rath, then looks away. "They will need to rest and eat – things that we do not need as much. We will go when they do."

Another person says, "Lura, I heard them speak of a watch system – others will replace those that leave so no area is left empty."

"But – " Again, Lura looks at Rath. Then she says, "It is not possible there are enough of them to be in every tunnel at all times. We will travel to where they are not and begin our studies again. We will finish our task." She begins to move and, wordlessly, those with her follow.

Rath asks, "Lura – I cannot speak for them, however, they may understand if you explain what you need to do."

"They will not listen to us. They are angry with us. Even if we had spoken to them before, they would not have listened. Most are disturbed or frightened of people from Ullia. Communicating with others is not our way. It is our way to not be seen and to accomplish what Erole sets for us." She pauses, then says, "I ask that you come with us now. We may need you if we fail."

"To … go to Ullia?"

She opens her mouth, shuts it, then nods.

"I cannot. Please – you need to speak with them."

"We have already done damage to your caves – some unintentional, but that will not matter to them."

"Then you must tell them that and help them restore the caves to how they were. I believe you all can."

The group is quiet. After a long moment, Lura says, "Will you come with me to speak with them?"

"Of course."

She exhales. "Must everyone come?"

"I believe it would be appropriate."

The others exchange uncomfortable looks.

Lura says, "If you are with us, we must be safe. We will be." To her group, she says, "We leave. Everyone."

They all move toward the back of the chamber, Rath with them.

Near the end of it, there is an incline. Lura leads them through a small narrow space that exits out into the Constellation Caves.

It does not take long before a blue-green light approaches them. They wait with Lura and Rath near the front.

A worker holding a Delphaen crystal jumps when she sees over a dozen pale yellow eyes looking at her. She holds up her bright crystal and says, "Y-You're the people we were told about! That were causing the cracks."

Rath, catching the winces in Lura's group, says, "May I ask that you lower your crystal? Their eyes are sensitive." The worker looks surprised. "Oh. Sorry." She does so.

Lura sends an appreciative look to Rath, then says to the worker, "What you say is true. We did cause them. However, the full extent of the damage was not our intent. We have been tasked with sending an accurate map of the Constellation Caves to our god, Erole. It is difficult to sense the caves with our traits when so many people are inside it. We thought the cracks would cause all to leave."

"I … I don't quite understand what you're saying, but if you're not dangerous … I think I should take you to Brinz. He's the one that heard from the person earlier that you all were causing this. He's taken charge of most of the groups nearby."

Lura bows. "Then, we will speak with him. Is this place where he is in … bright?"

"Yeah. We have a lot of lights up. None of us can see in the dark."

"Then we will adapt ourselves to your accommodations." With a single nod to the others, they all begin to unwrap the scarves around their waists to put over their eyes. Then, 'seeing' with Erole's Traits, Lura says, "We are ready now."

"O-Okay!"

As they begin to move, Rath says, "May I ask if the person you spoke of earlier was named One-Eye?"

"I think so."

"Was he all right?"

"He looked really angry." She rubs her arm. "But, then I heard that he hurt his back, so maybe that was why. I guess he was walking a little weird."

"Is he still with Brinz?"

"No. He asked for a map and compass and left."

"Do you know where?"

"I'm not sure. I'm sorry."

Lura, who has been listening to the conversation, suddenly touches Rath's shoulder, "Go. You do not need to come with us." She smiles a little. "I do not need to see your expression to know that One-Eye is very important to you – family. Perhaps not in the traditional sense, but a type of family that we know very well. If he was here recently, I am sure that he is in range for me to sense him. Would you like me to do so?"

"Please."

She concentrates. A strong, yellow pulse goes through the caves. She thinks, then says, "Are you familiar with these caves?"

"I am."

"One-Eye is going north. He is under the constellation you all attribute to Belle, the God of Selachuu."

Rath nods. "I understand. Thank you."

However, before he can leave, Lura says, "There is one more thing. If … If I may ask."

"Of course."

Very carefully, Lura takes out a small, intricately folded envelope. She holds it out to Rath. "For Evermore. When you see him again." Her voice is strained. "It is very old. I was always too afraid to send it. Will you give it to him?"

"Yes."

She looks relieved. "Thank you, Rath. Find your family."

The worker hands her crystal to him. "Here," she says, then also gives him her pack. "And this, too. You don't look like you have one with you. It was supposed to be my lunch. You'll need it if you're going further in the caves." Referring to Lura's group, she says, "You seem to trust them, so … I think I'll trust them, too. They don't seem so bad."

"Thank you very much."

Lura says to Rath, "Be careful. There are other groups from Ullia in these caves – "

The worker yelps, "R-Really?"

"Yes. It was needed to accomplish our task. The Constellation Caves are very large." She continues, "We are all very like-minded. They may have the same thought we did – to take you to Erole in Ullia. Do not let them."

"I will not."

They part at the next divide, Lura's group guiding the worker back to Brinz, and Rath walking further into the caves to find One-Eye.

At the same time, One-Eye walks with his Spirit Lion. His pace is slowing and – finally – he says, "We're sitting." He does so immediately, leaning heavily on the cave wall. His Lion watches him carefully, then butts One-Eye's hand, who starts petting him.

For a while, One-Eye looks up at the ceiling. He can see the reflective surface of the Miphrin, but it is not glowing right now.

He hears footsteps.

Sitting up, he glares down the tunnel from where he came. He relaxes when he sees a Delphaen crystal.

Then he sees familiar dark orange hair.

He gets up quickly.

One-Eye meets Rath before the other can fully see him and Rath starts when he suddenly sees someone in front of him. "One-Eye?"

Putting his hand over Rath's that is holding the crystal, he says, "Yeah. Are you all right? What happened?"

"I … " Rath suddenly flushes. "I am very hungry. May we eat while we talk?"

One-Eye laughs. "I'd love that."

They sit near the stream in the cave with the glowing crystal set between them. They are both eating half of a small baked vegetable and sharing the water.

While they eat, Rath tells One-Eye about Lura and the others from Ullia. " … I do not believe they intended to hurt the caves," he finishes.

One-Eye stares at him evenly. He takes another bite. "They still did. So Lura is talking with Brinz?"

"Yes. That is what she said they would do."

"Do you think they'll listen? Won't they just arrest them?"

"I do not know. However, I believe that Lura's group can help."

"How? With their map?"

"Yes – or, rather, that as well. It would be helpful to have a more detailed and recent map of the caves. I believe they could also make them more safe. They told me they made the cracks where they found hidden weak spots. If they would be willing to find others, it would allow us to make the caves far more stable and reduce the risk of cracks in the future."

"It could help them from getting arrested immediately, too. Lura said there were others here who might think their god would be interested in you?" he asks and Rath nods. "Didn't know Evermore couldn't sense you. Still don't know why that would make a god want to meet you."

"I cannot say either."

After they both finish their meals, One-Eye helps Rath with his cuts from when they fell. The pack the worker had given him contained medical supplies.

One-Eye says, "My Lion says I shouldn't use Sevran's Traits for anything else while it's healing my back." He pulls out a vial. "I don't know what a lot of these do, though."

"Carlos has taught me some healing. I can help." As One-Eye begins cleaning off one cut, he says, "Thank you for doing this."

"Sure. Why didn't you before?"

"I wanted to find you."

Reddening, One-Eye focuses on another cut.

Once they have all been cleaned and everything has been put away, they are quiet. One-Eye says, "You're all right? Besides the cuts."

"I believe so."

"The electricity … I don't know how it would affect you. I've never healed anything like that."

"Miv said they were always very careful with a … shock like that." One-Eye frowns. Rath asks, "How is your back?"

"Better. Sore. I can't walk for very long." He moves on,

"What is your plan? We should be close to an exit, right?"

"Yes. May I see your map?"

"Yeah."

They sit side-by-side. One-Eye holds the crystal over it for light while Rath holds the ends of the map down. He points. "We are here, under *Belle's Land*. The nearest exit would be further east."

"How long do you think?"

"Two hours. However, I would also like to ask the other groups if they would accompany us back. I am concerned about the structural integrity of the caves."

They stand up and One-Eye says, "Then we'll go to Brinz. Maybe you can talk some sense into him." At Rath's confused look, he says, "He seemed intent on staying to see if the cracks were being caused on purpose and find the people responsible."

They suddenly hear a gasp, then something clatters to the ground. They look forward to see someone has collapsed with a Delphaen crystal next to them. A black boot raises over the crystal, then smashes it and the light fades away. A pair of yellow eyes lifts up to them.

One-Eye grabs Rath's hand. "We're leaving."

"What?"

But One-Eye turns, pulling Rath with him. Just as they round a corner, a spark of electricity hits the wall behind them. Rath stares at it. One-Eye says, "Come on."

Another arc shoots toward them and he drags both of them out of the way.

"They should not be using their traits like that," Rath says in between breaths.

One-Eye ducks one aimed right at the back of his head. "Well they are."

"The person before. They may be hurt."

"Probably, but we can't go back to them. We'll make sure they get help later." Another spark flashes and One-Eye takes them down another tunnel. "I don't know how much their electricity will affect me, but my Lion says whatever they're doing is a lot stronger than whatever knocked you out. I don't have enough of Sevran's Traits left to heal you and I'm not sure I'd even know what to do … I don't want you to get hurt."

He looks back and sees Rath nods. "I understand."

He smiles briefly. "Where are we?"

Electricity sparks behind them, lighting up the Miphrin. Rath scans the constellation. "*Ara's Protection*. We are going in the right direction for the exit."

"Good. Which way next?"

"Right."

They turn. One-Eye abruptly halts. "Stop." He looks at the rubble ahead. "It's caved in," he explains. "Go the other way?"

"We cannot. It will take us to where we came."

One-Eye begins to reach for his knife when his Spirit Lion speaks to him urgently. He points his nose at the wall.

Going toward it, One-Eye tells Rath, "My Lion says there's a lower part of the cave behind there."

Rath holds up his crystal. "There was a similar entrance before. I believe I see it."

Quickly, they enter.

They have to crouch in the narrow passage and One-Eye grimaces, his back hurting. When they reach the bottom, a sea of yellow eyes is looking at them.

One-Eye moves back, shielding Rath. He says to his Spirit Lion, "You didn't say they were down here."

His Lion stares at him, then bats his paw at a small Spirit Eel poking out of the ground. They start to play, the Eel dodging and the Lion trying to catch him.

One-Eye listens. "He … told you about it." He steps aside so Rath can see.

As soon as he does, they see there is another dim glow in the cave – a blue-green one.

A worker comes forward and carefully uncovers their Delphaen crystal, holding it up to Rath and One-Eye's faces. "You're … You're not dressed like them."

A man in a hood joins them and the person dampens their crystal with their shirt. "Please move out of the way," he says. "We must block the entrance."

One-Eye says, "There's someone out there trying to shock us with Erole's Traits."

"We have heard. My Spirit Eel told me so. Who you saw is part of Lura's group." He shakes his head. "Erole always makes sure there is a deviant." He shrugs. "There is likely one in this chamber right now." He crawls up the tunnel.

One-Eye stares at him. "Is he going to be all right?"

Rath says, "He should be. I was taught that people with Erole's Traits are unaffected by electricity."

"That is true," a woman in a hood says. She pauses, realizing that she cannot sense Rath, then says instead, "Come further inside. We have food and other supplies. We were just about to leave."

One-Eye says, "How?"

"The underwater tunnels. Ah." She realizes. "Being from Pantha, you cannot breathe underwater. That may be a problem. People from Delphy and Ullia can."

Rath says, "I also cannot. If I remember correctly, this tunnel is very long. Even during this season, it is fully submerged in water."

"Correct. You know much. I enjoy people who do." She frowns. "However, that means neither of you can come with us."

One-Eye grits his teeth. Rath says, "Is there another exit back into the Constellation Caves from here?"

"Oh yes. Several. Which would you like?"

"One that would take us further east."

She looks back and the others step aside, revealing a

passageway. "There. I cannot guarantee its safety. I have felt more damages to the cave's structure to the east. My Spirit Eel tells me Lura and her group have sworn not to create any more cracks unless as a last resort and my group has as well, however, it would seem that those in the east have … deviated. Be careful now. We must leave."

"I understand. Thank you for your information."

She smiles. "Thank you for yours." She says to her group, "This way. You shall be out soon. We all shall be." The workers with them murmur their thanks and those from Ullia are relieved as they follow them.

As the cave empties out, Rath and One-Eye move toward the eastern exit. When they reach it, they find a small package is laying by it. One-Eye says, "What is it?"

Rath opens it. "Food."

"From one of them?"

Rath looks at the emblem on the package – an eel. "It would seem so." He tucks it in his bag.

Together, they crawl up the tunnel. One-Eye's Spirit Lion leaves for a few minutes and when he returns, his eyes are shining. One-Eye sighs, putting one hand in front of the other. "What did you find out?"

The Lion tells him.

By the end, One-Eye's mood is considerably brighter. He tells Rath, "My Lion found more Spirit Eels. He got some information from them" – he pauses, slowly frowning at his Lion – "in exchange for information." He stares. "*What* information?"

The Lion looks pointedly away.

"*Part of the contract?*" One-Eye huffs. "Whatever – as long as it didn't have to do with Rath. I'd say the less of them that know, the better." The Lion flicks his tail. "Yeah. I know you wouldn't." He listens some more, then continues to Rath, "He says that Lura's group was successful in convincing Brinz and the workers to leave. My Lion doesn't know about the others further on, but he did find out the entrance we're going to is still safe to exit from."

"That is good. May I … Would it be inappropriate to ask that you tell him – your Spirit Lion, that is – thank you for his efforts?"

The Lion puffs out his chest.

One-Eye laughs. "You just told him. He heard. He liked it a bit too much."

The Lion flattens his ears and One-Eye laughs again.

They reach the top of the tunnel. One-Eye says, "You can tell him those things. I don't mind."

"I see. I will do so."

He smiles, then says, "You said two hours?"

"Yes. I will find our location now."

One-Eye watches as Rath holds up his Delphaen crystal, making the Miphrin above glow with the same color. They slowly walk below the constellation. When they reach the end, Rath says, "We are currently at *Fierce's Gambit*." He references the map. "We will take this tunnel east."

While they travel, One-Eye says, "My Spirit Lion doesn't think we should encounter anyone – from Delphy or Ullia – for a while. It sounds like the person we met before delayed whoever attacked us by blocking that passageway. He says the person who had collapsed was rescued, too."

Rath sighs in relief. "I am very glad to hear that. Thank you for telling me." They turn down the next tunnel. "I hope that Franz, Velt, Well-Pagu, Bucket-Pagu, and Flower-Pagu are all right."

"They're outside. I'm sure they are."

11

Franz, Velt, Well-Pagu, Bucket-Pagu, and Flower-Pagu are traveling along the shore. They have already passed the caved in entrance and are going to the next when Franz and Velt see a General Delphaen Message in the ocean.

Velt says, "I'll see what it is!" and she hops over to the water. After she has retrieved the message, she tells the group, "The next entrance is still safe and people are leaving from it."

"That's great! We'll go there," Franz says. As they continue on, he asks, "Do you think Lord Garreth knows about all of this?"

"I'm pretty sure he's been keeping updated on things since Rath told him about the cracks in his letters."

Franz coughs. "No – I mean … do you think he knows about Rath and One-Eye … falling. Should we tell him?"

"I'm not sure." Velt bites her lip. "We don't really know him personally, so we can't send him a Delphaen message directly." She sighs. "I don't know, Franz. What do you think?" she asks the Pagu.

They turn to one another. Bucket-Pagu says, "We think he does know – or will soon."

Flower-Pagu says, "His Spirit Dolphin has been keeping him informed during this time."

Well-Pagu says, "Help."

Both exhale in relief and Velt says, "That's really good. I'm glad she is."

Franz says, "Me too. And not just because we won't be the ones to tell Lord Garreth."

"You're not afraid of him, are you?"

"He's … a little intimidating."

Further east, Garreth is on the beach behind his home, listening to his Spirit Dolphin. After the Dolphin relates one piece of information, Garreth says, "Rath … he … " He collects himself. "Are he and One-Eye all right?"

The Dolphin nods, then tells him more.

Garreth chuckles. "You say you heard of a Spirit Lion? *Hard* not to hear of one?" He sits back. "That has to be One-Eye's. I remember you telling me when they were here that he's a gossip." He nods. "He'll keep them safe. And Rath knows those caves well. One-Eye's Pertan blood will save him likely." He frowns. "What would Azalea say about all of this? Would she tell me to inform Marchand of what's going on?"

The Dolphin leans into his hand.

"Only I can make that decision?" He strokes the Dolphin for a while longer, thinking. "Maybe there is something I can do from here." He snorts. "Would teach those people that mean them harm a lesson at the least and help them find their way out at the most. Not that Rath needs the help, but I need to give it. Does that make sense?" The Dolphin looks at him fondly. "I'm doing it." He concentrates and his tattoos glow a bright blue-green. "Rath – you can't read the message in this anymore, so I'm not going to send one – it's just going to be emotion and I know you'll be able to read that." Then he sticks his arm into the ocean and the message shoots out quickly. Instead of removing his arm, he leaves it there, directing the message down the beach and toward an entrance to the Constellation Caves that he knows is there.

Rath and One-Eye are eating the meal that was left for them in the lower caves when the stream beside them erupts in light.

Rath looks up at the Miphrin with a gasp. "Grandfather," he says.

"Garreth?" One-Eye asks.

"Yes. Or, rather, he is the only person other than Marchand who is currently able to use his traits so powerfully." Above them, the stars still glowing with the bright message flowing through all parts of the cave.

After a few minutes, the light fades. Rath is smiling. As he picks up their bags and they both stand up, he says, "We are almost there. The exit is just – " He is cut off by a sudden spark of electricity.

One-Eye pulls him out of the way, but it grazes his arm and he stumbles. Rath catches him, then they both look down the tunnel.

A group of people, all with their scarves over their eyes, face them.

The one in front says to Rath, "It wasn't you who caused the light, was it? You have no traits at all. We ask that you come with us."

One-Eye takes Rath's hand and they start running.

The further they go, the more he stumbles and Rath supports him. The Spirit Lion runs alongside them both, urging them forward as more electricity flashes behind them.

After one more turn, they see a bright light ahead, growing brighter with each step. A line of people stand in front of the exit to the caves.

When Rath and One-Eye reach them, those in the middle calmly step out of the way. As they go through, they see the familiar uniform of the Selachuu Military. Then they are out on the beach and in the sunlight.

Behind them, the Selachuu soldiers reform their line and calmly hold up their gloved hands to catch the electricity shot out from those inside. The group from Ullia sees this and pauses, then turns and runs back into the caves.

Outside, One-Eye stumbles and Rath catches him.

They hear a familiar voice say, "Do not worry, Master Rath, I will tend to him."

"Carlos!" Rath says.

Rath's personal doctor and the doctor aboard *PearlHeart* nods. He begins checking One-Eye with Sevran's Traits, saying, "You strained your back. As well, you have greatly overused your traits."

One-Eye says, "I thought you were on Tema Island."

"I was, until recently. Phillip is here, too." He checks Rath as well. "These cuts are healing well."

Rath says, "One-Eye tended to them."

Carlos raises an eyebrow, looking at One-Eye, who says, "A worker gave him some medical supplies. I didn't know what most of them did. Rath told me."

"I see. Very good job. I believe it would be best for both of you to rest. I will show where you may."

As Rath helps One-Eye they both see their surroundings for the first time.

A small camp has been set up on the shore with tents supplied by the Butej Guard. Some cave workers are there, having recently exited. Phillip, the cook aboard *PearlHeart,* is cheerfully serving food from an outdoor kitchen.

Carlos leads them to a large tent away from the others. Inside, people are lying on pallets while doctors speak with them.

"They sustained injuries from those with Erole's Traits," Carlos says. "It would help if you were able to tend to them as well, One-Eye – your traits from Sevran are certainly strong enough – but only after you recover your strength."

After they sit down, One-Eye says, "They shocked Rath earlier. I don't know … "

Carlos looks startled and says, "Master Rath. May I check you again?"

"Of course."

While he does, he tells One-Eye, "For these injuries, you must check for disrupted nerves. It is delicate work." One-Eye nods. His Spirit Lion watches as well. Carlos is quiet for a moment as he finishes checking, then sighs. "There are no residual injuries. I did not feel any earlier either."

One-Eye frowns. "But he was unconscious." He glances over at the worker they had seen earlier who had been attacked, now in the tent with the others. "Them, too."

"Yes. And that is all. I am not finding any nerve damage which is very good, but also … troubling." He shakes his head. "How are you? Were you shocked as well?"

"Yeah. But not enough to make me pass out."

"Likely an underestimation on their part."

One-Eye holds his hand over his forearm. A weak yellow glow appears. He concentrates. "Delicate work, you said?" Carlos' eyes are on One-Eye's traits. "Yes. You should feel a tingling sensation if you pass over an area that has been affected." He presses his lips together. "You truly did overuse your traits."

One-Eye glares.

Carlos holds his hands up. "May I?"

He nods. He closes his eye while Carlos checks him again. His Lion rests his head in his lap.

Barely a minute later, Carlos pulls away. "Nothing, aside

from your back. I would like to check on that directly." He tells Rath, "You may rest while I do so. One-Eye, take off your shirt and lie down here."

While Rath goes to another pallet, One-Eye does so, wincing as he pulls his shirt over his torso. He lies on his stomach while Carlos opens his bag and pulls out a jar. "Eventide Leaves. Fresh from Tema Island," he says. "They bloom during late Spring." He leans over and begins applying it to a darkened area on One-Eye's lower back.

One-Eye relaxes. "What were you saying earlier? That it was troubling they didn't cause any nerve damage?"

Carlos applies a little more, then puts the lid back on the jar and sets it aside. He retrieves bandages from his pack and One-Eye carefully sits up so he can put them on. Carlos loops them around his torso. "Because doing so would take a high level of skill in using their traits *and* someone to teach them exactly how to do that." One-Eye's eye widens as he understands his meaning. Carlos nods, tying off the bandage.

"Yes. I am concerned their god, Erole, taught them."

"Self-defense?"

"From my understanding, Erole's people are never to be seen or heard. They are non-violent, or … supposed to be." He pauses, then rubs his eyes with his forefinger and thumb. "I have already informed the Selachuu soldiers of my findings and they will report the same to Belle."

"He's not here, is he?"

"No. He is currently traveling to Haliae and Pantha with the other gods. But, Belle has long been aware of Erole's troubling activities and has informed his people to be prepared should they be needed to intercept."

One-Eye remembers. "The electricity didn't affect them."

"It would have normally, however every soldier's clothing is made of Rellin – it protects from all forms of electricity."

"So if Belle knows, why hasn't he done anything about it?"

"He has done as much as he can. Even the Gods cannot overstep their bounds over one another's land or people. The only ones that may even attempt to do so are the Three Elder Gods, but it is still considered highly impolite." One-Eye snorts and Carlos continues, "Doing so would likely put them not in good favor with certain parties that they would rather not displease."

One-Eye stares at him, then has a thought on who. "Would think that making his people do things like this would also make them upset."

"They are displeased, but not always can they or other gods directly intervene. It was only because Erole's people were hurting those the Selachuu soldiers are sworn to protect that they were able to step in."

"Which is how they came here. What about you? And Phillip?"

Carlos smiles for a moment. "Rest first. Master Rath will likely be awake when you are and we can all speak together and not hear the same story twice." One-Eye huffs, but remains on his pallet. Carlos stands up, fixing him with a look. "And do not think this conversation has allowed me to forget the fact that you have overused your traits – both from Sevran and Lionel – and that it was highly irresponsible for you to do so." Reddening, One-Eye opens his mouth, but Carlos continues, "We will talk later. I will speak with Master Rath, as well, concerning his irresponsible choices in taking on such tasks as the cave workers have told me about when he was supposed to be taking a relaxing break. Perhaps I shall speak with both of you together." Then he says, "Rest well, One-Eye. Phillip and I will return later with food for you both."

"Thanks."

After he leaves, One-Eye looks at his Spirit Lion – the Lion seems a little uncomfortable, too – then he lies down on his stomach, his Lion flops down next to him, and they go to sleep.

12

Rath wakes up an hour later. He looks across the tent and sees One-Eye lying on his stomach with his torso wrapped. Rath gets up, then goes over to him. One-Eye is sleeping soundly.

The tent flap opens and Carlos enters. "Hello, Master Rath." He studies One-Eye. "I believe he needs more time to rest. Would you like to speak outside?"

"Yes, please."

They both exit quietly. Outside, the line of Selachuu soldiers is still standing at the entrance of the cave.

"Master Rath, would you tell me what has transpired on Delphy since your arrival? I have heard parts from the workers here, the Selachuu soldiers, and the Butej Guard in addition to the information that Phillip's Spirit Rabbit has been able to find out, but not the situation in its entirety."

"Of course."

They sit on some crates and Rath explains, starting with the first crack they heard about at the Wishing Fountain, to agreeing to help Leader Leytel, the group's decision to go to the Constellation Caves, and finally he and One-Eye falling into them and finding their way out.

Afterward, Carlos' lips are pursed. Then he says, "It is very good Lura found you." Sounding oddly hesitant, he continues, "Master Rath, I wish to fully disclose that Lady Azalea, Belle, Fierce, Marchand, and I have been concerned with Erole learning about the loss of your traits. I can tell you that – to our knowledge – Erole is unaware. I truly do not wish for you to meet him." He takes Rath's hand briefly, quiet, until he says, "Would you tell me more about the other parts of your time here? I would hope not all of it has been with the work you agreed to do for Leader Leytel."

Rath does and Carlos listens.

Just as he is finishing, One-Eye joins them and sits on the crate next to Rath. He looks a little sleepy, but less tense.

Carlos asks him, "How do you feel?"

"Fine." One-Eye says to Rath, "How are you?"

"I am well. I am glad to hear that you are, ah, fine."

One-Eye smiles.

Carlos clears his throat. "I believe, if you both will allow, it is time that I retrieved Phillip so that we can explain how we came to Delphy." He rises. "I will bring food as well. I would imagine both of you are very hungry."

He returns soon with two bowls, Phillip trotting beside him. "Rath! One-Eye!" the cook says. "It's good to see you both!"

"You as well," Rath says.

"You too," One-Eye says. "Thanks for the food."

"Definitely!"

As Rath and One-Eye begin eating, Phillip says, "I'm glad that we could help everyone here. Seems like we were really needed – just like my Spirit Rabbit said!"

One-Eye's Spirit Lion, who looks elated to see the Rabbit

again, paws the sand and the Rabbit hops off of Phillip's shoulder. They walk and hop away from the group, talking and passing on information from their travels.

Phillip laughs. "It seems like they're really happy to see each other again!"

One-Eye nods.

Carlos says, "Which brings us to how and why Phillip, his Spirit Rabbit, and I are here. To be short, Delphy is not the only area that has discovered Erole's people unofficially entering and being present in underground areas."

Phillip says, "They were in the underground garden on Tema Island. A few people were startled when they saw yellow eyes looking at them."

"The Selachuu Military was informed – there is a small customs port on the island – and they quickly discovered them by using Belle's Traits to sense the area and the traits of those in it. The soldiers told us that all they found were members of the Ullian Spies."

"The soldiers told us to stay out of the underground garden for a while," Phillip continues. "They said it didn't seem like they were doing anything with the herbs, just studying the place."

Carlos says to Rath, "When you told me the people here were tasked with creating an accurate map of the Constellation Caves, I wondered if they were doing the same on Tema Island."

Phillip says, "We stayed away like the soldiers told us to and not long afterward the spies were all gone. It was really weird. But, my Rabbit had a feeling that things might be happening in other places, too. Carlos brought up the Constellation Caves on Delphy and we were both worried about the Ullian Spies being there, too, so we asked the Selachuu soldiers on Tema Island if we could go with the ones who were already traveling to Delphy to help."

Carlos says, "The caves are very popular – especially during these months – and the Butej Guard far outnumber the Selachuu Military in Delphy, so it was unlikely they would be discovered as quickly as they were on Tema Island, given their traits would not allow them to find the spies as easily as those with Belle's Traits. We did not wish for sightings of them to cause a panic." He shakes his head. "We did not anticipate them creating structural damage with the cracks to convince people to leave. Or for them to start attacking others. I will not excuse their actions, however, it is correct that Erole would be very cruel in his punishments to his people if they were to fail their task. It is for this reason that Belle and the Selachuu Military have attempted to help Erole's own in different ways." He smiles a little. "The suggestion to have them stationed on different ships as a security measure was Belle's idea."

"Really?" Rath says.

"Yes. He believed it would allow them to live more normal lives with steady work around different people – kind captains like you. He also believed it would alleviate some of Fierce and the Butej Guard's stress of patrolling all of the areas in the South for those from Corxae. In the end, I feel that Erole only agreed to it because he believed it would allow him more spies on such vessels to report back to him, but Belle had faith that the people stationed on the ships would not wish to betray those they met." He continues, "I have spoken with the soldiers here and they intend to do what was done on Tema Island – allow the Ullian Spies to complete their task so that they may leave when they are finished. They may arrest those that directly attacked others, however."

Phillip says, "I've already heard some of the people here on Delphy not approving of that, though. They don't get why they need to give them access to the caves after all they've done. I kinda agree with them."

One-Eye says to Rath, "You thought they could help fix

them, right?"

"Yes. I had an idea of how they may be able to help, if they are willing."

Carlos says, "I am sure that certain groups would be – Lura's for one – and possibly the other group who aided in your escape." He looks over at the soldiers blocking the entrance. "All we can do for now is wait. Which brings me to two things – "

Phillip suddenly stands up. "Oh! I've gotta start cleaning up from dinner. I can take your bowls back."

After he leaves, Carlos says to Rath and One-Eye, "I would like to ask something of both of you. During this time period, you two are to do nothing but relax and recover."

Rath's eyebrows go up. One-Eye starts to frown, then seems to see the benefits of this. "All right," he says.

Rath turns to him, then back to Carlos. "Ah, I am not sure that I understand."

"Master Rath, from everything you have told me, you have not been taking this break as you intended. I cannot fault you for helping with the blankets, however, even that I believe is addressing an issue that we have spoken much on – you overwork. I ask that you do not offer to help or provide any aid or suggestions until the Ullian Spies have finished their task. Then, you may share your suggestion on how they can help repair the caves. Will you do this?"

"I … I will, Carlos."

"Thank you." He gives One-Eye a quick look as if to say, *Enforce this,* then says aloud, "I also ask you help me, One-Eye, with the recovery of the patients who sustained injuries from Erole's own – after you rest your traits for the next several days."

One-Eye says, "Understood." He stands up and offers Rath a hand. "Come on."

Rath takes it. "Of course. May I ask where?"

One-Eye asks Carlos, "We have a tent, right?"

He raises an eyebrow, then says, "Yes, the Butej guards will lead you to a vacant one."

One-Eye nods. "Thanks." Then to Rath, "I thought we could go rest."

Rath starts to say, "I am afraid I am not … Actually, I am rather tired." He says to Carlos, "I will do my best to not help, aid, or offer any suggestions."

"Thank you, Master Rath."

Later, Carlos and Phillip are speaking outside. Phillip is done with his kitchen duties for the day and his Spirit Rabbit has returned to his shoulder. One-Eye's Spirit Lion, too, has joined One-Eye in the tent where he and Rath are now sleeping.

"They really were tired," Phillip says.

"Indeed."

"Why do you think the Ullian Spies are doing this now? On Tema Island and Delphy?"

"I would think that it is likely due to many gods not being present in the South currently. They are all traveling to Haliae or Pantha."

Phillip nods. "On our way here, you told me the Gods had to follow a sort of … etiquette with each other and their people."

"That is correct."

"Wouldn't doing this overstep that? Or get them in trouble?"

Carlos frowns. "Unfortunately – alone – it does not. As I told One-Eye, it was only because Erole's people were directly attacking people on Delphy that the Selachuu Military could intervene. Such was not the case on Tema Island, so they did not. And … the underground is in some cases an extension of Erole's land. All tunnels, caves, and other subterranean areas are accepted to be his. It is somewhat of an inheritance of his."

He continues, "However, while this does not give him full permission to send his people to areas such as the underground garden we visited or the Delphaen Constellation Caves, in most cases, he and his people would not be disallowed either."

Phillip considers this, then frowns. "I'm confused." His Rabbit twitches her nose.

"Nearly everyone born with Erole as their god becomes one of his Ullian Spies. Their primary objective is finding out information and their history for non-violence makes it difficult to charge them for their transgressions. The law is rather lenient when it comes to them and their actions, I am afraid, as it can be claimed that their research would be helpful to others. Even Master Rath has said that it would be good to have a far more accurate map of the Constellation Caves and knowledge of where the weak areas are. I agree with him. The question is whether Erole's people will share this information with Delphy, or if it will remain confidential."

The next morning, One-Eye wakes and smiles when he sees Rath sleeping soundly on the pallet next to him.

He flushes suddenly, then abruptly sits up. His Spirit Lion moves off of his legs and stretches before following One-Eye outside.

Carlos is just exiting the healer's tent when he sees him. "One-Eye. Is Master Rath still sleeping?"

"Yeah. Thought I would get us both something to eat. Do we go to Phillip for that?"

"Indeed, the same as on *PearlHeart.*"

One-Eye looks at the growing line to the cook, who is busily working. "The line looks like the one on *PearlHeart.*"

Carlos smiles a little. "Phillip's talents are appreciated everywhere. Shall we join?"

The line is comprised of Selachuu soldiers, some cave workers, and a few stressed-looking members of the Butej

Guard. The guards grab their food and eat apart from everyone else, speaking quietly.

While One-Eye and Carlos wait, One-Eye asks, "How did you know that we would be at this entrance?"

"We did not know for sure. However, the Spirit Sharks provided frequent updates regarding the caves. And ... we encountered Lord Garreth's Spirit Dolphin on the way as well." They take a step forward. "His Spirit Dolphin had heard what happened to you and Master Rath, so we asked if the Selachuu Military would take us to an open entrance near there. We received word of several cave-ins on the way and I knew that Master Rath would attempt to leave from the nearest one. This was that one."

One-Eye nods. "He was knowledgeable inside. And resourceful." He gestures. "He used rocks – scraped them together – to make the Miphrin glow without traits. Knew where to go even when we were running from those people."

"You admire that."

"Yeah." One-Eye pauses right after he says it. He pets his Spirit Lion thoughtfully, quiet.

They get their food from Phillip and One-Eye immediately leaves for his and Rath's tent. He is still distracted when he opens the tent flap and starts to say something when he looks inside.

He stops. "What are you doing?"

Rath, who was sitting on his knees, starts. "Not thinking."

One-Eye stares for another moment, then holds up the bowls. "Food."

"Thank you very much."

Rath starts to stand, but One-Eye sits down across from him, handing him his meal. His Lion joins them, grinning. "And it's all right to eat in bed. Sometimes I think it's comfortable."

"I see. I will try it, then." Rath takes a bite.

One-Eye asks, "What were you trying to do earlier? The … not thinking."

"I was trying not to think about things that I believe may overstep what Carlos asked that I do." He frowns. "Or, not do." He takes another bite. "It is very difficult."

"What sort of things? Like help with the caves?"

"Yes. Initially, when I woke up, I thought I may ask to borrow a map of the caves to study it – I remember where the cave-in we discovered was – and think over my idea for how those from Ullia may help. However, then it occurred to me that Carlos asked me not to do so – to help, that is." He smiles, lifting his spoon. "However, I am enjoying this. It is far easier to not think about it when you are around, One-Eye. And eating wonderful food." He laughs. "You are right, it is rather comfortable to eat in bed."

One-Eye, tongue-tied, can only continue to eat and nod in agreement. His Lion rolls around next to them in delight.

Later, Brinz's group has exited the caves and Rath goes to speak with them.

"We left as soon as we heard about Eleira getting attacked," Brinz says. "Now I'm seeing how dangerous my plan was."

In the healer's tent, Carlos checks One-Eye's back and confirms it is recovering properly.

While One-Eye is pulling his shirt back on, Carlos pauses. "I wonder if at some point you might be interested in learning how to use different healing methods. Herbs, bandages, splints, for example."

"Never had to."

"I am not surprised. The traits you carry from Sevran are strong and the endurance you have received from Lionel's Traits certainly help, however … " He thinks. "As you know, my heritage is not fully from Pertes – I am also from Sudines, even if my Pertan blood is in the majority. Slightly," he says quickly. "However, on *PearlHeart,* if I relied only on Sevran's

Traits, they may become drained. They nearly did after our first encounter with Ara's Storm and healing Master Rath's dislocated shoulder. I am very grateful for your aid in that, One-Eye. Would you consider it?"

"I don't know how good I'd be with plants."

Carlos' lip quirks up. "It is not so much to do with them as knowing which would work." He puts his supplies back in his bag. "You do not have to answer now, but think on it. I believe it would help you – and those you care about."

One-Eye waits only one more moment before saying, "I'll learn." He flushes as he says, "Like you said, it would help."

"We can start after all of this, then. In fact, you could help me while Master Rath tells the others his idea for having Erole's people help – once they are done with their study, that is."

At dinner, Rath is bringing his and One-Eye's meals to their tent, speaking brightly to Carlos – "One-Eye has introduced me to eating meals in bed. It is very fun," – when they hear several voices say, "Rath!"

They both turn and see Franz, Velt, Well-Pagu, Bucket-Pagu, and Flower-Pagu coming toward them, waving.

The group reaches them and the Pagu fly to Rath, hugging him. "We missed you so much!" Flower-Pagu says.

"But, we knew that we would find you again!" Bucket-Pagu says.

"Hope!" Well-Pagu says.

Rath hugs them gently back. "It is so wonderful to see everyone. Are you all right?"

The Pagu nod and Velt says, "Definitely! We would have been here sooner, but we kept getting stopped by the cave workers asking why we were in the area."

Franz says, "We were surprised to see Carlos and Phillip were here. Is One-Eye with you, too?"

"Yes! I have food for us both. We have been having it in bed," Rath says.

Velt grins. "That sounds nice."

They reunite with Phillip and after Velt, Franz, and the Pagu get their food, they all eat as a group, sitting in the sand or on crates, talking with one another, happy to be together again. The Pagu look especially happy, sitting in the middle of everyone.

One-Eye says, "How did you know which way we were going?"

A little nervously, Velt says, "I used Belle's Traits. My father always told me that unless you're part of the Selachuu Military to only use them to find someone in case of an emergency – I thought this counted."

She, Franz, and the Pagu tell them about how more groups who entered the caves to investigate were exiting and Delphaen messages have been sent frequently to track their progress. While they are talking, Marn arrives as well as Dinra's team.

At the end of the day, one of the soldiers near the entrance to the caves looks at something – a Spirit Shark, to her eyes – then nods once, turns, and walks down to the beach. The other soldiers follow her.

Those in the camp see this and look toward the cave entrance.

Further inside, the spies are spread out in the caves. Spirit Eels communicate their positions to one another. Once they are all ready, they begin.

A wave of yellow wraps around every surface of the caves, outlining their surfaces. When it reaches the entrance, it crawls up the cliff and fades away.

A few of the workers move forward, concerned, but a look from the Selachuu soldiers stops them.

Inside, the spies concentrate, committing every part of their area to memory – hard rock and Miphrin deposits, weak areas, cracks, and cave-ins. They work through the night, the Spirit Eels with them. Near early morning, they come together and each draw out what they 'saw' in glowing ink on a section of a map. Then they sense the caves again for any discrepancies.

From outside, only intermittent waves of yellow are seen.

Once the information has been checked, they correct any errors. Afterward, their section of the map is complete.

A man named Loren will carry it to Erole. He is the one who chased Rath and One-Eye as they were exiting the caves.

As Lura gives him her piece of the map, he says, "You have my thanks. Will you rejoin the people of Delphy now? Erole will already be upset that we were discovered. But if you go further and aid them … "

"It is what I have promised. I feel it is only right, given what we have caused. Mera's group feels the same."

Loren shakes his head. "*They* were the ones interfering with our work." He narrows his eyes. "They may still interfere with other groups around Delphy – we have not yet finished the full map. We should have taken that curious man earlier. We almost did. However, I would think the Selachuu soldiers will prevent us as they did before."

"I agree. Will you tell Erole about him?"

For a moment, Loren hesitates. Finally, he says, "No. Erole would not appreciate the knowledge without it being confirmed. More than that … " He shifts uncomfortably, looking back at a woman who is speaking with a Spirit Eel held in her arms. "Grenian says her Spirit Eel believes the subject is not something we involve ourselves with. I cannot say I disagree." He steps back. "Go. Face your punishment with Erole later."

Lura only nods, thens walks away with her group.

Later that morning, Rath and the others are on the beach when One-Eye's Spirit Lion and Phillip's Spirit Rabbit suddenly turn and both look toward the cave entrance, their noses in the air.

A group of people exit, all with scarves covering their eyes to protect them from the sunlight. They approach the Selachuu soldiers first and the woman in front bows. Then they are led to a group of cave workers. It is not long before shouts come from that group and a Selachuu soldier – Azin – looks around, spots Rath, and swiftly walks over to him.

"Now would be a good time for your plan," he says.

"I understand." Rath quickly gets up.

Carlos, who was sitting next to him on a crate, drinking tea, watches this and sighs, knowing the break is over.

As Rath gets closer to the groups, he hears one of the workers say, "Why should we trust you? You'll likely bring the ceiling down over our heads! You've done enough to damage our caves. Just leave."

Grenian, the spy, says, "That is precisely why we wish to help. To make amends."

The worker, Evrin, huffs. Then he sees Rath and says, "You're the one who had the plan, wasn't it? Why would you think that they could help?"

"I am. And it is because they are capable of sensing where the weak areas of the caves are with Erole's Traits."

"We already knew that. Brinz and his group found the evidence of it. All they had to do was weaken the wall where one of those areas was and it traveled all the way to the surface, causing the cracks. I say we just arrest them."

"I do not believe that is possible. The law is non-specific on what the Ullian Spies may do on foreign land."

Before Evrin can say more, Azin clears his throat. "He's right. We can't try them for only damaging the caves. It would be possible with the ones who attacked others, but they've all left and we're under advisement the best course of action is not to pursue."

Evrin says, "But they nearly destroyed the caves! They put people in danger, destroyed ships, and disrupted waterways all for their … studies, or whatever they called them!"

"Minor injuries and property damage," Azin says. He looks at Grenian in front of the group from the Ullian Spies. "And, if I'm not mistaken, even those could be classified under accidents as there would be reasonable proof the areas were weak already and the cracks could have happened on their own. Isn't that right?"

She swallow, then nods.

Evrin stomps his boot in the sand. "Except they didn't! Rath, you're Councilman Georgio's son – inform your father or Garreth or have him message Marchand himself. Have these people tried for what they did."

Rath's eyes widen. "I … " He frowns. "I will inform all three, however, I cannot say what they will do given the circumstances."

"Even when your life was at risk?"

"I do not believe it was." Next to Rath, Grenian jolts in surprise. He turns to her. "May I ask if the people of Delphy would be allowed access to the map that was created?"

"I am afraid not. It was taken immediately."

"I understand. Would you be willing to find the weak areas in the caves so that they may be repaired before they become a danger?"

She bows outright. The others behind her do as well. "Of course. It would be our pleasure to do so. Many more groups, too, who are already speaking with others around Delphy."

"Thank you very much." Rath turns to Evrin, who looks calmer now, but his face is still red. "Would you be willing to go with them to see where these areas are?"

He has his arms crossed. "I suppose." He sighs then, releasing some of his anger. "But, this will take time. Even without some of the entrances being blocked, our messages would have to travel through the caves out to the ocean and back to Delphy to reach a group above ground to do these repairs and fortifications. It's not the most efficient."

However, Rath shakes his head. "I do not believe you will have to use the streams in the caves."

"Huh?"

"I have been trying not to think about it. May I now share my idea?"

They all nod. Azin smiles as Rath does.

Soon the groups are preparing to leave the beach. The workers and the spies to go back into the caves, the Butej Guard – having packed up the campsite – to depart on their skyships, and the Selachuu soldiers to their underwater ships.

Rath's group, too, is getting ready to return to Franz and Velt's homes when Evrin walks over and says to Rath, "I wanted to ask if you'd come with us. It was your idea, after all."

"Thank you for asking, however, I cannot." He flushes. "I am currently on break."

Evrin laughs. "I understand. It sounds like you and the others have already done a lot with this. I guess I was asking too much. You did explain your plan well – I trust that it'll work. Thanks again, all of you. I hope you have safe travels back."

Rath bows. "Thank you. And for your work."

Evrin smiles, then goes to join his group and the spies who are waiting at the cave entrance.

Before Rath's group can leave, the Butej Guard approaches them. They bow and the one in front, Fara, says, "Rath, if I may have a moment."

After they step aside, the guard says, "I have been asked to take you to Lord Garreth's home."

"May I ask why?"

"There have been concerns in regards to your safety. Both Lord Garreth and Fierce have been notified that several of Erole's own had intended to take you to Ullia to meet their god. They believe it would be best if you spent the duration of your time on Delphy with Lord Garreth and the Butej guards stationed in his house while the Ullian Spies are still present. As you know, this is only one area of the Constellation Caves and we have already received reports of similar cracks and cave-ins in other parts of Delphy that we believe – but have not confirmed – to be their activity. It seems likely, however, given the information that these people have been tasked to create a map of the entire Constellation Caves." She continues, "The Selachuu Military is currently traveling to these areas to discuss peaceful methods for the Ullian Spies to perform their task and the workers to have their aid in repairing the caves as they did here and afterward, confirm that none are present on Delphy. Their task is this. Ours, the Butej Guard's, is to ensure that you are safe."

Rath hesitates. "I apologize if this is rude to say, however, I believe I am safe staying in Meridelle Village."

Fara looks pained. "I am afraid this is not a request. It is a direct order from Fierce."

Rath looks surprised. "I understand."

He returns to the group to notify them. Franz and Velt's faces fall, but Carlos nods. "I cannot say I fully agree, however, I am concerned as well. Perhaps it would be best to go to Lord Garreth's for now. I will request to accompany you. One-Eye, it may be for you to as well. Your back has not made a full recovery yet and I will have more access to supplies there."

One-Eye frowns. "Fine."

Phillip says, "Do you think they would mind if I came? Carlos and I had planned to stay in Delphy until Vann's wedding."

Flower-Pagu says, "We would like to come, too, if that's all right." Bucket-Pagu and Well-Pagu nod.

Velt asks Rath, "Do you think you'll be able to make it back for the wedding?"

"I cannot say. I will let you know as soon as I do."

Franz says, "I hope so. I know both of our families have

really liked having you all around. Actually, I'm sure they'd like to see everyone before you leave."

Carlos clears his throat. "If I might offer a suggestion." He turns to Fara, who has been standing by. "I do not believe it would be unreasonable to allow all of us to go to Franz and Velt's homes so that their families may give a proper goodbye. I would imagine Master Rath and the others also have personal items there that would need to be acquired before we depart."

She hesitates, then nods. "You are right." To them all, she says, "We will take you there."

They go to the skyships, splitting up into three groups to fly with a Butej guard each – Carlos and Phillip, Franz and Velt, and Rath, One-Eye and the Pagu. As One-Eye lies down on his stomach in the skyship, Carlos says, "Flying will certainly be far better for your back than hiking would."

One-Eye stares up at him. "Right."

Carlos smiles for a moment, then says to all of them, "We shall see you there."

"Yup!" Velt calls.

Using Fierce's Traits, the guards lift their skyships into the air. Franz and Velt, who had never been on one before, cling to the hull or look on in amazement. Phillip does as well. Carlos, who has flown on them before, merely sits. One-Eye has not been on one, but cannot see anything except for the hull. He turns a little and can just see the Pagu, who are enjoying the wind while they hold onto Rath's collar, and Rath, who is looking at the sky.

They fly for a few minutes in silence until One-Eye says to Rath, "I don't like that I can't see your plan working. Can you see anything below?"

"Not yet."

"Let me know?"

"Of course."

In the Constellation Caves, Evrin and Grenian are walking through a tunnel with their respective groups when Grenian pauses and says, "Here." She points up, her Spirit Eel looking in the same direction. "There is a weakness just above us, three feet away from the northern wall in an eastern direction."

"I understand," Evrin says. He walks to one of the small waterfalls that run down the cave wall in certain areas. "Here goes nothing." His tattoos glow and he puts his hand into the water. A Delphaen message shoots upstream, disappearing into the ceiling.

It runs past hard rock and glittering Miphrin, through an opening and up further into another small waterfall with a tiled backdrop. Finally, it reaches the top of that and the water pouring out of a large glass globe.

A Signal Fountain glows brightly.

The group of workers assigned above ground see it.

"There!" one says and they quickly make their way over. They retrieve the message. "Three feet away from the northern wall in an eastern direction," they report to the others.

One consults a map, then another marks the ground with a small colored stone. "That would be here," they say.

Then they gather together, discussing. "We could move the bench there and reduce the weight," and "We could repave it as well." They nod, writing down the orders for construction workers to follow later.

Below, the worker receives a message back, reads it, then smiles at the spy. "It worked. They're coming up with ideas to improve it right now."

"That is good to hear."

They both turn to their groups. "Everyone," the worker says. "Go off in pairs. We'll cover this area. Listen to your partner and send instructions to those above."

"Yes, sir!" they say.

More quietly, the spy says to her people, "Go on."

They nod, then leave with their partners. The spy who left the food for Rath and One-Eye is among them and after using Erole's Traits, informs their partner of where the weakness is. Above, Dinra and her group see the Signal Fountain glowing with the message. Brinz receives the Delphaen message and relays it to Harton, who marks the area.

In the sky, Rath suddenly says, "Oh! I see one."

Flower-Pagu says, "I do too!"

Bucket-Pagu says, "It's working already!"

Well-Pagu says, "Helped!"

Rath flushes. "I am very happy to see they are working together."

The Pagu beam.

One-Eye smiles as well. His Lion is still lying on his legs, but seems restless. One-Eye says, "Go ahead. Tell me what you see. I won't move."

The Lion licks his face, then gets up and puts his paws over the railing.

Below them, the Delphaen landscape starts to light up with small blue-green orbs.

It takes only a few hours to reach Franz and Velt's homes, however during this time, much work is done on Delphy.

As pairs reach their assigned areas, more Signal Fountains begin lighting up – near a farm in northern Delphy, where Relanor is now working, his Spirit Lion trotting beside him; further south where Soren and his group have arrived for his brother Dereth and Mirani's wedding; and near one of the way stations Rath and the others stayed at, where the clerk is carefully folding completed blankets for the Haliae-Pantha Relief Effort.

In Kel City, Leader Leytel begins to receive reports on what must be done to strengthen the areas. "Please go to this area next," he says, handing instructions to Lana, the worker who had previously put out warning signs.

She takes them, looking brighter. "Yes, sir."

Leytel smiles, then continues writing a letter addressed to Rath.

At *Melta's*, Melta sees the Signal Fountains lighting up all over Archen Town. "Oh my! What in the world is going on?"

Luta says, "My Spirit Dolphin told me it's because of Franz, Velt, and the others."

"Huh?"

Luta quickly explains and afterward, his mother laughs. "Well! Never thought of using a Signal Fountain like that." She puts her arm over his shoulder. "But, it'll make all of us safer, that's for sure."

"And everyone's working together, too. I didn't know those people from Ullia were here, though."

"Me neither. Wish they'd be a bit more upfront about it. Now, come on, I see customers coming."

"Yes, Mom!"

Above, they are all looking at the Signal Fountains as well.

Rath says, "It concerns me there are so many weak areas."

Fara clears her throat. "If I may – "

"Of course."

She smiles briefly. "The Ullian Spies are very thorough. It is possible that some of these areas are truly no danger, but I am sure that even if there is a small chance, they wish to inform the people of Delphy."

"I see. I am very grateful to them for doing so."

The Spirit Lion rejoins One-Eye and begins telling him everything he saw. "Thanks," he says. Then to Rath, "Seems like it's working."

"I agree. It will take time, however, to make the necessary repairs."

One-Eye nods. "Still wish I got to see the caves with you and the others. And not … how we did."

"I do as well. I cannot say how long it will be until we are able to return to them, however, if they are finished before we leave, I would very much like to visit them with everyone as well."

One-Eye smiles. "Me too."

As he closes his eye to take a nap, Rath looks with the Pagu at the lights on Delphy.

13

When the Butej skyships arrive at Franz and Velt's homes, Franz's family runs to meet them.

Fiona is first to say, "Franz! What in the world … "

"It's all right, Aunt Fiona. It really is." He frowns. "Rath, One-Eye, and the Pagu are leaving, though."

Joseline gives a perplexed look. Then she sees the rest of the group and says, "Carlos, Phillip, you're here already."

Phillip smiles. "Hey, Joseline!"

Carlos nods respectfully. "It is very good to see you again."

"You two as well," she replies.

Rath, One-Eye, and the Pagu come over last. Joseline says to them, "I hear you're leaving?"

"Yes," Rath says. "I apologize that it is abrupt."

"No, no – may I ask why?"

After he explains, her eyes widen and Fiona squawks, "What!"

Joseline says, "Franz updated us as much as he could when

you were traveling, but I hadn't heard about the Ullian Spies yet."

Franz says, "Sorry, Mom. A lot happened after we reunited with him and One-Eye."

She tugs on his shirt. "It's all right." She turns back to the others. "How soon do you have to leave?"

Fana says, "We would prefer within the hour, however, if you would like to eat, we shall wait."

Joseline nods. "It is almost lunchtime. You're welcome to any food if you'd like."

"Th-That is all right, however, thank you."

"Of course. Velt – why don't you message your family? I'm sure they'd like to say goodbye as well."

Velt is already trotting off. "On it!"

Fiona claps her hands together. "Don't any of you worry – we'll have a feast prepared in no time!'

Franz sighs, but smiles. "Thanks."

Phillip says, "I can help, too, if you want!"

"Yes, please, Phillip dear," Fiona says.

Max, Mimi, and Mallo walk up to Rath and One-Eye.

Seeing how Rath is supporting him, Max says to One-Eye, "What happened to you?"

"Hurt my back."

"Fighting someone?"

One-Eye hesitates. He sighs. "No."

His Spirit Lion whips his tail furiously and One-Eye strokes his mane, saying, "I don't think falling in a cave counts as fighting the elements."

The Lion whips his tail even faster.

Mallo says, "I'm sorry you have to leave."

Mimi says, "Is it because we gave you breakfast in bed?"

Rath says, "No." He smiles. "Actually, I tried it and I find it very wonderful."

"See!"

While they are preparing lunch, Vann, Merlin, Niz, and Alfin arrive and help, then when it is finished, they sit around the table in Franz's family's home.

Vann says, "Sorry you all gotta go so soon." Merlin nods beside her.

Niz says, "It's this whole mess with the caves. I can't believe that it was the Ullian Spies who were causing the cracks." He shakes his head. "I hear they're expecting the caves won't be open until at least the end of the Summer. A lot of disappointed couples, I'm afraid … "

Beside him, Alfin says, "A lot of safe ones." Niz shrugs, agreeing. Alfin takes his hand, then says to Rath, "Niz took me to them before we got engaged. I think he still has special feelings about it."

Niz squeezes back. "And you don't?"

Alfin flushes, but does not say anything to deny it. Instead, he continues, "Rath, your parents did the same, right?"

"Yes. Mother had always wanted to see them. Father tells me she was unaware they were open to those who could not breathe underwater during the Summer until he told her."

Niz beams. "That must have been a wonderful gift to her."

"It was! She painted it right afterward – Father says she brought her supplies and did so on the beach outside of the entrance. It is one of their favorite memories, they tell me. The painting is currently hanging in my grandmother's home. My grandfather tells me that he wished to have it in his, however, at the time, he was not allowed to alter any of the furnishings."

Niz and Alfin frown. Niz says, "To ensure it stays a proper Delphaen home, hm?" He sighs. "I know what you've told me about where Lord Garreth lives – and I think that upholding tradition is a wonderful thing, however" – he looks at Alfin – "we both owe so much to the *changes* that Lord Garreth has brought. Alfin's descended from the Selachuu councilpeople, but not in the direct line to be one himself – even so, it would have been illegal for us to be married if Lord Garreth hadn't changed the law. We can never thank him enough for that."

Alfin nods quietly.

Rath says, "I am very grateful for it as well. It allowed Grandfather to marry Grandmother and Mother to marry Father."

Niz suddenly gets a spark in his eyes. "And have *you* anyone you'd like to marry thanks to the law, Captain?"

Velt shouts, "Dad!"

He chuckles. "Oh, I have a feeling … "

Alfin says, "Niz."

"Sorry."

Joseline covers a laugh, but Fiona dabs her mouth with her napkin, saying, "Goodness! It is true, however, that Lord Garreth has done much good for Delphy and Lord Georgio after him. Rath, you too have done well even if you will not inherit the title. Thank you." She raises her glass and the others do so quickly. The Pagu lift up theirs.

He flushes. "Y-You are welcome." He dips his head respectfully. "I am happy to help."

After they eat, he asks if they can help clean up, but Fiona shakes her head. "Absolutely not – we can take care of it just fine, Rath." She pauses, then smiles, saying instead, "Captain. It has been a pleasure seeing you again."

"You as well, Fiona."

Rath, One-Eye, and the Pagu retrieve their things from Velt's home, then they all gather by the skyships to say their goodbyes. "Safe travels, all of you," Joseline says. "I look forward to seeing you all again – hopefully sooner this time."

Rath says, "I agree."

The group boards the skyships and both families wave as they climb higher into the sky, heading southeast toward Garreth's home.

Up in the sky, Fana makes a quick hand signal to the

skyship next to her, then says to them, "We should arrive by late this evening."

One-Eye raises an eyebrow. "That's fast."

She smiles a little. "It helps when there are not waterways to worry over." She sobers. "Or cracks."

"Makes sense."

As she focuses on her flying, One-Eye asks Rath, "Do you see any more Signal Fountains lighting up?"

"I do, however there are not as many as before. I believe that is good."

For the rest of the journey, they are mostly quiet, stopping once to eat dinner before continuing on.

They arrive late that evening. The Spirit Lion wakes up One-Eye, who had been taking a nap and Rath helps him up.

A line of Butej guards has been waiting for them in front of Garreth's house, but it is abruptly broken when Garreth walks through them and strides forward to take Rath's hands. "How are you, Grandson?"

"I am all right. May I ask how you are, Grandfather?"

"Fine now. Good to see One-Eye, the Pagu, Carlos, and Phillip with you." To the whole group, he says, "Come on – we can talk for a bit, then you'll get the rest you need."

"Thank you, Grandfather," Rath says.

When they reach the front doors, Garreth says to one of the guards next to them, "And *don't* think about eavesdropping. I think your god would agree this is a subject that the fewer people who know, the better."

He looks surprised, then turns to the Spirit Hawk on his shoulder and nods. "We understand."

It is bright inside, with the Delphaen crystals hung all over the walls. One of the waterfalls on either side of the two staircases rushes down, but the other seems to sputter. Rath sees and his grandfather says, "Don't know what that's been about. Tried to find the source, but haven't had much time with the paperwork and keeping informed on the cracks. I'd ask you, but I'd rather you rest. We'll go to my sitting room to talk before that."

Carlos clears his throat.

"Yes, Carlos?"

"One-Eye has injured his back in the recent events. If I may take him to the infirmary instead to check it?"

"Absolutely." He rubs his chin. "Actually, I think I'd like to speak with my grandson in private – Rath, we'll go to my study – then we'll all reconvene for tea after?"

Carlos bows. "A fine idea."

Garreth turns to Phillip and the Pagu. "You're welcome to be anywhere you like. Phillip, if you want to see the kitchens, they're just down the hall to the left."

"Thank you, Lord Garreth!"

Bucket-Pagu says, "Thank you very much!"

While Phillip, Carlos, One-Eye, and the Pagu go in the direction of the infirmary and kitchen, Rath and his grandfather walk to his study. When they arrive, Garreth opens the door for them and Rath nods in thanks, then takes a look inside and pauses.

Garreth says, "Different, huh?"

"It is." Rath looks at the fireplace from Lotinx, the rug from Cunica, and the statues that were made in the forges on Grist. Garreth walks in and sits on the large Ursian chair, gesturing to its twin for Rath.

Once they are both settled, Garreth says, "This room used to be styled exactly how it was when this house was first built – Delphaen furniture and the like. Now, it's my own little sanctuary. Though, I'd imagine you haven't seen it since I started making my own changes."

"I have not."

"That would have been … eleven years ago, when you lost your traits, right?"

"Yes."

Garreth frowns. He sighs, leaning forward. "That time period is exactly why I agreed with Fierce's decision to have you brought here, Rath." He rubs his face. "I can't go through that again. None of us in your family or your friends or – I'm going to even say the Pagu – can handle it. I won't speak for you, because I think you took it the best out of all of us. Certainly far better than Marchand."

"Grandmother told me that nothing could be done and Carlos agreed. I trust them."

"I know you do. And if they were anyone else, I'd be angry with them, but they *know* what they're talking about – no matter how much I wished they weren't right." Garreth pauses for a long moment, then says, "I remember you telling me what happened when you sat in that chair – maybe not the same one it is now, but in that spot – before. You were so calm about it. I felt like I was ready to jump out the window and probably would have if it wasn't for Marchand behind me, with his hands on my shoulders, even though he was an absolute wreck, too. Then, not long after you finished, you gave us all a heart attack when you fell asleep."

"I-I apologize."

Garreth gives a half-smile. "Carlos declared you were merely exhausted and that we let you sleep until Fierce arrived with that skyship for him to take you and Carlos to Azalea's. The one that *I* should have taken with you." Rath begins to say something, but Garreth shakes his head. "I'm not saying this because of my own troubles, but for yours. I don't like that some god is interested in you and especially not that his people would go to such lengths to take you to him." He stops suddenly, looking concerned. "There were no lasting effects of those shocks you had?"

Rath shakes his head. "No. Carlos said there were none."

"I trust him." Garreth continues, "I don't like the thought of keeping you here – reminds me too much of my own situation – but it's not a bad idea until this whole situation is handled." He turns his eyes to the ceiling. "I'm already getting letters."

"Letters?"

Garreth waves his hand. "Petitions, pleas, however you want to call them. There are quite a few people on Delphy that want to ban people from Ullia coming here." He holds up his hand. "Now – officially, I'm not the one to be taking these requests, but with Marchand gone and Georgio still in the Council, I'm the highest authority figure on Delphy besides each of the leaders, even in my *retirement*. The reason I tell you is because things like this can easily spiral out of control – I've seen it happen. First it's people from Ullia, then it's some other group of people unlike us that people decide to have a problem with." He gestures around the room. "I want the cultures to come together – I want Merp to finally realize that's what we're meant to do. It's … part of why I've stayed on Delphy all these years. To help see that happen – even if it's just to make sure that marriages between the races continue to get approved. Call it stubborn, but it makes me feel like I'm doing good."

"I believe what you are doing is wonderful, Grandfather." Rath hesitates. "I … "

"Spit it out."

"I wish I could see you more." Garreth's eyes widen. "I-I … I hope it is not inappropriate to say, given the situation, that I am very glad to be with you right now, Grandfather. To be sitting in your study again."

Garreth is quiet for a long time after Rath stops speaking. Then he gives a broken chuckle and reaches out his arms. Rath stands up and goes over to him. Garreth hugs him tightly. "I am, too."

14

In the infirmary, Carlos has finished checking One-Eye's back.

One-Eye did not speak the entire time. As he sits up and puts his shirt back on, Carlos says, "He is all right."

One-Eye turns to him quickly, then frowns.

"Master Rath," Carlos says gently.

"I know that."

Carlos gives him a look, then decides to move on. "Your back is healing well. I would encourage you to not do anything strenuous – stairs, lifting any heavy weights, running – for another two days." He checks his pocket watch. "Now, I believe it is time I started tea. We will likely have it in the small dining room. Would you like me to retrieve Phillip and the Pagu or you?"

"I can. My Lion says he can guide me there. He's done talking with the others." The Lion, who had been with Garreth's Spirit Dolphin and Phillip's Spirit Rabbit, grins.

They leave the infirmary together, then go in opposite

directions. One-Eye's Lion takes him back to the foyer – they both stare at the sputtering waterfall – then down the left hallway to a set of double doors.

Phillip – his Spirit Rabbit has also returned to him – and the Pagu are inside, talking with a woman. However, when they see One-Eye, they thank her, then leave with him.

As they go back out into the hallway, Phillip says, "We were talking with the head chef. I kinda wondered this already, but it sounds like they're not allowed to cook *anything* that's not Delphaen or using Delphaen ingredients." He rubs the back of his head. "It's a good cuisine and I like it a lot, but I don't think I could do that."

Flower-Pagu says, "I thought it was very sad."

Bucket-Pagu says, "There are a lot of different types of food that are really good."

"Arbitrary," Well-Pagu says.

One-Eye looks at the Delphaen arches and crystals set in the walls. "A lot of things are in this place. I'm not surprised Garreth seems to hate it."

They turn the corner and see Rath, Carlos, and Garreth are already standing outside the door to the small dining room. After the others join them, they go inside.

The table is set into a curved out portion of the wall with windows behind it that overlook the ocean. The same waterways that run through all of the house are there, flowing over the window sill and down into holes that lead outside.

After Carlos serves everyone tea, Flower-Pagu takes a sip from their little teacup, then says, "We talked with the head chef."

Bucket-Pagu says, "We wish that they could cook more than Delphaen Cuisine."

Well-Pagu says, "Variety."

Garreth snorts. "You and me both, Honored Ones. It's just like the Phoenae airships in that regard, but at least she's able to pick from recent meals and not just the most traditional." He smiles a little. "Pretty sure Marchand *created* a few Delphaen dishes just so I wouldn't go crazy."

Carlos says, "I would not be surprised."

Garreth continues, "I told Rath this, but you should know, too – I've been getting more requests to strengthen the laws against those from other countries entering Delphy. Particularly people from Ullia."

One-Eye frowns. "Do you have the power to reject them?"

"Legally, no. That's now Georgio and Marchand's job. But … I do hold a certain amount of power, especially with neither of them here. Everywhere's different – Pantha has its king, Lionel, and soon a councilperson to act as authority figures, but here in Delphy, it's traditionally been my family and the leaders of each city, town, and village. Now, part of this is because of the Council. Georgio isn't on Delphy all that much and Marchand can only be in so many places at once, even as a god. The leaders help us keep track of everything that's going on here and their input is heavily taken into consideration when decisions are made regarding the country."

One-Eye nods. "If enough of them agree to not allow people from Ullia, then it's possible it would happen."

"Exactly. Even if we don't personally agree with it, we have to listen to the people here and – if it's something we'd rather not approve – try to alleviate the situation or find a compromise."

Phillip says, "So … would that be like only disallowing the people from Ullia who caused trouble? Because there were definitely a lot who wanted to help."

"Ideally, they would be treated just the same as anyone on Delphy. It's not as if our own people never cause problems. Often, they do." He finishes his tea. "The best outcome we can hope for is that the Ullian Spies finish their task, the Selachuu Military stops any fighting between them and the cave workers, and the latter remain patient while they do this." He sits back, crossing his arms. "Still a shame that it sounds like we will never get that map of the Constellation Caves they're making. Not that I don't trust Marchand's original, but … people with Erole's Traits would be far more precise and it's likely the caves have changed in ways we can't even guess since Marchand designed them."

"I agree," Rath says.

After a moment, Carlos says, "Lord Garreth, to my knowledge, Merp has only allowed Master Rath to visit your home for a single day every year. The circumstances are certainly extenuating, however, I am still surprised he agreed to this."

"That's because he didn't. In Fierce's words – 'mind, not my own – 'Merp's decision does not matter.'"

Rath looks shocked and even One-Eye is surprised.

"That's not exactly … respectful, is it?" Phillip says.

Carlos says, "No, however, I cannot disagree with the sentiment even if the choice of words was rather … brash."

"Sounded direct to me," One-Eye says.

Carlos frowns at him – One-Eye shrugs – then continues, "I do think it reveals Fierce's mood with the current situation. Did you speak with him directly, Lord Garreth?"

"No, no. A Butej guard forwarded the message to me. They seemed highly uncomfortable with it."

"I would imagine so. Fierce must be very stressed."

"Of course he is. He's currently one of the only gods in the South … Did Hep go, too?" he asks the Pagu.

The Pagu, who have been sitting in between Rath and One-Eye on the table, sipping their tea, lower their cups and are quiet for a moment as if listening. Then Flower-Pagu says, "Yes. He is traveling with the others to Haliae and Pantha."

Garreth says, "Well, there you have it. Fierce always seemed overwhelmed with the amount of work he gives himself patrolling the South – this just amplifies it." He gives a small laugh. "Bet he'd even be willing to have Vocalise's help right now."

Carlos narrows his eyes. "I do not believe that is appropriate, given the situation."

"It's the truth."

"Is it known whether Erole is still in the South? In Ullia or elsewhere?"

"Marchand never said anything about him coming along."

Flower-Pagu, after conferring with Bucket-Pagu and Well-Pagu, says, "We're not sure either."

Rath suddenly says, "Evermore."

Carlos turns to him. "I beg your pardon?"

"I apologize. I just remembered – when I was speaking with Lura, Evermore's mother, I was told that he was not being allowed to leave Erole's presence until he gave his full report of the previous year and a half. It was … punishment for him not going to Ullia during the Winter last year."

Garreth says, "I'm very sorry to hear that. Wasn't any of your faults. You were helping Ara and the rest of the world. Did she say where they were?"

"No, she did not."

One-Eye says, "When we arrived in Priage, I saw Evermore get on an Ullian ship like usual."

Garreth sighs. "Then he's likely on his way to Ullia. It takes over a month to get there. By the time he gets back to Delphy, you and everyone on *PearlHeart* will be leaving." He sets down his cup. "Well – enough of all that for now. The important thing is that you arrived here safely and there's at least a chance this whole situation can be resolved before too many of those petitions come through. I think you've all deserved your rest. We'll talk more in the morning."

As they leave, Garreth says to One-Eye, "Carlos told me that he and you will be sleeping in the infirmary to avoid the stairs. For Phillip, Rath, and the Pagu, I have rooms prepared upstairs. Honored Ones, I trust you'll want to sleep in Rath's room?"

"Yes, please!" Flower-Pagu says. "If that's all right with you, Rath?"

He smiles. "Of course. I would like that very much."

They beam and fly onto his shoulder to sit while they travel.

Now, outside Rath's door, Garreth says, "Good night, Grandson."

"Good night, Grandfather."

After Garreth leaves, Rath and the Pagu enter their room.

It is medium-sized, with a bed and a balcony that looks out over the ocean. The light from the Delphaen crystals is faint, having not been in water for some time. They quickly get ready for bed, then with the Pagu on one pillow and Rath resting on the other, they all fall asleep.

The next morning before breakfast, Rath, the Pagu, One-Eye, his Spirit Lion, Carlos, Phillip, and his Spirit Rabbit gather on one of the terraces overlooking the beach behind Garreth's home.

Garreth comes out not long afterward and sits down gruffly. "Sorry I'm late. More paperwork. Wedding Season."

One-Eye nods sagely, now knowing what this means.

Rath says, "It is all right, Grandfather. May I ask if you slept well?"

Garreth relaxes. "Yes, actually. Nice to have company – *different* company. What about you all?"

"I slept well, thank you," he says and the rest agree.

Garreth smiles, then becomes more serious. "I received a message this morning – there were some tremors late last night near Alianne Village. There wasn't too much damage – some older structures that were needing to be rebuilt anyways. Unfortunately, people are already starting to say it was caused by the Ullian Spies. Given the rainfall we've had and the location of Alianne Village, I would say it mostly likely wasn't. The Constellation Caves aren't the only structure beneath Delphy. The Old Delphaen Crystal Quarry is below them in certain areas."

One-Eye says, "How would it cause tremors?"

"It – well, Rath, why don't you explain?"

"Yes, Grandfather. Delphaen crystals can only grow in subterranean environments inside a water source. A great river runs through the quarry beneath Delphy, flowing west to east. At times in Delphy's history, it has flooded and caused tremors due to the force of the water against the floor of the lower caves. Alianne Village is above the quarry, so with the increase in rainfall, it is possible the river is flooded again."

One-Eye says, "Can it be checked? How do you get down there?"

"There were entrances to it from all of the leaders' homes that are above the river – including here in Grandfather's home. However, four hundred years ago, it was decided that they would be blocked. Marchand believed they were too dangerous due to the possible flooding. Since then, all Delphaen crystals have been harvested in the ocean depths to the north of Delphy."

While Rath speaks, his grandfather looks uncomfortable. Finally, Garreth says, "In the effort of full disclosure – the quarry *is* accessible from here." He huffs. "Blame a stubborn twenty-five-year-old version of me who wanted to impress Azalea and didn't understand the concept of *danger* when both of my mothers told me why it had been sealed."

Rath's eyebrows go up. "Grandfather."

"I've since blocked it again, but – I know how to open it. *Not* that I'm saying we go down there and investigate. To my knowledge, the tremors have always been temporary – the water level goes up, then filters back out to the ocean and goes down. But, like I said" – he looks at his grandson – "full disclosure."

Rath frowns. "That was very irresponsible."

Garreth sighs. "Azalea said the *exact* same thing. Similar expression, too." He shakes his head. "I don't think they're anything to be worried about, but it wouldn't hurt to remind the leaders the tremors are at least semi-normal – especially since some of them already think they have to do with the Ullian Spies." He hesitates. "I hate to ask you this, Rath – but would you be able to draft those letters to them? Explain how you did to us just now. I would and Georgio would if he were here, but he's not and I already have to go back to working on that paperwork."

"Of course. I would be happy to."

Garreth stands up and squeezes Rath's shoulder. "Thank you." He says to all of them, "I took a bit of a break yesterday, but today it'll be like it will be for the foreseeable future – I don't know how much I'll see all of you, but you're welcome to go wherever you want whenever you want. You have my full permission."

One-Eye nods. "Thanks."

"However, I wasn't able to get it cleared for you to leave the house beyond the immediate perimeter. I am sorry for that. Hopefully, the Ullian Spies will clear out of the nearby areas soon and you can all have your freedom again."

After Garreth heads back into the house, Carlos checks his watch. "Breakfast will be served at eight. One-Eye, I would like to check your back before then."

"Sure."

Phillip says, "My Rabbit and I are going to look at the plants outside the house." His Rabbit gives an excited hop on his shoulder.

Bucket-Pagu says, "We thought we would fly around. It's a really wonderful day." Flower-Pagu and Well-Pagu nod.

Rath smiles. "I hope that you enjoy and that everything goes well, One-Eye, Carlos. I will start on the letters for Grandfather, then see everyone at breakfast."

As Phillip and his Rabbit go down to the beach and the Pagu fly up into the sky, One-Eye and Carlos walk to the infirmary and Rath goes to Garreth's study. His grandfather had given him permission to use it whenever he needed the day before. There, he pulls out a log of the current leaders on Delphy and sits at the desk.

After he finishes writing the letters, he walks to the foyer to go out to the Paradi Message Tower, but when he approaches the front doors, a Butej guard near them says, "Rath, is there something you need outside?"

"I need to ask the Paradi messengers to deliver these letters I wrote for my grandfather."

The guard frowns. They do a quick hand gesture to the one on the other side of the doors, then say, "I will accompany you."

"Th-That is not necessary."

"I am afraid it is."

The guard opens the doors for them both to exit, then stays two paces behind Rath while they go down the stairs.

The Paradi messengers see them coming and descend the ladder quickly.

"Rath, it is so good to see you," Hera says. "I only wish the circumstances could have been better."

"You as well. And, I agree."

After he hands her the letters, she wraps them up so Morenid can carry them and they all watch him take off with them in his talons.

While Rath and the guard return to the house, the Pagu fly in the sky above them. They go over and through the different arches that make up the home, then settle on the roof and look at the long waterfalls that run down and into the ocean.

Flower-Pagu says, "I think Delphaen architecture is so pretty! I love the water and the plants do, too."

Bucket-Pagu says, "It is interesting to see how it has stayed the same here at Garreth's home, though. The design of Marchand's homes has changed over the years."

Well-Pagu sighs. "Merp."

They look at one another, then fly off again.

They pass by the windows of Garreth's office where he is working on paperwork. One window is open to allow in the breeze from outside. The Pagu wait by it politely while Garreth stamps another sheet, then Flower-Pagu says, "Excuse me. May we come in?"

Garreth jumps, then looks over. He smiles. "Well, of course. You don't need to ask that."

They enter and land on his desk, carefully avoiding his paperwork.

"It's the right thing to do," Bucket-Pagu says.

"Polite," Well-Pagu says.

Garreth chuckles. "You are right about that. What have you been doing?"

Flower-Pagu says, "We were looking around at the Delphaen architecture and all the water."

Bucket-Pagu says, "It's amazing to me that it looks the same here even after so long."

"Centuries," Well-Pagu says.

Garreth nods. "Well, yes – that's exactly how Merp likes it. Of course, it's been repaired over the years, but he would prefer that it looks just like how the first councilperson had it." He crosses his arms. "A long … *long* time ago." He pauses, then asks, "How are you three? I know you struggle to be here – my Spirit Dolphin told me. I give off too many negative feelings."

Flower-Pagu says, "It can make us tired."

Bucket-Pagu says, "But, it's better now."

"Others," Well-Pagu says.

Garreth says, "It's better with the others here?" Well-Pagu nods. "*I* feel better with them here. I wish … Well, Azalea was very firm that she didn't want to stay here. She has her island. And her gardens. I wonder how large they are now. How is the South Garden doing?" He sighs heavily. "One day I'll see them. I just feel like there's more good to be done here." He sits up. "Well, I hope I'm not being rude in saying that if I'm going to be there for breakfast, I'd best get these done."

Flower-Pagu says, "Of course not!"

Bucket-Pagu says, "But, before we go, we brought you something."

"Oh?" Garreth says.

They nod and Well-Pagu opens their little side satchel. "Berry," they say, holding out a small Delphy Berry.

Garreth grins. He takes it from Well-Pagu carefully. "Thank you very much, Honored Ones."

"You're welcome!" Flower-Pagu and Bucket-Pagu say.

"Happy!" Well-Pagu says.

As they exit through the window again – they give little waves before they do and Garreth waves back – he turns back to his work, popping the Delphy Berry in his mouth.

Downstairs, Rath meets the others by the small dining room.

"Hello, everyone," he says. "May I ask how your back is, One-Eye?"

"Yeah. Carlos says I should be fully healed in two days."

"That is wonderful to hear."

The staff admits them. As One-Eye sits down next to Rath, he asks, "What about those letters? Did you get them done?"

"Yes. I just sent them."

At that moment, Garreth enters and goes to the head of the table. "Sorry. Just finished."

Carlos says, "I believe you are on time, Lord Garreth."

He blinks. "Am I?" He looks at the clock and laughs. "Well!

That's a first. Must have been the Pagu's help. They came to visit me while I was working." He turns to them. "That Delphy Berry you gave me must have helped me finish up the rest a lot faster."

Flower-Pagu says, "I'm so glad to hear that!"

As their meal is brought in, Garreth tells them, "Not so many petitions today. I'm going to make some inquiries, but it sounds like it's possible the Selachuu Military is helping relations with the Ullian Spies and the people of Delphy."

One-Eye looks at his Spirit Lion, then says to Garreth, "You're busy – we can ask around instead."

Garreth raises his fork. "You all aren't allowed to leave the area, remember? Otherwise, I'd agree. *I* could use a walk outside."

"What about my Spirit Lion?"

Garreth snorts. "Only a true fool would try to tell the Spirit Animals what to do. Doubt even the Gods would."

One-Eye grins. "Good. My Lion's willing to see what he can find out. Let him know if you want any other answers."

"I'll do just that!" He looks to his side, where his Spirit Dolphin is. "Actually, would he mind company? My Dolphin is interested in going. I've already let her know everything I want to know."

"Definitely."

Phillip says, "My Spirit Rabbit, too! She also wants to explore Priage a little bit."

"He says that's fine." One-Eye turns to his Lion and ruffles his mane. "You off, then?"

The Lion looks ecstatic.

One-Eye laughs. "See you later."

The Lion licks his hand, then bounds off. Unseen by most of the group, a Dolphin and a Rabbit follow him as they pass right through the wall.

The Lion, the Rabbit, and the Dolphin arrive on the front porch. None of the Butej guards can see them, but a Spirit Hawk does look at them curiously. The Lion trots down the steps with purpose while the Rabbit hops onto each and the Dolphin swims in the air.

When they reach the bottom, they continue along the path in front of the home and up the hill. There, they pick up their pace and by the time they reach the top, they are running or diving.

Ahead is Priage Port, with sailors hauling crates, captains guiding them, and people reuniting after journeys. The trio of Spirit Animals moves on from the docks and go into the city itself to listen for news.

They slow as they come to a shop front. Two children are exiting with their mother.

" … my friend told me the Ullian Spies are all over. Wouldn't it be fun to go down into the caves?" one says.

The younger brother says, "I don't know … "

The mother turns around, shaking her head. "No. You've heard the Selachuu Military – no one is to go into the caves. We're to allow the Ullian Spies to make their map, *then* we can make our trip there." She sighs. "Well, after the repairs." Near them, a group of workers is checking a weak area in the ground.

"Yes, Mom," her sons say, then they walk off together.

The Spirit Animals watch them. Then the Rabbit flicks her ear and the Lion grins. They all go through the ground.

It is dark in the Constellation Caves, but the Spirit Animals can see. There is a cave worker and a spy in front of them. The worker says, "They've received the message. They're looking at the area right now."

The spy's eyes are bright in the dark. "I am glad to hear that."

"And … thanks for your help. It's been invaluable."

"It is my pleasure."

The worker smiles for a brief moment, then the pair moves on through the cave.

The trio comes across other workers and spies in pairs, some sending Delphaen messages to the areas above, others using Erole's Traits to determine the weak spots.

They turn around the next corner and see a spy, however, she is alone. She gazes far ahead, to where the Spirit Animals see another pair is working together. When they turn back to the lone spy, they see electricity spark at her fingertips.

Suddenly, a Spirit Eel curls around her arm and shakes their head. The spy and Eel have a private conversation, then she sighs and steps away from the wall. She hails the pair ahead and when they meet, she says, "I will be helping as well. Where am I to go?"

The spy already helping looks surprised. "To the nearest entrance. The Selachuu soldiers will direct you."

The worker says, "Thank you much. You've all been such a great help lately."

The spy who had been about to attack them hesitates. "Oh. I … " She nods. "I will do my best."

The Spirit Animals watch with approval.

As the spy and her Spirit Eel pass by them, the Eel arches their neck in their direction, then points down.

The Spirit Animals understand, however – after a brief discussion – they decide to go back up to the surface. Their information gathering is not quite finished.

Once there, they turn to one another. Then, with a unified nod, they move forward and disappear.

When they reappear, they are far further west – near the center of the southern coast of Delphy, in the largest port – Akkan City. Despite this, the docks are nearly empty. A large crack runs down the street leading into the city. Nearer to the water, the Spirit Animals hear shouting. They move toward it.

As they get closer, they see a man yelling at a Selachuu soldier. "They're destroying things down there! Arrest them!"

The soldier frowns. "We have been advised that our best course of action is to allow them to do what they have been tasked with, ask them to help fix the caves, and then see that they leave afterward."

"See that they leave now! And who advised you of this?"

"Belle."

"But he's on his way to the North, isn't he?"

The soldier glances at something near their feet. "A Spirit Shark relayed this."

The man calms down. "Spirit Shark." He pauses. "My wife says her Spirit Dolphin thinks we should allow the Ullian Spies to do what they need."

The soldier nods.

"I suppose … that's what we need to do. I'm sorry."

"It's fine. You will need to leave the docks now – I can't guarantee their safety."

"I understand."

The man walks away. The Spirit Animals watch him, then disappear again.

They travel to other parts of Delphy – going further west, then begin moving north.

As they do, they switch between the underground, watching the growing relations between the workers and spies, and the surface, looking on with the crowds as construction is underway or as soldiers explain to people why they cannot go into the caves. They see some arguments, but steadily more acceptance of the situation. They also see the Ullian Spies become more relaxed as they realize their task is finally being allowed.

When they are underground in northern Delphy, they see a spy standing with a worker who has just sent their Delphaen message. A Spirit Eel pokes her head over the spy's shoulder and looks at the Lion, the Rabbit, and the Dolphin.

At that moment, the spy turns. The worker does as well and gasps. "Oh! A Spirit Dolphin!"

The spy nods. "Yes. A Lion and a Rabbit as well, my Eel tells me."

"You didn't tell me you had a Spirit Eel."

He flushes. "Since the day of my birth."

"I've heard it often occurs like that," she says, smiling. "A Lion and a Rabbit, too, hmm … and your Eel." She sighs. "I've heard my friends want everyone from Ullia to leave. I would figure that would mean people from other countries would have to, too. That's what it was like here on Delphy centuries ago – my grandma told me. None but Marchand's own were allowed."

"On Ullia, it is still like that," the spy says after a moment.

"I hope that changes. I think it has only made Delphy far better to welcome others."

The spy starts to smile, but seems unsure.

The worker continues, "At the very least, knowing the Spirit Animals are together like this makes me even more sure we're doing the right thing by working with each other. Now, come on – let's keep going."

"Yes." As they walk away, the Eel looks over the spy's shoulder again. Like the other Spirit Eel, she points her head down.

The Spirit Animals hesitate.

Once the footsteps of the pair recede into the caves, the Dolphin speaks to the Lion and Rabbit – the latter two nod – then the Dolphin dives into the floor.

She continues through the lower caves, then comes out right below the craggy ceiling of another deeper cave.

Bright blue-green light glows under the surface of a rushing river, nearly as high as the cave itself. The color matches the Spirit Dolphin. She looks left, then right, gauging the water level of the river from both sides, then moves in the direction of the current.

When she returns to the Constellation Caves, she explains what she saw and they all think.

After a moment, the Lion says something and the others look alarmed. The Lion leads, running further into the tunnel. They move together, past the same pair from before. The Lion's ears are pricked forward, listening for where the rushing water is the strongest.

When he finds it, he tells the Dolphin, who swims below.

Here, the water is far higher, hitting the ceiling and eroding away pieces of it. The Dolphin goes back above. She speaks urgently with the Lion and Rabbit, then they all look toward the pair of people.

The Spirit Eel pops her head out again, listens, then her eyes grow large. She noses the spy urgently and he stops and the worker does as well.

"What is it?" the worker asks him.

"A weak area. One below." He kneels, touching the floor with his hand. A yellow pulse goes through the cave.

The worker hesitates. "But, we should only need to be concerned with those in the walls and ceiling."

The spy suddenly pulls his hand back. "No – it is weak here. If something is not done – " Suddenly, a small tremor goes through the cave floor and they hear the sound of rock crumbling, followed by a surge of water.

"The floor has collapsed in the lower tunnels," the spy says. He frowns, sensing again. "A river is there. Another cave."

"The Old Delphaen Crystal Quarry. We're right above them."

The ground trembles again, accompanied by another rush of water, now loud in their ears.

At the same time, the spy and the worker say to each other, "We have to let everyone know." Their eyes widen and – in spite of the situation – they smile for a brief moment.

Then the spy says to his Eel, "Stay here please. Inform me of the status." The Eel bobs her head and leaps to the floor. There, she watches it intently.

While she does, the spy and the worker go to find others to warn them.

The Lion, the Rabbit, and the Dolphin do the same, heading in the opposite direction. They find Spirit Dolphins and Eels who they can communicate with and as soon as they tell the humans they are with, they all hurry to warn everyone else in the caves.

The Spirit Animals look on in relief, then nod to each other and move forward, disappearing once more.

15

It is nearing lunch when the Spirit Lion, Spirit Rabbit, and Spirit Dolphin return to Garreth's house.

One-Eye is on the back terrace, lying in the sun while Rath reads a book in a chair beside him, and the Pagu sit on the table next to him doing the same.

When the Lion arrives, One-Eye reaches out to pet him. "What'd you find out?"

The Lion gives it in two short sentences.

One-Eye gets up with a startled sound.

Rath jumps. "I-Is everything all right?"

As the Lion fills in more details, One-Eye says, "Probably not."

At that moment, Garreth comes outside with his Spirit Dolphin. "One-Eye – "

"My Lion's told me."

Garreth nods. "And Rath?"

"Just about to."

Phillip rushes out, his Spirit Rabbit and Carlos with him. "Um – "

"We know. We're just talking about it. One-Eye, how about you fill in Rath? My Dolphin and I are going to check below the house."

After he goes back inside, One-Eye tells Rath, "That river you talked about below – the one in the old Delphaen Crystal Quarry – is eroding away the floor of the lower tunnels. My Lion, Garreth's Dolphin, and Phillip's Rabbit warned as many people as they could by communicating with the Spirit Dolphins and Eels they found. Most have left already."

"I am relieved to hear that. Thank you very much," he says to the Spirit Animals One-Eye and Phillip gesture to. The Lion and Rabbit nod crisply. "I will ask my grandfather to see if there is anything I can do to help."

Flower-Pagu says, "We'll go with you!"

"I'll go, too," One-Eye says. "Will we need to evacuate this place, too? If there's an entrance to the river below."

"It is possible."

Carlos and Phillip join them as they all go to the library, where Rath tells them the entrance is.

One-Eye says, "My Lion says if he saw the map of the Constellation Caves again, he could show us where the lower tunnel floor had collapsed."

"Yes, please. Thank you, One-Eye's Spirit Lion."

The Lion grins as he trots down the hallway.

When they reach the library, Rath says, "Grandfather?"

They hear a grunt and then the creak of boards. "Over here!"

They all go further into the circular room. Books and scrolls fill the curved shelves and a waterfall runs down the opposite wall. The windows are open next to it, allowing in a breeze.

Near the adjacent wall is a short set of stairs leading down to a boarded-up door that Garreth is currently uncovering. He pulls off one with a screech, then sets it aside in a growing pile. "I don't see any water down here – no tremors, either – so I'd say we're fine, but best to check."

"I agree," Rath says. "Grandfather, may we see the map of the Constellation Caves? One-Eye tells me his Spirit Lion can tell us the area where the lower tunnel floor collapsed if he saw it."

The Lion swishes his tail.

Garreth grins, then tackles another board. "Absolutely. Go get it and we'll see what he has to say."

After Rath returns, One-Eye says, "Set it on the floor like you did before."

"Of course." Rath does so, then he and One-Eye hold the map open on each side.

Unseen by Rath, One-Eye's Spirit Lion steps in between them. He studies the map, remembering where he and the other Spirit Animals were, then puts his paw down on one area. He looks at One-Eye, who copies the gesture with his hand so Rath can see.

"Here, he says."

Rath nods, thinking. He tells his grandfather, "It was under Meran Town where the floor collapsed today."

"That's not too far from here." He tosses the last board down. "My mother and Marchand tried to create tributaries to reduce the risk of flooding, but it still proved too dangerous and my mom finally convinced them it wasn't worth it. They did finish a few, though, between here and Meran Town. And, because it flows east, everyone in western Delphy should be fine. It's hard to say how fast a surge that strong will travel – all we can do right now is check the water level here while my Dolphin monitors it where the floor collapsed." He waves his hand. "Come on down, Rath. I trust your eyes. Let's see the level of it now."

"Yes, Grandfather."

Once Rath joins him, Garreth opens the door. A bright blue-green glow filters into the room.

A large river runs in front of them, Delphaen crystals shimmering beneath its surface. It stretches far into the distance to the left where it is only seen as a strip of blue-green, like a Delphaen message. To the right, it goes on until it flows out into the ocean.

Garreth clicks his tongue as he studies the water level. "Higher than it should be." He points. "Do you see that marking on the wall opposite us?"

Rath looks at a deep etching in the stone. "I do."

"That's the limit. We're in no danger now, but if enough doesn't drain by the time that surge reaches here, it'll be a problem."

"I understand. What can we do?"

He motions for them both to step back and closes the door. "For now, we'll keep this shut. If it does flood, it'll reach here first. We should check the home blueprints as well to make sure that if it does reach high enough, it won't be disrupting any supports. Will you help me with that?"

"Definitely."

They go back to the main level of the library where the others are. Garreth says, "My grandson and I are going to see if the house's supports will be safe here when the surge arrives. My Dolphin will keep us updated on when that'll happen. For now we'll be fine, but if you feel any sort of tremor, or – One-Eye, Phillip – either of your Spirit Animals think we should leave, we will. Butej Guard's approval or not."

Carlos gives a delicate cough. "I cannot imagine they would not do so if it was considered a danger to stay."

"You'd think so."

The Pagu silently confer with one another, then Bucket-Pagu says, "Garreth, if it would be all right with you and your

Spirit Dolphin, we would like to come with her."

Flower-Pagu says, "We may be needed to speak with people if there aren't any with Marchand's Traits or other Spirit Animals around."

Well-Pagu says, "Communicate."

Garreth's eyebrows go up and his Dolphin spins in a circle. He smiles at her, then says to the Pagu, "Absolutely. Thank you for your help, Honored Ones."

Flower-Pagu says, "We're happy to!"

Bucket-Pagu says to Rath, "I hope that you're able to figure out if Garreth's home is safe."

Well-Pagu says, "Luck."

"Thank you very much," Rath says. "And for offering to help communicate with others. I greatly appreciate it."

The Pagu beam and Flower-Pagu says, "Of course!"

Following the Spirit Dolphin, they fly through one of the open windows in the library.

While the others stay there, Rath and Garreth go upstairs to his study. Garreth says, "Unfortunately, I may have to set you up and leave you to it." He sighs when they reach the second floor. "Thought maybe you would get to rest when you came here."

"I do not mind helping."

Garreth looks at him, then shakes his head. "That might be the problem sometimes. Carlos told me a little about what's been going on – says you've hardly gotten a break since you arrived in Priage. Says he had to ask you to take one and set specific rules for it."

"He did."

They pause in front of the door to the study. "And? What did you think of it?"

"It was very nice. It was difficult not to think of anything that Carlos asked me not to, however, I enjoyed it." He smiles. "One-Eye introduced me to breakfast in bed."

"He…Hm. Maybe he is good to have around after all."

They enter and Garreth walks to the bookshelves. He pulls out an old tube. "Here it is – several documents for each floor but focus on the lower ones first and the supports."

"Yes, Grandfather."

Garreth sets the blueprints on his desk. "We'll talk at lunch if you're able to find anything. Right," he suddenly says. "You'll need this one as well." He goes back to the bookshelf and takes out one more map. He lays it on the desk, too. "The Old Delphaen Crystal Quarry." He opens it and points to a smaller diagram, comparing the height of the cave to the home. "Here's that line I showed you earlier. Do you remember about where the water was?"

"Yes, I do."

"Good. Use that when you study the structures. I don't think it'll cause any damage where it is now, but it's best to be sure. Then, test it with the water at its full capacity, like my Dolphin says it is now further west." Garreth takes his shoulder. "Thank you for doing this. I…" He shakes his head. "See you at lunch. Good luck."

"Thank you, Grandfather."

After he leaves, Rath sits down at the desk and begins to study the blueprints.

Inside the library, One-Eye, who had been listening to his Lion, says, "How far is the radius we can go around this house?"

Carlos says, "I estimate less than a mile."

"Is the exit to that river within it?"

"Certainly. Are you thinking of checking it?"

"Yeah. My Spirit Lion wanted to make sure nothing was blocking it and that no cracks had damaged the area around it."

"A very good idea. I can show you where it is."

Phillip says, "We'll come, too." His Rabbit nods.

They exit the library and go to the beach. The guards give them curious looks, but do not say anything.

When they reach the water, Carlos looks toward a grove of trees on their left. "It should be in that direction. However, it is underwater and I would advise you not to swim just yet."

Phillip raises his hand. "We can go! I don't know exactly what we're looking for, but we'll do our best." His Spirit Rabbit hops on his shoulder.

"Thank you. I would imagine the most important thing is to see if the opening is in any danger of being blocked. Look for cracks in the surrounding area or signs of rubble."

"Sure thing!" Phillip takes off his shirt and lays it on the sand. As he swims out into the ocean to dive underwater, a Butej guard approaches One-Eye and Carlos.

"Where is he going?" he asks.

"Not far," One-Eye says.

Carlos, with a patient look, says, "We had concerns about the Old Delphaen Crystal Quarry. Phillip and his Spirit Rabbit are ensuring the water from the river is able to leave uninhibited."

The guard's eyebrows go up. "I see." He coughs. "We…had heard of the possible danger to Lord Garreth's house."

One-Eye says, "Would you let us leave if it was?"

The guard looks aghast. "Of course. All of your safety is – "

"The first priority – I get it."

The guard frowns but gives a respectful nod to both of them, then returns to his post.

Carlos says, "You do not need to be so harsh with them. They are only doing their duty."

"Why is that? If Fierce told them to be here, what's his interest with Rath's family?"

"Because he was the one who found Master Rath after he lost his traits." One-Eye's eye widens and Carlos sighs, continuing, "He brought him to Marchand, of course, and he and the Pagu confirmed they were gone. I did my own assessment as well and came to the same conclusion. Even though Fierce was not directly involved, he very much blamed himself and promised that he would not let anything happen again. He is also Lady Marin's secondary god – her father was from Butej and part of the Butej Guard. While the Gods are not bound to aid all humans who carry their traits, oftentimes, they do. Fierce certainly does and that extends to Master Rath."

"What about the listening they do?"

"An order from Merp after he learned what had happened to Master Rath. Fierce agreed."

Not far from them, Phillip surfaces. "Hey!"

One-Eye says, "Did you find anything?"

He paddles to shore and steps out. "Um…I think so? Like I said, I wasn't totally sure what to look for. It was also hard to get close with the rush of the water."

Carlos sighs in relief. "Then, it must have been open."

"It looked like it, but I couldn't see inside all that much."

One-Eye says, "If water's coming out, that's good."

"That's true. But, then my Spirit Rabbit mentioned that it seemed kinda similar to something we've seen in Cunica – when we've gotten a lot of rainfall or snow that's melted and filled up the rivers. Because there's too much water in them, it rushes through really fast and does more harm to the plants than good because of the force and it also isn't able to sit long enough to soak into the ground."

Carlos says, "I see. What do you do in that case?"

Phillip shrugs. "We dam it up in areas to reduce the flow – the water level rises, but at least it's going slower and has time to be absorbed. But…"

One-Eye says, "We can't exactly do that here. We want less water in the caves, not more."

"Exactly."

Carlos says, "I believe we should notify Master Rath and

Lord Garreth of our findings. Lunch will be soon and we can speak with them then."

As they walk back to the house, One-Eye looks at the Butej guards at their posts, thinking.

Once they are in the library, Phillip says, "My Rabbit and I are going to see if we can help with lunch – if we're allowed to, I mean."

"Unfortunately, it is unlikely," Carlos says, frowning. "We'd best simply wait until it is served." He turns to One-Eye. "And you?"

One-Eye speaks silently with his Spirit Lion. A brief look of surprise crosses his features. "He wants to stay here. Said there are a few books he wants me to take out so he can read them." Carlos' eyebrows raise. "Truly? I wish you both the best of luck in your endeavors. Lord Garreth has given you full permission to whatever you may need in his home."

After Phillip and Carlos leave, One-Eye says to his Lion, "So what do you want to find?" He pauses, listening. "History?"

The Lion nods.

One-Eye looks at the books dubiously, then decides to just start with a shelf.

It takes them more time than the Lion would have liked to locate the history section and by the time One-Eye points at a set of shelves with promising titles, the Lion is pawing at the ground impatiently. "There. Now, which one?"

The Lion surveys the collection. He seems just as lost as One-Eye did a moment before.

"Just start with one," One-Eye says, ruffling his mane. "We'll go from there."

Almost immediately, the Lion lifts his paw to point to a title – *Weather Catalog and Conditions of Delphy.*

"Seems straightforward enough." He takes it out and sits against the shelf, laying the book in between them. "Any particular section?" The Lion stares. His eyes flick up at One-

Eye, who opens the book. "Let's just start at the beginning." The Lion nods, then settles down close to it.

One-Eye skips the preface and arrives at the first chapter. The dates listed are *Years 0 – 99 of the Fourth World*. They start reading.

The opening section is the catalog portion, noting temperatures and weather conditions. When they reach halfway through the first year, One-Eye says, "Is this stuff even useful?"

The Lion determinedly keeps reading.

One-Eye tries to as well for a while longer, but begins to lose patience by the end of the first year. He sits back against the shelves. "Who would even catalog all of this? Delphy's warm year-round."

The Lion noses the page.

Marchand's name is written at the bottom.

"*He* wrote all of this?" He flips back to the beginning. There, Marchand's name is written and below it are hundreds of others, all having contributed at one time or another. They do not recognize many, but near the bottom see Garreth and Georgio.

One-Eye nods, understanding. "Most of them were councilpeople." He flips back to the cover. "So Rath would have done this, too?" He frowns. "He probably would have enjoyed it." However, he smiles a little when they open it again.

After the catalog, there is another section listing the conditions, including instances of floods, droughts, and tremors. One-Eye looks at his Spirit Lion. "That's why you wanted to look at this."

The Lion stares back at him, then quickly licks his front paw.

One-Eye scratches behind his ear. "Thinking of seeing what people did before? Smart."

They begin to read, but little is written in regard to any

adverse conditions that year. As they turn the page to see the start of the second year's catalog, One-Eye asks his Lion, "Was there anything specific you wanted to find? Maybe there's a way to just look for years with heavy rainfall or storms."

The Lion thinks, swishing his tail.

They decide to continue reading as they are. The temperatures are nearly the same as the first year. When they reach the section on conditions, One-Eye suddenly stops. "Haliae," he says. "Two years ago, Rath said that the people there had been trapped inside because of a storm similar to Ara's. It happened this generation. What if we looked for it specifically?"

The Lion nods eagerly.

At that moment, the clock across the room begins to chime.

One-Eye grunts as he stands and picks up the book, returning it to the shelf. "We'll come back and check after lunch. I promise."

When they are with the others in the dining room, Garreth says to One-Eye, "Carlos told us that you and your Spirit Lion were looking at something in my library. Did you find anything?"

"Almost. We had to leave before we could."

Rath says, "May I ask what you were looking for?"

"Weather conditions in Delphy's history. Anytime it may have flooded like now."

Garreth's eyebrows raise, then he laughs. "Of course!"

Rath says, "That is brilliant, One-Eye."

Something nudges One-Eye and he says, "It was my Spirit Lion's idea." He gestures down to him.

Rath turns to the Lion instead. "That is brilliant, One-Eye's Spirit Lion."

The Lion sits up tall, his eyes shining.

Rath says to everyone, "I believe that would help with

what I found. According to the home blueprints, the supports will be affected if the water reaches the height Grandfather's Spirit Dolphin saw it at near Meran Town. Given the material they are made of, it is unlikely they would collapse, however they would be worn down considerably. Grandfather does not know if they have ever been replaced either. That would tell us if it would be a danger."

Garreth says, "There's a catalog in my library that's mostly written by people who lived or *are* living in this house and I can assure you they'd mention that sort of thing in the conditions section."

One-Eye grins and his Lion sits up even taller. "We found it. We were just going to look for another year there was a bad storm on Haliae. I remembered you telling us about it, Rath. Do you know the year?"

"Yes. The months it occurred, as well."

"Thanks. That'd help."

Garreth says, "Huh. Look at all of you – Carlos showing you all where the exit to the quarry was and Phillip and his Spirit Rabbit swimming down to look at it." He frowns. "And I've been doing paperwork."

Carlos says, "Which is required due to Merp's order."

"It does make me feel good – in a certain way. Definitely not the Merp part, however." He looks at all of them. "Thanks for your work. My Spirit Dolphin said she'd be back with the Pagu around this evening. Once we know how fast the surge is going we'll know when we should expect it. Rath, could you send more letters to the leaders? Just so they're informed. My Dolphin and the Pagu will make sure those in the Constellation Caves know to exit, but the more people who know, the better."

Rath agrees, then they all continue their meal.

While they eat, Well-Pagu, Bucket-Pagu, and Flower-Pagu travel with Garreth's Spirit Dolphin to where the water in the underground river has surged and broken through the floor of the lower levels. When they arrive, they all look into the bright blue-green light of the Delphaen crystals beneath the water.

Flower-Pagu asks the Spirit Dolphin, "You think the hole has grown larger since you were here?"

She nods.

Bucket-Pagu looks at the crumbling rock. "I don't think it can be repaired easily. The most important thing is that everyone left."

"Safe," Well-Pagu says.

Bucket-Pagu adjusts their glasses. "I'd like to go into the quarry. If we follow the river, it'll tell us better if there are any more danger spots." The Dolphin does a flip, speaking, and Bucket-Pagu smiles. "Thank you very much for going with me!"

Flower-Pagu says, "Then, Well-Pagu and I will go up into the Constellation Caves and warn people there!"

They all nod to each other, then Bucket-Pagu holds onto the Dolphin's dorsal fin and they go through the hole and into the quarry, where they begin to travel along the river. While they do, Flower-Pagu and Well-Pagu glow pink and purple and pass through the ceiling and arrive in the Constellation Caves. There they fly, still glowing.

After fifteen minutes, Flower-Pagu says, "We don't see anyone yet! Bucket-Pagu, what do you see down there?"

"The water is still really high!" they reply from the Dolphin's back. "We're going to see if it gets any lower ahead!"

Flower-Pagu and Well-Pagu silently speak, then Flower-Pagu says, "Yes, please! Well-Pagu would like to compare the locations on their map so they can calculate the speed!"

"Will do!"

They continue on but see no one, so Well-Pagu pauses and says, "Forward."

Flower-Pagu says, "Of course!"

Then they disappear, leaving pink and purple sparkles.

When they reappear, they are further east and in front of them, they see two people quietly talking with one another, one holding a Delphaen crystal and another with a black hood dimly lit by their pale yellow eyes.

The Pagu fly up to them. Flower-Pagu says, "Excuse me!"

They both start and the one with Erole's Traits looks particularly surprised, knowing that the Pagu were not there a moment before. His Spirit Eel tells him not to worry.

"Honored Pagu," he says.

"Hello! I'm Flower-Pagu and this is Well-Pagu. We've come to tell you that it may not be safe here! The river below is swelling due to the rainfall further west and causing the floor of the lower tunnel to break away! We ask that you leave the caves immediately!"

Both humans look startled. The worker says, "Of course!"

The spy bows. "We will do so. Thank you for informing us."

Well-Pagu says, "Welcome."

Flower-Pagu asks, "Do you know if there are any other people further on? We want to warn them, too!"

The spy's eyes become distant as he senses. "Yes, three more pairs ahead of us. We will tell them. We need to go that way – east – to reach the nearest exit."

"Thank you very much!"

The worker asks, "Will you both be all right?"

"Absolutely! We just want to make sure that everyone is safe!"

"Thanks. I do feel a lot better with you two around."

Well-Pagu says, "Three!"

"There's three of you?"

They nod. Flower-Pagu says, "Yes! Our friend is in the Old Delphaen Crystal Quarry with a Spirit Dolphin checking the water level."

"That's very brave of them."

Suddenly, a tremor goes through the ground.

The spy says, "We need to leave."

"I agree," the worker says. "Thanks again!" he tells the Pagu.

Well-Pagu says, "Course!"

The pair takes off, headed east.

Flower-Pagu asks Well-Pagu, "Should we leap forward again?"

"Yes!" They hold hands and disappear, leaving sparkles.

Below, Bucket-Pagu and Garreth's Spirit Dolphin are nearing the end of the swell in the river. They travel for a while longer before Bucket-Pagu – who had been studying the wall carefully – says, "There!" The Dolphin stops. "Well-Pagu! We've found where it's lower. It's at my location right now!"

Up above, Well-Pagu looks at their map. They focus and a green, glowing dot appears. They mark it with their pencil, then compare it with where they were before.

When Flower-Pagu sees their expression, they say, "Is everything all right?"

Well-Pagu shakes head. "Fast," they say. "Garreth… Tomorrow." They pause. "Evening."

"Oh dear! We should warn the rest here, then return to let them know and ask what they found out."

"Agree." Then they say, "Bucket…Pagu?"

Their friend responds, "We're going to check the rest of the river for any more danger spots!" They sigh. "It would be much easier if we had someone from Ullia to help, but I don't want any of them to be down here right now."

The other two Pagu look at each another. Well-Pagu says, "Eel!"

Flower-Pagu says, "You're right! Bucket-Pagu, what about a Spirit Eel?"

"Of course!" they say. "One that is not bonded to a human,

please!"

Flower-Pagu does a twirl. "Can do!" They and Well-Pagu put their hands together. "We would like to ask for your help if you are here, Spirit Eel!"

"Help!" Well-Pagu says.

Within moments, a wandering Spirit Eel appears before them. She looks reverently at the Pagu, eyes gleaming.

Flower-Pagu says, "We would like you to help Bucket-Pagu and Garreth's Spirit Dolphin. They are looking for weak points in the cave down in the Old Delphaen Crystal Quarry."

The Eel bobs her head eagerly.

Well-Pagu points to themself. "Report."

The Eel bobs again before diving down through the floor.

She finds Bucket-Pagu and the Spirit Dolphin, then swims beside them.

Bucket-Pagu smiles. "Thank you for your help!"

The Eel grins. She closes her eyes and concentrates. When she opens them, she shakes her head.

Bucket-Pagu says, "This area is safe?" The Eel winks. "All right! We'll keep moving forward."

They pick up their pace, the Dolphin moving faster and the Eel intermittently closing her eyes to sense the area.

Above them, Well-Pagu and Flower-Pagu move on as well, continuing to warn anyone who is still in the caves.

The Pagu and Spirit Animals work through the afternoon and by evening, they are near Garreth's home.

Flower-Pagu asks Well-Pagu, "Is it time to go back?"

They nod. "Hungry."

"Me too!"

Bucket-Pagu, Garreth's Spirit Dolphin, and the Spirit Eel pass through the cave floor to join them.

Flower-Pagu says, "Thank you for your help, Spirit Eel!"

The Eel looks invigorated. She tilts her head.

Bucket-Pagu shakes their head. "No, that's all we need for

right now. But, if you can, warn others that you come across. Keep them safe!"

The Eel dips respectfully, then disappears.

All of the Pagu climb aboard Garreth's Dolphin. Well-Pagu says, "Ready!" and the Dolphin flies up and through the ceiling. They come out near the hill in front of Garreth's home and the Dolphin swims in the air toward it.

16

When the Pagu and Garreth's Spirit Dolphin arrive, the Dolphin informs them that Garreth is in the library.

As soon as they enter, they see him, Rath, One-Eye, his Spirit Lion, Carlos, Phillip, and his Spirit Rabbit sitting on the cushions around a low circular table near the waterfall, deep in conversation.

Garreth notices his Spirit Dolphin first, then the Pagu. "Good. You're back," he says.

Flower-Pagu says, "Yes! Is everyone all right?"

They all exchange a look.

Garreth sighs and stands up. "We'll fill you in over dinner. I would bet you all are very hungry – you didn't have lunch, did you?"

The Pagu shake their heads. Well-Pagu says, "Forgot."

Dinner is already laid out in the small dining room when they arrive. While they eat, the Pagu tell the others about their journey.

When they finish, Rath says, "That is very concerning to hear how fast it is traveling."

Garreth says, "And none of it was going into any of the tributaries?"

Bucket-Pagu looks at the Spirit Dolphin, then shakes their head. "No. We didn't see any water deviating – it was all going in a straight line."

"They likely broke down then – their instability was part of the reason why my parents and Marchand decided to abandon the idea."

Then, Carlos, Phillip, and his Spirit Rabbit share that the exit to the river outside was unblocked, Rath tells them about how the supports would be endangered if the water level rose to the height near Meran Town, and One-Eye and his Spirit Lion continue with what they found in the weather catalog.

One-Eye says, "My Lion and I did some research on what the people living here did the last time Ara caused a large storm. Rath gave us the year and months for one."

Bucket-Pagu says, "That was a really good idea!"

He smiles, looking at his Lion. "It was his." The Lion glows with pride. "We didn't find any record of it and based on the temperatures and other information, Ara's storm from back then didn't have as many effects in the South so we kept looking back and found another one seventy years ago."

Carlos nods solemnly and the Pagu look sad, remembering the year.

One-Eye says, "The effects were worse here – Delphy even had *snow*. A few years later, there was flooding like there is now and some of it reached the house. The supports were eroded away and … Marchand had to help deviate the water. There was some note about him gathering it up. Garreth says it was likely similar to what he does with the messages from the Delphaen Celebration." The Pagu nod. "The supports were replaced with the same material they were originally built with. After that, the water levels went back down."

Flower-Pagu says, "We see. Thank you, One-Eye and Spirit Lion!"

Garreth says, "I agree. Thank you both." He turns to the Pagu. "Marchand isn't around and even if I sent a message to him right now, there isn't any way that dolphin could make it here by tomorrow evening, when you said that the surge would be here." He leans back. "It'll be bad enough trying to get the leaders along the quarry prepared for it, but here we'll be facing the immediate damage without Marchand's help." He sighs. "This home might not have become my favorite – in recent years, mind you – but it's still that, my home. I don't want to lose it."

Bucket-Pagu says, "We don't want you to either."

Garreth pats the table. "So – ideas. I suggested making the exit of the tunnel wider to accommodate for the high water flow. From what Phillip and his Rabbit told us about what they saw underwater, the amount of water in the cave is already too much for the size of the exit right now."

Phillip nods, petting his Spirit Rabbit on his shoulder. "We couldn't even get near it."

"However, Rath reasonably pointed out that doing so would disturb the integrity of the tunnel and I personally would rather not have to worry about it as well as the supports suddenly giving way. This house is built on the coast, after all."

Rath says, "We were just thinking of other ideas when everyone returned. May I ask if you would have any thoughts?"

"Not right now," Flower-Pagu says.

Bucket-Pagu says, "I would say we first need to reduce the water in the tunnel, but I'm not sure how it's possible to do safely."

"Problem," Well-Pagu says.

They all think for a while longer until Garreth says, "Well, I've avoided it long enough – even though they likely have heard our discussions already – I'm going to notify the Butej Guard. If we have to evacuate, they need to know." He looks around the table. "We'll figure it out and for tonight at least, we have nothing to worry about. Tuck the problem in the back of your head – it'll work itself out by morning."

After they all leave, Phillip says, "I feel like I have the … start of an idea, but nothing yet. Maybe like Lord Garreth said, it'll work itself out overnight."

Rath says, "I believe it will."

While they go to their rooms, Garreth goes to the guards on the back balcony. He walks up to the nearest one and says, "Hey."

The guard – despite seeing him coming – jumps. "Yes, Lord Garreth?"

"Got something to talk to you about."

"The … flooding?"

Anger crosses Garreth's face. "So you were listening."

"We have been told to."

For a moment, they are both silent. Then Garreth says, "Well, good – in this case. Means I don't have to repeat just about everything." He crosses his arms. "Well-Pagu says that it'll be here by tomorrow evening. All of us – my grandson and the rest of them – are trying to think of ways we can lower the water level, but if we don't and we can't … we need to leave."

"Understood."

Garreth's eyebrow raises. "That was remarkably easy to get you to agree."

"I am under your order as well, Lord Garreth, as Fierce has told me. Our duty is to keep everyone here safe. If the conditions will be as dangerous as we have heard, then we will aid in transporting everyone elsewhere." He pauses. "However, there is another reason."

"I knew it."

"We have been informed there have been unusual activities

nearby, possibly related to the Ullian Spies. We had already been told that negotiations had been slower in central Delphy, largely due to the travel times to reach the different entrances to the Constellation Caves around the coast – ”

“Get to the point.”

“Yes, Lord Garreth. We are concerned. There are many unaccounted spies – the ones we know of are certainly not enough to have covered all of the Constellation Caves. The Selachuu Military has sensed them with Belle’s Traits, however, because there have been no reports of attacks in the area, they have no cause to act.” He takes a breath. “These spies have not allied themselves with the workers or spoken with the military, nor have they hindered progress in the caves. All we know is those who are aiding the cave workers say these other spies are heading east.”

“You think they’re coming here.”

The guard nods. “We have given thought to relocation if the trend continues.”

Garreth pauses, thinking. Finally, he says, “Well, all right. We might be leaving anyways.” He looks at the home for a moment, looking sad. He turns back to the guard. “Keep me updated.”

“Yes, Lord Garreth.”

He leaves, going down the steps to the beach. He walks to the shoreline and sits. The sand is still warm from the day. His Spirit Dolphin appears in front of him and he strokes her head for a long time.

“You’ll be thinking, too?” he asks her.

The Dolphin’s eyes glitter.

Garreth laughs. “Yeah. We’ll figure out something.”

He stays with her for a while longer, then gets up to go back inside.

The next morning, the group gathers in the small dining room for breakfast. They are all quiet until Garreth sets down his glass and says, "Well? Any ideas?"

Rath says, "I am afraid not, Grandfather."

One-Eye says, arms crossed, "Not us, either." His Lion is pouting beside him.

Carlos clears his throat. "I had thought the Butej guards might be able to help. However, even with Fierce's Traits, they would need to exert themselves far too much to deviate the water from the supports."

Phillip pets his Spirit Rabbit. "We might have a thought. This all reminds us of something. Maybe in Cunica or … somewhere else?" He sighs. "Sorry."

Rath says, "It is all right, Phillip."

Garreth says, "Let us know if you think of it." He takes a bite. "Maybe what we need is a smaller victory – something to get our brains going on an easier problem. I should also let you know I spoke with a Butej guard last night. They're all right with leaving. Part of their agreeable nature is due to the fact they've heard an unaccounted group of the Ullian Spies that have neither allied themselves with the workers nor begun attacking others seem to be heading east – toward us."

Carlos says, "Do you believe they may be after Master Rath?"

"The guards seem to think so. The one I spoke with last night said they'd already considered relocation."

Phillip says, "To where? It doesn't seem like many places are safe in Delphy right now."

"Don't know. But I've asked they keep me updated."

The others nod.

Rath says, "May I ask if you would elaborate on what you said earlier? A, ah, 'smaller victory'?"

"Absolutely. How would you all like to figure out what's going on with that waterfall?"

They finish eating, then go to the foyer. The small waterfall to the right of the stairs is down to a trickle now. Garreth gestures to it. "Now, I don't think it would have any bearing on our problem belowground, but – like I said – figuring it out might get our minds working on a way to fix that, too. Haven't had much time to look into it with the paperwork, but … " He shakes his head. "Actually, I should get on that again now. I've already lost a lot of time in the past few days. Can I ask you all to look into it?" They all agree and he smiles. As he steps back, heading up the stairs, he continues, "Now, don't think I'm going to completely abandon these problems – I'll keep working on them in the back of my head. Let me know if you need anything. I'm still here to help."

"Thank you, Grandfather," Rath says.

After Garreth leaves, Phillip says, "How should we go about this?"

"We need to follow the water upstream. All of the waterways are connected in this home. If the others are unaffected, like the waterfall to the left, then the issue is likely not from the main source, but with this waterway specifically."

They follow Rath up the stairs and walk alongside the small waterway leading to the waterfall. It, too, is flowing at a slow rate.

They go on, but do not see anything that could be blocking the flow.

When they reach the end of the hallway, Rath leads them up the next set of stairs to the second floor. The waterway makes a sharp turn and disappears inside the wall, reappearing on the other side.

There, Phillip peers at the running stream in surprise. "It seems to be just fine here."

One-Eye looks at where the water disappears into the wall. "So the problem's in there."

Carlos sighs. "I believe I recall Marchand saying this was a design flaw, however Merp has not allowed him to change it. I am not aware of any way to open the wall, either. Are you,

Master Rath?"

"No, I am not." He leans over, peering inside. "It is very dark as well. I cannot see anything that could be blocking the water."

One-Eye says, "How could anything get in there, anyways?"

"I do not know."

Suddenly, Phillip's Spirit Rabbit begins sniffing the air. She says something to him, then he begins sniffing, too. "Hey, do you all smell that?"

They pause. Carlos says, "It does seem familiar," but Rath and One-Eye frown, not recognizing it. One-Eye's Spirit Lion sniffs near the slit, then wrinkles his nose and steps back, pawing his nose.

One-Eye listens to him. "A plant?"

Phillip gasps. "That's it! Carlos – do you remember? On Tema Island."

Carlos' eyebrows raise. "I do."

Flower-Pagu does a twirl. "I may know what it is! Rath, I think I can fit in there – would it be all right if I check?"

"Yes. Please be careful."

"I will!" Flower-Pagu flies into the slit. The others hear them gasp. "Oh! They're so pretty!" They fly out suddenly and – looking flushed – pat down their skirt. "But they're causing a problem!"

Phillip says, "They're Water Flowers, right? That's what my Spirit Rabbit and I think."

"You're right!"

Rath looks surprised. One-Eye, who sees his expression, says, "You know them?"

"Not personally. However, Grandmother has spoken of them. She does not have them in her gardens. She says they are, ah, 'greedy plants'. I was very surprised to hear her use such a word in regards to plants."

Carlos laughs gently. "I remember her speaking as such.

Water Plants … Phillip, Flower-Pagu, would you explain?"

"Definitely!" Phillip says. "Carlos and I saw them on Tema Island. They were to help prevent the underground garden from flooding. They're really good at storing up water – it's how they get their blossoms. I'd guess the 'greediness' comes from that – if they're not tended to frequently, they can use up water that other plants need and even make the environment around them a lot more dry."

Carlos says, "I was told it was an idea of Marchand's at the start of the Fourth World. To create flowers that bloomed in water."

Flower-Pagu beams. "I thought it was a wonderful idea! But … they do need a lot of water to grow. A little seed must have flown in here – they like dark places. It's doing well, but … it could maybe grow somewhere else."

Rath asks, "Is there a way to safely remove it?"

Flower-Pagu turns to Bucket-Pagu and Well-Pagu, then all three nod. "We think so, if we work together! We'll try right now!'

"Thank you very much."

The others wait while the Pagu fly into the slit. They hear Flower-Pagu talk softly to the plant and soon, the Pagu reappear holding a cluster of three Water Flowers. All have medium-sized blossoms with light blue petals and a shining bead of water in the center.

Rath leans forward, but does not touch them. "They look very delicate. Are they safe to travel? We need to find a place to transplant them to as well."

Phillip says, "What about the library? It doesn't get too much sun and there's that waterfall. I think with proper tending, they shouldn't absorb too much water."

"I would need to ask my grandfather, however, I believe that would be all right for now."

As they are talking, they hear someone say, "Well!" and

turn to see Garreth walking down the hallway, looking at the now flowing waterway. "You figured it out – " Then he sees what the Pagu are holding. "Those are … Water Flowers, right? Haven't seen them in a long time."

Rath says, "Phillip and his Spirit Rabbit smelled them, then Flower-Pagu flew inside and found the flowers in that slit over there."

Garreth looks at the enclosed part of the waterway. "Design flaw," he says. He turns back to the flowers. "I know Azalea's never liked these, but I always kind of did. Actually, Marchand tells me he used a similar idea for his Delphaen Palms – they both store their water in the center, right?"

"They do."

"Where were you all thinking of putting it?"

Phillip says, "I suggested the library, by the waterfall."

"Good idea. Every so often, it'll overflow when it rains, so maybe this'll keep it from … " He pauses. He asks Flower-Pagu, "Would that be possible?"

They tilt their head to the side. "Would what be possible?"

Garreth waves his hand. "Crazy idea. But … if we're trying to lower the water level below … "

Rath looks confused. One-Eye catches on, but says, "I don't think that one plant is going to do it."

"Okay – but *many*. A few dozen. Or hundred."

Carlos rubs his chin. "It would be a natural solution to the problem, however, I also do not know if – even with a great many of them – the water level would lower to what is needed."

Phillip says, "I could maybe help it out with Rella's Traits. My Rabbit says she could help, too." The Rabbit dips her head.

Rath still looks perplexed as Flower-Pagu gasps, saying, "Oh! I think it's a perfect idea! We'll fill the whole cave with them!"

"The … cave," Rath says. "Do you mean in the quarry?"

"Yes, imagine! Water Flowers everywhere! In the river by the crystals and along the wall and they'd help the water level go down and they'd be so happy and could grow so much more than in here or by the waterfall!"

As they speak, Rath's eyes grow wide. "That … that sounds very lovely. And I am glad they would be much happier there." He beams at the flower.

One-Eye stares at it. "We'd need more. How fast do they grow?"

Phillip says, "Pretty fast even without Rella's Traits, especially if their conditions are met – water and shade."

"Fast enough to grow by this evening?"

He frowns, but his Rabbit speaks to him and he says, "My Rabbit says it's possible."

"Fine. So where do we get more? Does it make more … " He gestures uselessly. " … seeds?" His Lion nods.

"Only when they're mature. They only give one each, too."

Rath says, "I believe seeds for them are sold in Priage."

One-Eye says, "But we can't go there, right? We have to stay in a mile radius."

"That is true. It is farther than that."

Garreth waves his hand. "Ask one of the Butej guards. I'll give you some gold to give them." He pulls out a heavy pouch and gives it to Rath. "Tell them to buy as much as they can with that amount."

"I will do so."

"And while you're doing that, we'll take these" – he nods to the flowers – "to the quarry and see what Phillip, his Spirit Rabbit, and Flower-Pagu say to do with it."

Phillip and his Rabbit nod. Flower-Pagu says, "I'm so excited!"

As they leave, Rath approaches one of the Butej guards to ask if they would purchase the seeds – they look startled by the weight of the pouch – then joins the others.

When he enters the library, he sees that the Water Flowers have been safely transplanted in a small pot next to the waterfall. As he goes down the stairs, where the group is gathered by the door, looking out into the quarry, he hears Flower-Pagu say, "If we put them all around here, I'm sure that there would be enough!"

"Good," Garreth says. "I'd think we'll get quite a few with the amount I gave Rath." He sees his grandson. "Welcome back."

"Thank you. The Butej guard has left to purchase the seeds."

"Glad to hear it." Garreth nods to Phillip and Flower-Pagu. "They have a plan. They also said we should let the Water Flowers we found acclimate to their new home and only use the new seeds in the quarry. Carlos as well says he has an idea on how to spread them." He looks at the rushing river. "Not exactly safe for any of us to be out there planting them."

Carlos explains, "I have suggested asking the Butej guards for their help. With Fierce's Traits, they will be able to carry the seeds to where they need to be planted. I am sure they will be willing."

"I see," Rath says. "That is a good idea."

Garreth nods. "So – that's the plan. We can't do much until we get those seeds. Did that guard say when they'd be back?"

"No, they did not."

"Shouldn't take too long with one of their skyships. Carlos – would you mind talking to the other guards about your idea? Tell them to meet us down here."

Carlos bows. "Certainly, Lord Garreth." He leaves, going up the stairs.

Garreth leans against the wall. He laughs abruptly. "Plants. I can't believe it."

One-Eye asks Flower-Pagu, "Is this going to work?"

"Absolutely!" They do a twirl.

Garreth says, "But, listen – if for whatever reason it doesn't, we're leaving. I'll be sad if we end up losing this home, but I'd rather everyone here be safe."

"Yes, Grandfather," Rath says.

Carlos returns not long afterward with half a dozen guards that seem surprised, but oddly excited.

One says, "We have come, Lord Garreth."

"I can see that," he snaps. Then, more calm, he says, "Come on down here. We're still waiting on the seeds, but we can explain what exactly you need to do."

Phillip and Flower-Pagu quickly explain their plan to the guards. Flower-Pagu finishes, "And you'll send them all around to their new homes!"

Phillip says, "The soil's pretty soft here because of the moisture – would that help you get the seeds beneath it?"

A guard nods. "Certainly. And we cover it with soil afterward?"

"That's right!"

Within the hour, the guard Rath spoke to returns with the seeds. She seems a little overwhelmed as she carries the heavy sack down the steps. "This is what I was given for the amount you provided, Lord Garreth. Is it … enough?"

"If it's not, I'd be amazed."

Phillip says, "It might be a bit too much. What do you think, Flower-Pagu?"

"Maybe. But – then we can just plant the others somewhere else!"

While Garreth holds the bag of seeds, Phillip takes out some and closes his hands over them. "Like this?" he asks his Spirit Rabbit and she nods. "All right … " He concentrates and a green glow emits from between his hands. When he reveals the seeds, they are still glowing. "Wow! Didn't know I could do that."

The Rabbit twitches her nose.

Phillip holds out the seeds to the guards. "Okay – they're ready to be planted."

"Yes, Phillip," one says. They turn to the others and make a quick hand gesture. The guards understand and step out onto a viewing platform within the cave. The water roars in front of them.

The guard makes one more hand gesture, then says to Phillip, "We will begin now. Hold them there."

"W-Will do!"

Phillip watches as, one by one, the seeds are plucked out of his hand by what feels like a small breeze as the guards delicately use their traits.

Flower-Pagu tells them, "We want the seeds all around the walls of the cave! Right at the water level, please!"

"Yes, Flower-Pagu," the guards say in unison.

The rest watch as the glowing green seeds fly around the cave in different directions. Once they reach their destinations, the guards give them a gentle press until they are in the ground, then another breeze to blow soil over them.

Flower-Pagu is delighted. "Yes! Just like that!"

The guards nod, focusing on their work. Once the seeds that Phillip had are planted, he reaches for another handful based on his Rabbit's instruction. He uses his traits to make them glow like the others, then the guards repeat the process.

After all of them are planted, Flower-Pagu says, "That should be enough!"

Phillip listens to his Spirit Rabbit, then says, "My Rabbit says she needs to do one more thing."

"Of course! Thank you, Spirit Rabbit!"

The Rabbit's nose quivers. She hops off of Phillip's shoulder onto the air in front of him. She flicks her ear, then bounds away. Starting on their right, she begins hopping on the soil surrounding the cave. Every place her paws touch glows for a brief moment with the bright, healthy green of Rella's Traits.

Rath gasps.

One-Eye, beside him, says, "You can see that, too?"

"Yes." Rath looks around the cave at the small green glows.

Flower-Pagu says, "That's because Phillip's Spirit Rabbit is using her traits! Even if you can't see her, you can see what she's doing with them."

"I understand," Rath says. He continues to watch.

The Rabbit hops around the whole perimeter, making sure to touch every place the guards planted a seed. She makes one final bound over the river and into Phillip's arms again. He hugs her tightly. "That was so neat! I don't know what you did, but it was really pretty!"

A Butej guard sees something and abruptly stumbles back.

The tiniest green leaf is poking out of the soil.

"It can't be growing already?" the guard says.

Flower-Pagu says, "It is! It knows we need its help!"

The guard only nods, still staring as the leaf turns into a stalk and a bud forms on top, rising above other small leaves that are just starting to emerge. It suddenly blossoms and the center fills with water, sparkling in the light from the Delphaen crystals in the cave.

The group watches as the whole cave erupts in green leaves and light blue flowers, swaying from the force of the river, but holding strong as they use the water to help them grow.

One-Eye says, "Is it ... working?"

Flower-Pagu says, "We won't know yet. We were able to help them grow, but they'll still need time to lower the water level."

Garreth ties up the bag of seeds. "Well then, it sounds like we've done all we can." He looks at the guards for a brief moment. "Thanks," he says quickly, then to all of them, "We'll let the flowers try until an hour before the surge is supposed to arrive. If it's safe, we'll stay. If not ... we'll evacuate." He rubs his chin. "Flowers ... Definitely something to tell Azalea one day." He smiles a little. "I wonder if she'd be surprised. Probably not." He says to the guards, "Well? We're done here. You can go back to your posts."

They jump and one says, "Yes, Lord Garreth." They leave the viewing platform, then go up the stairs and out of the library.

As Garreth shuts the door and hefts the bag of seeds to be taken upstairs, Rath says, "Grandfather, that was rather … abrupt."

"They're used to it." Rath frowns, but Garreth continues, "Come on. We'll put the rest of these seeds somewhere safe, then I'll have to return to my work and you all can try to relax until this evening."

Carlos says, "It would be prudent to check the water level regularly – perhaps every hour? Would that amount of time show any results, Flower-Pagu?"

"Maybe after two for this first check. They still need a little bit more time."

Rath says, "That is a good idea. I can check them."

On Phillip's suggestion, Garreth places the seeds outside, near the entrance to the library but away from the waterfall so they do not start growing. Garreth and Carlos go to have tea in his office and One-Eye and his Lion leave, both to take a nap, leaving Rath, the Pagu, Phillip, and his Spirit Rabbit in the library.

"That was incredible what you did, Phillip. And your Spirit Rabbit as well," Rath says.

"Thanks!" Phillip's Spirit Rabbit nuzzles his cheek and he laughs. "My Rabbit says thank you, too!"

Looking thoughtful, Rath says, "Marchand told me that his Spirit Dolphins could use his traits, however, only during dire moments."

"That's what Nan told me, too, with the Spirit Rabbits. I'd never really seen it before. I'm not sure I want to think too hard on what that means for us."

Flower-Pagu says, "There's nothing to worry about! Your Spirit Rabbit knew that it was time to help. Maybe … it would have been more dangerous if they hadn't, but that's why they did."

"To prevent it, huh? Well, I'm glad. I'm not sure I'll completely relax until we've seen the water level has been lowered enough by this evening. You won't be checking it for another two hours, right? What are you going to do until then?"

"I thought I would read. It has been a very long time since I have looked at the books in my grandfather's library and he told me that he has gained many since then that I may be interested in. I am very excited."

"That's great! Do you think he would mind if I looked at some of the cookbooks here? They're probably pretty old if he has any, so I think it'd be fun to see them."

"I believe he does – or, rather, he did when I was last here. I can show you where they were, if you would like."

They walk over to the bookcase to the right of the waterfall and windows. Rath scans the titles, then touches two shelves. "Yes. Here they are."

"Thanks!" Phillip pulls one out. "I can't wait to look at it. I hope you enjoy your reading, too!"

"Thank you. And you are welcome."

While Phillip walks over to one of the cushions laying on the floor, Flower-Pagu says, "What books were you thinking of looking at, Rath?"

"I thought I would find ones on minerals. I would like to learn more about them."

Bucket-Pagu says, "That sounds neat!" They nod to Flower-Pagu and Well-Pagu. "We thought we would look at the fiction section. Since we finished *Tales of Flight* this past month, we thought we would look for a new book club book!

Would you like to read it with us?"

"I would love to! Thank you very much for asking me. I truly enjoyed our book club before."

The Pagu beam and Well-Pagu says, "Too!"

Soon, they are all seated with their books. The Pagu have a small stack next to them of possible choices for their book club. They each start on one, looking excited.

Outside, One-Eye and his Spirit Lion are napping on the terrace in the sun. On the second floor, Carlos serves tea to Garreth in his office.

As Carlos sets down his teacup, Garreth says, "We can only pray this works."

Carlos sits in the chair across from him. He inclines his head. "Given Flower-Pagu's approval, it would seem that it will result in a positive outcome."

"That's true." He takes a sip, then pauses. He looks over a few pieces of paper, stamps a few, lays others to the side, then says as he is working, "What do you think of all of this, Carlos? Should we be worried about those members of the Ullian Spies trying to take Rath?"

"The Pagu have said nothing of it, however, I cannot imagine they approve."

"I'll make a bold comment and say they don't approve much of Ullia's God, Erole, at all. Marchand never seemed outwardly disapproving of his brother, but I know the situation in Ullia makes him sad."

Carlos nods. "Belle's efforts have helped greatly – before, those from Ullia would not dare speak or be seen by anyone outside of their culture, largely due to Erole and the tasks he gives them."

"Only does things for his own benefit, right?" Garreth shuffles through a few more papers. "Merp's like that."

Carlos' eyebrows shoot up. He shakes his head. "No, quite the opposite. Merp believes that all he does is for everyone *else's* benefit."

Garreth only snorts.

Carlos watches him closely, waits until Garreth takes another sip of tea, then says, "I will not press the issue, however, I will stress they are not the same."

"I'll take your word for it. You and Azalea knew him for far longer than I ever will." He stamps another sheet. "Though, I think I disliked him from the day I met him."

"I would agree. Lady Lenelle was quite displeased with your behavior, if I recall, and when she heard of it, Lady Meiberin was as well."

"Both were reconsidering even allowing me to inherit the title. I only told Merp what I thought of him."

"Which I am sure he appreciated on the basis of honesty if nothing else. Your choice of words was the issue, I believe."

"It hasn't changed much. I still think the same of him and I don't care him knowing – in fact, I'd prefer he did."

Carlos pauses. "Would you consider perhaps that view may do more harm?"

"Not to him. I've seen how he is. It wouldn't matter if he adored someone or outwardly hated them – he'd give them paperwork if they tried to change his rules, no matter what. That's something, at least, that you could call *fair* about him."

"I do not mean him. As you said, he will assign you exactly what he believes to be appropriate for changing his marriage laws. I mean, for you, Lord Garreth."

Garreth – who had reached for the next sheet – stops, looking confused.

Carlos continues, "Being antagonistic to him – or to the Butej guards – creates more harm for *you,* not necessarily them. However, you know full well the guards are primarily here by Fierce's order for *Master Rath's* safety. They do not deserve all that you say to them."

Frowning deeply, Garreth turns back to his paperwork. "I

get it, all right. I already know how the Pagu feel about this place and I know it's not just because of how tense the Butej guards can be." He stamps a few more papers, then sits back.

Carlos looks sympathetic.

Garreth finishes his tea and sets the teacup down gently. "Thanks for the tea, Carlos. I'll … consider what you said."

Carlos rises to take his cup. "Of course." He places it back on the tray to be carried out. "And I will say that allowing the Butej guards to help was a start."

"Yeah. They did … all right."

"I believe they were more than that." Garreth frowns and Carlos says, "Would you like another cup of tea?"

"No. Not right now. Thanks, Carlos."

"Certainly."

Carlos takes up the tea tray and Garreth goes to open the door for him. He watches him leave, then returns to his desk to continue working on his paperwork.

17

In the library, Rath and Phillip are still reading. Beside them, the Pagu are quietly discussing. They have narrowed the book selections for their book club to two.

The clock near the waterfall chimes and they all look up.

"It is time to check the water level," Rath says.

Phillip nods. "Let me know how it goes."

Flower-Pagu flies up. "I'll go with you! I want to see how the plants are doing."

"Of course."

They go down the steps to the door leading into the quarry and Rath opens it.

All of the seeds have sprouted, leafed out, and bloomed. Some even have two flowers and buds for more. A soft smell fills the cave as they wave their petals, catching the droplets from the river.

"They are beautiful," Rath says.

"It's so good to see them doing well!" Flower-Pagu says.

"I agree." Rath focuses on the marking on the wall across from them, recalling where the water level was before. "I believe it has lowered an inch."

"Will that be enough?"

"No, not from what we were told about the level further west."

"Oh."

"However, there is still time. I believe they can do it." He says to the flowers closest to them, "Thank you very much for your work. I greatly appreciate it." The water in the center of their blossoms glitters.

Flower-Pagu shoots up their arms. "Keep going!" they say. "You all can do it!"

After they return to the main library, Rath tells the others, "It has lowered an inch."

"That's not a whole lot," Phillip says. "Do you think it'll be enough by this evening?"

"I believe so."

Flower-Pagu, "Me too! We just have to be patient."

Upstairs, a guard informs Garreth that the Leader of Archen Town, Ehken, has asked to speak with him.

"We've had tremors," Ehken says, seated across from him in Garreth's office. "We've sent a petition, why haven't you – "

Garreth holds up a hand. " – done something? I have. My grandson did. Didn't you get that letter he sent you, explaining where the tremors were from and why they're not from the Ullian Spies and certainly nothing to be worried about?"

Ehken colors. "Yes, we have, however – "

" – then that's … " Garreth sighs. "Sorry. We're all stressed. Continue."

"Thank you. Have you seen the petition from Leader Leytel to ban those from Ullia on Delphy?"

"Of course. I didn't think anyone but him had signed it yet – and I would guess that was more because of the pressure from his people in Kel City."

"It's been a rather stressful month for them. They just had their repairs to the Constellation Caves settled out when the tremors began. It's put progress back and caused even more repairs to be needed."

"True, but I'm sure the Ullian Spies can help you determine exactly what needs to be done."

Ehken bites his lip.

"It was a *petition* – he hasn't kicked them out already, has he?"

"No. However, many of his people – not the workers that have been in close contact with the Ullian Spies – have voiced much displeasure by their presence. He's already told me he feels he will have to soon."

"Not without Georgio or Marchand's approval."

Ehken shifts uncomfortably. "As I recall, we do not need that in cases of emergency or … if all of the leaders in the area agree."

Garreth is quiet for a moment as the meaning sets in. He crosses his arms. "You've agreed." Ehken frowns and Garreth continues, "You know as well as I do that even with everything going on, there's not enough to justify a case of emergency for the presence of the Ullian Spies alone. If anything, it qualifies more as a natural disaster or a result of Ara's Storm."

Ehken throws up his hands. "Well, what was I supposed to do? Lord Garreth, my village is old and the cracks were enough to be concerned about, much less the tremors. The Ullian Spies shouldn't even be on Delphy." He suddenly realizes. "Rath. He sent those letters and you mentioned him just now. He isn't here, is he?"

"He is." He waves his hand before Ehken can ask any more. "Now, you know what my answer is – I may not have any official legal power on Delphy, but I do have my advice and I think you already know what it is."

"Allow the Ullian Spies to do what they need, like the Selachuu soldiers have said." At Garreth's nod, Ehken sighs. "We're doing our best, but the longer this goes on, the harder it is going to be to convince everyone they'll leave afterward."

"Do you know how far along they are with their map? I know there likely have been some delays with the tremors."

"Assuredly. But … " Ehken thinks. "I believe the caves around the coastline are finished. It's now central Delphy. Everything has been taking longer there."

"Then continue to do your best. Talk to your people. Assure them they're not here to harm anyone or Delphy – at least, not most of them."

"But, the cracks and … All right." Ehken meets Garreth's eyes. "I don't have any intent of withdrawing my name from the petition, but I will not go any further than that if the Ullian Spies leave once they're finished as promised. I cannot speak for the other leaders."

"That's fine. I appreciate you telling me."

"I had thought you already knew."

"I've had other things to deal with."

Ehken frowns, then gives a start. "The river … Your home is directly above it, isn't it?" He looks at his feet.

"Exactly. We're making preparations here if it turns out to be a problem."

Ehken's eyes widen. "Oh my." He stands up quickly. "Then – I'd best leave you to that. I apologize for delaying you."

"It's all right. It's … mostly my grandson and the others that are doing things. I've got my own work."

"As do we all. If Archen Town can help in any way … " He shakes his head. "I suppose it is a little ill-timed for me to be offering that now."

"A bit. But, not inappropriate. I thank you for it, but all we can do now is wait and see if our plan works."

Ehken seems curious, but does not ask. "I hope it does,

Lord Garreth."

"Thank you."

At the same time, Rath, Phillip, and the Pagu take a break from their reading to go outside.

As they look at the different plants that grow around the house, the Butej guards watch them, but say nothing.

When One-Eye wakes up, he joins them and they show him some ivy ground cover with small orange blossoms that his Lion sniffs.

One-Eye asks, "How was the water level?"

"It is lower – by an inch, I believe," Rath says.

"That's not much."

"No. However, I believe it will be enough by this evening."

Looking at a bush with purple flowers, Phillip says, "Those must be Ehrinels! Nan has a few recipes with them. There's a lot of older species here – it's neat to see them."

Rath smiles. "I agree."

When Rath and One-Eye are going back inside to check the water level together, One-Eye tells him, "Carlos says tomorrow I can start jogging. He says running might injure it again." He huffs. "I miss it. My Lion does, too."

"I am sure you will be able to soon."

When they reach the quarry, Rath studies the mark on the wall. "It is at least four inches lower than it was before."

"That's good," One-Eye says. "They seem to be happy. The plants, I mean."

"I agree. Flower-Pagu tells me they are working very hard,"

"How far down does it need to go? My Lion wants to know."

"Safely, I believe at least to where the rock outcropping is."

One-Eye peers over the railing. "That's far."

"Yes. However, there is time, especially if it continues at this rate or increases."

As they go back to the library, One-Eye says, "Would the

guards let us sail?"

"They may as long as it is within the mile radius. Grandfather has ships that we can use as well."

"Good. I want to do that with you tomorrow. Carlos said it should be fine."

"I would love to, One-Eye."

They have tea with Carlos, Phillip, and the Pagu, then they all check the water level. It has fallen by another four inches. Afterward, the Pagu show Rath the book they have selected for their book club – *A Dolphin's Journey*. He is delighted. When they check the water level later, they see it is six inches lower than before.

At lunch, Garreth hears about the difference.

"Fifteen inches!" he says. "Well, it's certainly not where it needs to be yet, but it's progress."

"I agree," Rath says.

Garreth asks Well-Pagu, "Do you still think that surge is coming at eight this evening?" They nod. "Well, it's possible then – as long as it stays at this rate. It doesn't look like we'll have any rain today, either, so that should help. With any luck, that surge will go through and flow back into the ocean and we can all sleep a lot easier tonight."

When Rath, One-Eye, and the Pagu next check the water level, they find it has only gone down by two more inches.

Flower-Pagu says, "It's a little more difficult with the water being lower. They need to take the moisture from the air instead of directly from the river. But, they'll get stronger as their roots grow further into the soil!"

One-Eye says, "However they do it, it'd better be enough."

"I think it will be!"

Bucket-Pagu and Well-Pagu nod.

The next hour, it is the same two inches, but on the following one, it has dropped by four inches. One-Eye exhales, relieved.

Flower-Pagu says, "They're doing so well!"

Rath says, "They are! There are so many flowers now as well. They are beautiful."

On the next check, the water level has gone down six inches.

"The roots must have extended further down," Rath says.

Flower-Pagu says, "I agree! Phillip's Spirit Rabbit gave them all the strength they needed for this!"

"That is very good to hear. I am glad that everyone has worked together in allowing Grandfather's idea to work. I think it is wonderful to see."

"Us too!' Flower-Pagu and Bucket-Pagu say.

"All!" Well-Pagu says.

In between checks, Rath and the others play cards, then he and the Pagu read with one another. He takes a walk with One-Eye around the house, staying within the radius and the watchful eye of the guards. From three to five, the water lowers by two feet in those hours alone.

That evening, Rath is in the quarry with Carlos. "It has gone down another six inches," he says.

Carlos sighs. "That is very good to hear. The surge will come through an hour from now."

Despite the steady progress, they are all tense at dinner. Garreth in particular seems on edge.

Finally, he says, "Should let you all know – a petition has been started to ban people from Ullia entering Delphy and several cities have already signed it."

Rath's eyes widen. "That is terrible."

One-Eye says, "We have enough problems already."

Carlos says calmly, "To them, they believe they are alleviating some of those problems. However, I agree – it is very short-sighted."

Phillip says, "Something like that wouldn't go into effect for a while though, right?"

Garreth says, "If I've got anything to say about it, it won't go into effect at all." He frowns. "But, that's now in Georgio and Marchand's hands. I doubt they'd agree with it, but if enough leaders sign, they will all but be forced to." He shakes his head. "Didn't mean to bring up more when we've not yet figured out our own, immediate problem. It's almost seven – why don't we check the level one last time and make our decision whether to stay or leave?"

They all agree and go to the library. The sun is beginning to set and the waterfall glints orange and yellow. Garreth walks purposefully down the steps to the quarry and opens the door. The others gather behind him.

The water level is far lower than when they first planted the Water Flowers and the group turns to Rath to see just how much. He looks over the river to check the mark on the opposite wall.

With relief, he says, "It went down by seven more inches. It is enough."

Phillip says, "Then we're safe staying?"

"Definitely."

Garreth pats his grandson on the back. "Even more so if it continues to go down." He smiles at Rath, then the group. "Thanks for doing this – for going with my crazy idea."

One-Eye says, "It worked."

"Now, I'd rather see it all the way through," Garreth says, shutting the door. "Why don't we stay in the library until the surge comes? No matter how low the water is, we're bound to get tremors. I've already informed the staff to secure anything that might fall. The rest of the home should be safe."

Phillip says, "I'm fine with staying, but maybe we could have some tea? I'm optimistic, but still a little nervous about this whole thing."

Carlos says, "I would be happy to oblige."

One-Eye says, "What about the guards? They helped, too."

Rath says, "That is true. I would like to thank them for doing so."

Crossing his arms, Garreth says, "Yeah, we should. Would you bring them in here, Carlos? Suppose they might like a cup, too."

"I will ask."

In the end, only three of the six guards who helped earlier arrive. The other three insisted on staying at their post, but thanked Garreth for the invitation.

Tea is prepared and they sit on the cushions near the waterfall to drink it. The guards look a little uncomfortable to be with the others and sit closer together in their trio, but relax more as the hour goes on.

One grows comfortable enough to offer into the conversation they had mostly remained quiet for, "I think my grandmother would like to hear about this – using Water Flowers, that is. She has always loved a good story. I think I will send a letter after this."

"That is a good idea," Rath says.

Garreth takes another sip, glancing at the guard. He sighs and looks at his empty cup.

After they finish, Garreth stands and says, "Got a minute, Carlos?"

"Certainly."

While the others continue talking, he and Garreth stand near the waterfall by the windows. The sun is lower and the Delphaen crystals have been dipped in water by the house staff, restoring their glow to ensure the library is well-lit.

Carlos waits until Garreth speaks.

When he does, it is not what he expects. "How did you feel when Azalea and I got married?"

"Overjoyed. I thought it was a fine match for you both." He adjusts his tie. "Although I have never had an interest in a similar relationship, I knew that Azalea wished for one."

Garreth nods. "Not long before we got married, she chose to complete her Natural Life Ceremony – said it was only right so that we could … grow older together. You did, too, not long afterward."

"I wished for the same with her and you – but in a different sense than you both. As you know, those from Sudines – even in part – have very long lifespans, however, for much of it we are asleep. It is why, before reaching adulthood, leaving Sudines and meeting others is discouraged. We will likely outlive them. Some will choose to keep their remaining years, no matter how long that may be while others believe it is time … to live." He smiles. "Although nine hundred and seven hundred, Azalea and I had only been awake for the same number of years as you – twenty-five – and after our ceremonies, we also now have a similar lifespan and one that I am truly grateful for. To see you both begin a family and Lord Georgio to begin his and" – he glances behind them – "to watch Master Rath grow and continue to. While alive for over seven hundred years, these most recent have been ones that I will never forget."

"You cherish your time. Whether it's long or short," Garreth says and Carlos nods. "I don't feel like I have been. I'm wondering when I can start changing that." He holds up his hand. "I know – that's only something that I can decide. Marchand's told me that, too. Just … " He sighs.

Carlos thinks, then says, "Another tenant of Sudines philosophy concerns regrets. I do not believe anyone could be at peace holding onto things that happened so many years prior."

"I'd bet."

"However, it does not matter how long ago it was or how many years you have yet to have. You may always change." He pauses. "To bring a recent example – while not from Sudines, one who has lived for a very, very long time and awake for far more of it – Ara. For many years, he grieved for his wife, North. However, since *PearlHeart* arrived with his family, he has begun to live again. He is starting more gardens in Draconi with his sister, Rella. Did you know that?"

"Rath told me. I thought it was a wonderful idea."

"I do as well," Carlos says. "It is never too late, Lord Garreth."

Garreth is very still for a long moment. Then he nods. Carlos stands with him by the window.

Near the end of the hour, One-Eye's Spirit Lion suddenly pricks his ears forward. Phillip's Spirit Rabbit does the same. Garreth's Spirit Dolphin flies over to him and he says, "About time?" The Dolphin nods.

As Garreth walks over, Rath asks, "What would you like us to do, Grandfather?"

He hesitates. "I'm going to go look. It'd probably be safer to leave the door shut, but ... I want to make sure the water doesn't hit the supports – maybe that *does* make it the safest option. Would you all come with me?"

They do and soon the large group has made it to the bottom of the steps. The ground begins to tremble beneath their feet and Rath looks to his grandfather in alarm. Garreth thrusts the door open.

Not a second afterward, there is a loud crash and water fills the cave to their left. It hits a wall and starts to shoot toward them. A moment later, a wall of water goes through.

Even though it nears the supports of the house, it does not reach them. For a few deafening seconds, the water rushes through, flowing out into the ocean. As it does, the water level lowers more and more, uncovering the Water Flowers around the cave. When it has settled, it is well below the etching in the wall.

They exhale a breath. Rath asks, "Is everyone all right?"

"We are!" Flower-Pagu says.

One-Eye says, "Us too." His Spirit Lion, however, shakes out his fur, disgruntled.

Phillip says with a small laugh, "Just a little wet." His Rabbit starts washing her ears.

The guards look startled. "It worked," one says.

Garreth starts, "Well – " He suddenly stops and says, more kindly, "Yeah. It did."

The guards nod to him. "We shall return to our posts, Lord Garreth."

After they leave, Garreth scans the river one more time, then steps back and shuts the door. He looks at the boards laying on the floor. "I'll replace those in the morning. Can't say we'll never have to go down there again, but I'd rather not have anyone wander in."

"Actually, could you leave it open?" Phillip says. "The Water Flowers will need someone to tend to them." His Rabbit nods.

Flower-Pagu says, "And they would love it if you and everyone said hello to them!"

"Yeah?" Garreth says. "Then, I'll leave it open. It's not like we've got any littles around here. You're all adults." He pokes the pile with his foot. "I'll dispose of these – but, in the morning. I think everyone here could use some rest."

Carlos says, "I would agree, Lord Garreth."

As they walk to their rooms, One-Eye says, "That's one less thing to worry about. Now it's just the petition."

"I hope that it does not go through," Rath says.

Phillip says, "It probably won't if the people from Ullia in the caves leave, right?"

Carlos says, "That should not be what it takes. However, at this time, it may be for the best."

Garreth says, "Things will calm down. But I agree with Carlos – I certainly don't mind the ones here that want to help or just live here, but it may be hard for the people on Delphy to separate them from those that created the cracks, attacked people, or tried to take you, Rath. I can talk to Georgio and Marchand and ask if they've given any thought to opening more relations with Ullia."

"Thank you, Grandfather," Rath says.

18

Before going to bed, Rath stands on his balcony, writing in his journal.

One-Eye and his Lion are out, too, on the balcony next to his. They have moved into the guest bedroom since Carlos cleared One-Eye to go up the stairs. As the Lion enjoys the ocean breeze, One-Eye waits for Rath to finish writing before saying, "Good night."

Rath looks over. "Good night, One-Eye." He pauses. "May I say 'good night' to your Spirit Lion? If he is available?"

"He is. He's right here."

Rath nods, focusing on the area. "Good night, One-Eye's Spirit Lion. I hope you both sleep wonderfully."

The Lion's eyes shine. One-Eye laughs. "He wants to tell you the same – and thank you."

"Of course."

One-Eye waves, then he and his Spirit Lion go back inside. Rath writes for another minute before turning around to do the same.

As soon as he does, a hand covers his mouth.

He looks into the bright yellow eyes of someone who appears to be from Ullia, but has Delphaen tattoos and clothes more similar to someone from Delphy.

The man turns Rath's head left and right, like Lura did before. "Amazing … if I was not in front of you, I could swear you were not even here by my traits alone."

Before Rath can move away, he feels a shock and falls forward. The man catches him, then carries him down the stairs leading off of the balcony to the ground. As he walks into the forest, he passes a Butej guard slumped against a tree.

Up in his room, One-Eye wakes up to a small voice. "One-Eye?"

He sits up. His Lion is yawning by his feet and Well-Pagu, Bucket-Pagu, and Flower-Pagu are flying near them.

Flower-Pagu looks embarrassed. "We're really sorry to disturb you. Rath never came back inside and we didn't see him on the balcony. Do you know where he is?"

One-Eye abruptly gets out of bed. He pulls on his boots and leaves the room. The Pagu and his Lion follow him. "No. It sounded like he was going to sleep." He opens Rath's door, then starts toward the balcony. Before he reaches it, his Lion stops and says something. "A Spirit Eel?" One-Eye asks.

The Lion nods.

Crouching, One-Eye and his Lion approach. One-Eye reaches for his knife. He opens one of the doors. Outside, an unfamiliar voice says, "Yes, I know. It seems we arrived too late." Whoever it is sighs.

One-Eye moves.

The man steps back a second before One-Eye appears. He has a hood over his head, shadowing his yellow eyes, but he lowers it, dimming their brightness. "I am not an enemy – at least, I do not believe so."

One-Eye does not lower his knife. "Why are you here?"

The man holds up Rath's journal and pen. "Likely a similar reason as you."

The Pagu fly out. Flower-Pagu says, "Do you know where Rath is? We're looking for him."

The man's Spirit Eel curls around his arm. "I do not. It seems I am now looking for him as well. Had I arrived sooner … " He shakes his head. "Best begin."

One-Eye hesitates, however the Pagu seem at ease and his Spirit Lion seems curious about the Spirit Eel, so he lowers, then puts away his knife. "I'm coming with you. Who are you, anyways?" Then, nodding to the journal and pen, "I'll carry those."

The man readily gives them to him – One-Eye tucks them in his pocket – then pulls up his hood and begins walking down the stairs. One-Eye follows. "Best we talk on the way. We haven't a moment to lose, not if my suspicions are correct." He pauses on a step, turning around. "Will you come with us, Honored Ones?"

They shake their heads. Bucket-Pagu says, "I think we need to notify the Butej guards."

Well-Pagu says, "Help."

The man looks surprised. "Oh. They may be able to … Yes. I suppose I could wait for them to arrive." He scans the forest. "I still sense them – not Rath, of course, but I have heard none can – but I do sense someone with Marchand's Traits among those with Erole's and Fierce's. That must be him."

As the Pagu fly away, One-Eye says, "Someone from Delphy took him?"

"I am afraid so. However, while Marchand is his god, his loyalty is fully with Erole. My god tries to have at least a handful of those with mixed blood in the different countries as spies."

They reach the bottom of the stairs. One-Eye frowns. "Start at the beginning."

The man extends his hand. "I am Relingel, son of Councilman Rittel of Ullia and successor to his title. I have not done so, as I am currently in training – usually in the presence of Erole."

"One-Eye," he says, taking his hand.

"Good to meet you. I will tell you more on the way. I sense the Butej guards are approaching."

A moment later, One-Eye hears footsteps and a dozen guards arrive, followed by the Pagu.

Relingel looks at them, clapping his hands together. "A good number. This shall suffice."

The guards look wary. "We are told that you are a friend."

"I would certainly hope to be."

They glance at the Pagu, then relax. "Why are we a good number? Suffice for what?"

"My apologies – people from Ullia rarely speak straightforward, but we always speak the truth. It is a good number because a man from Delphy with loyalty to Erole has made away with the man named Rath and he is trying to cover this with Ullian spies escaping in the same or similar directions." He smiles slightly. "He didn't expect me to come after him."

The guards nod to each other. "We will find the others with our skyships."

"Thank you. I cannot imagine this man will let anyone else take Rath, but it is best to be safe."

"We fully understand that," the lead guard says, then they make a hand gesture and the group leaves.

Relingel says to One-Eye, "I will reveal the man's path to you. It shall make this easier." Without another thought, he waves his hand and One-Eye suddenly sees faint yellow figures in the forest, walking away. They are all of the same man who has Delphaen tattoos and appears to be carrying someone, but no one is there.

One-Eye tenses.

Relingel sees and says, "Do not worry – they are only afterimages. That is what I was trying to do earlier – to find the man and Rath's path from the start on the balcony, but I am afraid it only works not long after the real people have been present." He frowns at the ghostly forms. "He was very careless to leave such a clear path."

He follows the figures and One-Eye starts to join him, then stops when he sees a Butej guard passed out against a tree.

He kneels next to them. He takes a deep breath, then puts his hands over them – now glowing yellow – to check them with Sevran's Traits.

Relingel says, "They are fine. We are always careful with those types of shocks."

One-Eye glares. "I don't believe that."

For a moment, Relingel seems startled, then sad. He says, "The longer we wait, the more these images will fade." One-Eye does not say anything as he finishes checking the guard. Afterward, he talks silently with his Spirit Lion and stands up. "My Spirit Lion will find a way to tell Carlos – he's a doctor."

"Very good." They walk for several seconds before Relingel says, "There are more guards like the one you found. I'm sure at least one of the spies the Butej guards are looking for will guide Carlos to them as well."

One-Eye glances at him, then nods. He then asks, "Did you know he'd come for Rath?"

"Unfortunately. I heard Erole tell him to. It seems he reported Rath's unusual characteristic to him and my god became interested, as all expected. As I said, I am often with Erole."

"But you're here on Delphy."

"Yes."

"Then Erole is – "

Relingel pauses for a moment. "On Delphy. Where else?" Then he looks ahead and suddenly gives an, "Ah." He walks forward quickly.

In front of them is the last ghostly image of the man. Relingel studies him. "Curious how Rath doesn't even appear in my afterimage. It asks many questions that … " He laughs a little. "Well, let's say if I was a fraction more like my god, I would be *very* interested in what that meant."

"Why aren't you? Like Erole, I mean?"

"Do you wish I was?"

"I don't know him. Just that … he doesn't do things that are right for his people."

"I fully agree." Relingel hesitates, as if considering how much to say. Finally, he says, "It is my goal to see an end to that – it may not come until I succeed my father. I've seen him and my grandmother before him reduced to people completely submissive to Erole as his spies. I do not intend to become that." Changing the subject, he looks up at the sky, saying, "I wonder if the Butej guards have found all of the spies. I do not sense them nearby anymore."

At that moment, they hear a rush of wind and a small Butej skyship descends. The guard aboard tells them, "We have apprehended all."

"I thought so."

"Your afterimages were helpful. Thank you."

Relingel bows. "My pleasure. Could you see the man carrying Rath from the sky?"

"No. However, we will continue to search."

Relingel waves a hand. "That will not be any good for much longer. They are going underground." At the guard's panicked look, Relingel pats the air with his hand. "Do not worry. We are on his trail – see?" He gestures to the ghostly figures.

The guard glances at them. "I do."

"I wanted to make sure you had found all of the spies before I let go of my traits here. One-Eye and I must continue further, it seems."

The skyship already begins to rise. "Do so. We will watch … for as long as we can from the sky."

"Many thanks."

After the guard flies off, Relingel waves his hand and the afterimages disappear. Then he faces where they were going and concentrates. He waves his hand and a new set of figures appear. Almost immediately after, Relingel's eyes widen and he buckles over.

One-Eye says, "Are you all right?"

Relingel grips his knees. "Fine." He moves forward, but with an effort. "Smart." He explains, "It seems the man has discovered – late – that I may track him. You will see why I may have over-exerted myself soon enough."

They continue through the forest. However, as they get closer to Priage Port, One-Eye starts to see other afterimages – guards and spies. When they reach the docks themselves, he stops, staring ahead.

Priage Port is full of images, sailors and travelers blending into each other in a muddled yellow glow. Further ahead in the city, shop owners, customers, and evening walkers appear where they were a few minutes prior.

The real people look at the images in fright and a few are already being calmed down by Selachuu soldiers that were in the area.

One soldier is speaking to a frightened man, saying, "Yes, sir, that's you." He points to the afterimage.

The man does not look comforted.

Then the soldier's Spirit Shark says something and he turns to see One-Eye walking and Relingel hobbling through the crowd. He goes over to them swiftly and says to Relingel,

"A public area might not have been the best place for this."

"I'm seeing that."

As the guard leaves to speak to another startled group of people, One-Eye searches for the man carrying Rath, but with the afterimages overlapping, it is impossible to see him.

Beside him, Relingel rubs his face. "Ugh, I feel ill."

One-Eye says, "Then make them disappear. We're not getting any further like this. Especially if you're like that."

"Point taken." He waves his hand and the afterimages disappear. He sighs. "Much better. I hadn't expected quite so many people – I'm accustomed to being out at night, but I thought other people preferred daylight."

"Do you have any other way of tracking him?"

Relingel raises an eyebrow. "Tracking one of Marchand's in a group of others with the same god?"

"He's also from Ullia, right? Can you sense that?"

"Yes, but he would have to be right in front of me and it takes concentration. The predominant god always appears first."

One-Eye's Spirit Lion returns and tells One-Eye that he was able to notify Carlos through Phillip's Spirit Rabbit, who woke up Phillip. One-Eye looks relieved, then says, "We'll keep going this way. I didn't see any afterimages off this road, so he must have kept to it."

"Very fine thinking." Relingel joins him. He glances back at the Selachuu soldier. "Maybe they can help. We've never been able to properly assess their traits, but they appear to be more adept at tracking someone of mixed blood."

"Then ask. I'm going to keep going this way."

Suddenly, they both see a Signal Fountain light up. One-Eye's Spirit Lion bounds toward it and the rest follow.

When they reach the fountain, they see a Butej guard is already there, speaking with a woman.

The guard – the same one from earlier – tells One-Eye and

Relingel, "A lead. She has seen Rath."

The woman nods. "Yes. Barely ten minutes ago. A man was carrying him. He seemed surprised when I recognized Rath – he usually comes here for supplies before he and *PearlHeart* set out, you see – and when I asked if Rath was all right, he didn't reply and left quickly. I got a weird feeling from the whole thing. Wasn't sure what to do, but I thought I'd get someone's attention in case it was something bad." Her eyes flick toward the guard. "It sounds like it is."

Relingel says, "That was very good thinking on your part. Where did Rath and this man go?"

She points. "That way." She wrings her hands. "Ohh, now I wish I followed them. Or offered for him to come inside until you all arrived."

One-Eye has already begun walking and the guard is boarding her skyship again. Relingel says to the woman, "He likely would not have accepted. You did your part. We'll now do ours."

She blinks. "Oh. Well, thank you."

As Relingel joins him, One-Eye says, "You're more optimistic than most people from Ullia I've met."

"I have to be. Otherwise, I have no chance of changing my country."

The Spirit Lion looks up at One-Eye as he says, "I've never met the King of Pantha. I wonder if he's anything like you."

Relingel's eyes glimmer. "Faerohr. I've heard of him. I would very much like to meet him."

When they reach a curve in the road, One-Eye says, "Where now?"

Relingel says, "I know where he is going – that is obvious – however, not the entrance he will be using. All entrances will lead there, but if we choose the one he did not, we could waste time that we do not have."

"Then where's the closest?"

Relingel swats the air with his hand. "Oh, that would be too obvious. He may be from Delphy, but he's from Ullia, too."

Then the Lion talks to the Eel and both speak to the human they are bonded with, who agree.

After the Spirit Animals run and swim off, Relingel says, "That was a good idea to ask the other Spirit Animals nearby. Your Lion would make a good spy."

One-Eye glares at him, but says nothing as they wait.

Once the Spirit Animals return with information, One-Eye scratches the Lion's ear. "Good work."

Relingel lets his Eel swirl around his shoulders, then pats their head. "As expected."

Following the Spirit Animals' directions, they enter the forest.

"Is there an entrance here?" One-Eye asks.

"Oh, several."

One-Eye almost stops, then keeps going. "Then we'll pick one. We've wasted enough time already."

"We'll waste more if we choose the wrong one."

They hear a bird call.

Relingel frowns. "A Paradi bird?"

One-Eye, however, rushes forward with his Spirit Lion. The bird calls again and they follow the sound. One-Eye searches the trees. His Lion suddenly points his nose up at one particular branch and One-Eye looks.

"Demeter?"

Melody's bird partner shakes out her feathers. She lifts off and lands on the ground, where she impatiently begins scratching at the grass with her talons. One-Eye kneels and feels around, his fingers immediately finding a handle.

Relingel and his Spirit Eel join them. "Ah – the correct entrance, I am guessing?"

"Probably." One-Eye opens it fully, revealing a long spiral staircase winding down into darkness.

Relingel hums, glancing at the Paradi bird. "Now, I would like to know how she knew this, however."

"She's Demeter, Melody's bird partner – someone on *PearlHeart*, Rath's ship. She knows Rath and would recognize him. She'd also want to help – especially if he was in danger."

"Excellent reasoning. However, why would she be here in the first place?"

"Because – " One-Eye huffs. "We have to go."

"No. *I* have to go." He waves his finger at One-Eye. "You're not going anywhere with that back of yours, friend." At One-Eye's expression, he continues, "Yes, I know of your injury. We don't simply rely on our traits. We're taught to read body language as well."

"I'm not letting you go down by yourself."

Relingel's shoulders fall. He raises both hands. "A compromise." Then without further explanation, he leaves, heading toward the city again.

One-Eye asks his Spirit Lion, "You're sure I can't?"

The Lion nods, looking upset as well.

Within minutes, Relingel returns with three Butej guards. "These fine guards have agreed to help. A very nice person with Marchand's Traits agreed to send a message for me to those Signal Fountains to alert them of a problem."

"Why three?"

"It's a very long way down."

One of the guards clears her throat. "We will create wind for you to travel down on. It should last for the journey given the distance Relingel has told us."

One-Eye's eye widens for a brief moment, then he says readily, "Sure." He stands on one side of the opening in the ground, across from Relingel. "We're ready."

The three guards nod, then begin to concentrate, focusing on the hole.

Slowly, a wind swirls up the gap in the center of the

staircase. After a few moments, Relingel tests his foot on it and finds it is semi-solid. He tells the guards, "It's perfect. Thank you."

The lead guard only nods.

One-Eye says, "So it's going to carry us down?"

Relingel shakes his head. "From my understanding, it will only slow our descent. Come on." Suddenly, he jumps into the hole. One-Eye looks down and sees him still falling, but not as fast as he should. "Wait a few seconds, then do the same!" Relingel calls up.

One-Eye glances at the guards one more time, then – with his Lion looking just as nervous beside him – leaps in.

Immediately, the wind hits them, sending One-Eye's hair and clothes flying. His eye adjusts to the dark, glowing blue with Lionel's Traits. He sees a pair of pale yellow glowing eyes peering up at him.

"Oh. You came. Good," Relingel says.

One-Eye glares at him,

"I'm also glad you can see. It will help for when we reach the bottom. It's completely black down there."

"I'll be fine." Something catches One-Eye's eye and he looks at small shiny flecks in the wall. "Miphrin?"

Relingel laughs. "A scholar as well?"

"Rath told me."

He sobers. "Yes. It's made this shaft a very good spying area. The mineral is transparent normally and opaque when lit by light, which we do not need to see by." He exhales. "My apologies. Some aspects of my heritage are hard to ignore. I would imagine it's the same for you?"

One-Eye does not reply.

"Come now. We'll be falling for at least ten more minutes. We should talk."

"I'm not talking to you about something like that."

Relingel seems almost pleased. "Fair enough. I wouldn't

expect you to when we only just met."

"What about you? You've told me nearly everything about yourself."

"You think? Well – my Spirit Eel has said that being more … open with people is something that will aid in making Ullia more open. It doesn't come naturally to me, I assure you."

"I wouldn't have known."

"Really? Why, thank you."

They are quiet for a few minutes. One-Eye hears the water of the Old Delphaen Crystal Quarry's river rushing by them. His Lion clings onto his back with sharp claws. "We're safe in here?" he asks Relingel.

"Oh absolutely. Erole made these shafts. They are completely secure."

"Where does this lead? I didn't know about anything lower than the quarry."

"Neither did Erole," Relingel replies after a moment. "But as soon as he did, he made these entrances quickly and quietly so we could access them. As for where they lead – more caves, of course. Ones that none of us have ever seen."

"What did you do while he was doing that? Did you know about the damages to the Constellation Caves?"

"Of course I did. If nothing else, I felt it. The tremors as well." He pauses. "I couldn't act on anything like that. Erole didn't find it important, but he's been engrossed with Evermore's information from *PearlHeart's* journey with Ara and exploring the caves below. However, it seems that Rath and the others managed to find compromises with some of my people to help those on Delphy repair the cracks. I'm glad." He does not say any more.

One-Eye frowns, but decides to leave it at that and they continue to fall in silence.

They arrive at the bottom. Relingel sighs as his feet make contact with the ground. "Not my preferred way of travel – I cannot sense anything while in the air. It was far faster than I expected, however. I must thank the guards."

One-Eye starts walking. "Do it later." He suddenly feels a hand on his shoulder.

"Wait." One-Eye sees his pale yellow eyes flick to their right. "Erole is beyond there. We must approach this carefully. But, first … " He raises his hand and concentrates. One-Eye sees several different patterns appear, all made out of electricity. Relingel holds onto one. "Yes. There it is." Then he flicks his hand, sending it flying up the shaft and out of sight.

"What was that?" One-Eye asks.

"The Butej hand symbol to let them know we've arrived safely and to pause their wind for five minutes – you can rescue Rath in five minutes, right?" One-Eye opens his mouth, but Relingel continues, grinning, "Oh, I would love to see the looks on their faces. Butej Guard hand symbols are carefully kept secrets. *Were*. Well, to me, at least – where are you going?"

One-Eye, who had already begun walking, says, "I have four minutes and fifty seconds. Come on."

Relingel smiles. "On the way."

"Did they come through here? Can you tell?"

"Let me see … " Relingel raises his hand and does a smaller gesture than what he did earlier. A few ghostly afterimages appear, but fade only a foot in front of them. "Yes. Very recently." He quickens his pace and One-Eye does the same. "After this turn, the tunnel goes straight. In fact … " His smile grows. "I sense him." It fades. "Yet, not Rath. Hmm … "

"Forget it. You can't sense him at all, right?"

"Yes and it is highly unusual. I don't think you can understand what an absolute surprise it is to be startled by someone who isn't supposed to be there when you can sense all around you."

"Then trust your eyes."

Relingel frowns. "Fair."

Ahead of them, the man with Delphaen tattoos carrying Rath, who is still unconscious, has arrived at the corner. He hesitates, then sets Rath down by it before entering the main tunnel. It does not take long for him to see two figures walking together, talking.

"Erole," the man says.

They both turn and the one who was speaking falls silent. The one who had been listening – a tall man in black with long blond hair and bright eyes – says, "You interrupted, Rellu."

Rellu, the man from Delphy, says, "For the task that you gave me."

"The man you're unable to sense? How fascinating," Erole, the God of Ullia, says. "But, I'm far more interested in Evermore's report right now. *And* these caves. Where do they go to? I want to know everything about them." He giggles.

The young man with him, Evermore – one of the sailors aboard *PearlHeart* – stares, unsure of what to do. Then he faces his god and says, "Shall I continue with my report?"

"Please do."

Rellu stomps his foot. "Erole, you had said – " He suddenly tries something else. "You truly do not sense him?"

At that, Erole – who had begun walking again – stops. "I sense you, Evermore, Relingel, and one of Lionel's."

Rellu gives an almost relieved laugh. "Then you cannot. Shall I show him to you?"

Erole glares at him, but nods. Instead of waiting for Rellu to lead him, he walks past him toward the corner.

At the same time, One-Eye and Relingel have just seen Rath. They quickly go to him and One-Eye kneels to check him with Sevran's Traits. He is relieved to see that he has no injuries. Then he gently brushes Rath's cheek with his hand and he begins to stir.

Just as he is opening his eyes, Relingel kneels and puts a finger up to his lips, indicating for Rath to be quiet. "You're safe now. Can you walk?”

Rath, who can see Relingel by the glow from his eyes, nods.

From the adjacent tunnel, Erole says, “Relingel.”

“Here.” Without another word or glance to Rath or One-Eye, Relingel stands and walks into the main tunnel. One-Eye helps Rath up, then guides both of them back to the staircase.

Erole turns the corner just as they enter it and the wind carries them back up.

Having heard two people running, but only sensing one, he studies the area. Relingel tenses as he waves his hand and afterimages appear, far stronger than his own. Ones of Rellu, Relingel, and One-Eye appear, but Rath does not. Erole frowns, however, when he sees the image of One-Eye leaving where he is very clearly holding someone’s hand.

Rellu points. “He must have taken him.” Then he realizes. “Relingel, you – ”

But Erole waves his hand impatiently, causing the images to disappear as he walks toward the staircase.

“Erole – ” Relingel starts to say.

Then a little voice says, “Stop.”

The god steps back as the area in front of him suddenly glows purple, green, and pink. Three Pagu – Well-Pagu, Bucket-Pagu, and Flower-Pagu appear.

“Enough,” Well-Pagu says.

Erole looks fearful for a moment, then recovers. He leans forward. “I only want to find something out.”

Well-Pagu shakes their head. They gesture to Evermore, who had followed with Relingel and Rellu. “Free.”

“But he hasn’t finished his report.”

Evermore says, “I have only one more minute to give, Honored One.”

Well-Pagu nods. They look toward Rellu. “Marchand.”

Erole grins. “But, he has loyalty to me.”

Rellu says, “Yes – for *years* and you wouldn’t even believe me when I told you I had found someone who – ” He shakes his head. “It doesn't matter anymore. I doubt there will ever be an opportunity to take him again.”

Beside him, Relingel nods. Softly, he says to Rellu, “This would be your time to exit. Take the staircase to the right, not the left.”

“You won't turn me in?”

“I already have. But, the Selachuu Military will be far kinder to you than Erole ever would. Go.”

Rellu gulps, then runs.

Erole watches, then turns his gaze back to the Pagu. “Why?” he asks. As he speaks, he continues to sense for anyone else in the tunnel.

“Protect.” Then they say, “Cracks.”

“I didn't do that to the caves.”

“Hurt.”

Erole recoils, understanding what they mean.

Relingel coughs. “The Ullian Spies have been under quite a bit of stress from your orders.”

Erole sends him a fierce glare. To Evermore, he says, “Finish your report,” but after he does, Erole does not seem happy. “Go,” he tells him. Then he begins walking, rounding the corner before continuing on the main tunnel.

Relingel follows automatically. As he and Evermore pass one another, he takes his arm for a moment. “For once, I agree with our god. Go. Be with those who care about you. You won't be required back until next year. Spend this time freely.”

“And you?”

Relingel's eyes are bright. “Not yet.” He releases Evermore and continues to the Pagu, bowing deeply, “I apologize for my lateness. This could have been avoided.”

They shake their heads. Well-Pagu smiles as Relingel rises. “Good.”

Relingel's eyebrows raise. He flushes, clearing his throat.

"Well … " His eyes drift further down the tunnel, where Erole has gone. He nods to the Pagu. "Honored Ones."

After he leaves, they look at one another and disappear.

During this time, Rath and One-Eye had been traveling back up to the surface, standing on the wind created by the Butej guards above.

Only after they have passed the Constellation Caves does One-Eye as, "Do you remember anything?"

"No. Only the man appearing on my balcony. Do you know what happened after that?"

"Most." He explains how the Pagu woke him and he met Relingel, then they and the Butej guards tracked Rellu, as well as the other members of the Ullian Spies. He tells him about finding the hatch with Demeter's help – Rath starts in surprise – going down to the caves that are lower than the quarry, and finding him near the corner.

"My Lion says Evermore and Erole were there, too," he finishes.

They reach the top not long afterward, where they step out of the wind and onto the grass.

The Butej guards all breathe a sigh of relief and release their traits. One says, "Are you well, Rath, One-Eye?"

"I am," Rath says. "Thank you very much to all of you for helping us."

One-Eye says, "I'll be all right. Thanks."

The guard smiles, but looks tired. "It is our pleasure." They gesture to a skyship not far from them. "Shall we take you back to Lord Garreth's?"

Rath says, "Yes, please."

While the guard retrieves their skyship, One-Eye and his Spirit Lion scan the surrounding trees. Rath sees and asks, "What is it?"

"Demeter. This is where she was." He turns to the two remaining guards. "Did you see her fly away?"

"The blue and purple Paradi bird? Yes. Not long after you and Relingel went down." They pause. "Is he … "

"Still there," One-Eye answers. "I don't think we'll see him again."

The guards nod. The third guard returns, then Rath and One-Eye board and the skyship lifts off.

As they are traveling, One-Eye gives Rath his journal and pen, then asks, "Will they want to move you again after this?"

"I cannot say."

One-Eye frowns, but says instead, "I had thought Melody and Demeter were on Paradi."

"That is what Melody told me as well." Rath thinks. "You had said Evermore was below. With Erole."

"Yeah. It sounds like they were here this entire time."

Rath nods.

They are quiet for the rest of the journey.

When they arrive, Garreth and the Butej guards are gathered out front. As the skyship descends, Garreth goes to meet them.

"Fierce wants to see you," he says. "He arrived not long after the Pagu told us that you had gone missing. He's with Carlos now. Tea," he says, as way of explanation.

They go inside. When they reach the door to the sitting room, Garreth says to One-Eye, "We'll wait outside. I'd imagine he wants to talk to only Rath right now."

Then he knocks and Carlos says, "Come in."

Fierce – the God of Butej – is sitting at the short table, looking pensive. An empty cup of tea is front of him. Carlos and the Pagu are with him.

"I didn't know the Pagu were here," Garreth says. Carlos says, "They just returned."

Fierce's eyes flick to One-Eye. "Good. I had wished to speak to you as well."

Garreth raises his hands. "Never mind then," he says to

One-Eye. "I'll be outside."

"If we may have a moment to talk as well, Garreth – after."

He frowns, but nods before leaving.

Fierce's look softens as he turns to Rath. "How are you?"

"I am better. May I ask how you are?"

Fierce smiles for a moment. "The same. Better." He sighs. "Most of that is due to Carlos' tea and … the Pagu. Come and sit for a moment. I will not be long – it is late, you must rest, and I need to return to my patrol."

One-Eye sits across from him. "Why is that important?"

"For reasons such as this." He extends his hand. "I am Fierce. It is good to meet you."

One-Eye shakes his hand, but does not say anything else.

Fierce does not seem offended as he continues to Rath, "My initial thought had been to move you again. I still think Garreth's home is the safest, however … I was rash. I did not think my decision through and I apologize for that. Despite my words from before, Merp is very capable of causing more trouble for your family should you stay here longer. I've already spoken to Garreth about this and he reluctantly agrees. Normally, given the situation with Erole's own, I would relocate you – possibly off of Delphy, however … it has been a long time since you have been on Marchand's land, hasn't it?"

Rath says, "Yes, it has."

Fierce looks sad for a moment. "Then, you will stay here – if that is what you wish." He coughs. "And, I am told that Erole and his people will not seek you out again. I can assure you that your travels will be safe from them. You are free to go where you will. Where that is you may keep to yourself, however – as a friend – I would like to ask where that may be?"

Rath thinks. "I would like to go west. One-Eye saw Demeter in Priage and I would like to see if Melody is here as well."

"I understand. I wish you the best of luck in doing so. Were they not supposed to be here?"

"No. Melody told me she and Demeter were traveling to Paradi during these months."

"Then, I hope it is for a good reason that she is here."

"I as well."

Fierce continues, "Carlos and Garreth have informed me about the petition to ban those from Ullia on Delphy. I can confirm that similar situations are happening in other countries. Carlos says it is likely due to my siblings being absent, having gone to the North to help Haliae and Pantha. I agree." He takes a breath. "However, it seems Belle's people are handling the situation well. Even so … I have advised that a temporary ban may be helpful – Erole has certainly overstepped his bounds. However, I can only speak for Butej – it is my siblings' decision regarding their own countries."

Rath says, "I apologize if this is rude, however, I disagree that a ban will be helpful. I do not believe that everyone should be responsible for actions they were not a part of."

One-Eye says, "If anything, they should be treated like everyone else who commits a crime. It was someone from Delphy who took Rath."

Sounding surprised, he says, "Someone … " He glances at Carlos, however he is just as startled. "Marchand will not like to hear of this."

Carlos clears his throat. "Likely one of Erole's spies. I can assure you Marchand is aware of them. He loves them as he does all of his own."

Fierce looks sympathetic. "Then, I must agree with One-Eye in this case – they must be tried. I would do the same if it was one of my own. I will look into this in other countries. I understand where you speak from Rath, however, banning them may be the safest course of action right now – until Marchand returns, at least." Rath frowns and Fierce's expression falls for a moment. He reaches over and squeezes Rath's upper arm. "Wherever you go, please let my guards know if you need any help. They are always there for you. As am I."

"Thank you, Fierce."

Afterward, the god steps out of the room, leaving them with Carlos and the Pagu. The Pagu hug Rath. "We're so glad to see you again!" Flower-Pagu says.

"I am as well." As they pull away, he says, "I believe I will go to sleep now. I am very tired."

Bucket-Pagu nods. "Us too!"

Well-Pagu says, "Rest!"

Carlos picks up the tea tray. "I fully agree, for all of you. Garreth has suggested that you all spend one more night here, then set out tomorrow."

One-Eye says, "What will you and Phillip do?"

"We thought we would stay here in Priage, then travel to Vann's wedding. Garreth has offered to arrange for us to stay at an inn for the duration of our stay in Priage, however, he did not know what your plans were."

One-Eye says to Rath, "I want to go with you – to find Melody and Demeter."

Flower-Pagu says, "May we come? We'd like to see them, too." Bucket-Pagu and Well-Pagu nod.

"Yes, I would love if you did," Rath says.

Carlos says to Rath and One-Eye. "I agree with Fierce – you will be safe from Erole and the Ullian Spies during the duration of our stay on Delphy, so you will not have to worry about that." He smiles. "I have enjoyed spending this time with you both."

"I have as well," Rath says.

One-Eye smiles a little, too. "Thanks for everything." He pauses. "Would you have time to … plants. And herbs."

Carlos raises an eyebrow. "Teach you other healing

methods? I believe so. Why not tomorrow morning?"

"Later – if we can." He glances at Rath. "We said we'd sail together tomorrow."

Carlos says, "I see. Then, after."

Below, in the foyer, Fierce is talking to Garreth. "I can assure you your grandson will be safe from Erole no matter where on Delphy he is. The Pagu themselves saw to it."

Garreth nods. "Even Erole wouldn't argue with them."

Fierce looks aghast. "Never. None of us do."

Raising an eyebrow, Garreth says, "Azalea would likely know more on *why* that's the case." He crosses his arms. "Guess I'll have to leave it to my own intuition."

"We all respect you, Garreth – I speak for my siblings as they have told me so. Azalea is – "

" – special. I get it. And I consider myself lucky every day for it."

Fierce studies him for a long moment, then says, "I would ask you a question, however I feel that it is up to Marchand to guide you on it."

"When I'm going to see Azalea again? Yeah. You're right. That's Marchand and I's business and then only barely the old dolphin's." He continues more calmly, "Thanks for having Rath and the others stay here. It was good to see all of them. Good to be in this home with others around."

Fierce hesitates. "I am glad to hear that." He sighs and lowers his voice. "I do ask that you be kinder to my own. They are under my orders to be here and aid how they can." Garreth frowns stubbornly and Fierce shakes his head. "Be well, Garreth."

"You too."

Fierce nods to the Butej guards near the front doors, then leaves. Not a moment later, Garreth hears a rush of wind and Fierce is gone, flying away in his hawk form.

19

The next morning, Rath and One-Eye sail.

Garreth, Carlos, Phillip, and the Pagu watch from the shore. The Butej guards, standing on the steps behind Garreth's house, do as well.

While Garreth and Carlos sit in chairs, Phillip, his Spirit Rabbit, and the Pagu sit in the sand. One-Eye's Spirit Lion, however, is not there.

On the small Delphaen ship, One-Eye sits by the tiller, watching Rath's movement. He says to his Spirit Lion, "Enjoying yourself?"

The Lion – who had climbed aboard with caution – now grins with his tongue lolling out and his mane blowing behind him. One-Eye laughs.

Rath says, "May I ask if he is having fun?"

"Yeah. He is."

"I am so glad!"

The Lion closes his eyes in bliss, taking in the sun and the salty wind.

When they return to shore, the Lion hops off the ship and happily trots over to where Phillip's Spirit Rabbit and Garreth's Spirit Dolphin are so he can confer with them about his short trip.

Rath says, "Thank you for letting us use your ship, Grandfather."

"Of course. You're not bad, One-Eye."

One-Eye starts to frown, then smiles a little instead. "Thanks."

They eat breakfast outside on the back terrace that day and afterward, Rath helps the Pagu build a sandcastle on the beach while Garreth watches them. One-Eye and Carlos have gone inside so Carlos can teach him about other methods of healing and Phillip and his Spirit Rabbit are in the quarry checking the Water Flowers.

Near the time the group has decided to leave, Carlos and One-Eye return. Garreth asks, "How did the lesson go?"

Carlos says, "Well. I have given them supplies for the rest of their journey and One-Eye is a fast learner – he knows how to use them."

"You're not … *expecting* they'll use them, right?"

"I would certainly hope not, however, it is always better to be prepared."

Garreth says to One-Eye, "And your back? How is it after last night?"

"Carlos says it'll take longer to fully heal, but it'll be all right as long as I'm walking for the next week."

"Good to hear it."

Phillip and his Spirit Rabbit come out later.

Garreth asks them, "How were the Water Flowers?"

"Great! I think they're going to do really well in the cave."

"I'm glad. I can't wait to show Marchand." He sits forward. "Phillip, Carlos, I've been thinking and … if you want, I'd like to offer you both to stay here. I know Rath, One-Eye, and the Pagu have already decided to leave and really … Merp's order is more about Rath than anyone else. Phillip, I'd like you to help tend to the plants while they acclimate and Carlos, I'd appreciate the tea – and the company. From both of you."

Carlos bows. "Certainly, Lord Garreth."

Phillip says, "I'd love to!"

Garreth laughs, looking relieved. "Now – I know you'll be heading to Vann's wedding and *PearlHeart* after that, but thank you. I'll be glad to have you for now." Then he calls, "Rath! Are you and the Pagu about ready?"

Rath looks up. He was just putting a small flag on top of the sandcastle. "Yes, I believe so." He beams. "We finished, Grandfather!"

Flower-Pagu flies in front of it. "Isn't it perfect?"

Bucket-Pagu says, "We built it very strong!"

Well-Pagu looks at the raised drawbridge. "Castle."

Garreth smiles. "It looks wonderful."

After Rath, One-Eye, and the Pagu retrieve their things, they all go to the front of the house to say their goodbyes. Garreth hugs his grandson tightly. "Take care," he says.

"You as well, Grandfather."

"And send me a letter when you find Melody and Demeter. Or, anytime, you know?"

"I will do so. And, I would love to."

Near them, One-Eye finishes saying goodbye to Carlos and Phillip while his Lion does the same with the other Spirit Animals. The Lion walks back to One-Eye looking sad. One-Eye scratches his ear. "I'm sure you'll meet others." His Lion flicks his tail.

Just as they are leaving, they hear a voice say, "Lord Garreth! Everyone!"

It is the Paradi messengers from the tower near Garreth's house. However, beside them is a young man with a purple scarf covering his eyes.

Hera says, "I found this young man in the forest, sleeping. Said he wasn't quite ready to greet everyone, but then we saw that you were all leaving."

"Evermore," Rath says. "It is so good to see you."

"It is for me as well," he replies, looking relieved. He bows low. "If I may be allowed to accompany you wherever you are going. I am told that I am not required in Ullia until this Winter, as is customary."

"Of course. That is all right with me."

One-Eye says, "We're looking for Melody and Demeter. Demeter is the one who found the entrance that led us to Rath."

Evermore starts. "Demeter … Melody. I-I had not known they were here."

Rath says, "We did not either."

"Then, please, I will accompany you. I wish to know that she and Demeter are all right." He flushes. "I believe I will be able to help find them, as well."

Hera claps her hands. "Glad this all worked out. Oh – and if Melody and Demeter are working as messengers here on Delphy, they'll be logged in the city's book where they're staying. I'd suggest starting there."

Rath says, "Thank you. We will."

Then, Garreth, Carlos, Phillip, and Hera wave to the small group as they travel up the hill, headed west.

Evermore asks, "Where will we go first?"

One-Eye says, "I thought where my Lion and I saw Demeter last. It's just off of the main road ahead. She was in the trees around the entrance to the caves." He shakes his head. "I can't believe Erole created those without anyone noticing."

Evermore presses his lips together. "My god is capable of doing many things. Did Demeter seem well? Unhurt?"

"If she flew off, I'd say she was all right. Just impatient."

Evermore smiles faintly. "That sounds like Demeter." His expression tightens. "I am concerned that she was in an area with so many entrances to the lowest caves – however, I am glad that she was there to lead the others to your location, Rath."

"As am I."

Despite the scare of Relingel's afterimages the previous night, the docks at Priage Port seem to be operating as normal.

As they continue into the city and walk down the street, they near the Signal Fountain that alerted One-Eye, his Lion, and Relingel of Rath's path and outside of it, the shopkeeper is filling the glass globe at the top. She sees them. "Rath! And I'm told you are One-Eye. I'm afraid I don't know the rest." After she climbs down her ladder, the Pagu and Evermore introduce themselves and she smiles. She says to Evermore, "Someone from your country – Relingel, his name was – was a great help. I don't think they would have found Rath otherwise."

"I am truly grateful for that."

Flower-Pagu says, "We heard that you helped, too!"

Bucket-Pagu says, "You sent a message with the Signal Fountain here!"

Well-Pagu says, "Guard."

The woman flushes. "Well – I just wanted to help. The situation didn't seem right to me."

Rath bows to her. "Thank you very much for doing so."

Her blush deepens. "You're welcome. I'm just glad to see you're all safe."

When they reach the curve in the street, One-Eye says, "We went into the forest here. My Spirit Lion remembers the area where Demeter was."

When they reach it, they stop and One-Eye points at a branch. "She was there last night." He turns to Evermore. "Can you do what Relingel did? Create those afterimages."

Evermore shakes his head. "I cannot. It is possible my traits are strong enough to do so for a few feet – certainly not as far as Relingel – but I am not trained in the technique."

One-Eye sighs. He and his Lion have a quick conversation, then he asks Rath, "What's the nearest town to here? Besides Priage. I don't think Melody or Demeter would want to stay in such a big city."

Rath thinks. "Ľoeile Village. I always thought it was a very beautiful place."

"Let's try there."

Evermore nods. "I agree with One-Eye and if it is as you say, Rath, I think Melody and Demeter would enjoy it. What direction do we go?"

"North. We should arrive near lunch." Rath smiles. "I cannot wait for you both to see it."

Flower-Pagu suddenly gasps. "Oh! Ľoeile Village! I remember now." They dance a little in the air. "Rath is right – it is the most beautiful place! It's been so long since I've seen it."

Bucket-Pagu tilts their head to the side. "Ľoeile … but I thought – "

"No, Bucket-Pagu! Not yet! They don't know!"

"Oh! So it'll be a surprise. I understand. I will not say a word."

Well-Pagu laughs gently next to them.

They start north. The forest extends for several miles ahead and they walk under the Delphy Berry trees. Two hours into their journey, they break and sit beside one particularly large stream, eating some of the berries that Rath and One-Eye picked.

While Rath gives a few to the Pagu, One-Eye offers some to Evermore. "Here," he says.

Evermore hesitates, then holds out his hand to accept them. Even in the shade, he has kept on his purple scarf to protect his eyes. "Thank you."

One-Eye sits beside him. "What is it?"

Evermore raises his head quickly. He frowns. "I am troubled by what happened to Rath."

"It's over. He knows that."

"That is true." Evermore sighs. "However, I was with Erole during that time – knowing about all of the damage being done and unable to stop it. I know how precious the Constellation Caves – and all of Delphy – are to Rath. I am sorry that … " He trails off, then eats some more berries.

One-Eye says, "You didn't act against your god?"

Evermore nods. He swallows, then says, "Even Relingel is afraid of doing so. But, his Spirit Eel gives him strength to intervene in smaller, more indirect ways, like he did with Rath. I am so grateful to him. He is always kind to me. Such things are normally avoided on Ullia, but he believes that it will only make all of us stronger as opposed to hiding these things." He smiles softly. "He once told me, when Erole was preoccupied in his thoughts, that our god would not be able to take us away from our friends if all of us were friends. I thought it was humorous."

"He's an optimist. And a weird one at that."

"The concept is foreign to him. And … us. But, it is nice. Hope."

Across from them, Rath suddenly gasps. "E-Evermore, I sincerely apologize."

He looks far more surprised. "Apologize … to me? No, I am the one … "

However, Rath comes over to them, begins to speak, then stops and says, "I should have asked – am I interrupting?"

One-Eye shakes his head and Evermore says, "No. What is it?"

In response, Rath carefully takes something out of his pocket – an intricately folded letter. "I have been asked to give this to you. From your mother, Lura."

All of the color drains from Evermore's face. His hand trembles as he holds it out, then he closes his fingers, and – finally – tentatively opens them again. He stays very still while Rath places the letter in his palm. He exhales and brings it close to him, running his thumb over the familiar folds before carefully placing it in his pocket. "Thank you, Rath. I will read it at a later time."

"Of course. I am sorry that I did not give it to you sooner."

"No, no – there has likely been much that has happened since you received this."

Throughout the next hour, the trees begin to thin out. Rath steps off of the path they have been on to show them a small sparkling stream. "We can follow this," he says. "It leads directly to the village."

They walk alongside it and on their next short break, the Pagu cool their feet in the water. When they move on again, it does not take them much longer to arrive.

L'oeile Village is set in a large bowl-shaped valley, surrounded by the forest. Other streams like the one they followed lead to a lake in the center of many homes. Children play nearby, running down the hill or along the lakeshore. The grass is fuller here than in other parts of Delphy and there are several cultivated areas next to the streams where grains are being grown. Two Paradi Message Towers stand on the east and west sides of the village.

Evermore softly taps his bare foot in the lush grass, sending an almost invisible pulse. "A valley," he says, reading the geography. "The streams all run into it?"

Rath says, "Yes, to a lake in the center."

Evermore nods. "I sense that, too." He pauses. "The location of it seems unusual."

As they start down, Rath says, "Marchand tells me that at the start of the Fourth World, this area was an inland sea.

However, as the water was rerouted to be used in waterways around Delphy, the water level grew lower. I found it sad to hear – Marchand had said that many Spirit Dolphins liked to swim in it. He tells me that its previous state as a sea made the soil here very unique. It is possible to grow many sorts of grains that are unable to elsewhere on Delphy. Penelope, the Goddess of Campi, gave her blessing to the lake to ensure it and the streams had fresh water for the people here. It seems Rella, the Goddess of Cunica, visited the area as well and, ah, said that it was better in this state, being used for farming."

One-Eye says, "From what I've heard, that sounds right for her."

Evermore says, "She does have great respect for cultivation."

Flower-Pagu says, "I think it is wonderful as both places! And, if there's anything I've noticed, it's that things always continue to change in the world. It doesn't mean it's good or bad."

Bucket-Pagu nods. "Flower-Pagu's right. What I almost said earlier was that I remembered this place as an inland sea – I had forgotten it was drained. But, so many people look happy with how it is!"

Well-Pagu says, "Home."

They reach the bottom of the bowl. There, a little boy is playing with his Spirit Dolphin near the stream. However, when they approach, he looks up and says, "Hello! If you're new here – you should talk to Leader. She told me to say that."

"Of course," Rath says. "Thank you for telling us."

"Sure!" He stands up – he is muddy from his knees down to his feet – and looks at Evermore. "Hey – are you from Ullia? Can you make those cool pictures like Laylin? I keep asking if she can make a dolphin, but she just says she's not sure, then runs off."

Evermore's eyebrows raise behind his scarf. "With … her traits?"

"Yeah! The electricity. It's so neat!"

Evermore seems perplexed by his words. "I … do know a Laylin. Many from Ullia know each other at least in name. And … " He brings up his hand. "I believe … " He concentrates for a moment.

However, as soon as a spark appears between his fingers, they hear a shout from ahead and Evermore instinctively closes his hand into a fist and puts it behind his back.

The boy seems unbothered as he turns around, facing the village. He frowns and pokes at the stream with his stick. "Oh. *He's* back again."

Rath, concerned about the raised voices, says, "May I ask who he is?"

"He's the leader from the town north of here – my friend lives there – it's called Yrina Town."

Rath nods. "I remember." The voices grow louder and he winces. "I believe I will go see what they are shouting about."

"It's just the whole Ullia thing again. Something like a … peytish … or … something-shun."

One-Eye says, "Petition?"

"Yeah! That's what it's called. We didn't sign it, so the other town is mad or something." He shrugs. "I don't get why. People from Ullia are neat. Anyways – Leader makes the leader from Yrina leave eventually. Come on, I'll take you to them." And he takes Rath's hand and pulls him along while One-Eye, Evermore, and the Pagu follow.

Following the stream on their right, the boy brings them nearer to the village. Ahead, they see a woman yelling at a man while some of the villagers look on and others go about their daily chores as if this were normal.

"I'm telling you – we've already made our decision!" the woman shouts. "So, if that's the only reason you came, then – " She stops suddenly, seeing the group approach. She seems to recognize Rath and clears her throat.

The man, however, does not notice and shouts back to her, "Then what? You'll just let those people cause a mess below ground and above?"

"Nel, mind who you're speaking around!"

The man recoils in confusion. The woman gestures to her right and he looks, then gives a start. Lowering his voice, he says, "Rath. We did not know that you were here."

The woman says, "I apologize you had to see us like that."

Rath says, "May I ask if you are talking about the petition to ban those from Ullia?"

"What else?" she says.

Nel, the man, only huffs.

The boy trots over to the woman and she kneels down. He points. "I brought them like you asked, Leader Leira. There's someone from Ullia with them, too!"

"Thank you, dear." She glances at Nel. "It's a *good* thing. They're welcome here." He huffs again. She turns back to the boy. "But Malin, I'm *Mom* to you, not Leader Leira."

"But … Yes, Mom. The other sounds so much neater, though."

Leira turns her eyes to the sky and sighs. She stands and says to Rath, "I am truly sorry you came at a time like this. Was there something you needed? I would bet it's far more important than this argument of ours."

Nel sputters. "Far more – this is about the *safety* of Delphy!" He turns to Rath. "What is your opinion on the petition?"

"I disagree with it."

"But – " Nel shakes his head. "I don't understand."

Leira says to him, "Why don't we talk a bit – away from our visitors?" She turns to the group. "I'm sorry – this will only take a minute. Malin can take you to one of the inns if you need somewhere to stay."

Rath says, "Yes, please. Thank you very much."

"Of course." Then she leaves with Nel, both talking more

quietly but clearly still arguing.

Malin tugs on Rath's hand. "This way."

They all introduce themselves as he leads them through the village. Beside them, the lake sparkles in the noon sun. Many of the villagers they see smile at them as they go by and a few wave.

Soon, they reach a tall three-story building. Malin lets go of Rath's hand and says, "There should be room for all of you. But the Pagu don't need much, do they?"

Flower-Pagu says, "Nope! We usually sleep next to Rath!"

Bucket-Pagu says, "We did at Garreth's home and when we're on our journeys!"

"*PearlHeart,*" Well-Pagu says.

Malin asks, "You mean, like on a ship?" They all nod and he grins. "That's amazing!" He suddenly frowns. "I thought sailors were always on the ocean, though."

Rath says, "We are for three seasons of the year. We are currently on break."

"Oh. Okay. So why'd you come here then? Leader Leira – I mean, Mom – would want me to ask you that."

"We are currently looking for two friends of ours. We were told that if they are employed here as Paradi messengers that they would be in the registry."

"The big book Mom has! She'd definitely let you look at it. Well, probably after she finishes talking with the other leader. She doesn't really like me touching her books while she's gone. Says I get mud on them."

A villager doing her laundry overhears and looks around the corner of a sheet, grinning. "Shouldn't you wash up before your mother returns, Malin? She might not like mud around her house at all."

Malin flushes. "I was just about to!" He starts to leave, then looks at the group. "Is there anything else I can help with?"

Rath shakes his head. "No. Thank you very much for

leading us here."

"Sure thing! I'll come get you when Mom's back so you can look at her book with the Paradi messengers." He runs off, saying, "See you then!" They all watch him throw off his shirt and leap into the lake, eliciting laughs from the other villagers. He surfaces, spitting out water, then begins playing with his Spirit Dolphin.

The group enters a dimly lit lobby with woven furniture and paintings hung up on the walls. Rath is looking at one when his eyebrows raise in surprise.

Before he can say anything, a man walks over to him and says, "Like the painting? We had it done by – " He suddenly gasps. "Rath! Well!" He chuckles. "This is a surprise. I bet I don't need to tell you who did that painting."

"It is by my mother, Marin Lewis. I did not know it was here, however."

The man nods. "Yes. We commissioned her several years ago. I keep asking Leader Leira to contact her again for a painting of our valley, but I don't know if she's gotten the chance – especially recently, with all of the trouble with the Constellation Caves." He extends his hand. "I know you, but I doubt you know me. I'm Deran, the innkeeper of Pin'et Inn, but I'm originally from Campi, like Marin."

Rath shakes it. "I see. It is good to meet you."

"And you. You look quite a bit like your mother – I'm surprised."

"Thank you," Rath says, flushing.

Deran looks at the rest of the group. "Looking for a room here?"

"Yes, please."

They all pay for a room to share, then Deran reaches under the counter for his keys. "I'll lead you there," he says.

As they go up the stairs, he continues, "The third floor is almost filled – still rather quiet, though. Most of them have

Erole's Traits, too, so we've been trying to keep the lights low for them. You don't mind, do you?"

"Not at all," Rath says.

Deran smiles. "One of them has been working at Ma'en Inn with two musicians. It's wonderful to see them together." He stops in front of a door and unlocks it. "But, this one is open and should be for a while. Four beds. Meals are served downstairs." He hands the key to Rath.

"Thank you very much."

"Of course. Let me know if you need anything else."

While Deran goes back downstairs, they enter the room and begin arranging their things. One-Eye sets his medical supplies from Carlos on the table and Evermore – who had taken off his scarf earlier – sees them and says, "Medicine?"

"From Carlos," One-Eye says. "He's … teaching me to use other methods besides Sevran's Traits."

"That is very good."

Once they are all settled, they go downstairs for lunch, where an inn helper brings them their meal.

Evermore slowly tucks into his. "The people here are all … very kind."

"They are," Rath says.

One-Eye says, "Seems like the leader is getting in trouble for being welcoming to people from Ullia, though. I can see why she talks to that other leader away from the village."

Flower-Pagu says, "It was troubling to hear about the petition. Why would so many leaders agree?"

Evermore says, "They are only doing what they believe is safest for their people. In light of what has been done … it is understandable."

Rath frowns. "I agree that those who intended to hurt Delphy or other people need to be tried, however, not everyone from Ullia was involved."

One-Eye says, "It's much how they handled people from

Pantha before it joined the Alliance. You could get arrested just for being from there. People assumed you were a pirate or bandit."

"I am very sorry to hear that."

Evermore shakes his head. "But, Ullia is part of the Alliance. We have been nearly since its creation." He sighs. "My mentors have told me they believe Erole only agreed to do so because it would allow him to gain more information from the countries in it."

Bucket-Pagu says, "That is true … but it does mean that everyone else in the Alliance is more aware of his actions."

Well-Pagu says, "Belle."

One-Eye says, "But he's not in the South right now. Although, the Selachuu Military has been helpful."

Rath nods. "They have."

While they are talking, a woman comes down the stairs. She hesitantly waits at the bottom, looking at their group. Evermore sees her and a silent message passes between them. She walks over and bows. "If I may join you for a moment? Evermore, isn't it? I am Laylin."

He smiles a little. "The one who has been asked to make dolphins?"

She flushes, then smiles a little as well. "Yes. You have spoken with Malin, I see. He is kind – all are here – but sometimes … " She raises her hands. "Overwhelming. I sensed another with Erole's Traits had arrived – we all did – and wished to introduce myself to all. May I ask for names?"

They give them and Laylin is amazed. "Pagu as well." She looks at Rath, having recognized his name, but says nothing. "It is good to meet you. Will you stay long?"

Rath says, "I cannot say. We are looking for two that we believe may be here."

"Oh. I hope that you are able to find them. And … perhaps … " She hesitates. "If you have a chance, go to Ma'en Inn –

it is across the lake. I perform with two friends there in the evening." Her eyes sparkle. "Such a thing is new to me, but I find it very fun."

Evermore says, "I would like to see that."

When the rest agree as well, Laylin brightens. "I am glad to hear this." She bows. "I will see you then." As she heads back up the stairs, she looks far lighter.

Evermore's smile fades.

Flower-Pagu notices and asks, "Is something wrong?"

"I am happy for Laylin – and those with her. I wonder why they are here, however, and … as established as they are."

One-Eye says, "It sounds like they weren't done with the map of the Constellation Caves yet. She might be from a group that's still working on it."

"That is true. Then why are they here and not … Perhaps they chose to stay?" He thinks on it.

Across the room, Malin trots into the inn.

Deran sees him first and calls out, "On an errand, Malin?"

"Yup!" He runs to Rath's group. "Leader Leira – I mean, my mom's back."

Rath says, "Thank you for letting us know. Is she available now?"

"Yeah – she says she wants to talk to you, too. Said that Evermore should come along. Or everyone, if you want."

One-Eye says, "I'll stay here. Thought I would take a nap." His Spirit Lion yawns beside him.

The Pagu nod and Bucket-Pagu says, "That sounds like a really good idea! We'll stay, too."

Evermore says, "I will go."

Malin says, "Great. Follow me!"

It does not take them long to reach a two-story home with waterfalls running out of both sides. Malin pokes his head through the curtain covering the doorway. "Mom! Rath and Evermore are here!"

"Thank you, dear!"

Leira is sitting at her desk. The light inside is dim, but enough to see by. As she stands to greet them, she asks, "Is it too bright for you, Evermore?"

Evermore – who had put his scarf back on while they traveled – pulls it down, testing, then takes it off. "No. It is perfect."

"I am glad to hear that." She extends her hand. "It's good to properly meet you both." Evermore shakes it after a moment of hesitation. "I hope to meet the others that are with you as well."

After she shakes Rath's hand, he says, "They are currently resting."

She nods. "It is a bit of a walk to our small village. Most of us like it that way." She pauses as if to say more, then says instead, "Right. My son tells me that you're looking for someone. I'm happy to help if I can."

"Thank you. May we look at the Paradi Messenger Registry? We believe it is possible that she and her bird partner have begun work here in the past month."

"Of course." Leira walks across the room to retrieve a bound book. She sets it down on the desk and opens it. "I don't think we've gotten anyone in that time frame, but you're welcome to look. With the petition, it's very possible I forgot."

"Thank you very much." Rath and Evermore look over the names, starting with the date when *PearlHeart* arrived at Priage Port. When they reach the end, both frown. "I am afraid they are not listed here. I appreciate you allowing us to see this."

"Definitely." Leira takes it up, shutting it. After she returns it to the shelf, she says, "May I ask what her and her partner's names are? If they passed through here, I'm sure someone around would know."

"I see. Their names are Melody and Demeter."

Leira's face lights with surprise and her son dashes in at that moment, bouncing near the desk in excitement. "That's the harpist! And her amazing Paradi bird!"

"It is!" Leira says, laughing. "They are both wonderful."

Evermore looks hopeful. "Then … they are here?"

"Yes! She, Demeter, and Laylin perform at Ma'en Inn across the lake. Have you met Laylin?"

Rath says, "Yes, just before we came here. She asked that we see her perform with her friends there."

"Perfect! This has all worked out then. Now, I can't say where Melody and Demeter go otherwise. She seemed a little troubled when I spoke with her the day she arrived in our village … oh, well, it would have been around two weeks ago."

"That is when *PearlHeart* – my ship – arrived at Priage and they disembarked."

Evermore says, "However, Melody had told others she and Demeter would be sailing to Paradi, not staying on Delphy."

Leira's eyebrows go up. "Really? I wonder why that is." She shrugs. "Well, she's a little quiet, but I can tell she's a strong girl. I'm sure she has her reasoning. Like I said, I don't know where she goes when she's not performing – my husband says it's likely she's off practicing where prying ears can't hear her. With how she plays, I wouldn't doubt she practices quite a bit. I would say your best bet of finding her is tonight when she and Demeter perform with Laylin."

Rath says, "I understand. Thank you again for your help."

"Defintely. I'm just glad we knew who you were looking for."

They thank Leira and Malin one more time, then leave.

Evermore puts back on his scarf to protect his eyes. He exhales. "I am relieved to hear they are indeed here."

"I am as well. Was there anywhere you wished to go before the performance tonight?" Rath thinks. "Actually, it may be best if we find Ma'en Inn beforehand."

"I agree."

They walk along the lake. Nearby, villagers are doing laundry or milling grain or cooking. One woman offers them some small sweet pastries and will not take their refusal, so both Rath and Evermore walk away with one each, happily eating.

After Evermore finishes his, he looks around and says, "So, Melody and Demeter are in a village like this. It is very peaceful here."

"I believe so as well. When I was training to be a councilman, I was able to visit here only once, however, I wished to do so again."

"I am glad you are able to then."

When they reach the other side of the lake, they find a wide, two-story building with a sign that reads *Ma'en Inn*.

Evermore says, "It will be hard to wait for tonight."

They continue to walk around, seeing more of the village

One of the streams has a bridge with designs carved in it depicting the ocean and dolphins. While Rath is looking at it, a group of childen – with Malin near the front – run up. As they run past, Malin calls amid his laughter, "Hey Rath, Evermore!"

Right afterward, the boy is tackled to the ground by one of his friends. They all laugh, then begin talking about what sorts of games to play next.

Evermore is quiet for a moment, then – as he and Rath continue on – he asks, "Did you have a childhood like that?"

"Ah – I cannot say I was as … rambunctious, but I did travel with the Pagu on Grandmother's island frequently and they would ask me to play games with them. We would talk for long periods of time, too, and often Carlos would wake me up for meals when I fell asleep while with them."

Evermore smiles briefly, then says, "It is very different on Ullia. It is training and learning that the more you bonded with one another, the more likely it would be that Erole would put you on different assignments. I … did not see my mother very often and I never knew my father – such things are also common on Ullia – so you bringing me her letter meant more to me than I can say." His cheek is wet.

Rath sees and says, "I am glad to hear that. I am sorry to hear that bonds are discouraged."

"That is what makes *PearlHeart* so different. I will forever be grateful for having been assigned to your crew."

"I as well. I am truly glad that I met you."

On their way back to the inn, they are given a basket of fruit native to this part of Delphy which they take back to the others.

When they arrive at Pin'et Inn, they offer one to Deran who takes it and thanks them, then they go up to their room.

One-Eye and the Pagu are awake now and playing cards with each other. One-Eye's Spirit Lion is also playing, with One-Eye adjusting his cards based on the Lion's instructions.

After one more turn, the Lion wins.

One-Eye pets him. "Yeah. Good job."

Flower-Pagu says, "Excellent job, Spirit Lion!"

The Lion starts grooming.

Rath, who had been about to offer them fruit, stops suddenly, surprised. Evermore says, "Your Spirit Lion was playing as well?"

One-Eye says, "Yeah. We found a way to."

While they eat the fruit Rath and Evermore brought, One-Eye says, "What'd you find out from the leader?"

"Melody and Demeter are here. Leader Leira says they perform at Ma'en Inn each night with Laylin. Evermore and I found where it is."

One-Eye nods. "That's the same one Laylin already invited us to. So Melody and Demeter are her friends. Were they there now?"

"No. We were told they are not often seen in the village outside of performances and that our best chance was to attend the one tonight."

"That's strange."

Evermore wraps his scarf back around his waist. "Not terribly. Melody has told me she would do something similar on Paradi and go into the caves there to practice alone. It seems the acoustics are good inside them as well."

After they finish eating, Rath picks up the basket, saying, "I thought I would offer the rest to those upstairs."

Evermore stands. "I would like to go with you as well, if that is all right."

One-Eye says, nodding to his Spirit Lion, "We thought we would explore the village, then be back later tonight. Are we eating at that inn for dinner?"

Rath says, "I would like to."

Bucket-Pagu says, "We thought we'd go sit by the lake for a while. It looks very relaxing." They wiggle their feet. "But, I'm really looking forward to this evening!"

Flower-Pagu twirls. "I can't wait!"

Well-Pagu says, "Event."

Rath says, "It is. And neither can I."

While One-Eye, his Lion, and the Pagu go outside, Rath and Evermore go up the next set of stairs to the third floor. After Rath knocks, a man in clothes similar to Evermore's answers the door. "Yes?"

Rath explains that they have brought fruit to share and the man brightens. He takes the basket. "Thank you very much." He nods to both of them. "Rath and Evermore? Laylin has told us about you. I am Vin. It is good to meet you."

They both reply, agreeing, then Evermore says, "Is Laylin here?"

Vin passes the basket to someone else who has approached the door in curiosity. "No. She is already at Ma'en Inn for her performance. She often goes early to steady her nerves."

"I had hoped to ask her about two friends of ours. We have been looking for them and discovered they perform with her."

"Oh. Do you mean Melody and Demeter? They are talented musicians."

"Are they all right?"

Vin pauses. Something passes between him and Evermore, then he nods slowly. "Yes. I believe so. However, Laylin said Melody was acting strange late yesterday evening and that Demeter had left for a long time. Even before that, Melody seemed concerned about something, but she did not share it with Laylin."

Rath says, "Leader Leira said Melody seemed troubled as well."

Evermore says, "It seems you all have been here for some time. Why is that?"

Vin's eyebrows go up. He hesitates. "Negotiations have been slow in this part of the Constellation Caves – we are all from the group tasked with creating our part of the map in Solene City, however we have since been banned by their leader. We have been told a Selachuu soldier will inform us when we will be allowed to enter the Constellation Caves in that area again."

Rath says, "I hope that you are able to soon."

Vin blinks. "Do you really? You are very kind." He studies Rath for a moment, then says, "I am glad that I met you both. Please let us know if there is anything that we may do. This village has been kind to us and we would like to do the same for others."

"Of course. Thank you."

As they go back to their room, Evermore seems thoughtful and sits by the window while Rath reads on his bed.

One-Eye, his Lion, and the Pagu return later, then they all travel together to Ma'en Inn for dinner.

Rath, who had been reading in *A Dolphin's Journey* earlier, is speaking with the Pagu, saying, "I just finished chapter four!"

Bucket-Pagu looks excited. "We're almost all there, too! Then we can have our first book club meeting!"

"Yes!"

Evermore asks One-Eye, "Did you find anything of interest?"

"Yeah. Everywhere we go is different from Pantha. Better."

"I could say the same for Ullia."

One-Eye's eye narrows.

Evermore raises his hand. "I do not mean to say they are the same. Or … comparable. Just that I have a similar feeling."

One-Eye nods. They are both quiet while Rath and the Pagu talk to one another until One-Eye says, "I'm not going to compare either, but it sounds like Ullia and its god treat you badly."

"They do."

For a brief moment, One-Eye's look loosens. "And … at least I don't have to return to my country every year."

"I had thought that I would be this year as well – late, though it was. It surprised me greatly when I remained on Delphy instead."

"I bet."

They fall into another silence, but seem more relaxed than before.

20

When they arrive, a crowd is already gathering outside with people talking excitedly. They join it and steadily move forward. Inside, the proprietor is speaking loudly. "Everyone – find a seat in the common room! We'll begin soon!"

Evermore says, "There are many people." He has taken off his scarf due to the dim lighting.

Rath says, "There are. I believe I see an available table over there." The Pagu, who have been sitting on his shoulder to not get lost in the crowd, agree.

They begin to make their way toward it, passing many full tables. A handful of people dressed in dark clothes are standing at the back of the room, scarves wrapped around their waists.

After Rath's group reaches the table and sits down, Evermore looks at the stage nervously. "When is it set to begin?"

Rath says, "The sign outside said it would start at seven.

However, dinner will be served now, at six."

Once the rest of the crowd gets settled, servers come around bearing meals. Little bowls go to Well-Pagu, Bucket-Pagu, and Flower-Pagu.

Bucket-Pagu and Flower-Pagu say, "Thank you!" and Well-Pagu says, "Thank!"

The man smiles. "You're welcome. I don't think I've ever seen Pagu here – I hope you enjoy the meal and the performance!"

While Rath and One-Eye begin to eat theirs, talking with one another, and the Pagu do the same, Evermore continues to glance at the stage as he eats.

As it gets closer to seven and the group is finishing their meals, the stage has remained empty and he frowns.

He hears a voice behind him. "Evermore."

When he turns, he sees Laylin is there. She has a panicked expression. "Could you … come with me?"

"Is something wrong? We could all help," he says. The others, who have since noticed her arrival, nod.

Laylin bites her lip. "All right. Over here, please." She walks away, slipping between the tables.

They follow her to a dark area backstage where she tells them, "Melody and Demeter have not arrived."

Evermore says, "Do you have any idea where they would be?"

"I do not. I tried sensing through the crowd, but … there are too many people. And others from Paradi here, besides. I do not understand. They have never done this."

"If they promised to be here, then they would be. If they are not here, they must be outside. Perhaps where they practice."

"That is a good thought. I do not know where that would be, however." She pauses. "Although … much of the village is here – fewer people would be outside. It would be easier to sense her now, I believe."

"Then I will do so."

Laylin peers through the stage curtain at the crowd. "I suppose I will … do my best here." She sighs and puts out both her hands, palms up. They all see a small dolphin made out of electricity leap from one hand to the other. It dives into her palm with an electric 'splash'.

Rath says, "That is beautiful."

She smiles. "Thank you. I have been practicing for Malin. The show is not set to start for another fifteen minutes. If you are able to find Melody and Demeter before then, we will begin as normal – if not, I will go out alone."

Evermore says, "We will find them, Laylin."

She thanks them, then shows them to a side door from the backstage area.

Once outside, One-Eye says, "Where do we start?"

Evermore says, "I believe the outskirts – perhaps the forest. It is more quiet there."

They start toward the edge of the bowl, following the nearest stream.

After they go up the hill and enter the forest, Evermore says, "I will try to sense them now," and he presses his bare foot into the grass. A yellow pulse goes through the ground and up the tree branches, making the leaves flash. They all wait quietly while Evermore processes it. "Not here."

When they reach the edge of where Evermore previously sensed, he sends out another pulse. "Not here, either," he says, moving ahead.

He does two more and on the fifth, he stops. "I sense them. Here!" The others follow him further into the forest.

Soon, they hear a voice ahead say, "I don't know, Demeter. It sounds like whoever it was is dangerous. But … if Evermore and Rath are down there … "

"*Caw!*"

"Th-Then, we'll do it."

Melody, speaking with Demeter on her shoulder, is standing next to an open hatch in the ground with a staircase leading to the lower tunnels.

Just as she is about to take her first step, Evermore grips her arm. "Melody, what are you doing?"

She jolts in surprise, then turns. "Evermore!" She looks behind him. "Rath! Everyone." She starts to tear up and rubs her eyes with her sleeve. Her harp case is slung around her back. "I-I thought … Demeter told me … "

Her bird partner gives them all a questioning look.

Evermore says, "It is all right. *We* are all right." Melody sniffles, but begins to calm down. "Right now, you need to help Laylin. She is alone at Ma'en Inn."

Melody gasps. "The performance! With everything … I forgot … " She rubs her eyes again. "Y-You're right. I can explain later. I'm just truly glad everyone is okay and that I don't have to … " She looks down at the shaft fearfully. Evermore kneels and shuts the hatch, then Melody says to the group, "I-I'm sorry. Let's go."

They move quickly to make it back to the inn in time. When they reach it, they go in through side door, Melody gives them a breathless farewell, then heads for the stage with Demeter on her shoulder. The group returns to their table just as the the performers walk out.

Laylin, very much relieved, sits on a stool beside Melody, who is seated with her harp propped on her knee. Demeter is on her shoulder, looking regal.

Melody lifts her free hand and plucks the first string.

After a few more notes, she begins to sing. Demeter trills beneath her voice, creating a harmony.

They tell a story about a Paradi bird flying through a storm, a speck of color among the gray, telling of the rainbow to come at the rain's end.

Beside Melody, Laylin has her hands lifted, creating the

scenes with her traits. The dim lights make her electricity glow even brighter. A small bird travels around the stage, sweeping around small droplets of rain and rising higher until it disappears in a shaft of light. A rainbow appears over them. Melody plays her final chord and all goes silent as the glowing arch fades.

As soon as it does, the crowd begins to applaud. Melody flushes at the whistles, but smiles in full when her eyes meet Evermore's and the rest at the table.

Rath and One-Eye clap while the Pagu stand on the table, doing the same. Evermore, who was too stunned to do anything for a moment, claps softly as well. He holds his hands in his lap as Melody, Demeter, and Laylin approach them.

He says, "I have never seen Erole's Traits used so delicately, Laylin." She looks appreciative. Evermore then turns to Melody. "It was beautiful," he says simply.

Hugging her harp close, Melody says, "Thank you. And everyone, for coming." She suddenly frowns. "I'm sorry to have worried everyone. And you especially, Laylin, for being late."

She shakes her head. "It all came out right."

Melody brightens. "It did." Turning to the group again, she says, "May we talk now? It's been a long day and I think I may go to sleep right after. I'm staying here at Ma'en Inn. Are you all as well?"

One-Eye says, "No, we're at Pin'et Inn across the lake."

"The same one that Laylin is at! Then, why … "

"We were looking for you. My Lion and I saw Demeter yesterday night in the forest near Priage. Knew you'd have to be somewhere on Delphy, but thought you had gone to Paradi." Melody strokes Demeter's chest. "We meant to. Demeter told me she saw you – and Rath – last night. That was why we … Well, we'll go with you to Pin'et Inn and let's talk there, if that's all right?"

While Laylin stays to speak with those from her group of the Ullian Spies who came to the performance, Rath and the others leave. The proprietor gives Melody and Demeter a wave as they do, thanking them for the performance.

Since the last time they were out, the sky has grown darker. Many Delphaen crystals have been dipped in water, causing them to glow. The group arrives at Pin'et Inn and go up to their room.

Melody sits on the bed next to Evermore's as she says, "I'll talk to Deran. It seems inappropriate to rent the room at Ma'en Inn when there's an extra bed here." Then she takes a deep breath and begins.

She starts with how she saw Evermore off at Priage and how he entered the Ullian ship like he did every year during the Winter, which then disappeared beneath the waves. "Demeter and I always watch until we can't see the ship anymore – "

Evermore turns to her quickly. "You do?"

Melody flushes. Demeter fluffs out her feathers. "Of course. But this time, we didn't see you go south. Demeter flew over the water and was sure that you were heading down. At first we worried that the ship had crashed or … We weren't sure. We finally asked a Selachuu soldier and he dove underneath, but said that no ship was there. However, he had heard there were several underground passages that lead to caves underneath Delphy. Demeter and I decided to wait at least the night to hear something. We couldn't go to Paradi, not knowing if you were all right."

"You should have gone, even so."

Melody frowns for a moment, then continues, "We ended up staying longer than I thought we would, but I wasn't sure what to do and the next ship to Paradi wouldn't be until the end of the week. Demeter told me she had seen a small village to the north of Priage, so we came here. Then, we started hearing about how the Ullian Spies were causing the cracks.

But, Leader Leira began welcoming them when they started to arrive in Ľoeile Village – I thought it was really kind of her. I met Laylin and when I told her I played the harp, she wanted to hear. She showed me what she could do with Erole's Traits with my music and we both decided to start performing at Ma'en Inn. People really seem to like it. I think it's made them feel safer around the Ullian Spies, too."

"I would agree," Evermore says. "However, why were you in the forest earlier? With the hatch … "

"Sometimes, Demeter would go out and look for you, thinking you might be with one of the groups from the Ullian Spies. Two days ago, she saw someone exit out of a hatch in the ground and decided to keep watch over the area in case you or another spy came out. Neither of us expected someone to take Rath down there. Demeter came back immediately and we were both worried about what had happened. We thought of going to the Selachuu soldiers again – and almost did – when Demeter suggested that we look for other hatches in the ground. She had just found another today. We almost went down it when you arrived."

"Why? What did you intend to do?"

"I-I wasn't sure. Demeter was ready to do whatever was needed to make sure you both were safe." She sighs. "I'm just glad that everyone is all right. But, where were you, Evermore? And where did that man take Rath?"

Evermore says, "To the lowest caves in Delphy. It is where I have been this entire time. The Ullian ship you saw did not take me south to Ullia, but to the underground tunnels the Selachuu soldier spoke of." He pauses. "It makes me wonder how long they have been looking into this." He shakes his head, continuing, "I was with Erole, telling him of our journey on *PearlHeart* to Draconi and finding Ara's Frost Flower seed. He was very upset when I did not return to Ullia last year to give my report."

"I'm so sorry."

"A man from Delphy who is loyal to Erole was tasked by my god to take Rath. Erole was very interested when he heard those with his traits are unable to sense him." He breathes deep. "I am very glad that others came in time so that Rath was never seen by Erole." He frowns suddenly. "That is, I do not believe he did."

The Pagu, who had been sitting in Rath's lap, speak. Flower-Pagu says, "He didn't. He sensed … something, but he was not sure what."

Bucket-Pagu says, "But, he will not try to look for Rath now."

Well-Pagu says, "Left."

Evermore sighs. "I am very glad to hear that." He turns to Melody. "You have been doing tremendous things here. I am sure that you are a large part of why the Ullian Spies have been so welcomed here and this village has not signed the petition to ban us."

Melody shakes her head, flushing. "No, no – Leader Leira is the one who did that."

A small smile lifts Evermore's lips. "And you have shown them how beautiful Erole's Traits can be with your music – you and Laylin both. Thank you."

Melody swallows, but nods.

Afterward, she officially moves her and Demeter's things from Ma'en Inn to Pin'et Inn and into the room Rath and the others are sharing. Laylin is back at that time and they talk briefly before they all retire to their rooms.

21

The next day, Rath, Melody, and Demeter are looking at a painting in the lobby area.

Melody clasps her hands together. "Oh, I thought it was your mother's!"

"Yes. I was very surprised to see it here."

At that moment, the door opens and Deran says, "Leader Leira, Malin! How can I help you?"

They look over to see the two enter. "We're here to see Melody, Demeter, and Laylin," Leira says.

Seeing Melody and Demeter, Malin says, "You both were amazing last night!"

"Oh! Thank you," she says while Demeter lifts her head gracefully.

Deran smiles. "I'll get Laylin. One moment."

After he returns, Leira speaks with her, Melody, and Demeter. Malin, meanwhile, plays a board game with Rath, One-Eye, and the Pagu. Evermore stands by, watching.

Malin takes his turn. "Laylin showed me the dolphin she made last night again! It was so neat!"

Rath says, "I agree."

One-Eye glances down at his Spirit Lion, who is looking at the discussion at the table across the room. He says to the Lion, "We'll find out if it has to do with us."

The Lion does a tight circle and lies down, but keeps his ears angled forward.

Just as Malin wins the game, Leira and the others walk up to them. Melody looks nervous, Demeter is preening, and Laylin seems thoughtful. Evermore steps away from the wall, joining them as well.

Leira asks her son, "Did you have fun?"

"Definitely! I won!"

She laughs. "That's great!" She picks him up, then says to the others, "I've asked Melody, Demeter, and Laylin if they would do something for me. However, they had a feeling – and I agree – that if we go through with it, you'd all like to come with." She grins. "I thought we'd do another performance, but this time for the people of Ymira Town. They're one of the towns who signed the petition. I thought seeing someone from the Ullian Spies working together with others would inspire them to pull their name from the ban. We'd stay here, of course – people from Ullia are not currently allowed in Ymira – and invite Leader Nel and his people. If it goes well with them, I thought maybe we'd send you all to other parts in Delphy. I don't know what your plans were, so I hope it wouldn't be too out of the way."

Rath says, "We would be able to. The wedding we are going to is at the end of the month, in Meridelle Village."

"That's not too far. And I'll make sure anywhere else I send you to isn't either. I'll tell you more about that later – I just wanted to let you know that it would be a possibility. But, for now, we'll focus on the performance here. It'll be this evening

– same time as last night – but we'll have it outside instead. That way our whole village as well as his – or, anyone that shows up – will have room. We'll have to prepare a lot more food depending on who all is coming, which … is what I need to go do right now."

"Is there anything that can be done to help?" Rath asks.

Leira blinks. "Well." She smiles. "Thank you very much. I'll give it some thought – all of this is dependent on Leader Nel's acceptance. I'm going to send him a Delphaen message right now. I'll let you know what he says and we'll go from there."

Afterward, she and Malin leave and the rest go their separate ways – Rath and the Pagu to have their book club in their room upstairs, One-Eye and his Lion to go for a walk, and Melody and Demeter to practice outside in the forest. Before they leave, Melody takes Evermore's hand. "I promise we'll stay within reach."

"I trust you."

Once she and Demeter have left, he starts to go back inside, then sees Laylin sitting on a bench in the shade of the inn's awning. She is openly practicing new electrical shapes with her traits.

When Evermore sits down with her, she tells him, "I am very excited for this. I have grown to … quite enjoy these performances. It is satisfying when others do as well."

"You cannot stay here in this village, Laylin."

The electric dolphin disappears. She closes her hands. "I realize this. I will leave when negotiations are finished to perform my task creating the map of the Constellation Caves. I believe our piece is to be the last part. However … I have grown to like this place – and the people especially. They are all so welcoming."

Evermore nods.

For a moment, they sense around them the different

people about their daily business, their light voices carrying over the sound of the breeze through the tall grass and the lap of the lake around the shore.

Laylin says, "What of you? Will you … " She inclines her head in the direction where Melody and Demeter left.

Evermore's cheeks color a little, but he shakes his head. "No. Not while Ullia is the way it is."

"I understand."

When the others return, Laylin stays outside while Evermore joins them inside for lunch.

One-Eye asks Rath and the Pagu, "How was your … book club?"

Flower-Pagu says, "It was amazing!"

Bucket-Pagu says, "I really enjoyed hearing everyone's input."

Well-Pagu says, "Next."

Rath says, "I agree. It was truly wonderful. And, I cannot wait for the next one as well, Well-Pagu. How was your walk with your Spirit Lion, One-Eye, if I may ask?"

"Good. We're looking forward to running again, though." The Lion nods in fervent agreement.

Across the table, Evermore asks Melody, "Your practice went well?"

"Yes! I'm … I'm really looking forward to tonight. If we do it, that is." Demeter's eyes gleam.

They have just finished when the door opens and Leira comes in. She sees them and says, "Good. You're here. I just spoke with Laylin outside. Leader Nel has agreed to come." She holds up a hand. "Now, I can't guarantee how many from his town will – he wasn't sure either – but at the very least he'll get to see what you three have created. Thank you again for agreeing."

"Of course!" Melody says.

Leira looks over the whole group. "Now, you had asked

what you all might do." She pulls out a list, chuckling a little. "Quite a few things, actually. Would you mind?"

Rath takes it. "Not at all."

After she leaves, they all look over the list.

One-Eye says, "That's a lot of things."

"Indeed," Rath says.

They start with the Weaver's Guild for blankets that people can sit on. Well-Pagu spots the building quickly.

"Definitely," the Lead Weaver says. "I was wondering if we would be needed. It's passed through the whole village what you and Laylin are doing, Melody and Demeter. Thank you."

"You're welcome," she says and her bird partner gives a nod.

They go to the village hall for chairs and tables, then to a local craftswoman for some of the decorations.

While they go around the village, a few Spirit Dolphins pass by, offering to chat with One-Eye's Spirit Lion, but he only talks a little, then focuses on the task at hand. The Dolphins grin and swim off.

It takes them two hours to get through all of the items on the list and after they do, they return to Leira's home to inform her.

As Rath hands the list to her, she says, "Thank you for all of your help. It's greatly appreciated." She sits back. "I have the food sorted out and I even heard from Leader Nel that at least two or three people from his town are interested in coming tonight. If they could just see Melody, Demeter, and Laylin together, I'm sure they'll change their minds." She shakes her head, then leans forward. "Well, I'll release you from duties. I don't expect you all to work tonight either – minus you, Melody and Demeter – so relax and enjoy yourselves."

After they exit, Melody says, "Demeter and I are going to go practice. We'll probably be gone until this evening, so we'll see everyone then." Demeter gives an affirmative "Caw!"

Evermore says, "I will speak with Laylin and those in her group upstairs. We have not spoken at length since we arrived."

Flower-Pagu says, nodding to Bucket-Pagu and Well-Pagu, "We thought we would fly around the village some more, then relax by the lake."

Bucket-Pagu says, "I'm really glad we've gotten to see so much of it already!"

"Explore," Well-Pagu says.

While they leave, One-Eye says to Rath, "Would you have time now? My Spirit Lion wants to know if you would play a board game with him."

"I would love to." One-Eye gestures to the Lion and Rath says, "Thank you very much for inviting me."

The Lion paws the ground in excitement. Without waiting for them, he bounds off toward the inn.

One-Eye laughs. "He's excited. Come on."

In their room, they set up a board game from Delphy using shells and Delphaen crystals in various shapes. Rath and the Spirit Lion sit across from one another, with One-Eye in between them.

"He's going to tell me the moves he wants to do, then I'll do them," One-Eye says.

"I understand," Rath says. "I am truly excited for this."

The Lion's eyes brighten. Then he grows serious and says something to One-Eye, who nods and moves a crystal. Rath thinks, then does so as well.

They play back and forth for half an hour until, on Rath's next turn, he pauses. He smiles and, looking straight in front of him, says, "Excellent job, One-Eye's Spirit Lion."

The Lion licks his paw. One-Eye laughs beside him. "He says you did well, too."

Rath's eyebrows go up. "Ah, thank you."

"He's asking if you want to play again?" One-Eye translates.

"Yes, please."

They play for much of the afternoon, each taking wins. Closer to evening, One-Eye tells Rath, "He's going to sleep a little now. Do you want to play a few rounds with me?"

"I would love to."

While his Spirit Lion sleeps next to them, peaceful in the setting sun, One-Eye and Rath play. After a few more moves, One-Eye begins to say something, then does not. It is only when they have played several rounds, each winning some, and are packing away the board game that One-Eye lightly touches Rath's hand, who stops, looking at him quickly.

One-Eye flushes and glances to his left. "He really appreciated that. My Spirit Lion. I think … it meant a lot to him."

"I am very glad to hear that. I truly enjoyed playing with him. And with you."

"Me too."

Just as One-Eye's Spirit Lion is rousing from his nap, the others enter the room and they all get ready to leave.

The Pagu change into clothes more befitting an evening concert. Flower-Pagu does a spin. "What do you think?"

Bucket-Pagu says, "We thought it would be nice to dress up."

Well-Pagu adjusts their hat. "Appropriate."

Rath nods. "I agree. It is very appropriate for the occasion."

When they go down to the lobby, Deran meets them at the front doors. "Thought I'd go out there, too. Have my daughter minding the inn for anyone who'll be inside, but" – he chuckles – "I can't imagine there will be many."

Outside, the supplies they helped gather – the blankets, chairs, and tables for the food – have been set up and others have done all they can to make the village more festive. Curling blue-green ribbons are strung in between the homes and Delphaen crystals have been placed in baskets near the lake.

As their group goes toward the stage, the crowd becomes more dense. Already, people have lined up for food and groups sit on the blankets, awaiting the performance. It will be held on a small stage made up of a blanket, two stools, and strung Delphaen crystals twinkling in the late evening light.

As Rath looks at it, One-Eye takes his hand. "Let's get the food for everyone."

"Of course."

Evermore glances at the two of them, then says, "The Honored Pagu and I shall secure the blanket."

Flower-Pagu says, "We'll select a really pretty one!"

Rath smiles. "Thank you, everyone." Then, with One-Eye and the Spirit Lion beside him, they leave to join one of the lines.

Afterward, they find Evermore and the Pagu on one of the blankets. They sit down and open up the food baskets, then begin to pass them around. Some of the fruit they had earlier – as well as the sweet pastries – are inside. There are also small bread rolls and Delphy Berries.

As they eat, Rath, One-Eye, and the Pagu share with Evermore their journey on Delphy so far which he had not heard, traveling with Franz and Velt, reuniting with Carlos and Phillip, and staying at Garreth's home for a time.

Evermore listens. He frowns, however, when they finish. "There is not much I can share. I have been in Erole's presence during all of the time you spoke of." He hesitates. "I am truly so sorry, for all that my people have done."

"You are not responsible," Rath says.

One-Eye says, "If anything, you helped us save Rath. Thank you."

Evermore's head raises in surprise. He pauses, then nods as he slowly finishes his food.

Almost as soon as he does, a voice calls from the direction of the stage, "Thank you all for coming!"

They turn to see Leira there. "I especially wish to thank Leader Nel and those from Ymira Town who have joined us," she says, nodding to a group near the front. "Now – please welcome Melody, Demeter, and Laylin who will be giving a special performance tonight."

Everyone claps as she leaves the stage, then Melody, with Demeter on her shoulder, and Laylin walk on.

They both sit on their stools, look at each other once, then begin.

It is a different song than they played the previous night – about a cave with glowing gems and bright lights from openings above.

Evermore tenses, then relaxes.

Laylin creates the lights and small crystals to glow around her and Melody. Demeter trills under Melody's long sung note and reverberating harp chord, then they let it fade as Laylin's light disappears, too.

After a beat, the audience applauds. Melody and Laylin stand and bow, then exit.

Evermore is still looking at the stage long after they have left.

One-Eye says, "It was beautiful."

Rath nods next to him. "It was."

The Pagu sigh, having greatly enjoyed it.

Melody and Demeter join them. She sits by Evermore and as soon as she does, he reaches out his hand to gently touch hers. "That was the first song you and Demeter played for me."

Melody blushes, then turns her hand around and squeezes his. "It's my favorite."

"Mine as well."

For the rest of the evening, people stay on the blankets and talk, enjoying the cool breeze in the valley.

As it grows darker and the group is thinking of leaving, Leira and Nel approach them. Laylin is behind them.

Leira says, "If I could have a minute of all of your time?" Rath says, "Of course."

After they sit on the blanket, Nel says, "I would first like to apologize for my behavior the previous day. It is not how I wish to present myself. And while this performance was wonderful, my feelings have not changed. We will not take ourselves off of the petition. Laylin, I hope you know that it is not against you personally. It is just what I believe to be the safest for our town at the moment."

She nods.

"Now, before we signed the petition, we *did* allow the Ullian Spies there to complete their task – create the map of the Constellation Caves as has been ordered by their god, Erole." He shakes his head. "Those fools in other parts of Delphy, however, have *not* allowed even that and gone through with their petition as well, creating a standstill. That" – he clears his throat – "is something I *can* help you with."

Laylin's eyes widen. "Truly?"

He smiles more kindly at her. "Yes." He nods to Leira. "To my knowledge, we can grant you temporary access on the basis of us vouching for you on a work-related aspect that we think would benefit Delphy overall. It takes two leaders to sign off on it. I am willing to do this with Leira."

Laylin brings her hand up to her chest. "That would be … Thank you very much. I will not forget this."

"And I hope you will not forget us," Nel says.

Leira continues, "My original plan had been to send all of you off to another place, but … Nel talked me out of it, saying perhaps that would be something better for the future, when all of the business with the Constellation Caves is over and not as a way to convince the people of Delphy to allow the Ullian Spies to be in them."

Nel says, "After all, as fine of a performance as it was, it is only one example and while there are sure to be spies that mean no harm, there certainly are those that do. Not that we haven't had trouble with the people of our own country as well."

Leira sighs. "That's something else … But first, Laylin, do you think you and your group would be willing to go back to Solene City? I remember you telling me that was the area you and your group were assigned to. I've already notified the Selachuu soldier that will travel with you of our plan and he's agreed to come tomorrow morning to see you get there." She frowns. "It seems … there was a sizeable crack not too long ago that's made access to the Constellation Caves possible from inside the city instead of the regular entrances on the coastline. Leader Minta is furious about it. It seems it's still being repaired, but for now … it's an entrance."

For a moment, Laylin looks pained. "I recall its creation." She nods. "It would be more efficient than traveling to the coast. I will inform the others that we will travel there tomorrow morning to complete our task."

"Great." Leira looks to the others. "Did you have any idea of what you will do?"

Melody says, "If it's all right with everyone, I want to go with. I want to support you, Laylin, and everyone."

She looks touched. "Thank you, Melody."

Evermore says, "As will I."

One-Eye and the Pagu nod and Rath says, "I agree. I would also like to see if there is anything that can be done to help. It concerns me there is such a large crack there."

Leira smiles a little. "I thought you all might. Let us know if you need anything for the journey."

"Thank you."

After they take care of their food baskets and blanket, they try to help take down the tables, stage, and other decorations put up for the night, but Leira sends them off. "No, no – we have this and you've got to wake up early tomorrow. It'll be a long way to Solene City and no waterways that ships are allowed on either."

Malin says, "We can do it!"

"It's about bedtime for you, too, dear."

"Aww … "

While the rest of the village cleans up, the group returns to Pin'et Inn, walking next to the glowing Delphaen crystals.

22

At dawn, Laylin knocks on their door.

The group is already awake and have their packs on. Laylin sees this and nods approvingly. "The Selachuu soldier has arrived. It is time to leave."

When they reach the common room, they see the soldier and the Ullian spies speaking with Deran, who is saying, "It was truly a pleasure to have you all." He sees Rath's group and says, "And you all as well. Take care on your journey."

"Thank you," Rath says.

Many of the villagers, including Leira and Malin come out to see them off.

Leira gives Rath the agreement signed by her and Nel, saying, "Take care. And good luck."

Malin says, "Please come again! I want to see a chimpanzee next time, Laylin!"

She hesitates. "I hope to see you again, too, Malin."

They follow the streams out of the valley, then enter the

surrounding forest.

After they have traveled for a few hours, they have breakfast in a clearing. Rath looks up at the sky through the branches of the trees around them.

He suddenly sees a hand in front of him. "Lance," the soldier says in introduction. As Rath shakes his hand, he says, "Forgot to tell you earlier. Laylin and the others already know, but I figured your group didn't. Rath, correct?"

"Yes. It is good to meet you. Thank you for traveling with us."

"Pleasure."

As they continue on, the forest becomes more dense and the Pagu see some mushrooms at the base of the trees. Lance sees them too and nods. "Yeah. They're edible," he says, then picks a few to tuck into his bag.

One-Eye stares at him for a moment.

Lance sees and shrugs. "You learn a few things when you've been stationed here for a while. I do mushroom foraging in my off-hours."

"How long have you been on Delphy?"

"Eight years now? I like it a lot. Might as well be home for me. Is it the same for you?"

"Don't know. My citizenship is from Pantha."

"You can change that, you know. I suggested it to the others, too, who've really taken to Delphy. No petition can change anything like that – especially if it has Marchand's approval."

"Have you?"

"Thinking about it. It's a bit of a decision. I'd still be with the military, of course, and I'd still be required to be on Selachuu at times, but when I get older? Or want to retire? I think I'd like to stay on Delphy."

One-Eye nods, thinking. "I'm on the ocean most of the year – I don't see how it would be worth it."

"That makes sense – but, like I said, for later? Either way, it's nice to have a more stable home to come back to."

They stop again for lunch. One-Eye is sitting next to Rath with his Lion pacing beside him when he finally says, "What's the process to gain citizenship here?"

Rath puts down the fruit he was eating and opens his mouth to answer when he suddenly flushes. "I ... I am so sorry, One-Eye."

"Why?"

"Marchand said to ask if you would like to live on Delphy and I have not. He wished to let you know that he would approve it and that my father would also." He turns a deeper shade of red. "I apologize, I have not answered your original question."

"It's fine. So I'd need their approval."

"Yes. And to fill out paperwork."

One-Eye sighs. "Of course."

"Then, it would need to be processed so that your address is formally changed."

One-Eye begins to nod, then stops. "Your address isn't on Delphy, is it?"

"No, it is not. Actually, it is on my grandmother's island. However, given it is part of Marchand's land, I am still considered a citizen of Delphy. I was very relieved to hear as such."

"Your grandmother's island ... " One-Eye pauses. His Lion peers up at him.

"Would you like me to direct you to where to find the paperwork?"

"No – not right now. I'm still thinking." He shakes his head. "It would make it easier to stay here over the Winters – I have to fill out extra paperwork with my employer because of being from Pantha – but ... I don't know if it's where I want to stay forever."

Solene City is seven days away by foot. Fewer waterways are in central Delphy and Rath explains to One-Eye and his Spirit Lion that any present are used primarily for messages, not travel.

Midway through the week, early in the morning, One-Eye climbs out of his and Rath's tent and begins stretching, his Lion doing the same beside him. They go on a jog in the surrounding forest, rejoining the group later before they set out.

When Rath – who had been talking with Melody and Demeter – sees One-Eye return, smiling as he talks with his Spirit Lion and looking far brighter than he has for almost a month, Rath turns a very bright red.

On their last day of travel, they go up a hill and find a wide stream with a bridge over it. They cross it and look ahead.

A waterfall runs down, filling a pool at the bottom that in turn supplies dozens of smaller waterways that all lead to Solene City, its buildings glinting in the sunlight.

Seeing One-Eye's expression, Lance says, "First time seeing this place?"

One-Eye nods. His Lion is taking it all in beside him.

Lance starts down the hill, the others following him. "Told you it was nice here. Thinking Solene might be a good place to settle down eventually, but … " He shrugs. "We'll see."

One-Eye says, "Rath told me these waterways were only used for messages?"

"That's right. Ships aren't allowed here. The city is far removed from the ocean, so many waterways were created to connect them. It's also why L'oeile Village is no longer an inland sea, due to much of the water being diverted here instead."

They pass the waterfall and reach the bottom of the hill where Lance meets with another Selachuu soldier. They speak, then the second soldier tells them all, "This way. Best get you there quickly."

However, as soon as they are walking through two stone arches, a man approaches them, saying, "I did not give my approval! I told you – "

Lance quickly walks back over to Rath. "The agreement?"

"Of course." Rath pulls it out.

The man ahead is continuing, "Selachuu soldiers or not, it does not give you the right to – " He stops suddenly, then frowns. "Rath. It has been some time."

"Yes, Leader Minta." Rath holds out a letter. "I have been asked to deliver this to you. It is from Leaders Leira and Nel of L'oeile Village and Ymira Town."

Minta takes it quickly. "So, I've been told." He opens it and reads it over. He sighs heavily. "The fools have really gone and done it. They have no idea just how much damage the Ullian Spies have caused here. The crack near my home nearly destroyed its foundations!" He crosses his arms, studying Rath. "I *am* surprised to see you here. Why are you?" He glances at the soldiers. "And I don't want anyone from the Ullian Spies in my city."

But Lance shakes his head. "To my understanding, that agreement you're holding is absolute."

The other soldier says, "We'll be escorting Laylin and her group to the crack now." Then, without another word, she walks ahead, gesturing to the spies to follow. They hesitate, but Laylin and Vin step forward first and the others join them.

Minta moves toward the group, but Lance stands firmly in between them.

He glares at him, then finally looks away and at Rath. "I'd like to speak with you. We'll talk now." He points. "And why isn't that spy following them?"

Evermore frowns back at him.

Rath says, "Evermore is not with Laylin's group. He has been traveling with all of us."

"Then – "

Lance says, "That agreement allows all members of the Ullian Spies to enter Solene City."

"On a *work*-related … Fine. He can come, too." Minta says to Rath, "However, do not think I will let him stay any longer than the others just because he is with you."

"I do not – "

Minta turns around and begins walking. "This way."

Those with Rath look startled, but he and Lance follow, then the others do as well.

They walk by homes and businesses surrounded by waterways. There are multiple fountains and many bridges all leading to the largest house in the city.

Minta's home is a tall three-story building made of white stone. All of the waterways join into one larger one that wraps around the front of the house, enters it, and continues out.

Lance parts ways with them, going instead to a large area nearby that has been concealed by cloth, where other Selachuu soldiers and the Ullian spies are speaking.

Minta says, "Can't believe they're being allowed to do this. Haven't they caused enough trouble?" He starts up the steps, then suddenly stops. "Solette! What are you doing?"

His daughter, who had been speaking with the soldier who escorted Laylin's group, says, "I'm – "

"Do not speak with them. Come inside."

She frowns, but nods.

Servants open the doors and Minta says to them, "Rath comes with me. The others stay in here. Do not let them out of your sight."

"Yes, Leader Minta."

After he and Rath go up the stairs, one of the servants says to the others, "You may sit on the benches here. Can we offer you anything?"

One-Eye glares, but not at the servants. "We're fine," he tells them. "What's wrong with him?"

They exchange a look. "We'd … " one says.

The other coughs. "Best not say."

Melody says, "We wouldn't want to get you into any trouble."

Evermore says, "Your employer is a very disagreeable person. I do not appreciate how he speaks to those around him."

The servants glance at one another again, but stay quiet and return to their tasks cleaning the foyer or sending Delphaen messages through the home's smaller waterways.

The doors open again, this time to let in Solette. She thanks them, then brushes her hair out of her eyes, looking frustrated, but thinking.

She notices the others and says, "I apologize. Did my father ask to speak with you?"

"Only Rath," One-Eye says.

She blinks in surprise. "I had thought it was him." She extends her hand to each of them. "I am Solette, Leader Minta's daughter. What brings you to Solene City, if I may ask?"

After they tell her, she smiles. "That is very good of you to support the Ullian Spies. I could not believe Father when he told Laylin and the others … " She coughs abruptly. "That is, I should leave. Please let me know if … " However, she stops, nods to them respectfully, then goes down the hallway.

While they wait, One-Eye's Spirit Lion looks around. He flicks his ears and says something to One-Eye, who replies, "Yeah. You're right. The layout is similar."

Melody asks, "To what? Oh, I'm sorry – were you talking to your Spirit Lion?"

"I was. It's all right." He explains, "This place looks almost exactly like Garreth's. From the outside, too."

Melody looks surprised and Demeter begins to scrutinize the furniture.

Evermore's eyebrows raise. "Does it?" He frowns, thinking.

Upstairs, Rath and Minta have arrived in his office and now sit on either side of his desk.

Minta says, "Now – if I may ask a question – is Marchand on Haliae? Or Pantha, currently?"

"He is on his way to both with the other gods."

"And you, Rath? I hear you are often traveling. It isn't often you stay on Delphy."

"That is true. I will be boarding *PearlHeart* late next month with my crew for our seventh journey."

"Seven years." Minta laces his fingers. "Seven years you've been doing this and … Marchand still has not found a replacement, has he?"

"Pardon?"

"For your position – excuse me, what *would* have been your position – as councilman. What Councilman Georgio now holds."

Rath frowns. "I cannot say. I have not been told as such."

Minta nods. "I offered my services – my whole family's, as you may recall – but Marchand refused to make any decisions at that time." He fixes Rath with a look. "He seems to hold onto this vain hope that you will miraculously regain your traits and assume the role that you were born into. They are not back, are they? Your traits?"

"No. Carlos has told me they will not return. I trust him."

"I am sure you do. Even Marchand has high regard for him, so I do as well. Then, why is it that he and Councilman Georgio have refused to choose someone to fill your place? My family is plenty worthy – we have only carried Marchand's Traits for generations. I will not disparage your own heritage because Marchand approves of mixed cultures and thus will I, however, I do recall your traits from him not being very strong even when you did carry them." He shakes his head. "Why *are* you on Delphy? I have heard of your presence here in nearly every message I've received regarding this whole situation –

you reporting the cracks to Leader Leytel, him *asking* for your advice even though you are not a councilman, then being tasked to find their cause and being allowed to despite your lack of official rank. Helping others use their traits in ways that you would not have known if Marchand hadn't taught you and eventually aiding the groups to re-enter the caves and begin their restoration and repair. *Then,* I receive a letter from you – because, we too, are on the river that flows over the Old Delphaen Crystal Quarry – saying the tremors are nothing to be worried about and that they are not being caused by the Ullian Spies, then afterward – I am told by Leader Ehken of Archen Town – you and your friends found a way of saving former Councilman Garreth's home from the surge." He exhales. "That isn't even to count the work that you have done in L'oeile Village or its relations with Ymira Town and the spies that used to be there but are now right below us. *Why* are you here on Delphy, Rath?"

"I am on break."

Minta stops, his mouth open slightly. He slumps back in his chair. "That makes … an odd sort of sense."

Rath clears his throat. "May I leave? I have told you my reason."

Minta frowns at him. "Yes … " He hesitates. "Yes, you may go."

Rath finds the group still in the foyer and they all leave.

As they go down the front steps, Evermore says, "Did he listen to your reasoning?"

"I believe so," Rath says. "He seemed … very angry, however. He wondered why I was on Delphy."

Melody pets Demeter, who is beginning to look back at the house rapidly. "Why couldn't you? It's your home."

"It is. Although, he is right that I am not often here."

One-Eye says, "Because you're on *PearlHeart.* Working."

They decide to stay at Akelle Inn, a tall building surrounded by a flower garden, with most rooms on the upper floors, their windows open to keep them cool.

The owner, Indrif, tells them, "We only have smaller rooms here. It is a popular spot for people during the Wedding Season. However, not this year." He sighs and moves on, "How many would you like?"

Rath says, "I am all right with sharing."

One-Eye says, "Me too. Just two, then?"

Indrif pulls out some keys. "Or four, depending on … well, if any of you would mind sharing a bed – there's only one in each room."

One-Eye flushes. He takes a key. "Four. We'll all pay."

"Understood."

They each go to their room. The Pagu, who are staying with Rath in his room, fly off of his shoulder to look out one of the windows.

Flower-Pagu says, "It's a really pretty view from here!"

Bucket-Pagu says, "I like all the waterways everywhere."

Rath walks over. "It is, indeed. Solene City is very beautiful."

Well-Pagu frowns. "Empty."

"The inn, you mean? It is unusual given the Wedding Season. However, I am thankful there were enough rooms for everyone."

"Us too!" Flower-Pagu says.

While the Pagu go outside to explore and check in with how Laylin and the others are doing, Rath and One-Eye sit at the table in Rath's room, talking. The Spirit Lion has his paws up on the windowsill, looking out on the city.

One-Eye says, "My Spirit Lion has really enjoyed seeing more of Delphy this past month. We hadn't seen as much as he wanted during the Winter two years ago."

Rath brightens. "I am glad that he is, then. I have very much enjoyed traveling with him – " He suddenly stops, then continues, "That is, I cannot see or hear him, however, when you tell me that he is around, I am far happier."

One-Eye is surprised and even his Lion looks startled by the statement. Then he begins grooming and One-Eye smiles. "He likes being around you, too," he says. "Franz's mother told me something while we were with him and Velt. She said you told her your grandmother and grandfather can see each other's Spirit Animals. She also said you didn't know how that was the case."

"I do not. Grandmother has only said it often happens with those with heritage from Sudines."

"Not traits?"

Rath thinks. "No. She said heritage."

One-Eye nods, then moves on, "Minta seems to know you. When did you two meet?"

"It was when I was traveling on Delphy meeting the different leaders in preparation to work with them in the future as councilman. We also met at my grandfather's when I had lost my traits."

"Why was he there?"

"Grandfather tells me that he came immediately to Priage to help when he heard no one knew where I was." He frowns. "Grandfather told me he does not believe his intent was honest. I did not know how to feel about that." He continues, "By the time he arrived, Fierce had already brought me there. It was after Marchand, the Pagu, and Carlos confirmed my traits were gone. When Leader Minta learned this, he asked Marchand if he might be my father's successor as councilman."

One-Eye's eye widens. "He *what?*"

"He said that if I could not use my traits and Marchand could no longer sense me that I would be unable to perform my role."

"You already have been. Everywhere. Since we've been here. Whether or not you're inheriting that title, people respect you. You're helpful and kind and you think things through before you jump into them. You're smart and your advice is actually good. I respect you for all those things."

Rath looks surprised, then flushes deeply. "Th-Thank you. I am happy to help."

One-Eye smiles for a moment, then asks, "What did Marchand say?"

"He said … he did not wish to make any decisions. My grandfather was furious that Leader Minta asked for such a thing. Marchand also did not appreciate Leader Minta's timing."

"I'm not surprised. He doesn't still want that position, does he? As councilman?"

"I cannot say. However, today he asked if my father or Marchand had chosen someone else. I have not been told they have."

One-Eye exchanges a look with his Lion, then asks Rath, "Was there anything you wanted to do here? It sounds like Laylin and the others were able to get back down into the Constellation Caves. I don't know how long it'll take them to finish, though."

"I do not know either. Well-Pagu, Bucket-Pagu, and Flower-Pagu told me they were going to check on how they were doing and would tell me when they returned."

One-Eye stands and offers his hand. "Then we have some time and I have a feeling the Pagu would be able to find you no matter where we went. I want to spend today with you. Do you?" Rath smiles, taking his hand. "Yes, I would."

For the rest of the morning, they explore the city together. They start at the waterfall. Rath explains how it was carved and they both enjoy looking at the flowers growing near it. One-Eye's Spirit Lion finds a restaurant nearby and they eat lunch there while the Lion talks with the local Spirit Dolphins. He joins them as Rath and One-Eye are leaving, looking very satisfied with his discussions.

As they are looking at some of the fountains, they all hear from the sky, "Rath! One-Eye! Spirit Lion!"

Well-Pagu, Bucket-Pagu, and Flower-Pagu fly down. Bucket-Pagu says, "We just had lunch with Lance."

Flower-Pagu says, "We also got an update on how Laylin and the others are doing!"

"News," Well-Pagu says.

Flower-Pagu continues, "They're all working very hard to finish their part of the map. Based on what Lance has heard from the other Selachuu soldiers, he thinks they'll finish their first version this afternoon, then the revised one by this evening."

"I am very glad to hear that. Thank you," Rath says.

"Of course!"

One-Eye says, "What then? Do they just go back to Ullia?"

The Pagu look at each other. Bucket-Pagu says, "We're not sure. Erole is no longer here and I'm not entirely sure what spies who are not assigned to ships do during this time. Often, it is work for Erole, but that would be complete now."

Well-Pagu says thoughtfully, "Perform?"

Rath says, "Yes. I believe Laylin would like to return to performing."

They decide to go back to the inn and play cards in the main room on the first floor. One-Eye helps his Lion play as well. As they are finishing their fourth round, Melody, Demeter, and Evermore join them. He is able to take off his scarf due to them sitting in the corner of the room, away from the bright windows.

As Melody picks up her cards, she says, "It's very different from L'oeile here. People seem afraid of Evermore."

He takes his turn. "They are." He sighs. "I pray that Laylin and the others are able to finish their work."

Bucket-Pagu says, "We heard they will likely finish their part of the Constellation Caves map by this evening."

Flower-Pagu says, "It sounds like they're working very hard!"

Well-Pagu nods.

Evermore says, "Then … Well, they will likely go to Ullia."

One-Eye says, "Why is that? The Pagu didn't seem to be sure where they'd go either."

"Where could they? Places like Ľoeile Village are an exception, not just on Delphy, but everywhere. My people are not banned from any countries in the Alliance, but our activities make us unwelcome and untrusted." He lays a card down. "I am certain Erole makes it as such so that we have nowhere to go between the tasks we are given."

Rath thinks. Then, after they are finished playing, he says, "I hope that some day after this, everyone will feel as though they are welcome here on Delphy, Evermore. I think it is a beautiful place with many kind people. And, I believe Marchand would like it as well."

Evermore smiles. "Thank you for your words. I would hope so as well. But, Ullia is far and even if we are allowed to leave at other times, we are always required back at the Winter. It limits the areas we can go to during the other seasons. In some ways, I am uncertain if it is worth it to live in another place, as Lance has suggested to Laylin and the others. I am content and grateful to be on *PearlHeart* for the majority of my days."

One-Eye listens, thinking. "Regardless, it sounds like they'll be finished by tomorrow and with that agreement, they'll have to leave Solene City as soon as their work is finished."

"That is true," Rath says.

Melody says, "Do you think we'll see them before they leave? Demeter and I would like to see Laylin again."

Evermore says, "It is unlikely." At Melody's disheartened expression, he touches her arm gently. "However, I am certain she has enjoyed this time and – perhaps – one day will return, when people from Ullia are more welcome, as Rath says."

Melody nods.

They spend the rest of the afternoon together, then eat dinner at the inn. After they pay for their meal, Indrif says, "I really am grateful for you all here. Many decided to cancel their plans after the cracks started to appear and" – he clears his throat abruptly – "even more when Leader Minta began voicing his displeasure over the situation. It does not lend itself to a peaceful, romantic environment, you know?"

One-Eye says, "He should be done with that soon, shouldn't he?"

"You would think. He's always been irritated about something and well … I shouldn't say so much. Anyway, the other inns have been booked by people who either don't care about the situation or are interested in it, leaving mine forgotten by any couples."

"I am sorry to hear that," Rath says.

"Oh, it's all right. The season is always up and down, even without things like this. There's another month until Summer officially starts, which is when it's the busiest – I'm sure it'll all be made up."

That night, as everyone in Solene City sleeps, the Ullian spies come together in the Constellation Caves.

Laylin looks over their piece of the map for the final check. She nods, relieved. "It is finished."

They sense someone approach them and turn.

Laylin bows. "Relingel."

He raises his hand. "No need for that."

Vin hesitates. "You … are not with Erole?"

"He finally tired of my company." He frowns. "I would have liked to have seen those caves further … " His eyes flick to what is in her hand. "Your piece of the map?"

Laylin gives it to him. "That is right. Is it now … complete?"

Relingel, in the middle of looking it over, hums. "Yes, it

is." He tucks it under the scarf wrapped around his waist. "We shall see if our god has an interest in it now." The others tense and he says, "I am sure that he will one day and he will be … pleased that we have finished it." He looks up at the Miphrin. "I do wonder what they look like all lit up. Our map only gives us an idea, but I have a feeling the light would be too bright for our eyes." He then asks, "What will you do now?"

"Leave," Laylin says immediately. "I … *We* wish to stay, however – "

"Your agreement only covers this work. I understand." He thinks. "What about the repairs? There is a large crack here and many weak spots in the city – too much water, I am sure. Will you not help with that?"

"As you said, the agreement covers only our task with the map."

"Then ask for it."

Laylin starts. "But – "

Relingel shakes his head. "Use the Selachuu soldiers as intermediaries if you need, but – we need to start this, Laylin, all of you. They will not accept us if we continue to do things the way we are used to." He continues, "I have heard that elsewhere on Delphy that some wish to create a new position for us here, like Belle did on the ships – but to test for weak areas and give building advice." He knocks on the wall. "They need it."

Laylin smiles faintly. She bows. "We will try. However, I cannot guarantee … "

"I do not need that. Nor will I get upset with you like our god would. But – if my time on Delphy has taught me anything, it is that the people here value communication. Ideally, both parties would come together, but" – he shrugs – "it wouldn't be a bad idea to be the initiator."

"We shall see."

Relingel smiles. Without another word, he walks away.

The others look to Laylin. She takes a breath, then says, "We shall wait until morning. People from Delphy would prefer that." The others quickly agree, nodding.

They exit the caves, going up the ropes the Selachuu soldiers secured for them near the crack. Lance helps Laylin up. "Done?"

"Yes. However … We wish to extend our stay to aid in the repairs. Of this crack and others. We are told there are many weak areas in this city."

"Wouldn't be a bad idea. You'll have to ask Leader Minta. In the morning, I'd suggest."

"That was our plan."

Lance smiles briefly. He bids them all good night with a wave and the Ullian spies cluster together in the small area set aside for them. They look up at the stars, which are not too bright for their eyes, and fall asleep.

23

Rath and the others wake up to shouting outside. They go down the stairs, then to the front door, where Indrif is standing, rubbing his face. The sky is overcast and a low rumble of thunder comes from the west.

Indrif sees them and asks, "Did it wake you up, too?"

Melody nods. "Who is it?"

A particularly loud shout makes them all jump.

"You can probably guess. Is there anything I can get for you all?"

Rath says, "No, I do not think so."

"Do let me know," he says, then returns inside.

After he does, they decide to follow the voice.

There are not many people outside, with the rain starting. A mother is talking to a pair of twins – one boy and one girl – who are near a waterway, saying, "Come back inside. It looks like it'll be a downpour."

The boy says, "But, Mom!"

"No. You know the waterway floods and scares your sister."

The sister nods, taking her mother's hand more readily.

As the group nears the source, they see Minta is standing under the portico of his home to shield himself from the rain while he shouts at Laylin and the other Ullian spies, who are standing at the bottom of the front steps. It is dim enough that while their hoods are up, their scarves are around their waists as opposed to over their eyes. The Selachuu soldiers stand by and watch. Lance sees Rath and his group and waves them over.

When they meet him, Rath asks, "Is everything all right?"

Lance glances at Minta, then at Laylin, then pauses and says, "Not exactly." He looks up. "*That* isn't helping."

"The rain?" One-Eye asks.

"Yeah – if it keeps coming down, it'll flood Solene's waterways badly. Minta should be accepting their help and start preparing for it."

Melody says, "What are they asking to help with?"

The other soldier says, "To repair the crack and help strengthen any weak areas in Solene's architecture. As you can tell, he's refused."

Another crack of thunder sounds overhead, muting Minta for a moment. Then the downpour starts, drenching all of them.

Rath looks back at the city, concerned. "I have seen Solene City flooded – it can be very dangerous. I would like to see if there is anything to be done to help."

While Minta continues to argue with Laylin in the heavy rain, they go back into the city. Rath finds the mother from earlier placing sandbags by the waterway near her house and they all offer to bring out the rest.

"Thank you so much," she says. "My husband and I usually work together on this, but he was asked to help with repairs east of here."

As they set them down, the woman's son watches One-Eye and when they are finished, he stares up at him before dashing back inside at the call of his mother.

The group goes to the house next door to help, moving down the street until they are far away from Minta's shouting.

Suddenly, thunder booms above and the rain doubles in amount. The Pagu gasp and Rath shields them with both hands.

A door opens not far from them and an older woman calls, "Come, come! The rest has been done!"

They enter and find a small room with a warm fireplace, blankets draped over every chair.

"Go on and sit wherever you like. I'll get you all something warm to drink. I'm Emmerin, by the way."

"Thank you," Rath says, finding a seat by the fire. The Pagu are on his hands, holding out their own to the warmth while One-Eye and Evermore do the same.

When Emmerin returns, she nearly drops her tray. "Oh my!" She quickly sets it down on a table near them. "I didn't know there were Pagu with you! I haven't seen one in so long."

The Pagu, now warmed up, fly over to her and introduce themselves.

Afterward, Well-Pagu extends their little hand. "Meet."

Emmerin holds out her finger to theirs, but frowns. "Meet?" Well-Pagu looks up at Rath, who says, "I believe Well-Pagu means that it is good to meet you."

She smiles. "Ah, I see. And you as well, Most Honored One."

Well-Pagu beams.

Bundled up in blankets Emmerin knitted, the others give their names. She says, "Leader Minta has been upset ever since that crack appeared by his home. However, I cannot believe he would have neglected to send out the Delphaen message to begin fortifying the waterways for this storm."

One-Eye sips his tea. "Sounds like he was too busy yelling."

She frowns. "Is that right? I thought it was the thunder." She drinks from her own cup. "Although, I *did* hear him yesterday when the Ullian spies arrived." She turns to Evermore. "Were you among them?"

He shakes his head. He seems a little uncomfortable in the home. "I arrived as well, however, I am not part of their group."

"I see." She smiles. "And you do not need to look so tense – Minta's made many in this city cautious of the Ullian Spies, claiming they'll do to our homes what they did to his, but I believe the Selachuu soldiers when they say that it was not their intent. I've always heard people from Ullia love caves and tunnels."

Evermore nods. "They are fascinating. To hold up so much with comparatively little."

"You wouldn't want to destroy them." She sits back. "I also simply don't agree with faulting a whole group of people just for the actions of some – or even many." She looks at One-Eye. "I am sure you have faced much prejudice as well, haven't you? You're rather different from other people from Pantha I've met. They've told me how hard it is to even get a job with how some people view them." She continues, "Being so closed off to others is not how Marchand taught us to live. The simple act of reaching out to different people can often be the most important effort."

Rath says, "I remember him telling me this."

Her eyes crinkle. "I do not believe we ever met, but I remember you, Rath. Younger, perhaps, with your father, Councilman Georgio, and Marchand. Meeting Leader Minta for the first time." She sighs. "I am afraid he has not changed since then. All of us know that he covets the position in the Council. I find it to be very inappropriate. Regardless, from what I hear, your father is in very good health. I do not see any reason for there to be a question of who may succeed him for many years still." She suddenly says, "I apologize. Is this a painful subject for you? I should have asked."

"No. I have accepted it. I have a new path in life."

"The captain of a Pan ship, correct?" Rath nods. "Would you tell me some of your tales? I can't think of leaving my home in Solene, but I do miss being so close to the ocean."

"I would be happy to."

While Rath begins to tell her about their journeys on *PearlHeart,* the rain continues outside, thunder rumbling in between flashes of lightning. One-Eye's Spirit Lion listens to Rath speak, but also keeps one ear pivoted toward the window.

At Minta's home, he finally retreats inside, saying, "And if I were a member of the Council, I would ensure that anyone from Ullia is never welcome again on Delphy after this!" His servants shut the doors for him.

The Ullian spies pause, then Laylin turns, looking at the waterways that are already flooding.

Minta, who had begun drying off his hair, sees them from the window. "What are they still doing here? I told them to leave!"

His wife, Tana, near the other window, watches the downpour. "I thought you said this rain was nothing to worry about."

"It's not! If it had been, I would have – "

Suddenly, Solette – who had also been looking outside – gasps. "Minet Street has flooded!"

Tana says, "Have the people left?"

"The Selachuu soldiers just escorted them away." She looks at her father. "We should have sent out the message. It is a very good thing people seemed to have prepared regardless and … I believe I saw Rath and his group helping as well." She pauses, then begins to tie up her hair.

Minta says, "Where are you going?"

"To help them! To help *our city!*" Then she is out the doors.

Minta starts toward them. "Solette!"

But she is already outside. She dips her hand into an overflowing bowl nearby and sends a strong Delphaen message. It shoots through the water and into the city's waterways, then to each home.

Once it is sent, she joins the Ullian spies.

"You are Laylin?" she asks.

Laylin starts, not from her presence, but from her tone. "Yes."

Solette hesitates, then dips her head respectfully. "Would you help me? You can … sense other people, right? I want to make sure that everyone in the city leaves. I realize that it may not be appropriate to ask for such a thing when – "

Laylin shakes her head. "We will help. Truly, it was our decision to cause the crack here. We may not be at fault for all that has happened on Delphy, but this, we are responsible for. And more … we would like to see that everyone is safe as well."

Solette looks relieved. "Thank you. If you would all take a street" – she blushes – "well, I suppose you would be more adept at organizing yourselves."

"We will be all right. Be safe."

"You as well."

Solette runs ahead into the city. Laylin and her group start to move when the front doors open and Minta calls out, "Solette! Where – " He turns a furious look at Laylin. "What did you say to her? Where is my daughter going?"

Before she can respond, Tana tells him, "To help. That is what she said." She turns to Laylin. "Did she say anything to you?"

"She asked us to ensure everyone exits the city."

Minta blurts, "An evacuation?" Then he seems to see the

rain and the flooded waterways for the first time. "Oh. Yes. A wise course of action."

Tana says to Laylin, "Do as she says. And ... I am sorry for how you have been treated. Thank you for being willing to help."

"It is the least that we can do." Without speaking to her group, they all begin to head down different streets.

While they do, Tana turns to Minta. "We are leaving – immediately."

Minta gapes. "Why? Our home is well-fortified. We didn't have to when this happened before – "

She gives him a withering look. "We will not stay in this house while our people have to be in the forest again – and that was only thanks to the supplies the Butej Guard provided for them. We will help Solette and the others evacuate them and *you* will need to do something else."

"What?"

She takes his hand gently. "Warn – no, *tell* the others that the Ullian spies are there to help. There are those that are afraid of them and I cannot say that they do not unsettle me, either, but ... Solette's a good judge of character. If she believes they can help, then so do I." At Minta's hesitation, she says, "I am not telling you to accept them just yet – but let us please not cause any unneccessary panic with them *trying* to help. Solette will tell them, I'm sure, but as their leader, they need to hear it from you."

Minta is quiet for one more moment, then puts his hand in the bowl, sending a message.

Rath is just finishing with their journey to Haliae when the well in Emmerin's home glows. "Oh!" She gets up quickly and places her hand in, reading the message. She says to the others, "It's from Solette – Leader Minta's daughter. She's ordering an evacuation to the hill for everyone." A few seconds later, a second message arrives. "Another!" she says. "From ... Leader

Minta? To trust the Ullian spies. My goodness … ”

At that moment, there is a knock on the door. One-Eye opens it and sees Lance there. He looks inside, sees the glowing bowl, and says, “Delphaen message?”

Emmerin pulls on a shawl and a hat. “Yes, sir. We are ready to leave.”

Lance smiles. “Great. This way.”

He escorts them out. Already, the water is up to six inches outside and the flooded waterways press against the sandbags, nearly reaching over them.

As Melody helps Emmerin through the water, Rath hears a familiar voice say, “Everyone, this way! Yes, it will be all right. I apologize the message was late. It will be all right.”

He turns and sees Solette, drenched, but guiding two more families in the street near theirs. She makes eye contact with him, looks embarrassed for a moment, then walks over. “I apologize for my father's careless action – or, lack of action, as it may be.”

“You do not need to.”

She grits her teeth. “Yes, I *do*, Rath. This isn't even just about his disrespect to you and your family that I am very much aware of. He's endangered our city – what he's *supposed* to be responsible for, not whatever he thinks about joining the Council.” She exhales. “I'm sorry. I'm stressed. Will you help me evacuate everyone?”

“Of course.”

One-Eye and Evermore decide to stay as well to help them.

Evermore says to Solette, “With your permission, I would be able to sense for anyone still around.”

“Granted – no matter what my father says. I've already asked Laylin and the others to help – I am grateful they accepted.”

“I see. I will join them.”

Melody touches his arm. “Please be careful,” she says.

Emmerin says, "And tell them thank you for us."

Evermore swallows, unable to say anything, then leaves, walking carefully through the rushing waters.

Melody and Demeter go with Emmerin and the Pagu – who are seated on her shoulder beneath her large-brimmed hat – while Lance continues to direct other families out of their homes and to the hill nearby. Rath, One-Eye, and Solette separate, going toward different streets to do the same.

One-Eye is going to the next home when he sees the small boy from earlier peering over the sandbags at the waterway.

"Hey!" One-Eye says. "You need to leave!"

The boy glares at him. He starts to say something, but his mother arrives, holding onto his sister's hand. "Tolin, we need to go!"

"Yes, Mom!"

One-Eye points, telling her, "Go in that direction. Everyone's heading to the hill."

"Thank you," she says, then leaves with her children.

Later, the three reconvene. Solette says, "That should be everyone in this area. The Ullian spies should be checking – " She stops and says, "Everyone! Stay away from the waterway!" Near them, the water is sloshing over the sandbags and into the already flooded streets where the people are traveling. Solette turns back to Rath and One-Eye. "Thank you both for your help. We'll start on the next – "

They hear a shout. "Tolin! Lettie!"

Ahead, the sandbags have given way, releasing the water and pulling the children away from the mother One-Eye spoke to earlier.

They all run toward them. With a growl, Solette lunges over and grips Tolin's hand. "Grab your sister's hand *now!*"

Tolin reaches out. "I-I can't – "

Rath tries to rescue the girl, but she desperately flails, just out of reach. He leans out further, then takes her hand. "It will be all right," he says.

Suddenly, they hear a dull *crack* and the water level abruptly drops. The remaining sandbags collapse, crashing into the waterway. Rath looses his grip and Lettie goes under. Without hesitation, he dives in after her.

One-Eye prepares to leap in, but Solette grabs his shoulder. He shirks it off immediately.

In front of them, a whirlpool has formed. Rath and Lettie are no where to be seen.

Laylin runs toward them, sees it, and turns pale. She bows to Solette. "I am sorry – I was warned about weaknesses, but without permission to check – "

Solette shakes her head. "It's all right. I'm sure … "

Next to them, One-Eye speaks silently with his Spirit Lion. The Lion prepares himself, then jumps in, passing through the water.

Rath and Lettie fall through the large crack that caused the whirlpool into one of the pools of the Constellation Caves.

He quickly finds her and carries her to the shore, where they both collapse, coughing.

After he recovers, he asks, "Are you all right? Are you hurt anywhere?"

Lettie trembles. "I-I don't – " Large tears run down her face, then she swallows and says, "I … I think I'm okay."

Rath exhales in relief. "I am very glad that you are."

"Are you?"

"Yes, I am." As the water level rises, he stands, saying, "We should leave this area. Are you able to walk?"

She nods. She reaches for Rath's hand and he takes it.

As they walk away from the pool, Lettie asks, "Do you know how to get out?"

"I know of two exits that are near here. One is the crack by Leader Minta's home and the other is in the base of the waterfall. The first would be in that direction." He looks back at where they came.

Lettie stares at the pouring water. "I don't want to go that way."

Rath nods and they turn in the opposite direction. "Then we will go to the waterfall."

"The … Oh! The tunnel underwater. My brother swam in it once. Mom got mad. But, that's … " She hesitates. Finally, she says, "I can't breathe underwater."

Rath says, "That is all right. I cannot either. However, it is not a far distance. If you take a deep breath, you can swim through it."

She frowns, nervous.

They continue through the tunnel, the water becoming more shallow the further they go.

One-Eye's Spirit Lion watches them, then disappears.

Above, the Lion reappears beside One-Eye, who listens. He tells the others, "My Spirit Lion says they're down there. They don't seem to be hurt."

Selined – the twin's mother – looks hopeful.

Tolin, however, clutches his mother's hand and says, "And why didn't *you* do anything? I thought people from Pantha were supposed to be strong!"

"I'm doing what I can now. I don't think going down there is going to help."

Evermore runs over. "Where is – "

Laylin explains, "Rath and a young girl named Lettie are down there."

"We could try to sense for them – or, for Lettie."

Selined says, "Would that … hurt her?"

"No. Not at all."

Tolin says, "He's just saying that. They just don't want to get in trouble."

Evermore stares at him, then kneels and says, "I'm sensing you right now."

Tolin jumps.

"Do you feel anything?"

Tolin pats himself down. "Well … no."

Evermore smiles. "Then your sister will not feel anything either. Please allow me a moment to concentrate." Then he taps his foot on the submerged stone and sends a pale yellow pulse all the way to the bottom of the waterway and through the crack at the bottom into the caves. After a moment, he says, "They're heading east." He frowns. "Lettie is heading east. I am afraid I cannot confirm if Rath is with her."

One-Eye says, "My Lion saw him with her."

"That is good." To Solette, Selined, and Tolin, he says, "It is all right. None can sense Rath with Erole's Traits."

Tolin says, "That's kind of weird."

One-Eye says, "No, it's inconvenient right now." He starts moving through the water. "Come on – don't you want to save your sister?"

Tolin lets go of his mother's hand and splashes after him. "Hey!"

The others follow. One-Eye asks, "Solette – is there an exit in that direction? Besides the one on the coast?"

Solette says, "Only the waterfall. The other one would be the crack near my home."

"I'm guessing they decided not to go to that one."

They continue on for a few moments until Solette gasps, "Oh! Lettie … " At One-Eye's questioning look, she says, "She can't breathe underwater – or, she hasn't been taught to."

"She can hold her breath, can't she?"

"Of course, but … Maybe one of us can dive in and help her."

Below, Rath and Lettie have continued to walk. They enter a smaller room with another pool. "Here it is," Rath says.

Lettie gulps, looking at the dark tunnel. "I-It isn't far?"

"No. It is only twenty feet to the other side."

"I … " As they grow closer to the water, Lettie suddenly digs in her heels and pulls back. "I can't! I'll run out of air!" She starts to cry.

Rath stops and kneels in front of her. She grips his hand tighter, rubbing at her eyes with her other hand.

She hiccups. "If … If I could breathe underwater like Tolin and Mom, I … I could go back to them." She sobs, "Leader Minta said my traits were too weak and that I shouldn't try to learn!"

Rath's eyes widen. When she lowers her other hand, he takes it in his. He looks at her Delphaen tattoos extending halfway up her forearm. He shakes his head. "Lettie, what Leader Minta told you was not true."

"What?"

Rath points at his wrist. "My traits were far weaker than yours – my tattoos only curled around here. I was able to breathe underwater. Marchand tells me he gives it as the most basic trait next to message sending."

"Really?" She rubs her nose with her arm. "What happened to yours?"

"I lost them."

"I'm sorry."

Rath pauses, surprised, then nods. "May I teach you how to breathe underwater? I am trained to do so by Marchand."

"Please!"

They walk over to the pool and he climbs in. Lettie hesitates, then follows. Her feet just reach the bottom. "Wh-What do I do? I see Tolin touching his neck."

"That is correct." He brings his hand up to his own neck. "You will touch right here and take a deep breath."

She starts to, then says, "What if I can't do it?"

"We will try again. I believe you can do it, Lettie."

She shuts her eyes tightly and takes a deep breath. Her tattoos start to glow and she gasps.

"You did it!" Rath says. "Now you will be able to breathe underwater."

"But – what if it didn't work? What if I can't breathe and I'm down there and I can't get back up? Or I messed up?"

"I'll be there to help you. I promise to keep you safe."

Lettie studies him, then extends her pinky. Rath holds out his and they shake. She smiles, still looking nervous. She ducks down into the water and stays there for a few seconds, trembling, before she begins to relax. She comes back up. "I … I did it! They *are* strong enough!"

"Congratulations, Lettie."

She hugs him tightly around his waist. When she pulls away, he asks, "Are you ready to swim through the tunnel?"

"I … I think so. You'll be there the whole time?"

"Definitely."

She smiles again, then dives under. Rath takes a deep breath and joins her. She looks back at him right before going through the tunnel, then continues on and Rath follows her. They travel for ten seconds in the dark, Lettie's tattoos the only light.

Distantly, they hear voices.

Lettie recognizes one.

"Mom!" she shouts and swims faster.

By the time Rath surfaces, Selined is already pulling her daughter out of the water. As she holds Lettie, she looks at Rath, opening her mouth to say something, then gasps.

Rath hears an odd sound. He turns around just as the mud from the hill starts to dislodge and come down.

One-Eye – who was also there – reaches for him, but something else is faster.

Rath feels teeth bite into the back of his shirt, then he is abruptly thrown out of the water. He collides into One-Eye and they both go rolling through the wet grass. Behind them, the mudslide fills the pool, blocking the entrance.

When they stop, their eyes are wide and they breathe heavily. Rath sits up, then touches the back of his shirt. "Did you … "

One-Eye stares at something padding over to them. "My Lion did that."

"He – " Rath looks around. "May I ask where he is? Is he all right?"

"You can't see – " One-Eye sighs. "He's here. And yeah – he's fine." He studies his Lion, but for once, the Lion is quiet.

After he gestures to where he is, Rath says, "Thank you very much, One-Eye's Spirit Lion. I am glad to hear that you are fine."

The Lion comes closer, but it is clear that Rath cannot see him. He puts his paw on Rath's hand, but he does not react.

One-Eye sees and frowns, confused. His Lion tells him something and he stands, offering Rath a hand. "He's right – he says we should get out of here. Go somewhere safe. You're not hurt, are you?"

Rath takes it, standing as well. "I do not believe – " He suddenly hisses in pain. One-Eye lets go of Rath's hand and kneels quickly. The back of Rath's calf is covered in mud and part of it is bleeding.

One-Eye turns to his Lion. "You could have been more careful."

The Lion stares at him.

"Yeah. I know. He's alive."

A Butej guard who had seen them from the forest arrives with medical supplies and One-Eye surprises him by asking for them.

While One-Eye works, Lettie says to Rath, "Thank you for teaching me."

"Of course. I am happy to see you are safe."

She grins for the first time.

Selined says, "Lettie told me you taught her how to breathe underwater. And … she shared with me what Leader Minta told her. I can't believe … " She shakes her head. "The important thing is that everyone is safe now."

Tolin says, "How did you suddenly fly out of the water?"

Rath says, "One-Eye tells me his Spirit Lion pulled me out."

"Is One-Eye really his name?"

"Yes."

Selined pats her son's shoulder. "I think we should go join everyone else up on the hill."

After they leave, Solette says, "I'm sorry for all of this – if my father hadn't … " She sighs. "Like she said, the most important thing is that everyone is safe. My father even sent out a message that the Ullian spies were trying to help. He didn't say they were to be *trusted,* but it's … a start." She moves on, "You two rest. Laylin, Evermore, and I are going to do a final check of the city. We'll see you up on the hill later."

"Thank you. You as well."

They all leave. One-Eye finishes tying off the bandage around Rath's calf, then asks, "Is that … all right?"

"Yes. You did a very good job. Thank you."

One-Eye offers his hand and they walk the rest of the way to the forest.

When they reach the shelter of the trees, they see that tents – supplied by the Butej Guard, who arrived not too long ago – are being put up while families sit around with blankets.

They sit together against a tree. A Butej guard comes by with a blanket, which One-Eye wraps around both of them. His Spirit Lion settles on his legs.

24

Melody and Demeter find them later. The Pagu are with them.

"Are you both all right?" Flower-Pagu says. "We heard about what happened."

Bucket-Pagu says, "The crack and … "

"Lion," Well-Pagu says, looking at One-Eye.

He nods.

Rath says, "Yes. We are all right. How is everyone?"

Melody says, "I'm worried about Evermore, Laylin, and the others, but I'm sure they'll be safe." She frowns. "What did Well-Pagu mean about your Lion, One-Eye?"

"He saved Rath by … biting into his shirt. He won't tell me how he did it."

"Oh my."

Another Butej guard comes over to them. "The tents are prepared. There are enough for all."

Rath says, "Thank you very much."

As they go to them, One-Eye talks silently with his Spirit

Lion. The Lion raises his eyebrows, giving One-Eye a look and he frowns. Finally, the Lion snorts and answers One-Eye's question.

He stops.

Rath notices and says, "What is it?"

One-Eye turns to him quickly, now a bright red. "It's … I don't want to talk about it right now. I'll let you know, all right?"

"Of course."

One-Eye shoots one last look at his Spirit Lion – the Lion grins smugly – then walks with Rath and the others to the tents.

They have lunch provided by the Butej Guard, then most go to take naps. One-Eye passes out next to Rath in their tent.

While they sleep, Melody and Demeter stand at the edge of the forest, waiting for Evermore and the other Ullian spies to return.

When they finally see them coming up the hill, they both relax. Evermore sees them immediately and takes Melody's hand briefly.

Nearby, Solette speaks with Laylin. Leader Minta and Tana are behind their daughter. Solette asks, "Everyone has left?"

"Yes. The city is empty."

Minta says, "It is *ruined*. The repairs will take … " Tana frowns at him and he says, with a sigh, "The most important thing is that everyone is safe. Thank … you for your help."

Laylin says, "It is the least that we can do."

Solette says, "Come. I'd like to discuss plans. Father, with your permission – "

"No, Solette."

"Father!"

"Not right now." Looking exhausted, he continues, "We'll discuss more tomorrow. Please."

Surprised, she replies, "Of course."

Laylin says, "You should get some rest as well. You look tired."

"And you?"

She shrugs. "We are accustomed to long hours. When night comes, we will rest." Then she and her group go off to some tents further away from the others, where Lance and the Selachuu soldiers greet them.

Minta takes his daughter's shoulder. "Right now, let's focus on everyone being the most comfortable they can be. It's … unlikely we'll be able to return tonight. Or tomorrow. Or … "

Tana smiles slightly. "We'll make the best of what we have. Which is a great deal thanks to the Butej Guard."

Solette says, "They are quite helpful. The Ullian spies, too."

Her father frowns, then gives a slight nod. Together, they leave to organize the food distribution and check in with their people.

Rath and One-Eye wake up later that evening, near dinner time. As they wait in line for their food, they see Minta is unpacking boxes of provisions, complaining loudly, "Shouldn't have to be doing this … " He hands out the next boxes. "Here. One for each person."

The man who takes them says, "Thank you, Leader Minta."

Minta does not reply. He bends over again and when he rises, he begins to speak, then stops. "Rath. And … One-Eye, was it?" He thrusts two boxes at them. "Here. One for each person."

Rath says, "Thank you, Leader Minta."

One-Eye frowns and takes his.

They join the Pagu, Melody, Demeter, and Evermore by their tents. The Butej guards have now set up small shelters to further block the rain.

One-Eye says, "He hasn't learned anything."

Evermore says, "Leader Minta?"

"Yeah."

Melody says, "He … seems to be trying to help. But, I agree that doesn't make up for what he did before."

The Pagu look at each other, then Well-Pagu says, "Trying."

Later that night, Solette walks around the camp, speaking with everyone. When she arrives at Rath's group, she asks, "Are you all going to sleep now?"

Rath says, "I believe so."

"Thank you for your help today. How's your leg?"

"Better. One-Eye did a very good job with healing it."

"I can see that." To all of them, she says, "I don't know what your plans are after this, but I wanted to ask if you would be willing to help tomorrow. The rain is expected to let up overnight so we can start rebuilding in the morning." They all agree to and she smiles, but looks tired. "Thank you. You've already done a lot – everyone has, but … " She sighs. "My mother and father are sleeping already – the day's exhausted them, so that's why I'm checking on everyone now. Did you need anything?"

"No. However, thank you for asking," Rath says.

She wishes them good night and they do the same before she moves on to the next group.

They wake up to brighter skies the next day. The breakfast line has started and this time, Tana is serving them. She hands Rath and One-Eye their boxes, saying, "Here. And thank you for all of your help."

"Of course. Thank you," Rath says.

Nearby, Minta is meeting with Solette and Laylin. Tana arrives after her duty distributing meals and joins them.

After welcoming her, Minta turns back to Laylin, who he was speaking to. "I still do not trust you or your people. You have made a mess of my city and all of Delphy."

"We are aware of this. We wish to offer our apology for doing so."

Minta's jaw tightens, then loosens. "My daughter is

convinced that you can help us in rebuilding Solene City and strengthening it against further disasters."

"Certainly. We are able to identify weak points in the architecture so that modifications may be made."

"Would it be able to stop the flooding from breaking through the waterways again?"

"It is possible with enough advance knowledge."

"Then I will give you my permission to begin. It is a beautiful city, but it does have its problems, all of which Marchand and I – and all those before me – are aware of. We need the waterways, but they wear down the stone over time – it's unavoidable, especially with a downpour like this. However, if I hear about you doing anything untoward, I'll – " Before his daughter or wife can speak, he stops himself, then says gruffly, but less angrily, "Well, like you said, this is the least that you can do for the damage you caused."

"We understand."

Solette suddenly asks, "Did you finish your map of the Constellation Caves? I had heard that was the original reason you were here."

Minta scratches his jaw. "I had heard about that as well."

Laylin says, "Yes. We finished the previous night. It has been taken to Erole, who ordered us to bring it."

Solette frowns and Minta says, "Ordered? I had heard odd things about the God of Ullia, but … "

Tana says, "Dear." She says to Laylin, "We understand that other gods and their people are different – their relationship with one another is."

Laylin smiles faintly. "Very much so."

Minta shifts uncomfortably. "Then … if Erole ordered you to do this, the matter is more between him and Marchand than you and us."

"He did not order us to create the cracks – that was our decision and one that I sincerely regret." She dips her head.

"We will take responsibility."

Minta studies her, then nods. "Well, good. I would hope that Rath – no, Councilman Georgio would let Marchand know."

Solette says, "I am sure that he will be made aware of the situation if he hasn't been already."

"True. Former Councilman Garreth would also be able to notify him." He looks at the flooded waterways and homes that are submerged up to their doors. "We should focus on our part. My – our city." His family smiles. He stands, brushing off his dirty clothes. He says to Laylin, "Now, don't think that I am pulling my name out of the ban for this aid you're giving us – I still stand firm on that decision." Sounding more calm, he says, "It is the best for the time being. I truly think that."

Laylin rises. "I believe so as well."

Minta then says, "Solette – I will leave you in charge of the overall efforts and distribution of labor, do you understand?"

She grins. "Yes, Father. I have many ideas."

Solette goes to speak with Rath and the others and finds them outside of their tents, having just finished their breakfast.

"Good. You're all here," she says. "You had asked what you could do. My father, mother, Laylin, and I just discussed and father is willing to let the Ullian spies help. He has tasked me with the division of labor. I think the first task is to clear any rubble or damage."

While she goes to talk to other groups, they start down the hill. However, when they pass by the waterfall, Rath stops. Both the waterways leading into it and those being supplied by it have been blocked off to not allow any more water in the pool. "We'd best start with this," he says, indicating the mudslide. "If we can clean it, the waterways can be opened again."

He carefully steps closer to the mud-filled pool, studying it. The Pagu offer to go ask for supplies and quickly return with a Butej guard, who hands them shovels. "Please let us know if you need anything else. We are staying to help with the restoration efforts," they say.

"I understand. Thank you very much," Rath says.

Together, they work at emptying the pool of mud and putting it in barrels to be used in gardens. The Pagu fly around, pointing out where there is still mud and watching the hillside carefully for any more landslides. Evermore also checks the hill routinely with Erole's Traits.

Tolin arrives late that morning and watches One-Eye shovel. He makes eye contact with him, looks away, then says to Rath, "Thanks for saving my sister."

"I am glad that she is safe."

"Yeah. Me too." He shifts. When One-Eye comes around again, he says, "Why are you helping? This isn't your city."

One-Eye stares at him. "Because it's the right thing to do. Probably some stuff you can do, too, if you ask." Then he goes back into the water to shovel more.

Tolin flushes. "I … I was just about to do that!" He runs the rest of the way down the hill. "And I'm gonna do way more work than you, One-Eye!"

Evermore raises an eyebrow, having heard the conversation.

Rath, who had been speaking with the Pagu at the time, sees Tolin and asks, "Where is he going?"

One-Eye says, "Hopefully to work."

"I see. That would be very kind of him."

One-Eye gives a noncommittal grunt.

By lunchtime, they have cleared out the pool. Evermore checks the hill one more time, his hand pressed against it. He pulls away. "It is stable now."

"That is good to hear," Rath says.

From the top of the hill, Selined calls, "Lunch!"

They turn and see her, Lettie, and many of the parents and younger children of the city coming down behind her.

As Lettie trots, she says, "Lunch, lunch, lunch … " She arrives in front of Rath and holds out a box. "I brought lunch!"

"Thank you very much for doing so."

Lettie beams.

Next to them, Emmerin hands three small boxes that fit in the palm of her hand to the Pagu. "These are for you, Honored Ones," she says.

"Thank you!" Flower-Pagu replies.

Emmerin looks overjoyed. "All of us need to help. Speaking of which … " She says to all of them, "Solette told me Tolin went down to the city to demand – her word, not mine – that he help and to give him the jobs that would take the most strength. I don't know what's gotten into him, but I'm glad he's finally putting that energy he's always had to good use."

Others carefully unblock the waterways and they all watch the clear water run freely.

They clean up, then sit down to eat. Lettie joins them after helping her mother give out food to everyone and sits next to Rath while she eats her own meal.

She says to him, "I told Mom that after we go home, I want to practice breathing underwater. She said we could go to Merian Lake – it's really close to where Dad is right now so we can see him, too! And I thought I would practice message sending, too. I can't send them very far, but I want to try."

"That is wonderful to hear. Marchand told me that Delphaen messages work best when they are sent together. Even if you cannot send yours far, you can help someone else send theirs or they can help you. It is part of what led to the Delphaen Relay."

Lettie looks elated by the idea. She nods quickly.

Tolin arrives with his lunch not long after and she waves to him happily. The boy looks embarassed for a moment, then sits down with One-Eye. He makes a show of rolling his arm. "I carried rubble for Solette down in the city."

"That was helpful," One-Eye says.

Tolin frowns up at him. "Well, where are you going next? I want to work where you are!"

Lettie suddenly giggles. She says to Rath, "My brother really likes One-Eye!"

Rath smiles. "I like him as well."

One-Eye drops his spoon, flushing deeply.

Tolin is red as well. "I-I do not! Just thought … people from Pantha are supposed to be strong, so … " He glances up at One-Eye again, then shovels food into his mouth while One-Eye focuses on his own.

Later, Solette sends them down into the city to clear away the sandbags. Selined sets Lettie on one of the walls. "You can sit here and we'll watch them together."

"Yes, Mom!" She kicks her feet.

Nearby, Tolin is with them as well and is trying to pick up a sandbag. One-Eye, who has already carried several, comes back, sees him, then lifts up the one next to him with ease.

Tolin glares at him, kicks the other sandbag, then follows him. "How do I get strong like you?"

"You work." He dumps the bag in a cart full of them to be taken away and repurposed. "Like you are."

"So – I just keep doing this?" Tolin looks at his hands.

"Yeah."

"But I've been doing stuff all morning! I still can't lift up a sandbag."

One-Eye turns Rath. "What do you think Tolin could help with?"

Tolin says, "It's not that I can't do the sandbags, but … One-Eye and you all are already doing them, so … "

Rath nods. "I understand." He looks around. "Actually, there were many sandbags that broke last night. There are scraps and some dry sand around. Would you find a broom and sweep them up? That would help greatly."

"I can do that! Mom! I need the broom!"

Selined is startled by his eagerness. "O-Of course!" She says to Lettie, "Do you want to come with?"

"No! I'll be all right here. I'm up on my wall!"

She laughs. "My brave girl." She looks at the group still working and the Pagu supervising, then decides that Lettie is perfectly safe.

She leaves with Tolin, who is tugging her arm and saying, "Come on, Mom! I need to help so I can be strong like – so I can get strong!"

"All right."

They come back not long after. Tolin proudly wields his broom, sweeping up sand and other small debris onto small scraps of cloth which the Pagu wrap up and carry away. One-Eye walks over to grab another sandbag and Tolin looks up at him. One-Eye glances at him, but neither say anything as Tolin keeps on working.

Soon, they are able to move on to the next area. The waterway with the hole has been dammed off and drained of water. There is a group of workers and Ullian spies standing inside the waterway, discussing the best ways of repairing it.

From on top of the hill, Minta sees them and frowns, but does not interfere. He leaves to check on his people.

When Rath and the others move on again, Lettie yawns and her mother picks her up off of the wall. She calls to her son, "Tolin! I'm taking Lettie for a nap! Do you want to come, too?"

"I'm working! I don't need to – " He stumbles forward a little.

Rath, nearby with a sandbag in one arm, steadies Tolin with his free one. "Are you all right?"

"Y-Yeah. Thanks. Just … tired, I guess."

"You have been working hard."

Tolin perks up. "You think?" He looks at One-Eye.

One-Eye pauses, then gives a very slight nod.

The boy jolts, then – clutching the broom to his chest – runs to his mother. "I'm going to go nap – I mean, go take a break! I'll be back later!"

Rath says, "I see. Sleep or – ah, please enjoy your break!"

"Thanks!" Then he takes his mother's hand and says excitedly, "He *nodded* at me!"

His mother smiles, a little confused, but pleased to see him so happy.

One-Eye says to Rath, "Move on after that one?" He nods to the bag in Rath's arm.

"Yes. I believe so."

At that moment, Solette runs up to them. "You won't believe – " She suddenly clears her throat, slowing down. "That is, how is the work here?"

"It is going well," Rath says.

"It looks like it. Thank you all." As the others gather, she says, "I wanted to tell you that not only are the workers fine cooperating with the Ullian spies – they have heard good things from their friends, they told me, from other parts of Delphy – but they already have ideas for fixing the hole in the waterway and strengthening all of them so that this will be far less likely to happen in the future." She sighs. "I'm relieved. I had thought … Well, it seems my father hasn't influenced everyone. I'm glad. And, relieved – like I said." She giggles. "Sorry – I'm rather tired. I've been up since early this morning." Her smile fades. "However, I can't help but think how Marchand will react to all of this. Does he know? Did your – may I ask if your grandfather sent a message to him? I'm sure it would reach him."

Rath shakes his head. "I cannot say. My grandfather did not tell me."

She rubs her arms. "I'm not sure which is worse – him not knowing or him coming back to … well, I was about to say 'coming back to things in such disrepair', but maybe things won't be like that. Maybe," she says, looking at those working in the waterway, "things will be much better. We can only hope."

Throughout the day, the group works at clearing the sandbags around the waterway. They take a break later that afternoon, eating some berries that some of the residents brought down, including Lettie, Melody, Demeter, Tolin, and Selined. When they all go back to work, Tolin happily sweeps, then pokes his muscles, then sweeps again with more vigor.

While they stay by the waterway, other workers see if any repairs need to be done to the homes. Having a history of flooding, the bases are all reinforced, but a few are starting to show damage, as confirmed by the Ullian spies.

One pair is looking at Emmerin's home, where there is a small crack to the right of the front door. "What do you think?" the worker, Gerin, asks.

Talas – the spy – kneels and touches the wall, sending a pulse around the house. He concentrates, then says, pointing, "Internally, it runs all the way to the roof. I would recommend reinforcing it immediately. It would not handle a second flood."

"I'll let Solette know – " However, as he turns around, he suddenly sees someone else behind them. "Oh. Leader Minta."

Minta glares at both of them. He focuses on Gerin as he says, "I may have tasked my daughter with organizing everything, but I do still have the final say as this city's leader for any architectural changes."

"I fully understand." He gestures to the crack. "We'll need to do some repairs here. Talas says that internally this crack goes up to the roof."

Minta's eyebrows raise. He looks at Talas suspiciously. "You can tell all that?"

"Yes."

"Then why – " He makes an effort to calm down. "So you *knew* that crack near my home would be as large as it was?"

Talas stiffens. He shakes his head. "No, we did not. It became what it did because of others creating cracks nearby at a similar time. We did not anticipate it."

Minta huffs. "If that's true, how can you be sure about *this?*" He gestures to the home.

"It is very different."

"How – "

Gerin raises his hand. "Leader Minta, if I may – if Talas believes this could be a problem, I am willing to do it."

Minta crosses his arms. "And I suppose I'll have to be willing to pay for it. Fine. Do it." He says to Talas, "But do not think that I will change my mind on the ban just because you're being *safe* and *thorough* and making me spend more money than I already will be with this mess."

"I speak only the truth," Talas calmly says.

Minta gives him one last look, then stomps away,

Gerin says, "Well, I'm ready to get started when you are. You just tell me where to work."

Talas smiles. "Thank you."

As evening comes, progress slows until only the most critical workers remain in the city, ensuring that everything is fortified for the night.

While Rath and the others are eating dinner near their tents, Flower-Pagu says, "It's so wonderful to see everyone working together! We got so much done in the city."

"Indeed. And, I believe so as well," Rath says.

Bucket-Pagu says, "It seemed like Tolin did a lot of work, too, and Lettie and Selined brought us meals and watched!"

Well-Pagu says, "All."

Rath asks, "Where is Tolin? He had said he would eat with us."

One-Eye says, "I think he ate and passed out. Tired." He

finishes his bite. "Sleep is good for him."

"It is."

Melody says, "I'm just glad that we've been able to help so much. I'm really happy that Demeter and I stayed on Delphy after all" – she glances at Evermore, flushing – "for a few reasons."

Evermore, now able to take off his scarf due to the evening light, meets her look and smiles. "I am as well. I think … much good is being done here. I look forward to what the future may bring with it."

"Me too!"

Minta walks over to them. He only glances at the others before he says, "Rath, I would like to speak" – he coughs abruptly – "*after* your dinner, if you are available."

"Of course."

One-Eye, sitting next to Rath, frowns.

Once they finish eating, Evermore, Melody, and Demeter take a walk while One-Eye sits, petting his Spirit Lion, and the Pagu look up at the stars through the tree branches.

Rath finds Minta at the edge of the forest, facing the city. Minta turns, sees him, then waves his arm. "Well, get over here."

"Yes, Leader Minta." Rath steps beside him.

Minta glances at him and sighs. "Always so polite." Then he says, "What do you think of the repairs down there? What would Marchand say about this?"

"I think it is wonderful. I am very happy to see everyone working together. I cannot speak for Marchand, however."

"But – you've been with him most of your life! From your training to that … trip with the gods on *PearlHeart*." He shakes his head. "How did you manage that?"

"They asked me."

Minta pauses, then rubs his eyes. Finally, he says, "I do not plan to step down any time soon, but I know that when I do,

Solette will be a wonderful leader."

"I think so as well. She is very talented."

For a moment, Minta smiles, but it disappears as he says, "You've accepted your new path in life, is that right?"

Rath blinks at the subject change. "Yes, I have."

"No regrets?"

"No."

Minta studies him for a moment. "I think … I could stand to learn from that – doing the best with what I have. That's probably what Marchand would hope for, too."

"If I may … "

"Speak."

"Thank you. Marchand has always told me that when everyone does so – their best, that is – and works together, that it is very beautiful to see. It is how he always wished Delphy would one day be."

"When he told you this … did he say specifically his people or everyone?"

"Everyone."

Minta thinks. "Together." He frowns, but his anger seems spent as he looks at the Ullian spies, Delphaen workers, Butej guards, and Selachuu soldiers alongside one another. He settles back on his heels. "I'll ask him the next time I see him to clarify, but … I have a feeling he'll just say what you did right now. Thank you for the talk. I wish you the best with your future."

"I wish for you the same."

Minta is quiet for a moment, nods once more, then goes to rejoin his family. Rath looks down at the city, then returns to the others.

25

The next morning, they eat breakfast and go back down to the city. Tolin, Lettie, and Selined join them. Tolin talks amicably with One-Eye. "My arms are sore!"

"That happens. You're … building muscle. That's what they do."

Tolin listens, then seems hesitant.

It is only when they reach the base of the hill that he says, "Sorry about … I'm sorry for the things I said earlier. About you not being strong enough to save my sister or about your name … I'm sorry."

One-Eye, whose expression went from neutral to confused to accepting, simply nods.

Tolin asks, "So – you're okay with me?"

"I … guess. What do you mean by that?"

"Well, I really like you – I want to be strong like you some day."

"Just be as strong as you want. Doesn't have to be like me."

"But – " As they continue on, Tolin thinks. "Huh. I guess that makes sense."

Once they reach the city, Lettie says to Rath, "Could you put me on my wall?"

"Of course. Are you ready?"

"Yes!"

Rath kneels down and picks her up, then sets her gently on top. "There."

She hugs him. "Thank you!"

"You are welcome."

While Lettie swings her feet, Selined says, "Thank you for all the work you and the others have been doing."

"I am happy to help. Thank you as well for bringing food yesterday."

"Of course!"

Lettie says, "Lunch! I can't wait for lunch!"

Rath and her mother laugh.

They work through the morning, then eat at the campsite at the top of the hill. Lettie tells Rath, "Mom and I practiced message sending this morning. I think I'm getting better at it!"

"That is wonderful to hear. When I was learning to use my traits, I would practice with my grandfather on his beach. We would send back the same message to each other."

Lettie gasps. "That's what we do!" She giggles. "It's so fun! Back and forth and back and forth!"

"It was fun for me as well! We would both send them quickly, like *plip plip!*" He demonstrates by patting the ground.

"*Plip plip!*" Lettie says.

They are on their way back down to the city when Solette catches up with them. Walking alongside Rath, she says, "I think most of the families should be able to return late this afternoon. Much of the fortification is done. With the Ullian spies showing us where the issues are, it has gone much faster."

"That is good to hear," Rath says.

"What about you all? I'm deeply grateful for your help, but I can't imagine that you came here expecting such an extended stay. Was there a date you needed to leave?"

"Yes. We will need to by the end of this week. We are going to the wedding of a friend of mine."

"Oh, how wonderful! I heard some of them that had been cancelled are now rescheduled. I think Indrif at the inn will be happy. I also heard they're opening the Constellation Caves again in the areas where the repairs have been finished, starting with the entrance near Meridelle Village."

"That is where my friend lives!"

Solette beams, eyes sparkling. "Were they thinking of going to the caves?"

"Yes, we all wished to. However, we did not know when they would be safe to enter."

"I'd say it would be possible by the time you arrive, if you would all like."

Rath looks ahead, to where One-Eye is talking with Evermore. "I would love to."

Solette catches his expression and smiles, but decides to say nothing.

To the northeast in Meridelle Village, Vann and Merlin return home early for lunch. They collapse on the grass on one of the hills nearby.

"Think we can sleep during the wedding?" Vann asks.

Merlin hugs her around the waist. "Fine by me."

She snorts and hugs him back.

Velt comes running up, with Franz close behind. They are both grinning. "Vann, Merlin! You're back!"

Vann says, "Our parents gave us the rest of the day off."

"Wedding plans," Merlin says with a shrug.

Franz says, "You've got everything ready though, right?"

Vann says, "Pretty much."

Sitting next to her sister, Velt says, "Yeah – but have you accounted for this?"

"What?"

"The Constellation Caves are open again! Well, the ones nearest to us."

Both sit up immediately.

"Really?" Merlin says.

Velt beams while Franz sits next to her. "Yeah! Franz just heard about it today."

He says, "You both could go like you originally planned."

Vann says, "That'd be great." She touches Merlin's cheek. "You could finally see them." To Velt and Franz, she says, "Thanks for letting us know. I bet Rath and the others will be excited, too. They're still coming, right?"

Velt nods. "I'm sure of it. They would let us know otherwise."

Her sister leans back. "Wonder what they've been doing since they left. They still at Garreth's?"

Franz says, "That was the last I heard."

"Hope he's doing well, too. Bet all of this and it being the Wedding Season has been a lot of work for him. Hopefully he gets some rest, too."

Velt says, "Agreed!"

At Garreth's home, Phillip and his Spirit Rabbit have just finished checking on the Water Flowers in the Old Delphaen Crystal Quarry.

Garreth, who is having a cup of tea with Carlos in the library, asks, "How are they?"

"Great! We had to do a little trimming, like Flower-Pagu suggested, but they're all growing well. I don't think the water level has changed much either – even with that swell we got this morning."

Garreth nods. "I checked on it – rain to the west. Hit

Solene City the worst. Heard their leader didn't make the appropriate preparations, either. I'm not surprised." He takes a sip. "But – his daughter, Solette, is talented. I like her. She'll do well when she inherits the title. Helps that I doubt she has any *other* aspirations beyond that."

Phillip looks perplexed. "Huh?" His Spirit Rabbit twitches her ear, curious.

Garreth waves his hand. "History."

At Phillip's continued confusion, Carlos clears his throat and says, "Leader Minta of Solene City is not seen to be very … competent, to Lord Garreth."

"And *you* think he is?"

"I would refrain from speaking of him."

"*That* says more than anything else you could say." Garreth turns back to Phillip. "It's fine. And thanks for helping out. I really do mean it when I say I like having you both around."

"Sure thing!"

Garreth's Spirit Dolphin appears beside him and he strokes her back. He says to her, "Nice having another Spirit Animal around, huh?"

The Dolphin bobs her head.

Petting his own Spirit Rabbit, Phillip says, "I hope One-Eye's Spirit Lion is all right – my Rabbit says he struggles without a lot of interaction."

Garreth laughs. "If Rath could see him, I'm sure he would unknowingly spoil him to the ends of the world."

Carlos raises an eyebrow. "And what would lead you to believe such would be a possibility?"

But Garreth only shrugs and takes another sip of tea. He sets it down on the tray. "Thanks for the tea, Carlos. Always enjoy it."

"You are welcome." Carlos puts his cup down as well, then says, "I do not mean to voice displeasure, however, you and Lady Azalea are rather … vague when it comes to that subject

– others seeing Spirit Animals that are not directly their own."

Garreth snorts. "Not much to say. I'm sure Azalea understands it a lot better than I do. And it's not like my Dolphin was any clearer either." The Dolphin's eyes shine next to him.

"I see." Carlos continues, "I do hope that Master Rath, One-Eye, the Pagu, and Evermore were able to find Melody and Demeter. It is concerning to think they remained on Delphy during this time."

Garreth nods. "Especially with everything going on."

Phillip says, "I'm sure they found them. My Rabbit says that with the Pagu with them, there's no way they wouldn't."

Carlos and Garreth agree. Then Garreth says, "Well, we'll all find out soon enough – they'll be arriving by the end of this week, right? For all of you to go to Vann and Merlin's wedding?"

Carlos says, "That is correct."

At that moment, a servant walks in. "Lord Garreth, you have a letter from your grandson, Rath."

He grins as he stands up. "Looks like I'll find out sooner than the both of you. I told him to send a letter when they found Melody and Demeter. That must be it." He leaves.

When he comes back, he sits down gruffly, muttering to himself.

"Lord Garreth?" Carlos says.

"That misguided, irresponsible … "

Carlos looks aghast. "I cannot imagine you are speaking of Master Rath."

"Of course not!" Garreth snaps. "However, I would like to speak to him about so readily accepting to help."

"I see," Carlos says with a polite cough.

"They're fine. Melody and Demeter were found. They're in L'oeile Village. They *were*." Phillip and Carlos exchange a glance, then continue to listen. "They all went on to Solene

City."

Carlos' eyebrows go up and Phillip gasps. "Where they had the flood?" he says.

"Yeah. And like I'd heard, Minta hadn't prepared at all." He rubs his face. "There's some things that may be better shared in person when they arrive, but they're all right and the city is undergoing repairs, which they're helping with. They're still planning on returning to Priage by the end of the week and Solette – who, like I thought, is heading the restoration – believes that most of the work will be done by then, too." Then, to Carlos, he says, "He's got a scratch on his leg, but One-Eye's healed it with medical supplies from the Butej Guard."

Carlos looks relieved for a moment, then his eyes narrow. "Just a scratch?"

"Better to talk in person."

Carlos frowns.

"There's … also a few things that Rath said about Solene City that I think Marchand should know about. I knew Minta was a bad influence – and I'm sure Georgio's aware of it, too – but … " He shakes his head. "It seems Minta hasn't given up that notion of succeeding Georgio." His eyes flare with anger. "Can you believe that he actually *asked* Rath if his traits had returned?"

Carlos lifts his chin just slightly, but makes no other comment.

Garreth sighs. "And knowing Rath, he just answered politely." He shakes his head again.

After a moment, Carlos asks, "Will you tell Marchand everything that has been occurring on Delphy?"

Phillip jumps. "He doesn't know?"

Garreth answers, "No, as far as we know, he doesn't. And … for a time, I thought that was for the best – I didn't want him distracted from helping Elvin and Lionel and the others with their countries. But, now … I think it might be time."

Carlos thinks. "He is likely just arriving in the North."

Garreth nods. "I might be a while. Anything I can get for you two before then?"

Carlos shakes his head and Phillip says, "Nope! But, thanks!"

"Sure thing." He smiles at them, then goes out the glass doors next to the waterfall.

He walks up the short hill, then down to the beach. The Butej guards watch from their posts. Then, with his Spirit Dolphin beside him, Garreth sits in the sand next to the ocean. His tattoos are already glowing as he decides on what to say. When he is satisfied, he puts his hand in the water and a strong Delphaen message takes off, traveling northeast to Haliae and Pantha.

The message exits Delphy's territory, then makes its way past Paradi and its rainbows and Unys and its fog, then Pica Pica, whose inhabitants are still partying. It follows the coastline of Pantha, crossing the part of the ocean where Berceuse's Isles of Oct are hidden, then finally to Haliae, where it shimmers at the coast.

Marchand is speaking with Elvin and Belle at the time, saying, "It looks like far more of the snow has melted since we've been here," when his tattoos glow brightly and he pauses. "It's from Garreth. I'm sorry – I need to check this."

Elvin smiles. "Of course."

Belle says, "We'll be here."

Marchand goes to the shore quickly, dipping his hand in the water.

When he returns to the others, Elvin asks, "Is everything all right?"

Marchand opens his mouth, then shuts it. He runs a hand through his hair. "Yes?"

Elvin looks concerned.

His brother explains the message the best he can. "The Ullian Spies have been on Delphy. Erole tasked them with creating a map of the Constellation Caves, but with people there, they couldn't do so accurately, so they created cracks to cause them to leave … "

"Isn't that dangerous?"

"Very. Rath and One-Eye fell down one." He pauses. "Actually, Rath fell down twice – the second with a young girl named Lettie, but I'm getting ahead of myself."

He goes on to tell them about the plan to work together – Elvin nods approvingly – with people from Delphy and Ullia helping to fix the cracks and strengthen the caves, then how the extra rainfall from Ara's Storm caused the river in the Old Delphaen Crystal Quarry to have a powerful surge that caused tremors – "They used Water Flowers to lower the water level underneath Garreth's house! I wonder what Azalea would think of that … " – then Erole tasking a man from Delphy with heritage from Ullia to bring Rath to him.

Elvin starts in surprise.

Belle frowns deeply. "I had heard of that."

Marchand says, "You did?"

Belle nods, then gestures to a Spirit Shark who is poking his nose up through the ground beside them. "Our own decided to inform us at a similar time. He arrived while you were reading your message – not exactly the same report, but the same events from different perspectives."

"I see. I'll admit, that detail alone – Erole tasking someone to take Rath – almost made me go back to Delphy immediately. It seems Erole's First, Relingel, helped Rath. And One-Eye and his Spirit Lion, of course, along with Fierce's Butej Guard."

"I've met Relingel. He's good. Did you know of Erole's spy?"

Marchand winces. "Of course I know Rellu. He's my own. I never imagined he would do something like this, however."

"From what I've heard, he's been apprehended by my own and is being taken to the Selachuu prisons right now. My soldiers don't think he'll be working with Erole again."

Marchand nods quietly.

Elvin says, "Why would Erole wish to meet the Captain? And go to such means to do so?"

Belle says, "His lack of traits. People with Erole's Traits – and Erole himself – can't sense him. My own have difficulty tracking him for similar reasons."

"Really? I had no idea."

Marchand says, "I can't sense him, either. It's what made him going missing before so … " He shakes his head, then takes a deep breath. "Garreth didn't say as such in his message, but I can only imagine the Pagu also intervened. It seems Well-Pagu said Erole had … left."

Both gods tense. Elvin coughs. "Well … "

Belle says, "Sounds conclusive."

Marchand says, "I can only hope it remains that way. It's amazing Erole has only found out about Rath's lack of traits now."

Belle sighs. "I'd imagine Fierce will be keeping that in mind along with his other tasks. Do you want to return to Delphy?"

Elvin says, "It would be completely understandable if you do."

"I thought about it," Marchand says. "Especially when Garreth told me of what was happening in Solene City concerning the views Leader Minta has been pressing. They were very concerning to hear and not at all how I taught him. However, I've decided to stay here. From everything Garreth told me, everyone – or, at least the majority – have worked together to help one another during this time. I still can't believe they would consider banning Erole's people, but Garreth seems to think that with the clear effort the Ullian Spies are making to repair the damage they've caused and their growing reputation with the workers on Delphy, that the petition will likely not go through. I'm glad – if there had been a majority, Georgio and I would have had to agree with them."

Elvin nods. "Such is listening to the voice of your own."

"Exactly." Marchand pauses. "It sounds like they have everything in hand and we can't be everywhere all the time – we have to depend on our own, each other, and the Pagu to help when we can't." He frowns. "However, it wouldn't hurt to discuss with Erole boundaries when we return."

The other two nod.

As they walk together on the beach, Belle says, "According to my soldiers, the Ullian Spies have been seen all over the South."

Marchand hums. "Garreth said Fierce told him the same."

Elvin says, "Really? Goodness … what is Erole after?"

Belle says, "Knowledge. On those grounds, we can't order him out. The underground … is an inheritance of his, as well. However, it sounds like it was only on Delphy that my own had enough cause to intervene – other situations were or are currently being handled peaceably."

"That is good to hear."

Marchand sighs. "And all of this during the Wedding Season … I wonder if Vann decided to go through with her and Merlin's. I told her that I wouldn't be there and gave them my blessing before we left – Merlin's wonderful. She invited Rath, One-Eye, the Pagu, and some others from *PearlHeart* to the wedding, too. I hope they're able to have it – after all, they're supposed to be on break."

The others agree, then they rejoin the rest of the gods to continue to help rebuild Haliae and Pantha.

That evening, in Solene City on Delphy, everyone who had been working turns in for the night. As Solette had told them, many people were able to return to the city and sleep in their own homes, Tolin and his family among them. However, Tolin begged his mother for one more night in the forest and she agreed. Lettie was too tired to say much and crawled into their tent without another word. Clutching his pillow under his arm, Tolin waved brightly at One-Eye – who just raised a hand in reply – then, beaming, went to bed as well. His mother smiled at all of them, then entered their tent, too.

The next morning, the small family helps the Butej guards take down their tent. While Selined was taking down the poles, a pair of Paradi messengers arrive. "A letter for you, from your husband, Selined."

"Oh. Thank you." She quickly reads.

The Paradi messengers go over to Rath's group, who are getting ready to go down the hill. "A letter for you from your grandfather, Rath."

"Thank you very much."

Across from them, Selined gasps. Lettie looks up at her. "What is it, Mom?"

"This is wonderful news! Lettie, Tolin, your father's coming home early!"

"Really?" Tolin says.

"Dad! Dad! Dad!" Lettie says.

"Yes!" Selined says. "They say the repairs have gone far more quickly than expected and after hearing about the flooding here he is determined to help." She laughs. "Your father is very strong, Tolin."

He holds up his arms. "I'm going to be, too, when he comes back! That's what One-Eye says – that if I work, I'll build muscle."

Selined listens, then smiles at One-Eye as well, thanking him.

One-Eye just nods.

As they are going down the hill, Tolin says, "How long are you all staying, One-Eye?"

"Until the end of the week."

Then he says, "Mom! When is Dad supposed to be here?"

"About four days, he says."

Tolin's face falls. "You won't meet him, then ... " He suddenly looks hopeful. "Will you come back?"

One-Eye asks, "To Solene City?"

"Yeah. Or ... Delphy. I'm sorry – where do you live?"

"Technically Pantha, but I haven't been there in over ten years."

"Do you not like it?"

"Other places are better. Delphy is."

"I really like it. Though, I guess I haven't been anywhere else. Just Priage once – and that's still Delphy. Do you like traveling?"

"I do." One-Eye glances at Rath, who is speaking with Melody. "I've seen a lot of countries since leaving Pantha."

Tolin follows his look, then focuses on Evermore. "Does ... doing that make you ... less afraid of things? Or people?"

"People from Ullia?"

He jumps. "How did you know?"

In response, One-Eye pauses. They have reached the bottom of the hill and he says to the others, "Go on. We'll be there." Then he crouches down and Tolin stands in front of him. "Listen, you're going to meet people who are good and bad no matter where they're from. People have different cultures that you need to be aware of – they're not anything to be afraid of. I've met people like that everywhere I've been. Good people are wherever they are – they're not tied to any one country."

He thinks. "So ... Evermore's good. He's been helping."

"Yeah. He is. Talk to him and you'll see that for yourself."

Tolin chews on his lower lip. Then he nods decisively and holds out his hand. One-Eye stares at it as he says, "Dad says it's what adults do. I understand what you're saying, One-Eye."

After a moment, One-Eye shakes it. "Good." He stands back up and they continue walking.

Tolin says, "I really wish you could meet my dad. He's really strong, like you. And I definitely want you to come back – do you think you will? I'm going to be a lot stronger whenever you do."

One-Eye smiles a little. "Yeah. I might."

Tolin grins.

For the rest of the week, they work together. The sandbags have all been carried away, so they help clear up other debris that piled up from the flood. During one of their breaks, Tolin attempts to talk to Evermore while they sit in the shade of a nearby tree. Evermore seems surprised by his effort, but appreciative. Lettie, who was near Rath, says, "That's … Evermore?"

"Yes. He is a dear friend of mine."

"Mom says that he … sensed where we were, so everyone knew where we were going. When we were … below."

"That is what I was told as well."

She nods. Then she gets up and walks over to join her brother. She very quietly says to Evermore, "Thank you for helping us. Before and now."

He looks startled. "You are welcome."

Lettie smiles.

That evening after dinner, they are able to return to the inn where they were staying. Indrif seems particularly pleased as he holds open the door. "Welcome back. It is so good to see you all."

"You as well," Rath says.

They gather in his room to talk before going to bed. He says, "Solette has assured me that everything is nearly repaired or in the process of being so and that she will release us from our duties tomorrow."

Melody says, "We did finish with those sandbags. Tolin

was a lot of help, too."

Evermore nods.

Rath says, "He was. It was wonderful to see everyone working together." Next to him, the Pagu happily agree.

The next day, they walk through the city with Solette. "Nearly everything is complete," she says. "Honestly, I'm surprised my father has delayed fixing the crack near our home until now." As they approach it, they see Minta is talking with the workers and spies.

They hear one worker say, " … that's the plan. With your approval, Leader Minta, we'll begin immediately."

Minta's mouth is pressed into a thin line. Finally, he says, "Very well. All right. It seems … sound. But, if you – " He directs this at the spies, raising his finger toward them. However, it drops and he instead looks at the city, still with repairs to be done but in a far better state than at the start of the week. "Good … work," he says instead. "But do not … " He huffs. "Just get started!"

"Yes, Leader Minta."

While the group approaches the large crack, Solette, Rath and the others go over to Minta, who is glaring at the ground.

Solette says, "They should be done soon."

"That is what they said. Hopefully, I will not regret this."

"I don't think you will."

Minta looks at the group behind his daughter and crosses his arms. "I suppose I should let you know – in my official capacity as leader – that my fellow leaders in the area have … dropped their names from the ban, causing the whole matter to become null and void." He jerks his chin. "I tell this to Evermore specifically, as it will affect where in Delphy he may go to and I don't know your travel plans."

Evermore says, "Thank you for telling me."

Minta does not seem pleased. He turns to his daughter. "The city?"

"Only smaller repairs are still underway," she says. "Everyone has moved back into their homes." Before her father can ask, she says, "Rath and his friends have returned to the inn where they'll be staying for the night, then leaving."

"I see." Minta studies them all for a long moment. His expression seems to loosen, then tightens again as he turns on his heel and walks up the stairs to his home. He shuts the door behind him.

Solette sighs. "I didn't expect a goodbye, but … " She shakes her head. "I apologize for his rude dismissal. I think this will all take him some time to get used to and … I doubt that hearing about the other leaders removing their names from the ban has helped his mood."

One-Eye says, "That shouldn't be something to be upset about."

"No, I agree." She looks at the crack near her home. "I hope they're all safe down there." Then, to all of them, "Thanks again for your help, on behalf of the people of Solene City. I release you from your duties and ask that you take today to rest before your journey in the morning."

Rath says, "You are welcome. Thank you for all that you have done."

She smiles. "I am happy to."

As the group eats dinner at a nearby restaurant, Flower-Pagu asks, "Where will you go after this, Evermore?"

He blinks, uncertain. "I do not know. Erole has not called me back and … what Leader Minta has said has allowed me to go to other places here. We will be departing on *PearlHeart* soon, so I cannot imagine leaving Delphy."

Bucket-Pagu says, "Why not go to Vann's wedding with all of us?"

Well-Pagu nods. "Go?"

Evermore hesitates. "I am not sure … " He reaches over the small table, not taking Melody's hand, but resting his close to hers. "Actually, if you would allow, I would very much like to see more of Delphy with you and Demeter. Unless you would like to go to the wedding?"

Melody takes his hand. "No, I … I don't know Vann very well. I would feel a little awkward." She smiles. "I would love to see more of Delphy with you."

He smiles in full. Then he says to Rath, One-Eye, and the Pagu, "If Melody and Demeter are all right with it, I think we may stay here in Solene City until the repairs are finished. I would also like to see Laylin and the others again, if possible."

Melody nods. "Me too. I thought I would ask Indrif if I could play my harp for the people here."

Bucket-Pagu says, "I'm sure he would be happy to have you both stay! Do you think we could hear your harp, too?"

"Of course!" Melody beams. "I'll ask him in the morning."

When she does, Indrif is delighted by the idea. "Oh, how romantic! A harpist and her bird partner … " He grins. "And I've recently received so many messages inquiring about open rooms or requesting their previously cancelled ones – I think you'll have quite the audience to play for!"

Melody flushes. "Oh!" Demeter begins preening.

Indrif says to the others. "I am grateful that you chose here to stay – and thank you all for your work in restoring Solene City! I hope you have safe travels where you're going."

Rath says, "Thank you very much."

They make their final goodbyes to Evermore, Melody, Demeter, and Indrif before leaving Akelle Inn. Solette, who is speaking with some workers and Ullian spies, sees them and wishes them well. Tolin and his family come out, too. "Hope to see you again soon!" he says, waving, and they all wave back.

<h1 style="text-align:center">26</h1>

They meet Lance up the hill in the forest, where the last few Butej guards are cleaning up the temporary camp.

Lance asks them, "Heading out?"

Rath says, "Yes. To Priage, then Meridelle Village."

Glancing down at a Spirit Shark, he says, "Thought I'd let you know I informed Belle of the situation – everything. Spirit Sharks knew a lot more than I did. Seems like you've all been through more of this than any of us. Anyways, thought you should know the gods have been informed. Haven't heard of any of them coming back, so they must think they don't need to. Belle doesn't. Sounds like things should be settled on Delphy by the end of this month, too. Take care."

Rath says, "You as well."

As they travel through the forest, One-Eye asks, "What did your grandfather's letter from yesterday say?"

"He said he had informed Marchand of the situation as well, through a Delphaen message. He had not heard a reply yet, however, he did not expect to until today at least."

Flower-Pagu says, "I'm sure it was a surprise for Marchand."

Bucket-Pagu says, "I hope he's all right."

Well-Pagu says, "Family."

Throughout the day, they walk through the forest, going toward L'oeile Village. They stop briefly in a clearing to have breakfast, then later to have lunch – Selined packed it for them – and afterward, set off again. They pass by L'oeile Village, but do not stop there, instead moving in the direction of Priage.

As they are nearing the city that evening, they see two Butej guards are by the hatch in the ground.

One sees them and says, "Good evening."

One-Eye says, "What's with the hatch?"

They look temporarily startled that he knows about it. They exchange a quick look, then the other guard steps over the area. "It's gone. We've discovered that in other places as well, where there were similar shafts. They've all been filled in."

The first guard says, "We just spoke with Relingel, the leader of the Ullian Spies. He said his god has made them inaccessible."

Rath says, "I see."

One-Eye says, "It's probably better that way."

They continue on to the main street. Ahead, ships are coming into port. They can just see the masts of *PearlHeart* past the other ships, still undergoing maintenance, bobbing happily.

Bucket-Pagu, sitting on Rath's shoulder with Flower-Pagu and Well-Pagu, says, "Just one more month right? Before we can go on *PearlHeart* again?"

Rath smiles. "Yes. I cannot wait."

Flower-Pagu shoots their arms up, saying, "Us too!"

One-Eye smiles as well and his Lion grins beside him.

They find Carlos, Phillip, and Garreth waiting for them

at the base of the hill leading to Garreth's home. Rath's grandfather hugs Rath when they arrive. "Good to see you're all right."

"You as well, Grandfather. May I ask how the Water Flowers are doing?"

"Great. Thanks to Phillip and his Spirit Rabbit over here."

Phillip blushes. "It's been really fun." His Rabbit hops in agreement, then sniffs in the direction of One-Eye's Spirit Lion, who sniffs back.

One-Eye pets his Spirit Lion, saying, "You can talk later. We have to find a ship now."

Garreth nods. "Better do that soon so you can make it to a way station before the sun goes down."

One-Eye offers to find one for them and returns quickly so they can all say their goodbyes. As they walk toward the waterways and their ship, Garreth watches them, his Spirit Dolphin at his side. He strokes her head, then – with a small smile – heads back up the hill to his home.

On the ship, Rath handles the lines and One-Eye is at the tiller. Carlos, Phillip, and the Pagu sit next to them, relaxing. Phillip's Spirit Rabbit and One-Eye's Spirit Lion are already conversing, their ears flicking madly.

Once they are underway, Carlos clears his throat. "Master Rath, we heard from Lord Garreth that you went to Solene City and were unfortunately there during their flood. As well as that you had sustained a scratch. Is it healing properly?"

Rath says, "Yes, on my lower right calf. I believe it happened when One-Eye's Spirit Lion pulled me out of the pool near the waterfall. One-Eye healed it very well."

Carlos, who had already started to gape at the second sentence, only dimly hears the last. "One-Eye … " He suddenly looks at the bandage, studying it, then nods to One-Eye. "Fine work."

"Thanks."

Phillip says, "One-Eye's Spirit Lion … pulled you? How?"

Rath says, "I do not know. It was very surprising."

One-Eye gives a cough, but says nothing. Carlos glances at him, but he looks away.

Carlos says, "It has been known to happen before. Master Rath's grandmother and grandfather can see and interact with one another's Spirit Animals, despite one being a Turtle and the other a Dolphin."

Phillip says, "I remember hearing about that!"

Carlos says to One-Eye, "May I ask if your Spirit Lion elucidated it any further?"

One-Eye keeps his eye on the waterway. "I don't want to talk about it."

"I see." Carlos lets it drop, asking instead, "Why was it needed for you to be pulled out of the water, Master Rath?"

Rath shares with them their travels while One-Eye and the Pagu add in their own comments.

By the end, both Carlos and Phillip are startled. Carlos says, "Better in person," remembering what Garreth had said.

Phillip says, "But, you're all right? That sounds really scary."

"We are," Rath says.

Carlos says, "I can only imagine what Fierce will think of this when he hears of it. Or Marchand." He continues, "Master Rath, Lord Garreth received a reply from Marchand today. He has chosen to stay on Haliae. He believes that all is being taken care of, although he was greatly concerned to hear much of it. He also asks that you and everyone be careful – and to relax now that it seems things are in repair."

Rath says, "Marchand told me the same before he left – that is, to relax."

With a brief smile, Carlos says, "I understand this trip has likely not yielded itself to such, however, I believe that now – Vann's wedding – will be a very appropriate time."

They arrive at a way station later that night near Archen Town. While Rath, the Pagu, and Phillip go find dinner, Carlos sits with One-Eye in the group's shared room. "If I may ask for further clarification from earlier," Carlos says. "Regarding how your Spirit Lion was able to 'pull' Master Rath out of the water."

One-Eye reddens. "He only told me one thing that would affect it."

Carlos raises an eyebrow, waiting.

"My … bond with Rath."

Both eyebrows go up, then down. "Have you told him?"

"No."

"I believe you should." Before One-Eye can respond, Carlos raises his hand. "I do not believe he will take it as … you seem to be." He thinks. "Did your Lion specifically use *romantic bond* in his description?" One-Eye's face turns a further shade of red and Carlos says, "I see. Regardless, I do think that Master Rath would be quite happy to hear that your bond has grown strong. He enjoys your company very much."

One-Eye looks at him quickly.

"Which … I will not elaborate on as this is between you two." He pauses. "And your Spirit Lion." He sighs. "I am afraid my earlier reaction to Lord Garreth was misplaced. I am beginning to believe that the humans associated with their Spirit Animals are not given full information as to the nature of this bond – it seems that the Spirit Animals would prefer not to say what exactly causes this to happen."

"I don't know about that." One-Eye glances at his Lion, lying on the ground beside them. "He is trying to – he just thinks it should be obvious. But … he does say that Rath having heritage from Sudines is a factor of it."

"I have heard the same."

"You're also from Sudines in part. Do you know why that would have an effect?"

Carlos presses his lips together.

The door opens and Rath, the Pagu, and Phillip come in. Rath says, "We brought food."

One-Eye stands up to help. "Thanks." As he holds out his hands to carry some of Rath's boxes, he starts to say something more, but does not.

After they eat, Rath, the Pagu, and Phillip offer to take the boxes away.

Carlos – continuing his converstion with One-Eye – says, "Hep's people from Sudines are a very old race."

One-Eye takes a moment to track what he is saying, then nods.

"I cannot say that is exactly why some from there are able to see other Spirit Animals, but it would be a factor. Most people in the present are descended from three groups of the Third World – Ara's people, Amara's people, and their brother Alan's people."

"Haven't heard of Alan."

"He is no longer here," Carlos says quickly. "However, those from Sudines – or, the race they were before they came under Hep's protection – are from the Second World, at least. Lady Azalea would know more."

Both One-Eye and his Spirit Lion take in the information. Then One-Eye says, "Thank you for answering."

Carlos smiles a little. "I would wish to know as well. Especially as it may concern Master Rath's safety, which your Spirit Lion was important in protecting."

"Would the Pagu know any more?"

"Assuredly. However, they may not be able to say."

One-Eye thinks as he pets his Lion. "Then I won't ask. It doesn't exactly matter why it happened. I would like it if Rath could see him one day. Or talk to him. Not just for his protection. They like each other." His Lion grins and One-Eye smiles.

"To share in that part of your life?"

"Yeah."

Carlos' look softens.

Rath and the others return soon and they all go to bed early that night. One-Eye is in the one across from Rath's with his Lion curled up beside him. Rath is already asleep with the Pagu lying on his chest on their own little bed. One-Eye pets his Lion once more, then closes his eye and goes to sleep as well.

It takes them three days to reach Franz and Velt's homes.

They pass by the Wishing Fountain – the crack has since been repaired – and Kel City. While they stop at the way station near there, Rath receives a letter.

"It is from Leader Leytel," the Paradi messenger says and their bird partner gives a "Caw."

After Rath reads it, he tells the others, "He would like to thank everyone for their efforts with the cracks. I will tell Franz and Velt as well when we arrive."

As they travel, Phillip – having not seen much of Delphy – looks around at the landscape excitedly. Carlos reads a book with the Pagu sitting next to him doing the same. Rath and One-Eye sail, enjoying the sun. The Spirit Lion and the Spirit Rabbit nap together, having finally caught one another up.

On the second day, they near the divide where the crack had appeared in the waterway and they needed to camp on land for the night. The crack is completely fixed now.

While they are having dinner in their room at the next way station, Flower-Pagu says, "I haven't seen any Ullian spies around."

Rath says, "Neither have I."

One-Eye says, "It's possible they left."

Bucket-Pagu says, "We had hoped … a few had stayed."

Well-Pagu nods.

Carlos says, "I am afraid I agree with Fierce – perhaps not

all are ready for them to. However, from everything you both told me of your continued travels, it seems there is room for that to change, given time."

They arrive at Franz and Velt's homes early the next morning. While Rath and One-Eye are tying off the lines, the pair runs to greet them.

Velt says, "You made it!"

"Yes!" Rath says.

As they walk up the hill together, Franz asks, "So – how was Lord Garreth's? Were you there the entire time?"

Rath says, "No. We were only there for two days."

After they tell Velt and Franz what had happened since they parted ways, the latter two look stunned.

Franz rubs his neck uncomfortably. "You … might want to wait until after the wedding to tell both families about all of that."

Velt says, "I don't know – it might be best to tell them now."

Vann comes to meet them. "Tell us what?"

"Let's wait until everyone's gathered. That way they only have to tell it once more."

They have a late breakfast with everyone. Niz and Alfin have closed the boat shop for the day due to the wedding being that evening and join them in Franz's family home.

When the group finishes telling the story the second time, they are all quiet. Then Fiona dabs her chin with her napkin and says, "Well! It is good to see you are all safe now."

Rath nods. "Indeed."

Franz does a double take. "A-Aunt Fiona, you're … all right with this?"

"Oh, certainly not, but given the past month, it unfortunately does not surprise me."

Even Joseline looks suprised by her reaction.

Fiona waves her fork. "And you all did a very good thing, helping those Ullian spies. It's heartening to know that who will one day be the Councilman of Ullia – Relingel, was it? – not only has a Spirit Eel but seems to have a *very* good head on his shoulders."

Mimi says, "That thing you talked about with the afterimages sounded really neat."

Max says, "I wish I was there!"

Carlos frowns. "It seems it frightened many people."

Joseline says, "True. However, it did help. And, I didn't know people with Erole's Traits were capable of doing such a thing. It seems there's much we don't know about those from Ullia."

Velt says, "I can't believe Evermore was with Erole this whole time. Or Melody and Demeter, looking for him. They must have been so worried."

Franz says, "It's good Demeter was there to see you, Rath."

"I agree."

Niz says, "We had heard some parts – the river and the tremors, of course, as well as the flooding in Solene City – but it's quite different to hear it firsthand. It was good that you were all there to help."

Alfin says, "We've seen Ullian spies around here helping with the repairs – but not as many now. Seems they've all left."

Then, Mattias – Franz's grandfather – who had barely said a word either time during their visits, says, "They're a private people. Interaction is still very new to them. And they are very new to Delphy. It will take time, but I believe one day, it will come." He smiles softly and continues to eat his meal.

The Pagu nod and Flower-Pagu says, "I think so, too!"

Bucket-Pagu says, "After all, we remember when there weren't any other races except for Marchand's on Delphy."

Well-Pagu says, "Long."

Niz holds Alfin's hand. "I can't imagine – for multiple reasons."

Alfin colors, but smiles.

Rath says, "I am very happy that so many different people may live here now."

One-Eye says, "Me too."

Phillip says, "Rella says she likes it on Cunica, too. She says it's always good to have an extra pair of hands to help."

Carlos nods. "That sounds very appropriate for her."

Vann winks at Merlin. "Can't say I mind it either."

He grins. "It's pretty nice." He leans over and kisses her cheek.

Niz raises his glass. "To opening up borders?"

The rest lift up theirs.

Well-Pagu quietly says, "Together."

The rest look at them, then smile.

Niz says, "I like that far better." They clink their glasses. "Together."

"Together!" everyone says and they drink.

Throughout the rest of the day, all of them help with any last minute preparations for the wedding. Melta, Tierth, and their son Luta are already there and preparing the food. Merlin's family arrives and tackles him to the ground, laughing, then calmly updates one another about what has been happening in their lives.

Merlin's younger cousin tells Rath and One-Eye while they are carrying chairs, "There were Ullian spies on Pantrog, too. But" – he shrugs – "they discovered there are no caves, so they left immediately."

As the sun starts to dip, Rath and One-Eye begin decorating tables. One-Eye flips a cloth over one and Rath places flowers on top, smiling at them as he does so. One-Eye sees, then hesitates. Afterward, they sit on one of the hills near Franz and Velt's homes. The wedding is being held in between them, where there is a large clearing and a waterway that rounds it. It has been filled with tables, glowing Delphaen crystals, and bright flowers.

"What are Delphaen weddings like?" One-Eye asks.

"They can vary per couple, however, traditionally a meal is served, then the couple exchanges their Delphaen scarves which they have worn during their engagement. Then they send their first message together, sharing their announcement. However, Marchand has since adjusted it so that this part is optional depending on the traits of the people. My father sent a message for him and my mother when they were married. After, there is dancing and talking with one another and sometimes games."

One-Eye nods, his Spirit Lion doing the same beside him. "Thanks. Never been to anything like this. Pantha doesn't exactly have marriage."

"I see."

One-Eye pauses and they both relax in the evening breeze. Finally, he says, "I'm glad for that, too – being … together, like Well-Pagu said. Being able to see different places and meet people. I'm glad that I met you because of it."

A little flustered, Rath says, "I am truly glad to have met you as well, One-Eye. And your Spirit Lion as well."

"He is, too. He enjoys listening to you. You know a lot of things and he likes that. You're also kind to him." He pets his Lion. "I think … because there aren't many people from Pantha here and definitely not as many as there were on Pantrog – " His Lion stares at him and One-Eye says, "Fine. And there were none there compared to in Pantha … I think he misses so many people being able to see him and interact with him. It's why he's been so excited to see other Spirit Animals here on Delphy. Still – it's not exactly the same as another human. I think that's why it was so important to him that you played games with him and talk to him directly. Thank you for doing that. It means a lot to me, too."

Rath looks stunned. "Of … of course. My relationship with both of you is something I hold very dear. Thank you for allowing me to be a part of your lives."

In response, One-Eye squeezes Rath's hand and his Lion puts his paw over both of theirs. Rath squeezes back, then they watch the preparations conclude.

For the rest of the night, they watch Vann and Merlin exchange their vows – Merlin appears to forget for a second, then grins and tells them perfectly – and they exchange their scarves. They go to the waterway and Vann sends a message while holding Merlin's hand, who smiles at her softly while she does.

Then they eat and dance together with their friends and family. The Pagu join in, mingling with one another and the dozens of Spirit Animals – Dolphins, mostly, but some Seahorses, Rabbits, Birds, and Sharks, too. One-Eye, who has decided to remain seated with Rath, Carlos, and his Spirit Lion – Phillip has opted to dance – says, "Aren't there any Spirit Chimpanzees?"

His Lion flicks his ear in annoyance.

Carlos sighs. "According to Vocalise, they are not needed."

Merlin, being spun by Vann, leans back and says, "He says they don't need to help, but we know the truth!" Then he is dragged off by Vann, both laughing.

One-Eye says to his Spirit Lion, "You can go talk with them."

But his Lion hesitates, then lifts his chin, and plops it on the table in between Rath and One-Eye. He glances at both of them, then grins. One-Eye laughs. "He wants to stay with us. Maybe play some cards."

Rath says, "Yes, please."

Carlos says, "I would like to join as well." He gives a quick look to One-Eye.

He says, "Sure," then goes to retrieve them.

While they play together, the others dance or eat, enjoying the evening.

They all set out early the next morning.

Fiona, who is wheeling Joseline's chair, says, "Are you sure about this?"

Joseline grins back at her. "I should be asking you that."

"Oh, I'll be fine."

As Fiona pushes her, Joseline says, "I haven't seen the Constellation Caves in years – not since I lost the use of my legs. I want to see them again."

Fiona looks at the group. "I'm sure those who haven't seen them will be excited as well. It is a very good thing they are open again."

Ahead, Niz and Alfin are talking with Rath and One-Eye. Alfin is saying, " … I don't think your friend Evermore should be concerned about his stay on Delphy. Most other petitions I've heard about to ban those from Ullia have been dropped for lack of signatures."

Rath exhales. "That is very good to hear."

Niz says, "I'm glad that people have come to their senses. Otherwise, who knows what it would have led to?"

As they continue to travel, Alfin says, "Have you seen the caves, One-Eye? Glowing, I mean."

"Once," he says. "When Garreth sent a message through them."

Niz's eyes widen. "That must have been a sight. Lord Garreth's traits are very strong." He nudges Alfin. "Don't worry, I'll do my best to create something for us to enjoy as well."

Alfin lifts their held hands and kisses the back of Niz's. "Looking forward to it."

Niz blushes, beaming.

They pause for breakfast later that morning. Franz talks with his mother, saying, "I'm so glad you're getting to see them again!"

"Me too! Thanks for being willing to do this, Fi."

Fiona is distributing the meals, tidily wrapped up in

checkered cloth. "Of course," she says.

They travel for several more hours before having lunch, then continue on. By that afternoon, they reach the crest of a cliff overlooking the ocean. The sisters pause for a moment and Joseline says, "Beautiful … "

Alfin walks over to her and asks, "Are you ready?"

"Yes. Thank you."

He nods, then carefully picks her up, carrying her down the steep steps while Fiona quickly folds up the wheelchair and follows them. When they reach the bottom, Fiona puts the chair back together just as fast and Alfin sets Joseline in it. She thanks him again, then they all look at the cave entrance.

It has been fully repaired and the rocks have been cleared out of the way, allowing the water from the ocean to flow through it easily.

Before they enter, Vann and Merlin both take Delphaen crystals from a basket near the entrance. They dip them in the stream and the crystals begin to glow blue-green.

One-Eye takes Rath's hand as they all enter and the Pagu lift off of Rath's shoulder to fly next to them. One-Eye's Spirit Lion looks up at the reflective Miphrin in anticipation.

The group walks until the light from outside fades.

Then, Vann and Merlin step away and go toward a raised bowl set in the wall that catches water from the ceiling.

While Merlin holds their crystals, Vann thinks about her message and her tattoos start to glow. Holding onto Merlin's hand with her right hand, she lowers her left into the water, sending a message through the cave.

At the same time, Niz sends his message from the opposite wall and Velt, Franz, Joseline, Fiona, Mattias, Mallo, Mimi, and Max send theirs together from the stream.

Rath, One-Eye, the Pagu, Carlos, and Phillip watch as the whole cave fills with blue-green light from the messages traveling through the water.

As the Miphrin begins to glow, the Pagu spin happily next to Carlos and Phillip, who look around in appreciation and awe. On Phillip's shoulder, his Spirit Rabbit sniffs, her eyes wide. Rath lifts his free hand to trace the illuminated constellation and One-Eye smiles at him while his Spirit Lion sits in front of them.

Acknowledgements

The Constellation Caves was the third book I wrote in the *PearlHeart* series. What began as a more insular story became more complex as I put my mind back to where the characters were in between book one and the original book two (that is now book three). It was very confusing and I am very happy with how it all turned out.

Thank you so much to my family for always listening to my drafts and for being willing to listen to this after I finished reading aloud what we all thought was book two. I am so grateful for the immediate positive reaction when I told you what I was writing.

Thank you to my beta readers for supporting the world and the characters. I appreciate your time and care with this story so much!

Thank you to my friends and everyone reading this series! I hope that these stories bring you hope and joy as they do for me.

About the Author

Keilani McConnell has always enjoyed creating stories and sharing them with friends and family. She has a Bachelor of Music in Flute Performance and both teaches and performs in her local area. She also draws comics, animates, and makes jewelry. To relax, she likes to read, be outside, and play with her kitty, Midna. She is the author of the *PearlHeart* series of novels, two silent comic compilations (*Gem Music and Other Silent Comics* and *Turtle Journey and Other Silent Comics*), and an art book (*Snakes in Hats: 2024 Artwork*). She lives in Colorado. For more information, please see her website keilanimcconnellart.com

www.ingramcontent.com/pod-product-compliance
Lightning Source LLC
Chambersburg PA
CBHW020905060726

47591CB00004B/1088